DEAR
MR. PRESIDENT

HALLIE ISRAEL

For additional copies or information contact:
East Meadow Publishing
eastmeadowpublishing@gmail.com

ISBN 978-0-615-47838-8

Carlisle Printing
OF WALNUT CREEK LTD.
2673 Township Road 421
Sugarcreek, OH 44681
800.927.4196

Layout & Design | Abigail Troyer

table of contents

chapter

chapter

*This book is dedicated
in loving memory of my mother, Karin Israel*

prologue

It's funny how a simple idea can take control of a life.

It begins its existence as a spark, the smallest form of light. It cannot warm you; nor can it guide you in the dark. If it is not kindled, it will die. Yet, the understanding of one such spark that evades most is how quickly it can turn into a fire, and how powerful a fire can be—how dangerous its potential truly is.

If a spark catches, it won't take long to spread—clearing a path as it swells from head to heart, leaving nothing untouched by its smoldering glow in-between. In an instant, heat consumes the body, sets the spirit ablaze. Flames envelop the mind with flickering fingers, searing a fiery imprint into the flesh as they tighten their grasp, branding you as their creation. After this, they are unforgettable, something that no amount of water could ever put out. Something very real, that only *you* could create.

Once an idea is realized, it seems to develop an agenda of its own. You can no longer manipulate its potency, but rather the other way around. It is in control of you. And in this, a simple thought at first, a spark nearly useless, takes control.

Captives of the flame are carried along on its journey, a changed world the destined product of its magic. Those who play victim to these thoughts have accomplished tasks said to be impossible.

I was one of them, and this is my story.

They tell you not to play with fire, but sometimes it's hard to resist.

chapter one

I was sitting at a desk, vacant expression fixed absentmindedly to my face. A boy in the back row was sleeping, while another had resorted to counting the tiles on the floor. Two girls in the corner were passing notes. Most of us were doodling in our notebooks, praying for the timeliness of the lunch bell. Oblivious to all this activity, somewhere in the background, a teacher's voice was droning on like an overworked cassette. She cleared her throat.

"Students, I have to make an announcement."

We all knew what was coming.

It was nearly mid-autumn. Enthusiasm for academics had faded faster than the color of the leaves. Pencils grew dull, smiles flattened out, jackets got heavier, and as was customary for the season, the America Project would be assigned to us, the newest crop of seventh graders. It was the only upstanding school tradition approved by the Mapleview Board of Education, and until just recently, something that held an infamous reputation for being the easiest project in history. For my sake, I hoped that this year would be no different. Instructions were given and guidelines passed out. I skimmed the paper, and the room around me became quiet for the first time all day.

How was it that the project's workload only became substantial once it was my turn to complete it?

You could bet I was less than thrilled.

Apparently, the theme of this year's project was called 'ONE Nation, MANY Opinions'. The idea was to find someone in the nation, think of a political topic, and discuss it. We were then supposed to present our findings in the form of a two page report as well as an oral presentation. I sighed—the assignment given the *previous* year was to bake a classic American dish and bring it in. Microwave macaroni and cheese with pre-made apple pie had never seemed so unfair.

Still, it was just an average school project. It couldn't have been any less notable, right? *Wrong.*

That's the funny thing about a fire. Sure, its flames can be found in dragons and fairy tales, but they can also come from two sticks. Inspiration can originate from even the most ordinary and insignificant of sources—you just have to know where to look. As of that time however, I had no idea where to turn for anything that could make the project more than what it seemed—a pain. I was just about as unresponsive to its prospects as I would have been to a glass of water.

It was only on the bus ride home, after the school day had come and gone, when I was hit with an idea. Something too problematic to be possible, and far too foolish to be probable. I was instantly in love with it.

I was going to talk to the President of the United States. No, not just talk. We were going to *discuss*; exchange each other's opinions of various issues, and demonstrate them in the form of 'a two page report and an oral presentation'. In other words, the one person in the nation I chose to do my project with was Bob Deerun (a.k.a. Mr. President).

Just like that, the spark in my mind was formed. It was basic to the point of being laughable.

Exactly how were we going to communicate, you ask? Well, at that point there only seemed like one option—you guessed it: *snail mail.*

Don't get me wrong here; I don't discriminate against modern technology. It just didn't seem right that I could dial up the White House number and say

'Hi, this is Cara Greybird, is Mr. President home?' Then the person working the phone would say 'Sure, I'll connect you right away.' Yeah, like that would happen. So I could rule out the phone. I also didn't think that I could reach the President by computer. As far as I knew, I hadn't seen him in any chat rooms lately and an email message seemed far too impersonal. I couldn't get the President by fax either, because…well, to be honest, I didn't know the number—nor anybody who kept it safe at home, tucked away in their address books. Ruling out all of the alternative choices, to me, mail seemed like the only answer.

The spark had caught and grown into a fire. Its flames were quickly multiplying, and I was in no rush to put them out.

I was too excited to even consider that my plan could fail, although that would have probably been a logical thought to have. Instead, the main question to me at the time was, well, *what do I write?*

After a few minutes of daydreaming, I was interrupted by a sudden jolt of the school bus.

"Sit down!" the driver snapped. Her voice was rigid, and thankfully, not directed towards me.

After a faint pause, there was a polite "Sorry."

"Go sit with Cara," she sighed, gunning the acceleration just in time for us to reach a speed bump. The bus shook.

Just my luck.

I leaned over the side of my seat, partially curious to see the kid that had caused all of the commotion, and partially to get a look at who I would have to sit with for the rest of the ride home. I had *definitely* never seen her before.

She looked about my age, but was considerably taller. Her build was lanky, but she didn't seem like the type of girl who you worry can't keep her balance in a strong wind. Nothing about her was average, and yet nothing seemed abnormal. Assuming that the driver wouldn't crash the bus, there was a good chance that I would survive the ride home.

It only took a moment for me to realize the error in my thought. Sure the girl looked just normal—from the ankles up that was. Her shoes told a whole other story.

A mix between a combat boot and a clown shoe, they were large and bulky, almost not a match for such a slender girl. Each looked like a 100-pound block of concrete, and I was amazed that they didn't weigh her down as she walked.

I smiled to myself: there was no need for anyone to worry about this frail girl blowing away; she was safely anchored to the ground.

The shoes themselves had been spray painted all different colors, and the amusing thing was that for a long time, I couldn't decide whether I loved or hated them. In the end, it was her shoelaces that helped me to make up my mind. Each was about an inch wide, and it appeared as if the girl had colored them with a highlighter and then stepped in a large mud puddle.

Before I knew it, the ride home had become something of a questionable normality. I slid deeper into my seat.

"Where does Cara sit?" she asked helplessly, scanning the bus for a sign of some sort, as to where I was. I leaned into the aisle and gave a small wave in her direction. The bus was packed with the usual rule-violators, the kind of kids that can force a bus driver into an early retirement. Yet, somehow among the yellers, the aisle-hangers, the seat-switchers and the gum-chewers, she managed to spot me relatively quickly. "Oh."

She hurriedly clunked her boots towards the back of the bus where I sat. After a moment of exchanging vague, uninspired smiles, I halfheartedly scooted over in my seat to make room for the new girl. She accepted my gesture and gracefully slid into the available space, setting a glitter-smeared bag onto her lap.

"Hey," I drew out the word in one long breath. "I'm Cara."

"I'm Sandy," the girl shyly replied.

"Sandy?" I repeated, making sure I had heard correctly. Alone, it was a perfectly normal name. Short and simple. Not too contemporary or unusual: simply *unfitting*.

Sandy was one of those people who must spend a small fortune on sunscreen. Her skin was whiter than the tips of my fingernails and its tone was perfectly even. No sunburn, no freckles; something uncharacteristic for a kid within the months following summer vacation. Her hair was even more atypical. It was *red*; not orange or auburn or ginger. Traffic light, brand new convertible, tomato red, and natural too. It was somehow obvious that she hadn't dyed it, yet, with the way it stood out so prominently against her skin, the common name she had provided as her own just couldn't belong. In truth, she looked more like an *Apple* or a *Strawberry* than she ever would a *Sandy*.

"Yeah." She was blushing, her skin slowly beginning to blend with the color of her hair. "You see, my real name is Sandra." She sighed, and with a small eye roll mumbled, "Sandra *Guinevere Vivian*. I just wanted to shorten it a *little* when I moved here." I fought back laughter. If this girl was Sandra Guinevere Vivian, the next heir of the royal family would be named Madonna. For a lack of anything to say, I nodded back at her. The bus, choosing an inconvenient time to defy the laws of nature, had become silent.

I'm sure it was not by coincidence that Sandy had chosen that moment to become deeply fascinated with her shoes. She was staring down at them, concentrated only on clicking their spray painted heels together. The more time went by, the faster she clicked, and the more desperately I searched for small talk.

Click Click Click Click Click.

"I like your shoes—" I blurted, starting to lie in an attempt to fill the quiet.

Click. Click. She slowly gave up her role as Dorothy and settled her heels back into the floor. I watched as she bent to tighten their laces, her hands working them into a knot without the use of her eyes, which were pointed up towards me. "Thanks, but you don't have to." She glanced down, tapping the spray painted leather with her fingertips. "I like being different."

Click; It only took a second for me to change my mind. Sandy wasn't misunderstood and nothing about her was trendy or shallow. She was just herself. *And that couldn't be bad.*

"It's the truth!" I found myself laughing, realizing the sincerity in my own voice. From her smile alone, I could tell she had recognized it too.

I heard the squeal of a brake that was pushed with too much force, and my body was flung into the adjoining seatback. Recovering quickly, I looked out the window to find the bus parked at my street corner, its front wheels exceeding the stop sign by yards. *Click Click Click.* Her shoes were at it again.

"This is my stop," I explained, squeezing into the overcrowded aisle. I slid my backpack over one shoulder. "Nice meeting you, Sandy."

"You too."

I almost didn't recognize her voice. Something in its tone had changed, the timid sound having disappeared and left something solid, almost *warm*, in its place. "Maybe I'll see you around sometime."

"Definitely."

I kind of hoped I would. *She had good taste in shoes.*

chapter two

There was nothing better than a Friday afternoon. With all problems on hold for as long as a weekend can allow, it was the perfect time to relax—*or so I thought*. Nonetheless, one look outside on that particular day would surely make any pleasant notion appear as factual. The sun was shining and the air was filled with the lingering scents of summertime. Although it was predicted to rain later, for the moment, the weather couldn't have been nicer.

"Cara, hey, Cara!" My neighbor waved from where she had been kneeling over a flowerbed, her fingers smudged with dirt. "Cara, hi there!" I took another step in the direction of my driveway.

"Hello Mrs. Hamstering."

"Beautiful day we're having isn't it? Perfect to get my gardening done!" I nodded. If anyone could plant a garden on soil as thin and dry as tissue paper, it would be her—she loved a good challenge.

A deep, throaty, snarl ripped through the air. I couldn't help but jump. Mrs. Hamstering laughed. "Down, Jawsie. Good dog. Yes…that's right. You recognize Cara, don't you? Good boy…"

I turned in the direction of the noise to face *Jawsie. Speaking of challenges…*

For such nice people, I could never understand why the Hamsterings would want a dog that was completely the opposite. They adopted Jawsie from a local shelter last year, and ever since then, he's been a permanent fixture on the lawn— literally permanent, because he's stuck there. Fixed to a chain soldered to a stake that runs down until the ground turns to rock, Jawsie growls and barks at pretty much everything that goes by. Squirrels, rabbits, and even birds have learned to keep their distance from him the hard way, and now, I only wished I had caught on more quickly. I took a step back, wondering if my fear was obvious. Jawsie bared his teeth.

"Isn't he just the sweetest?" Mrs. Hamstering smiled. It was beyond me how she managed to love Jawsie, but I decided not to hold it against her.

"*Adorable.*"

"So how are you doing, Cara?" she called over to me, wiping her brow with a corner of her dusty sleeve.

"Fine, thanks, and you?" I replied almost instantly, putting more effort than was necessary into a forced smile.

"Fantastic. I haven't seen you since this summer, you know. I think Jawsie's missed all of the kids from the neighborhood too, now that school has started up again. You're welcome to stop by anytime to play with hi—"

"Great!" I cut her off, pretending to appreciate the offer. If all of the neighborhood kids decided to play with Jawsie, I doubted if there would be any neighborhood kids left. "I will definitely, um, have to take you up on that sometime soon. It's very tempting now, but I really should be getting home, so I guess I'll see you later then. Bye!"

Jawsie growled and I was off like NASA's fastest rocket, speeding up the rest of the driveway, through the open garage door and into my house within seconds. A new personal record.

Once inside, I slid off my shoes and tossed my coat and backpack into the hall closet, leaving all reminders of my past school day collapsed in a wrinkled heap. My body had become accustomed to carrying the added weight of my textbooks but reacted quickly to their dispatch, and I could feel as my muscles began to relax. Spine arching into a contented slump, I made my way down the hall and into the family room. I grabbed the TV remote from the coffee table and was just about to dive into the couch when I found that it was already occupied.

"Hey, J.J.," I mumbled.

It wasn't that I actually needed a babysitter. She was more of a household help, a twenty-something-year-old paid to start dinner when my parents would be coming home late from work, or to pick me up from school if I needed a ride. When she wasn't doing that however, which was most of the time, she enjoyed taking on the part-time identity of a prison warden.

"Hey, kiddo!" she exclaimed, giving her best impersonation of someone who was actually excited to see me come home.

"I'm so glad you're home!" she added, reading my mind. If J.J. had anything other than an IQ of 12, it was her talent for acting. I gave a weak smile, half-expecting her to put me in a half-nelson, tousle my hair, and invite me out for ice-cream. Instead, she swiped the remote from my hand.

"Nah-uh…," she shook her head, tossing it gently aside. Her aim was off and it widely overshot the couch, tumbling down the armrest and onto the carpet. She shrugged, not bothering to retrieve it. "Television is only for kids who do their homework," she explained, settling deeper into her seat.

"Since when do we have that rule?"

"Since I decided I needed a little quiet time today," she answered, as if that were a justifiable response.

"Whatever you say," I didn't bother to argue, turning back towards the hall. I suppose I could have reminded J.J. that it was a Friday, and therefore I didn't really have any homework that needed to be completed right away, but I decided to let her win whatever clever argument she was having.

It was only after I had retrieved my backpack from what I hoped might be its final resting place for the day that she called me again.

"Hey wait, do you think you could grab me a bag of chips while you're up?"

"Absolutely!" I yelled back, with no real intention of actually doing it.

J.J. was probably proud of what she had done, knowing that she had just managed to secure herself a calorie-filled afternoon of all the stain-remover commercials and *Desperate Housewives* reruns that daytime television had to offer. What she didn't know about, however, was located in the one room of the house that she had never bothered to visit. In other words, I also had a TV in my room. Score one for Cara.

Despite insistent protests from my back, I did my best to hurry up the stairs and into my bedroom. Within another moment, I was leaning against my headboard, remote in hand and an old box of *Froot Loops* at my side. Feeling triumphant in my outsmarting of J.J., (not that this was anything to be proud of—I estimated that 99% of the population could have easily done the same), I opened the box, and began to munch on the cereal. The stale taste it left behind in my mouth was evident, but I hardly minded.

I suppose meeting Sandy had caught me a little off-guard, and in all the excitement, I'd taken my attention off of the spark which had excited me just moments ago.

My project.

The President.

The idea came back to me with just as much animation as before. In seconds I was up again, scurrying about my room and looking for the necessary materials to keep the fire going. I collected them within moments and was soon back on my bed, positive that what I had gathered was the perfect means for kindling. I had nearly fallen into my normal afternoon routine, but now my mind's focus was far from the ordinary. In fact, my concentration did not stray away from the objects that I had gathered in my lap: a pen, a pencil, and most importantly, a piece of paper on which I had scrawled the greeting, '*Dear Mr. President*'.

Whether I cared to admit it or not, J.J. had made some sense downstairs. I smiled as I realized the irony of this statement. Although she had no way of knowing why, what she had said before was true.

I desperately needed to get to work.

I picked up the pencil and began to feed the fire. After an uninterrupted hour of writing, crumpling and erasing, I was ready with my final project. I laid the paper out in front of me to give it a final evaluation:

Dear Mr. President,

Hello, my name is Cara Greybird. I attend Mapleview Middle School, located in New Castle, Pennsylvania, and am a proud citizen of this nation. This year, I am doing a project for my 7th grade class and it would be greatly appreciated if you could answer a few questions for me. (The idea of the project is to discuss various political outlooks on topics of interest and then share the results of the conversation in class. The point is to try and understand other people's views and perspectives.) The questions are as follows:

Would you rather make a decision that everyone else supports but you do not believe in, or make a decision that everyone else is against, but you know is right? Please explain.

If you could make ANY new law what would it be, and why?

If you were able to double the budget of a national department, which of the following choices would it be?
a) NASA
b) Military
c) FBI and CIA
d) Animal Rights Division
e) Public Education
Please explain your thinking below.

Thank you so much for your time. I am really glad that I chose you for my project!

Sincerely,
Cara Greybird

It was perfect. The handwriting wasn't bad either, which for me especially, was a real miracle.

"Caraaa!" I heard the voice before the knocking at the door and was left with no time to appreciate the rarity of my legible penmanship.

"Who is it?" I sighed, already knowing the answer.

"It's *me*, Cara, let me in!"

"Door's opened, Nad."

Before I could react, the door gave way to a seven year old who had shoved it aside with more force than intended. You could tell that her hair had once been twisted into a bun, but by now more pieces were hanging around her face than were actually tied back from it.

For sisters, Nadia and I look nothing alike. My hair falls to the middle of my back in long, messy waves; not quite black, but too dark to be considered otherwise. Nadia's is the color of brown sugar, and sits an inch or so above her shoulders. It's naturally pin-straight, but you'd never know it, since it often goes un-brushed. I'm an average height for my age, while she is short for a second-grader. My eyes are hazel, and hers are electric-blue. I might be talkative, but a fog horn is probably quieter than Nadia. The list goes on.

Obviously, the two of us don't share many physical traits. What we do share however, is a bedroom, which is divided in half by a large sliding curtain. Even though the room belongs to the both of us, if one has the door closed, the other is supposed to knock. This is a rule that Nadia usually either forgets, or neglects to follow, and so I was naturally impressed to see her sudden acceptance of it. I'll be the first to admit that sharing a smaller space can be difficult, especially with someone whose personality itself fills up a room. Yet, the two of us managed to survive, and against all odds, get along pretty well too.

Bounding past the doorway, Nadia moved further into the room and sat down at my side, sloppily folding her pink ballet skirt beneath her.

"How was ballet?" I asked, although her expression alone answered my question.

"Watch," she answered, her voice implying that I was about to be impressed. "My teacher says I'm pretty advanced, especially after just one class." I nodded as she stood from her spot on the bed and without warning, hurled herself into a dramatic leap, thrashing her small body back and forth at random, following no apparent pattern or rhythm. Teeth clamped tight to her lower lip in an attempt to mask her exaggerated effort, and eyes filled with a serious focus, she ended her routine with her head up high and arms extending upward, much like an Olympic gymnast.

"Bravo!" I cried, hoping that she wouldn't catch the amusement bubbling up in my tone.

Pleased with the attention, Nadia bowed before adding an encore cartwheel to her piece, and when that didn't work, toppling down onto me, erupting into a fit of laughter.

"Wasn't that great!" she gasped. I nodded as her eyes scanned the room, no doubt bored already and eager to do something new. "Want to go downstairs?" That was another thing about Nadia; she often changed from one subject to another without realizing it.

"No thanks." I held my breath, rolling her onto the carpet before pushing myself upright.

"Fine then, I guess."

"I've really got to finish some homework," I added quickly, noticing the hurt look that was beginning to form on her face. Scrambling closer, Nadia leaned over my shoulder to get a better look at what I was working on. She grabbed a fistful of her short hair and tugged it behind her ear, ignoring it when it fell back again, framing her cheeks seconds later.

"It's a project for school." I reassured her. I watched my sisters face twist as she attempted to read my cursive writing. Giving up after a few seconds, she adopted her previous topic.

"Are you sure you don't want to go downstairs?" she pleaded. "Mom is almost home, and J.J.'s getting ready for a party. You should see her; she has on a pair of hoop earrings that are so big, they could fit over her head!"

At this I laughed. Nadia always had a special way of making everything seem exciting and new. No detail was ever left out, or an action considered too small. She was always the center of attention—the host of the party, but if invited, you were forever her special guest of honor. Now was a rare exception. I shook my head 'no', turning her down once again.

"Sorry, Nad, but I've really got to work on my project right now."

"Alright," she sighed, pausing briefly before snapping right back into action.

I watched with a smile as my sister picked herself up, and with a few choice ballet moves, danced out of the room, recovered from her disappointment. I knew Nadia all too well. Not only did she change subjects at the blink of an eye, but hobbies as well. Last month she and her violin were inseparable, then she loved karate, and now it was ballet. I wouldn't be surprised if she went off to be a NASCAR racer by the end of the week.

As the sounds of Nadia's footsteps became more and more distant, I pulled an envelope from my dresser drawer and began to search the room for a stamp. Unsuccessful, I opened my history binder and instead, began to copy down the White House address in a careful print. Just as I had inserted my letter inside and was licking the envelope closed, I heard the sounds of the early evening news coming from the television, which I had forgotten to turn off. I glanced up to catch the opening story.

In our community, we have a 5:00 news program that mainly covers local subjects, like who won the district spelling bee, who got the highest test scores, and if any schools were closing for the day. Most of the time, however, the opening story had to do with political issues affecting the area. It usually wasn't that interesting, but the theme music always seemed to grab my attention. Out of habit, I fixed my gaze on the screen to see a woman with an obvious spray tan standing behind the anchor desk. She was smiling in such a way that it looked almost uncomfortable, grin clinging to her face even as she began to talk.

"Hello," she said a bit too enthusiastically, "and welcome to the 5:00 news report." A long gap of silence followed these words, initiating what she seemed to think was a dramatic pause. "Tonight's story," she began after quite some time, "is short, but truly rousing." She stopped to stare exaggeratedly into the camera, flashing us all another *charming* smile. "The President of the United States," she continued, "will be attending the ribbon-cutting ceremony opening the Giraffing Children's Hospital's new 2-acre therapeutic garden, right here in our city. The project has been in progress for 7 months, and has only just recently been completed. The hard work of the hospital families, patients, and staff, will be unveiled to the public and officially opened by our President in exactly sixteen days. An exclusive invitation-only party will follow the ceremony, *which is also invitation-only.*" She shot a quick, irritated glare at someone behind the cameras, as if she were angry with them for failing to get her a personal invitation. After a moment, she started up again, informing us with the details of the story, the phony smile returning to her face.

"This is a very big deal for everyone involved with the ceremony because the President will be clearing an entire day of his busy schedule, just for us. It's simply marvelous," she murmured, dabbing the corner of her eye with a monogrammed handkerchief. "Well Pete's giving me the signal to 'wrap it up here' so I guess that's all the details for now! Find out whether number three pencils will be allowed in Mapleview Middle School next year after this short break!" she exclaimed suddenly, abandoning her tissue and beaming. The theme music returned and a commercial popped onto the screen.

I stood to collect my jaw, which was hanging somewhere near the floor. The room felt suddenly hotter, but my blood ran cold. I reached for the television remote, fumbling with it for a moment before a clammy finger could connect with the off button. Without thinking, I snatched my letter to the President from the floor and my portable scooter from under the bed. I knew that I had to get my letter mailed before the President left the White House and was determined to do just that. Then, pulling on last year's outgrown tennis shoes from the closet, I did something I thought I would never do—I climbed out of my second-story window.

chapter three

Desperate times call for desperate measures. I'd heard this phrase countless times, but never did I think that it would cause me to end up on my roof-top, toes aching from my too-small shoes, and chest aching from my pounding heart. Desperate times call for desperate measures, but in my case, it was the time itself that propelled me to such an act. It was not on my side.

Usually, I'm not the one who does the whole sneak-out-of-the-house-and-don't-tell-anyone thing. My stomach alone, now having lodged itself somewhere up near my throat, was enough to remind me of why. I did my best to choke it down, swallowing hard as I closed the window behind me. I wasn't sure which scared me more, the idea that I couldn't calm it, or the realization that it had good reason to be afraid.

In my neighborhood, at approximately 5:30 p.m., Jawsie is not in his usual place (fixed firmly to the ground). Instead, he is on a walk. Under normal circumstances, I suppose that this would be quite fine—that is, it *would* be if his owner possessed some type of superhuman strength. Jawsie is a husky and rottweiler mix with an energetic personality and a mad impulse to chase everything in sight. For a heavyweight wrestler or the strong man of a circus to keep hold of his leash is possible, but it's obvious that Mrs. Hamstering is neither of the two. At four-foot-eleven, she's less than 100 pounds soaking wet, equipped with the muscular abilities of a toothpick.

To make a long story short, usually within the first three minutes of the outing, Jawsie ends up escaping his owner's light grasp, running around like a maniac and damaging everything within his reach. This would explain why at precisely 5:30 p.m., every garage, door, and window in the neighborhood is sealed tightly closed. All kids come in from playing outside. Vases are positioned in higher places, and couples new to the area soon learn that patio furniture is an overrated investment. It is sort of an unwritten rule that no one is to leave their houses from 5:30 to 6:00 in order to avoid damage to their property or themselves—and at my house, being outside when Jawsie is loose will get you a punishment equivalent to running through an acid rainstorm. Many people in the neighborhood have complained of Jawsie's habits to Mrs. Hamstering, and after about the thousandth call, Jawsie had finally been signed up for obedience classes which were to start in a week's time.

Well, I needed my letter mailed by today, not the following week, or even the following morning if I wanted the chances of the President receiving it before his trip to Pennsylvania to be good. If it was delivered too late and he got it after he had already gone, the response would get back to me way after the project was due, which was three weeks from the time. The bottom line was that I needed to mail my letter, even though, you guessed it, the time on my clock now read 5:27. I knew that even J.J. had the sense to keep me indoors during this period of unpredictable danger and it seemed to me that all other options were closed.

As far as my plan went, I'll be the first to acknowledge that maybe jumping out a window doesn't qualify as the most brilliant of activities—especially when you're as afraid of heights as I am. In fact, under normal circumstances, it wouldn't have taken much persuasion at all to keep me from considering such a leap. This time was different; *a compelling exception.* The resolution to act had overpowered my fear in a coup so sudden that my better judgment could do little in protest. Instinct had forced my consciousness into submission, its motives vague but uncompromising. For some reason I couldn't yet place, the project felt important to me—a task no less necessary to preform than breathing, and equally important in function. My mind was made up, and by that point, not even reason could turn me away. How did I survive jumping out a second story window, you might wonder? The answer is simpler than you would think.

My bedroom window faces the backyard of my house. Although the house is composed of two-stories it is not fashioned in a way that most traditional two-story houses are. In fact, it's built in a somewhat pear-like shape, with a wide rectangular first floor, a narrow roof tilted slightly towards the ground, and in the center of that first roof, the smaller and more square-like second story of the house. It is on this floor that my bedroom is located, and above it is the uppermost roof, formed into a shape that roughly resembles a trapezoid. This makes it the perfect house for escaping from a high height because from my bedroom window, I could climb down the minor slope of my roof, and then— well, come to think of it, I really hadn't planned my escape much farther than reaching the bottom of the roof. However, seeing as the more I thought about the whole ordeal, the more my stomach seemed to be twisting itself into knots, I decided that I would figure out the rest of my plan as I went along.

I slid the letter into the safety of my pocket, ignoring how clammy my fingers had become. Blood was coursing hot through my veins, threatening to boil if I thought too carefully about what I was doing—or worse still, all of the ways that it could go wrong. Even so, I tried to keep calm as I climbed out of my window and onto the roof, dragging my scooter along with me. The afternoon sun was long gone, the winds having picked up in its place. The clouds above looked more like a shadow, gathering and growing dark as they crawled closer overhead. Turning my attention away from the sky, I carefully inched my way towards the edge of the roof—half of my mind busy trying to keep me from slipping, the other frantically considering my options for getting down.

Tense, I examined the backyard for any ideas. I could not simply jump, the roof was at least 12 feet in the air, and the ground below me was inflexible. There was a large pine tree next to the house, but its branches seemed too frail to support my body if I were to climb down from them. Then there were the two jump ropes that Nadia and her friend had left outside from the day before. For a moment I believed that I would be able to tie the ropes together and use them as a sort of ladder to get me down, but soon came to the glum realization that the jump ropes were already on the ground, and tauntingly out of my reach. There was really nothing else in the yard, besides the trampoline…*the trampoline!* Putting my fear aside for a moment, and ignoring the painful thumping of my heart, I allowed myself a smile. I had found my answer.

During the summer when I had bounced on it with Nadia or a couple of my friends, it had always seemed so close to the roof. Almost like I could reach it with a good jump. Now, however, from the opposite perspective, I began to have second thoughts. *Come on, Cara,* I urged myself. *Just a little farther.* I bit my lip, grasping onto the shingles as I inched forward. *I can still turn around at anytime,* I thought, hoping the reassurance would keep my hands from shaking. *I'll just get a little further before I decide. A little further. A little further.*

WHAM!!!!!!!

The next thing I knew, I was lying flat on my back. The air had been knocked clear out of my lungs and I gasped for breath, struggling to fill them again. I opened my eyes, fighting nausea as I lifted my head.

It took me a moment to realize where I had fallen—smack-dab in the center of the trampoline.

Rolling over onto one side, I held a shaking arm up to my eyes, scanning it for any apparent injuries. My hands felt for the envelope in my pocket, somehow still smooth and un-creased. Aside from my heart, now pounding itself into overdrive, the rest of my body seemed unaffected by the fall. I leaned back and pressed a hand to my chest, closing my eyes. As the pigment slowly returned to my skin, the details of the fall came back to my head. Let me tell you, they were not pretty. I hate to admit it, but I was probably no more graceful than a three-year-old, jumping off the high board for the first time at a swimming pool. To put it short, my daring jump was just as pathetic as it was insane. Yet, other than the shock that comes with falling from the second story of a house, I felt alright.

Trying not to draw attention to myself, I celebrated my good luck by cherishing on my own ignorance, more than happy not to know how close I had come to missing the trampoline altogether and falling onto a much less forgiving surface. Shaking off the idea, I pushed myself upright, and when my legs seemed steady enough, lowered them to the ground. Once standing, I began to search for my scooter, wondering where it had landed. I found it nearby in surprisingly good condition, lying sideways among a patch of stubborn grass seed that wouldn't take to the dirt. My mom had been attempting to cover the dusty soil of our backyard with greenery, but one summer and a very large sprinkler bill later, the chances of her success in the endeavor were looking slim. Carefully, I knelt to pick up the scooter, patting the dirt off of its handlebars before trampling back across the so-called lawn and towards the street.

On my way, I snuck a quick glance through the side window to see if anybody had heard me leave, realizing that, to my relief, I probably wouldn't be missed so much. J.J. was completely zoned out of reality, watching soap opera reruns in the same spot I had left her in that afternoon, unconsciously adjusting her party attire. Nadia, as well, was in her own little world, thoughtfully flipping through the pages of a coloring book with a package of dull-tipped crayons at her side. I took a deep breath, unnervingly certain that there was no turning back, and continued to make my way towards the post office.

With one hand dragging my scooter and the other pressed flat against the envelope in my pocket, I crept down the driveway and onto the merging street. Each door I passed was shut tight, no doubt locked and ready for Jawsie. Just looking around, one might think that some sort of disaster had struck and I was the only one left on Earth. Everything around me was still, deserted and quiet. I suppose that when Jawsie is running free however, even the slightest hint of tranquility is a good sign. Hoping I was safe, I stood up and adjusted my scooter, breathing hard as I kicked off from the ground. It wasn't long before I reached the first intersection and turned onto Acorn Boulevard. The Friday rush-hour traffic was thickening, but I continued to push myself down the road, switching to the sidewalks when they began down towards Maple Street.

By the time I pulled into the post office entryway, my knees were aching and my knuckles had gone white from gripping the handlebars. Speeding across the empty parking lot, I skidded to a stop in front of the door, propping my scooter up against the side wall before running inside.

Almost instantly, I was attacked with the overwhelming odor of glue and moist paper. The air was stuffy, and its weight felt heavy on my skin. About eight feet from the door stood a bored looking teenager with hair dyed a pinkish color, matching the shade of her fingernails almost exactly. She looked up at me without concern and then back down at the counter, fiddling with a key that was strung around her neck.

"If you're gonna mail something, do it now," she smacked through a wad of gum, twirling the fluorescent mess on her head with a now-camouflaged index finger. I didn't answer, and the girl rolled her eyes. "Last pickup is in two minutes, so you'd better hurry up." She looked down at me from her place behind the counter, her eyes searching my face like she was trying to figure out if I could speak English or not.

"Do you have any stamps?" I asked her, realizing that I had forgotten to stick one onto my letter. "I think I'm going to need two of them."

"Whatever," she grunted, checking her wristwatch. "That will be 88 cents." Anxiously, I dug into my pockets and I pulled out a dollar bill. I gave the money to the girl, who handed me my change along with two American flag/bald eagle stamps. (Very patriotic, don't you think?)

"Is that all?" she asked, taking another look at her watch. "My shift is up."

"Yeah," I answered. "Thanks." As if she had just been released from a prison, the girl swung open the plastic flip door of the counter and went stomping off to a room labeled 'Employees Only', mumbling to herself about a paycheck and someone named Dan.

As soon as she left, I fastened the stamps to my envelope, realizing only moments later that my letter still needed to be mailed. As if he had heard my thoughts, a smiling man strode out from the same room where the previous girl had disappeared. He was dressed in a postal uniform which appeared to have been washed with so much starch that it would not allow him to move any portion of his upper back, and was trying his best to hide the apparent look of annoyance on his face. His nametag, which was pinned proudly to the chest pocket of his shirt, labeled him as 'Dan, Assistant Manager.'

"I'm so sorry for the delay," Dan smiled, revealing a mouth of braces. "There was a minor problem in the—*um*—*the mailroom*, sure, yes that's it, the *mailroom*, which needed our immediate attention. We hope you understand. Is there anything else I can do for you?"

"Yes, if you could mail this, that would be great," I answered, sliding the envelope across the counter, its future now out of my hands.

"My pleasure," he answered. "You're in luck, the last pick-up today is late, and so your letter won't have to wait until tomorrow. Well, you should probably be on your way home; I hear there's a big storm coming this way." And with one last smile, Dan turned his attention from me and began to sort some other envelopes into a large plastic bin, my own letter untouched.

Normally, I tend to be quite a talkative kid, but today, chatting it up with Dan the Postal Worker, when every minute I spent away from home was bringing me closer to Jawsie, was not exactly a dream come true. In fact, the only thing that kept me standing there was the need to watch my letter as it traveled from the greasy looking counter to the hands of the man and finally into some mailroom in the back of the building where it would wait to be sent. As soon as it was safe, I could go. Until then however, I had to keep our conversation going, purely to ease my own paranoia.

Searching for something to say, I chose the first and possibly the blandest thing that came to mind. "Excuse me," I began, drawing out the word as I watched him pick up the plastic bin containing the letters, depositing my own into the mix. I suppose that to him it seemed just like any other in there; a letter to some pen pal in southern Peru, a subscription to a bird-watching magazine— nothing too important. Nevertheless, to me, it looked like a leaf of pure gold jumbled together with an array of ordinary yellow paper.

Only a few more seconds now until it made its way to safety.

"Do you know the time?" I blurted after a moment, more concentrated on the gold in the bin than the person holding it.

"Certainly," Dan recited, dropping his oversized container leisurely on the floor to get a good look at his watch. I tried to hide the pain in my face, silently kicking myself for not supplying a question that required an effortless answer.

Never had I felt so displeased for not simply noting that indeed, the sky did look rather dark, or that yes, I really should be getting home. It was the hardest I had ever tried to look moderately pleasant in an everyday situation.

My efforts, however, instantly failed when I heard what came next.

"5:50 on the dot," he reported. My jaw became stiff and my smile tightened into a thin line. Mind racing, I watched powerlessly as Dan picked up the bin and piled it into the back room. I was afraid. So much so in fact that I wasn't aware when Dan re-entered the room. I had been trying so hard to calm the dizzying whirr of my thoughts that I didn't notice when he gave me the same look as the girl with the pink hair had when she couldn't decide if I spoke English or not.

I was reassured at last that my letter would be alright, but alarmed because I didn't know if I would be.

I was wrong to have been so worried about Jawsie, for he was now far from my mind, the least of my worries. Sure, 5:50 put me right in the middle of Jawsie Danger Zone, but it also meant something else. *My mom would be on her way home.* It was this new thought that scared me most. If I didn't make it home before she did, I might as well just feed myself to Jawsie first in order to save her the trouble. It was nearly six o'clock, and if I had listened to the man now in possession of my letter, my gold, the thing sitting lonely in a bin in the back of some stuffy room, maybe the dark nausea that was beginning to creep through my stomach and nestle itself into the back of my throat wouldn't be so strong. I should have been getting home. *Who knew that such a commonplace question deserved such a terrifying answer?*

"Thank you." I nodded and ran for the door, hoping to leave my uneasiness behind like the powdery dirt from my sneakers, gathering in a dusty trail on the post office floor.

Once outside, the cold air greeted me callously, clearing the warmth and humidity from the post office out of my mind with one powerful gust, its thick chill piling into my lungs like an iron weight. Ignoring the cold, I rushed to my unattended scooter and wheeled it down the street, hoping that if I paid no attention to the blustering winds whipping past my raw skin, or the cold, or the weary exhaustion of my body, or even my will to give up, it would go away.

Instead, it got worse.

As luck would have it, about five seconds into my trip home, it started to drizzle, little needle-like droplets of water that swell and sharpen, and it wasn't long before this shower became a cold, hard, rain. Soon enough, it began to pour. Another ten or fifteen seconds and my entire body was drenched, my hair so thoroughly soaked it would appear as if I had just been thrown into a pool. My clothes themselves had practically melted into my body, leaving me feeling like I were on some sort of cruel conveyor belt, using all of my strength to push myself forward, but remaining right where I had started—trapped. The rain itself seemed to be seeping into my very skin, with each pellet of water having very little trouble penetrating my body and sinking right in, leaving only the tremors of their chill after they had gone.

By the time I reached Acorn Boulevard, I had to trudge through the flooded grass and drag my scooter behind me through the puddles because the water was starting to submerge the streets. No matter how great my resistance, despite the fight I might put up, I knew that this wasn't going to be easy.

A few moments of struggle later and I was nearing my street, almost home. Of course I wasn't there yet, but on the other hand, I was so close that I couldn't help but celebrate. I tilted my head downwards, away from the rain, and attempted to dry my face with my sleeve. Since both were thoroughly drenched by this time anyway, my efforts had little effect. I shrugged, pulling my scooter closer towards the intersection. The storm hardly mattered, anymore. *I had succeeded.*

I rounded the corner and stopped dead in my tracks, my recent mistake becoming overwhelmingly clear. *I had spoken too soon.* My heart was the first to notice, pounding, panicking, ramming itself against my chest as if trying to break through.

Much like myself at that moment, it was unable to escape. I was trembling, but this time it was for reasons which had nothing to do with the cold. My lungs were bursting, but when I opened my mouth for air, only the rain seemed to settle inside. Gasping, I choked it down, nerves searing with the unsettling sensation that I was drowning as the water rushed past my throat. My eyes were unblinking, terrified of what lay ahead, blocking my passage out of harm's way.

I had just seen Jawsie, raging down the pavement with only one obstacle in his path—*me*.

chapter four

Jawsie's face was dripping with water, his ears flying far behind him as if they were having trouble keeping up. Either that, or they too, just wanted to keep their distance. The sounds of the storm were gone, and in their place was that of his nails as they met the pavement, paws smashing through the flooded streets, choke leash snaking itself through the water in his wake.

I wanted to run, but my body felt like lead, suddenly weighed down by the water I had swallowed. I tried to scream, but the sound got caught in my throat just before it could surface, gagging me as I struggled for another breath. All I could do was watch the eyes of the animal now approaching, their wild emotion becoming more and more clear with each step he took. He looked numb here, emotionless almost, running for the sole reason of not wanting to be still. He didn't mean to hurt me, yet there was still a good possibility he might. He wouldn't consider his actions, and there were no thoughts behind them. He was coming closer.

I felt almost like I was trapped in a dream, one of those dreams where you can't escape. The only difference was that in a dream, your mind and your body are unconnected. Somewhere deep inside, a part of you knows that you're sleeping, and if you just lie still, you'll wake up before anything gets the chance to hurt you.

This right now, was not the case.

Seeing as my body, in those last few moments, had chosen to fail me, I turned to my brain. Luckily, it hadn't given up on me just yet, and after a few fear-filled seconds of searching, I had come up with a plan. It wasn't a great plan, and actually, not a good one, either, but a plan nonetheless. When you're on the street alone in the rain with a wild dog running straight toward you, any course of action is better than none.

My thoughts were cut short by the sound of Jawsie's manic breaths.

I had no more time to think.

I had to do something, but I had hesitated, and by that time it was too late.

A sharp pain cut its way into my left leg. Within a moment, my nerves were exploding with heat, my skin practically on fire. I was afraid to look down, scared of what I might see. After all, I didn't need any visual evidence to know that I had been bitten, nor to comprehend that it wasn't good.

Powerlessly, I shook my leg away from the dog, begging it not to come near me, not to touch me again. I could feel the part of my jeans that had been ripped with the bite, and worse, the knot in my stomach as I realized that the warm sappy liquid accumulating at the wound was not the rain, but rather blood.

As this realization came, so did the fright.

"OUCH!" I screamed, finding my voice wavering somewhere between shock and fear. I panicked. "Help!" I yelled to nobody. It was impossible for anyone to hear me. Everyone was in Jawsie-lockdown. I needed to carry out my plan alone.

"Jawsie!" I called shakily, trying to blink back tears. "Please," I bit my lip. "JAWSIE, OVER HERE!" He glanced up impatiently, curious as to what I was doing, or confused as to why I would be distracting him from his game of leg tug-of-war.

"Jawsie look!" Using all of my might, I hurled my scooter down the street towards the direction I had come, and as far away from me as I could possibly make it go. It clattered to the ground helplessly a few yards away, handlebars scraping against the curb. I watched as the front wheel unattached and rolled to the other side of the road.

"GO GET IT BOY! FETCH!" I somehow managed to sound excited through the apparent unevenness of my tone. Spotting the spinning wheel, Jawsie lost interest in me and ran in pursuit of the scooter.

I didn't get to see what happened next. I mean, I probably could have stuck around to watch, but I was too busy running down the street as fast as I could possibly manage in the opposite direction of the event. Actually, I don't really think you could call it running. It was more of a cross between a hobble and a sprint, my injured leg dragging limply behind me like a child's toy being pulled by a string.

After a minute or so, I thought I heard the click of claws behind me, but I didn't dare look back. I forced myself to keep moving until I had reached my destination, whether it be back at home or clamped between Jawsie's teeth. If there was still hope, I wouldn't surrender yet.

Using all of my remaining strength, I raced up my driveway, ducking under windows and attempting to dodge the falling raindrops as I went. I looked back for the first time just before I had reached the side of the house. In the corner of my vision, a faint outline of my mother's car was making its way down the street. I could only hope that she hadn't seen me, but at that point, the reassurance felt empty. Whether it was the sweat, blood, rain, or tears, or perhaps the combination of them all settling into my skin, something at that moment made me realize that despite my reluctance to surrender, my time was up. I had to get inside—quick.

My first instinct was to run in through the back door. I had actually made it about two-thirds of the way there once I realized that this would probably cause more harm than good, considering that the door would be locked and I would have to knock to get inside. I could just see my mom's face if she were to open it, returning from work to find her daughter standing outside in the rain with a huge gash in her leg, undoubtedly because she broke every rule ever set forth for her. *That would end well.*

Maybe I can crawl through the basement window, I thought to myself as I ran over to the place on the ground below my bedroom. The window was small and sat right at ground level, but if I were able to squeeze in through it my effort would be little in comparison to the price I would otherwise have to pay. Kneeling down, I tried unsuccessfully to slide the pane open, realizing within a moment that it was bolted shut, locked in preparation for the storm. Trying to pick through it would only be a waste of time.

After a few seconds of frustration, I gave up on the basement window and decided to find another way in. As I began to stand, my foot slid on the fluid-like dirt. About as quickly as I had gotten to my feet, I was sent straight back to the ground, now a thin, watery mud, oozing through the yard like some sort of runny soup. Yet, as my body hit the Earth and icy drops of mud consumed every trace of heat that still clung to my body, falling into a bowl of soup didn't seem so bad. At least soup was warm, and unlike the gritty sludge now in my mouth, soup did not taste like dirt.

By this time, there were more areas on my body covered in the mud than not, and so not particularly caring if one more mark would spoil my outfit, I made no resistance to the fall, nor any remarkable efforts to stand quickly afterwards. Instead, for the first time all afternoon, I began to wonder if what I was doing was actually worth it. It was a lot to risk for a letter, a letter that in all truth might have already been sent too late. It was a strange time for logic to kick in; leaving me to wonder what exactly I was doing after most of the damage had been done. In all actuality, I didn't understand it myself. In fact, from all the events of the entire afternoon, only one thing I knew was for certain. Something was compelling me to risk facing a huge punishment, losing virtually all of the heat in my body, and even becoming dinner, and it wasn't just for one letter. There had to be more to the story—parts that even I was yet to figure out.

I sighed. There was no use in fighting for an answer, just as there was no use in fighting a mud that was somehow watery enough to splatter my entire body, but failed to cushion a fall. I wiped my eyes, shifting my weight onto my knees.

That was the key. I couldn't fight the mud, but rather, find a way to make it play to my advantage.

I smiled, deciding against the idea only when the rain against my face sent its dirt-streaked runoff seeping into my mouth.

I still had one hope.

Without wasting time, I shuffled over to the trampoline, sitting unaffected by the chaos in its familiar and now strangely fear-affiliated spot. Once I had reached it, I positioned myself at its side, and then, using all of my strength, began pushing it closer towards the roof. Under normal conditions, the trampoline wouldn't have budged if I had tried to move it. That day however, the mud below me acted as a sort of massive dolly, helping me to slide it into place. As I worked, it suddenly became clear just how close I had come to missing the trampoline altogether when I had fallen earlier. Just a few inches closer towards the side of the house and I would have plummeted straight to the ground. I did my best to ignore the shiver this thought sent up my spine and tried to shake off the idea. With a side of the trampoline pushed directly underneath the roof, I wouldn't have to worry about falling and hitting the ground if I slipped again. This time, I would be sure to have a safety net.

When the trampoline had at last been settled into its desired spot, I crawled onto it, stomach-first, as to not irritate my aching leg any more than necessary. Leading with my right leg, I began to stand, distributing my weight onto the side of my body which hadn't previously served as a Jawsie chew-toy. Once my balance was set, I began to jump, aligning myself with the edge of the roof as I did so. The muscles in my legs were burning, my right knee threatening to buckle without the help of its counterpart to absorb half of the pressure. Nonetheless, despite the arguments of my body and brain, warning me that I couldn't make it, I felt strangely untroubled. Of course I knew that what I was doing was dangerous, especially since I would be using only one leg. Yet somehow, each passing warning I received had a near opposite affect from the one intended. *I simply didn't have time for hesitation or worry.* Sure enough, as soon as I had reached the perfect height, I flung my feet outwards, thrusting myself towards the roof.

I suddenly understood just how good hesitation could be. It stops you from having second thoughts after your actions are too late to change.

Only as I was flying through the air did it occur to me that I had jumped on an angle, and that if I missed the roof now, the result would probably earn me a broken ankle. No trampoline lay underneath me to break my fall. However, seeing as I was about ten feet off the ground at the moment—the peak of my jump, I realized that I wasn't exactly in a good position to change my mind. Practically able to hear the sirens of the ambulances that I was convinced would soon be lined up in my driveway, I closed my eyes, unable to watch. Blindly, I reached out my arms, desperate for them to clutch onto something before I began the long trip back towards the mud. After what seemed like an eternity of frantic grasping, I felt my shoulder scraping the side of a rain soaked shingle. I opened my eyes, surprised to see my arms pressed against the edge of the roof, holding me upright. Not daring to look down at my dangling legs, I shifted my weight onto my elbows, using them as leverage to propel the rest of my body into safety.

Heart still pounding in my chest with what appeared to be a very painful expression of relief, I squirmed my way forward until both of my feet were a safe distance away from the edge. The hardest of my journey was over *at last*. Then again, I had learned the hard way not to speak too soon. The wet roof was rushing with water, but I made it to my window with little strain. As quietly as I could, I lifted its unlocked latch and climbed inside.

I took my first step into safety, unaware that in spite of all the dangers I had avoided, one had been left ignored. Now it sat before me, a rather large unforeseen setback in the form of two widening blue eyes. Frozen in place, all I could do was stare back in astonishment. To my misfortune, the eyes continued to return my gaze. Unblinking, they watched as I staggered the rest of my way into the room, shutting the window behind me. Slowly, I found my voice.

"Nadia?"

chapter five

Stunned, I took a step toward my sister.

"Cara!" she nearly screamed, both hands clasped dramatically over her mouth, feet glued to the floor. I didn't dare move towards her. Her eyes were wide with nervous curiosity and skin white as a sheet—who could blame her; I probably looked like a wreck, if not like some kind of swamp monster. She still recognized me at least, which was a good sign. Nonetheless, her face told me that she'd just had a surprise encounter with aliens from another planet, much less a sibling. Before I could manage a word to explain myself, Nadia was back in full-swing, as sharp as ever.

"Come sit here," she instructed. Her jaw had relaxed, and the surprise was gone from her eyes. Typical Nadia. Only the color in her cheeks couldn't manage to keep up, but it was quickly returning, the blood rushing back to her face. When I didn't respond, she took control. Grabbing me by the hand, she led me to her bed and motioned for me to take a seat on top of the comforter, shoving stuffed animals, crayons and stray puzzle pieces out of the way as we went.

"On second thought, maybe you ought to sit down in the bathroom," she decided, eyeing her white blankets and giving me a once-over. "No offence, but you look kind of gross."

"None taken Nad," I murmured, following her across the hall.

"So?" she demanded once I was seated on the edge of the bathtub. "What happened? Where were you? Did you sneak out? Well, you must have! But *why*? You know it's Jawsie's walking time, don't you? I mean, really, Cara, he could be outside on the streets right this very second!"

I wondered how long she had been watching me, how much she had seen, but I was afraid to know the answer. I could just imagine how I must have looked; navigating through my own lawn like it was some sort of brilliantly constructed deathtrap, falling victim to the mud and acting as a helpless object to the rain.

Maybe I'll be able to avoid her, I thought to myself as Nadia went on shooting off questions, almost faster than the rate at which she could think them up. *Maybe if I just sit here she won't even notice that I'm not answering, or my leg.* I sighed; there was no longer any point to my optimism. By that time, there was nothing I could really do to hide my secret from Nadia.

Right then, as if on cue, Nadia validated my fears:

"EWW!" she wailed. "Look at your knee! It's your whole leg, look at it! What happened?" Aware that I had never had the chance to look at the bite, I reluctantly glanced down to see the damage.

I don't really want to get into details, both for my sake and yours, but I will say this: it was BAD. My knee was skinned pretty terribly, and with the rips in my jeans from my fall in the mud, it wasn't difficult to see the small tooth marks where Jawsie had punctured my leg. The bleeding had stopped, but it had left its fair share of stains.

Almost instantly, I felt a stinging pain where I had been looking, as if my body had been waiting to punish me until I could see what I had done to it. I reached over to touch the bite, wondering if it had been infected, but all I could feel was the raw and tender skin around the mud-coated gash.

I rolled up the leg of my jeans and pressed my fingers in closer to the bite, wiping away the mud that covered it, which was now more crimson than brown. As my fingers finally made contact with the wound, my body instantly responded, and my hand recoiled automatically. Pain from the bite itself was sent exploding throughout my body like thunder to the sky, and the searing heat my nerves sent was enough to make every other ache and tenderness of my body feel insignificant to its superior sting. I winced and forced my eyes to look away from the bite, as if not seeing it would make it go away. I'm no expert, but even then, I was still pretty sure that ignoring my wound was probably not the most effective way of treating it. Then again, coating it in dirt and letting the wet denim of my pants rub against it as I crawled out in the rain might not have been a fantastic way to ease the pain either.

Nadia cringed slightly at the sight, but then unfolded herself to get a better look. "Wait just one second, Cara. I'll help you." Her voice was urgent but sweet, and I figured that she was mimicking the doctors on TV. Deciding that her newest adventure would be playing the part of the nurse, Nadia stood and walked towards the closet, returning to my side moments later with a wash cloth. She leaned over the tub and turned the water on high, letting it warm before I could clean my cuts.

It wasn't long before I found myself explaining everything to Nadia. Relaying the events of the afternoon actually felt better than I thought it would. In fact, fitting my feelings into words also helped me to sort out parts of the story for myself. Looking back on it then, I realized that my letter and the project which had begun it were now two unrelated things, although I was sure that they hadn't started out that way. I was yet to understand the reason for this split, but was too involved in my story to sort out the details, much less to notice the sound of the garage door as my father returned home from work. When I had finally finished, Nadia's eyes were wider than ever and her mouth was slightly open. This time though, she didn't look afraid.

"So what do you think, Nad?" I asked, hoping she would somehow understand. My sister, who as always was trying to dramatically boost the situation, was silent for a moment. Slowly, she opened her mouth.

"Wow." The silence that followed seeming almost unnatural, considering who it was that had left it. This from Nadia, who couldn't keep quiet for a minute if her life depended on it, was not something to be ignored. It was a compliment much bigger than I'd expected. I turned off the water and dried my leg, tossing my dirty washcloth into the wastebasket for fear of explaining its condition to my mom on laundry day. Through it all, Nadia was still struggling to regain her speech. "Cara? Can I help?" she whispered, swallowing hard.

Ignoring the stinging in my knee, I felt myself smiling, surprised at how the past few moments had matured her. Then again, Nadia never ceased to amaze me. I felt the pain numb, and my smile grew larger as I realized that this second-grader was now dressing my leg with the ease of a trained professional. Nadia was really something else. Either that, or she watched too many hospital shows.

"Thanks, Nad," I beamed, feeling good now that I had told my secret, and even better knowing that now, I wasn't alone. "For the gauze, I mean. And for listening and wanting to help out too. That really means a lot."

"Cara? Nadia? I need you two in the kitchen!" I could hear my mom yelling from downstairs. I jumped a little at the sound of my name. Nadia seemed not to notice.

"Coming!" she stood, moving towards the hall.

"Nad!" I called her back. "What should I do?"

"About what?"

I motioned to my muddy clothes.

"Ohh, right." She bit her thumbnail. "One second." I watched as she left the room , returning seconds later with a set of pajamas and a bathrobe. "Put these on."

"Thanks, you're a lifesav—"

"Girls! In the kitchen, please!"

"We're on our way!" I pressed a hand against the shower wall and forced myself back to my feet. "Nad, why don't you go ahead?" She didn't argue, shutting the door behind her. Hastily, I pulled off my wet clothes and tossed them into the bathtub, hoping that the water might wash away some of the stains. I then reached for the pajamas Nadia had brought and slipped them on, wrapping a towel over my wet hair when I was finished to give the impression that I had been in the shower. Of course I would eventually have to tell my parents about my dangerous outing that afternoon. In fact, I was sure that there would be a time when we would all look back on the incident and laugh. (I would be waiting until *that time* to tell them.)

I opened the door and found Nadia waiting on the other side with a box of tic tacs. "Take a handful," she shrugged, pouring them into my palm. "I forgot to tell you earlier, but your breath smells like dirt."

There was nothing I could say.

Nadia had never been good with keeping secrets but she was always a good friend, and I knew I could trust her with what she now knew. The rest would be up to me. I just had to get through the night, have dinner with a moderately pleasant disposition, and I would be home-free. The day would soon be behind me, and above all, the letter would be safely on its way to Washington.

"Come on, Nad," I waved her towards the hall, eager to put the afternoon behind me. *Just put on a happy face,* I thought to myself as we headed down the stairs. *The letter will be delivered, your leg is fine. Just put on a happy face…*

We reached the foyer within a few seconds, and turned quickly into the kitchen. Automatically, we each grabbed ourselves a plate from the stack that was sitting on the island in the middle of the room and helped ourselves to the different foods that were laid out, buffet style. Our plates heaping with food, we trudged into the dining room where our family usually ate dinner.

The table itself was unusually elegant, draped in a silky red tablecloth, with a lacey placemat set out in front of each seat. Mom's good silver salad bowl was out, and cloth napkins had been placed at each setting as opposed to the usual paper ones. Three cream-colored candles served as the table's centerpiece, the tallest in the middle. The small blue flowers randomly etched into the wax perfectly matched the décor of the rest of the room.

"It's beautiful in here," I said, quickly running through all the important dates I could remember and trying to decide what the cause of the celebration might be. *It wasn't anyone's birthday, not an anniversary, couldn't be a holiday…*

"Thank you, Cara," I heard my mom call from behind, pushing past me to set a napkin down on the table. She was still in her work outfit, and I could see the faint spots on her blouse where the rain had pelted her on her way to the parking lot. She never had a substantial liking for jewelry, but tonight, a thin string of crystal beads were looped twice around her neck. My dad followed her into the room. I hardly ever saw him dress up, but he was looking his very best tonight in kaki pants and a dress shirt that Nadia and I had bought him for Father's Day. This was definitely a special occasion.

"Happy, uh, congratulations…," I stammered, hoping that this might cover it.

My mom wrinkled her nose the way she always did when she had no idea what I was talking about. She looked down at the table and then back at me. Noticing my bathrobe, Nadia's ballet outfit, and our plates, they hurriedly explained that a family new to the neighborhood was coming to join us that night. As it turned out, my mom had met them at the supermarket on her way home from work and had invited them over to dinner. For the first time that night, I became aware of the four extra chairs set around the table. *Perfect timing.*

"Girls, will you do me a favor and put on some nicer clothes?" my mother asked, rushing the plates Nadia and I had taken back into the kitchen. "And no costumes, Nadia," she added as an afterthought, seeing it necessary to clarify. I lingered for a moment, watching her set our untouched dinners aside on the countertop.

"Hurry," my father added searching an overhead cupboard for a match to light the candles. "They'll be here soon."

So much for my casual evening.

I hope these new people will be nice, I thought to myself as I hurried upstairs to get dressed, relieved that I would at least be changing into something dry and not caked in mud. I stopped for a minute to adjust the bandage on my leg. *And if they have a pet, please let it be a miniature poodle.* I'd had enough of big dogs for awhile. Within a few minutes, a properly clothed Nadia and I were seated on the living room couches near the front of the house, nervously awaiting the arrival of our guests.

"I don't think I match," I complained to Nadia, crossing my arms and looking down at my outfit. She nodded in agreement and I chucked a throw pillow at her, aiming to miss. I had decided to wear a yellow cotton t-shirt and a maxi skirt I couldn't remember buying, so assumed that it must have once belonged to an older cousin. The skirt was simple, mostly white with a few red and blue flowers stitched on towards the hem.

"You look great sweetie, love the skirt!" I could hear my mom, always one to vouch for hand-me-downs, yelling from the kitchen.

"Thanks, Mom." I rolled my eyes. Although the skirt wasn't one of my favorite things to wear, I had chosen it because it was the longest one I had, stretching nearly to the floor. I figured that this would be good to hide my leg, which surprisingly hadn't been aching as much after Nadia had cleaned it up. I had originally tried on a pair of jeans, but at least for now, they were too stiff to wear over my leg, rubbing like sandpaper against the swollen skin.

Nadia had thrown on a printed sundress that she had gotten on a family trip to Florida. She had attempted to braid her short hair, but it came out looking more like a mess.

I was so distracted by the sound of the doorbell that I didn't notice the throw pillow being tossed back to me, hitting me square in the chest.

"They're here!—Ouch!—Nadia that wasn't funny!" I threw the pillow aside and stood up to race a near hysterical Nadia to the foyer. The second I shifted my weight onto my injured foot, I knew I was going to pay for it. I did my best to cover up the wincing that followed with a fake sneeze, remembering the hard way that it hurt to walk.

Doing my best not to appear as if I was limping, I hobbled my way over to the front door, which my sister had reached a good ten seconds beforehand. Still laughing, she undid the lock and swung it open. On the other side, I saw Sandy standing with three others I assumed were her family.

"Hi, please come in! Welcome to the neighborhood!" I gestured towards the house. The first to step inside were Sandy's parents. Both were smiling, but they somehow seemed cold. Maybe the fact that they were dressed from head-to-toe in matching gray polyester suits had something to do with it, but seeing the two of them couldn't help but make me feel like I was about to get in trouble for something. The only distinguishable difference between their pinstriped outfits was what they wore around their necks: Sandy's father was sporting a stiff gray tie while her mother styled a short boring necklace made of unpolished stones. Not to my surprise, the woman's graying hair was pulled into a painfully tight bun which was tied with a (you guessed it) gray scrunchy at the back of her neck. After saying hello and introducing myself, I took a good look at the pair of them. Instantly, I had no question whatsoever as to why Sandy wanted to stand out.

Following behind her parents, she and a smaller girl stepped through the doorway. Sandy was wearing a purple tunic so florescent that I assumed it must be able to glow in the dark. Her top was belted with a teal sash, and below this was a pair of midnight-blue leggings, tucked into her spray painted shoes. Her ears sported the most sparkly chandelier earrings I had ever seen anyone wear before. The smaller girl, a redhead who looked younger than me and a little bit older than Nadia, had on a corduroy jumper with a pair of argyle socks, all incorporating similar shades of pink. The thick scrunchies she used to fasten the ends of the world's most flawless pigtail braids were made of the exact same color fabric as the rest of her outfit. If perfection had a store, she was a frequent shopper there.

"Hello," my sister chirped, eager to play the part of the hostess. "My name is Nadia. What's yours?"

The smaller girl stepped forward from behind Sandy, straightening her already perfect posture. She opened her mouth to introduce herself. "My name is Cornelia Ann V. Giraffing. The V. stands for Victoria," she replied, almost out of breath from saying the longest name in history. *So that's where 'Sandra Guinevere Vivian' came from!* I thought to myself as the younger girl extended her arm towards me for a business-like handshake. Sandy looked apologetic. Nadia just seemed confused.

"*Okaay*," she spoke my mind, dragging out the word in one long breath as she searched for a response. "That's quite a name you've got there," she managed after a second. "Can I call you Cornelia, or maybe Nellie for short?"

Cornelia Ann V. Giraffing (the V. stands for Victoria) shook her head in a slow nod as she thought of a proper compromise. "You may call me Cornelia V.," she said at last, like that was a better alternative.

"That sounds great." I smiled, trying not to sound too amused. Cornelia V. agreed, and I introduced myself to her, and Sandy and Nadia to each other. After we had all met, Nadia and I led Sandy and her sister into the kitchen.

"Everything is delicious, so don't be afraid to try as much as you want," I offered, reclaiming my dish from the island.

"As you can see, Cara certainly wasn't shy about that," Nadia added, eyeing my full plate as she added a breadstick to her own. "I guess I'm not either."

While I sifted through my pasta salad, tossing the mushrooms into the sink when nobody was looking, the Giraffing sisters moved through the buffet mechanically, taking small, equally-sized portions of each dish.

Once everybody's plates had been filled, we made our way toward the dining room, where the adults were already waiting with large portions of food set out in front of each of them. We took our places at the table and began to eat, consuming our food like it was the elixir of life. At first, the parents were the only ones who were talking, swapping big, phony smiles and exchanging the classic, *So how do you like the neighborhood?* and, *Oh, your house is so lovely* gibberish. Not to mention the periodic, *Thank you so much for inviting us,* and ever popular, *Thank you for joining us.*

When meeting new people, I usually relied on Nadia to start up a conversation, and I couldn't remember a time when she had let me down. Unfortunately, the earlier events of the evening had quieted her, just moments before I could put her gift of extreme chattiness to use. Now it seemed as if Nadia, Sandy, Cornelia V., and I were competing in a round of the silent contest, all trapped in a four-way tie.

After what seemed like hours of listening to the adults' discussions, I grew tired of pretending to be interested and began a series of pathetic attempts to start up a conversation among the kids. The small-talk was bland, starting with a series of unimportant questions, and ending with a few observations about the weather. I'm not sure how, but thankfully my efforts were somehow successful, and the conversation moved from forced to natural within a few moments. Things at the table soon grew far from awkward and I was actually beginning to enjoy myself.

Strangely enough, Nadia and Cornelia V. instantly clicked; Nadia finding some quality in Cornelia V. that she couldn't get from a bottle of clothing starch, and even more surprisingly, Cornelia V. coming to terms with Nadia's energy. The two were inseparable before they were halfway done with their dinners.

Once the ice was broken, the same went for Sandy and me. The conversations multiplied almost as quickly as the food on our plates disappeared, and after dinner, Nadia led the four of us upstairs to the guest bedroom.

In reality, there was nothing really out of the ordinary about my guest bedroom. Due to our house's lack of an attic, it had become more of a storage place than anything else, filled with abandoned exercise equipment, and stacks of old books, toys, games, and boxes of clothes nobody had gotten around to donating. I couldn't count the number of times my mom had tried to clean it up, but the stacks of old or outgrown things always seemed to be accumulating, and after awhile, she would always give up. In the back of the room, however, there was a large walk-in closet with strong shelves capable of supporting me if I wanted to climb them. I had spent many hours after school or on weekends reading, perched comfortably on the shelves, or playing solitaire down below on the carpet. The closet could probably hold five or six people comfortably, which made it a perfect place for Nadia, Sandy, Cornelia V., and I to sit.

Eagerly, Nadia dragged Monopoly, her favorite game, off from one of the closet's shelves and began to set it up on the floor. After insisting that we play it, the four of us gathered around the board. Nadia's game piece was always the train, and I usually chose the dog. Cornelia V. claimed the battleship, and Sandy took the top hat. Once we were situated, the game began.

It wasn't exactly as fun as I had hoped because Cornelia V. stopped us every couple minutes to check the instructions and see if we were playing fairly. We had each gotten in about three or four turns in when my mother appeared in the hall. She made her way toward the closet, trying not to trip over a pile of Dr. Seuss books as she did so. After maneuvering around the treadmill, she announced to us that dessert was ready downstairs and available if we wanted it. Instantly, seeing as these were the magic words that could snap anyone under the age of ten into a completely different mindset, Nadia and Cornelia V. quickly abandoned our game and bounded towards the stairs. Halfway there, Cornelia V. remembered her manners and slowed to a walk, pulling up her wrinkled socks and fixing her faultless braids. Despite her intentions, she appeared about as elegant as a dog trying to impersonate the Queen of England.

Having successfully delivered her message, my mother turned and headed back in the direction of the kitchen, leaving Sandy and I alone. The room was silent with Nadia and Cornelia V. gone, and the quiet reawakened my memories from earlier that day. Leaning against the side wall, I began to play them over in my mind. I remembered Jawsie's bite, the letter, and my broken scooter. I remembered Sandy's smile, and our connection on the bus. With all of the new excitement, I remembered what had been so important to me just a few hours back. With these memories came a strong urge to tell someone my secret. Telling Nadia had not been enough. She could only grasp the concept in the way that little sisters can. Right now I was in desperate need of someone who would *really* understand me. Someone I could trust. *Someone like Sandy.*

chapter six

"Sandy," I thought out loud.

"Yeah?" she replied as she tried to rub out a wrinkle that had formed near the bottom of her shirt.

"Can I tell you something?" I asked her, unable to stop excitement from seeping into my voice

"Sure." She deserted the wrinkle and fixed her attention on me. It was quiet for a moment as I racked my brain, searching to find the words that could describe the whirlwind the past few hours had put me through. She waited patiently for me to speak, forks scraping the last crumbs of dessert from their plates downstairs the only sound to be heard.

"Come here," I motioned, my mind still unable to sort out the day's events. As she got up to follow me, I pushed a box of doll clothes off of one of the closet's shelves, leaving it bare.

There's something about elevation that helps people think clearly. Whether it's the top of a mountain or the uppermost shelf of a walk-in closet, being away from the ground, even for a little while, can really help a person to gather their thoughts. When you're up there, everything has a way of making sense. I was hoping that this perceptiveness would rub off on Sandy—to help her understand a day I was only just beginning to comprehend.

Moving to where the box had once rested, I jumped up, grasping the board with my fingertips. I tried to swing a leg over the shelf to get me into a sitting position, but it was physically impossible with my skirt. Moving on to Plan B, I reached up to the second shelf and began to pull down some of my mom's old magazines. Once their pages had created a stack on the floor that was a good height, I hopped onto the pile like a stepstool and tried again. Successfully, I wormed my way up onto the shelf, squirming around until I had positioned myself sitting fully upright. Above my head now, there were two other horizontal rows of shelves, spaced much closer together than the ones below the panel I had just mounted. I continued climbing up until I had scampered my way up to the top shelf, with my head just a foot or so away from the high ceiling.

"Do you think you can climb this?" I called down to Sandy, making myself comfortable.

Looking genuinely surprised with the whole ordeal, she shrugged, deciding to cooperate. "I can try." She stood on the magazines and grabbed onto the shelving, scaling the wall with humble effortlessness. She ascended slowly but surely, losing her footing once or twice, but reaching the top shelf with little difficulty. Once seated, I began to explain my letter to the President for the second time that day. I told Sandy about how I wanted my opinions to influence changes in the government, or anywhere, actually, for the better.

I have to admit that going over my story again made the whole thing seem crazy, impossible almost, unlike when it unfolded; when it had seemed just as simple as breathing. The bottom line was that I knew I could help and didn't want to wait a decade or so until I was 'eligible' to do so. Maybe it was a bit extreme, but when your hopes are as high as the place you have to sit to sort them out, there's really no perspective that can stop you anyway.

I finished talking and the room fell silent. Sandy let each detail soak in, going over every fact until she came to a personal conclusion. Turns out she decided my idea wasn't so crazy after all. I thanked the elevation of the closet. For awhile, we sat in its strangely comforting humidity, excitedly fawning over the possibilities that come with the power to change, the 'maybes' and 'what ifs', creating thrilling situations that could feasibly become our future. I suppose that in this moment, Sandy had seamlessly merged with my story, becoming not its listener, but a piece of its plot. A part of the plan. We went on with this game for a long time, until the faint sounds of voices began to enter our ears.

"Cara, did you hear that?" Sandy asked, the lightness in her tone disappearing as she spoke.

I nodded, feeling relieved that I wasn't the only one hearing voices, but a bit fearful in knowing that they weren't just my imagination. Just then, another bout of voices echoed softly through the walls, the noise they brought drifting about the room like some sort of wandering ghost. I cupped a hand over my ear and leaned forwards away from the shelf in hopes of deciphering the sounds.

"That's my dad's voice," Sandy concluded after I had given up interpreting.

"Of course!" I exclaimed, doing my best to hide the relief in my voice. "The noises are coming from that vent."

I climbed down the shelves slowly and sat near the far corner of the closet.

"Here it is," I said, lifting the metal grill that was covering the vent by its hinges and allowing the muffled sounds to become clear voices. Curious, Sandy crawled off from the shelf as well, crouching next to me. Sandy rolled onto her side and I pressed my ear to the wall, hoping to get a better listen. Sure enough, Sandy was right. As I leaned in closer to the vent, I could hear both of our parents chatting steadily on some subject unknown to me.

"What are they *talking* about?" I whispered to Sandy. Our parents were spitting out national-level spelling bee words like bullets and I could only understand every other word that left their mouths. I couldn't help wondering why they used such big vocabularies when talking to new people.

"I can't tell," Sandy whispered as she moved herself closer to the vent, intent on comprehending something worthwhile. She nodded after a moment, wrapping up her thoughts. "I'm pretty sure that they're talking about work and their jobs, but I'm not positive." She propped herself up on an elbow to face me.

"Oh," I said, disappointed, covering the vent with the grill. The voices were instantly reduced again to nothing but an indistinct hum.

"So where *do* your parents work?" Sandy asked, playing off of the adults' conversation.

"My dad owns the Violet Turtle." I answered, "It's a little restaurant downtown, about twenty minutes from here. My dad did a lot of traveling before I was born, and so the foods he serves are from all over the world. You know, like French, Italian, Chinese, Mexican, and American too."

"I've heard of that place! It's supposed to be awesome!"

"Well, the food tonight was right off their menu, so if you liked it, you should definitely come see the restaurant sometime."

"Absolutely, dinner was fantastic! Does your mom work at the restaurant too?" Sandy asked.

"No, to be honest she's not much of a cook." I smiled, setting my injured leg out in front of me. "She's an English professor at the New Castle Community College. Most of her students are college-age but she has evening classes for adults too." Sandy nodded.

"That's really great."

"Thanks. And, what about your parents—what do they do?" I asked, giving her a shot at the question.

"Well, both of them have the same job," she started. "They're CEOs at the Giraffing Children's Hospital."

"Wow," I stared in admiration. "Are you talking about that huge clinic in West Liberty?"

"Yeah," She blushed, now timid, "My grandparents donated the money to build it, so it was named after them." Having nothing more to add to the discussion, she shyly steered the conversation away from her family. "Do you want to go downstairs and get some dessert?"

"Sure!" I exclaimed, standing to brush off the dust that had collected on my clothes from our climb before the two of us hurried downstairs.

Long before we had even reached the dining room, the overpowering essence of coffee struck us, and the soft sounds of classical music rang drowsily through the halls. In the living room, Sandy's parents, as well as my own, were seated across from one another in twin loveseats, still talking about work and picking at a small tin of caramel-covered popcorn. Nearest to the fireplace, Nadia and Cornelia V. were practically being swallowed up by two oversize armchairs. Each one sat hunched, stooped over a notebook and scribbling frantically into it. Once we approached them further, they gave no sign of acknowledgment towards us, and their manic writing continued on.

"What are you doing?" I asked Cornelia V., who now looked like a mad scientist trying to record an extensive formula before she forgot it. After a moment or two, they put down their books and looked up.

"We are playing a game," Cornelia V. answered, her tone similar to the one a mother might use to tell her child that they are too little to understand something. Seeing my less-then-amused expression, Nadia continued to explain.

"You see," she began, "we both rummaged around *my side* of our room and collected little trinkets that were lying around, like a tennis ball or a pencil eraser. Then, we put everything in a box, and now we're picking them out one at a time to write short stories about them."

"After we have finished writing, the respective narrator of each story will read their creation out loud, and we as a group will decide which one is best," Cornelia V. chimed in. "The person with the best story is awarded one point, and the first person who gets three points is the winner of the game!"

"Sounds *interesting*," I murmured, more to Sandy than the younger girls.

"Actually, that looks kind of fun," she shrugged. "Want to join in?" I didn't feel much like spending quality time with Cornelia V., but I nodded anyway, trying to be a good hostess. Besides, my leg was starting to hurt again, and resting it for a little while would probably do some good.

"Are we allowed to play too?" I asked Nadia, my voice making clear that Sandy and I were going to play no matter what her answer was.

"Yeah, sure," she bit her lip, glancing back at Cornelia V. to get her consent before turning to face me. "Before you can play though, you'll need some notebooks."

"We'll be right back then…and nice journals you've got there," I added, recognizing them as something from my backpack. Nadia and Cornelia V. didn't respond, having already gone back to their writing, so I let it go. Turning towards the direction we had come, I led Sandy back up the stairs and into my bedroom where we launched a hunt for something to write on. After a few minutes, I found a couple of old school journals resting under my bed and pulled them out, pleased with the discovery. There was a small purple one with a silver spiral going up the side, and an orange one with a mustard yellow elastic band wrapped around it to keep the pages together. Both of the notebooks were used, so I ripped out a few doodles and old homework assignments before offering Sandy a choice between them. Not much to my surprise, Sandy picked out the orange and yellow journal, the brighter of the two, leaving me with the purple one. Having found our notebooks, we sifted through the rest of the bedroom until we came across two relatively sharp pencils and then returned downstairs.

Our sisters hadn't moved from where they were seated near the fireplace and were now laughing at something Nadia had undoubtedly written. By the time we were seated, the laughter had died down and she was digging her hand around in the small box of ornaments, already impatient for the new game to begin.

"Alright, its time to start." She smiled as her hand connected with an object, concentration building visibly in her face as she worked to wrap her fingers around it. "Cornelia V. has set her watch to go off in ten minutes. When I reveal whatever it is I have in my hand, we'll have that amount of time to write. Got it?"

"Yeah," the rest of us chanted in unison, except for Cornelia V., who (of course) replied, "Yes, I do."

"Okay!" cried Nadia, the excitement in her voice growing with each word. "Ready, *set, GO!*"

As soon as the words left her mouth, Nadia unclenched her fist to reveal a small peppermint candy, aged to about four years. Energetically, she set it down on the table and then bent herself back over her notebook, already writing.

Still smirking at the trivial object placed before me, I looked over my shoulder at Sandy, wondering if she still wanted to play.

"Why not?" she whispered, shrugging her shoulders before opening to a fresh page in her journal. After a moment's hesitation, I turned towards my own notebook and did the same. In the ten minutes that followed, the room remained silent, except for the sounds of lead scratching against our pads of paper. Once in awhile, someone would crane their neck to get another glance at the candy, but other than that, we all remained protectively on top of our papers. When the quiet was finally broken by Cornelia V.'s watch alarm, the sound was enough to make me flinch. Seeing the need for new instruction, Nadia tossed her notebook aside and jumped back into her role as teacher.

"Time is up!" she cried, as if we hadn't already noticed. "Everyone put your pencils down! Now it's time for the fun part of the game. We'll go in a circle, and when it's your turn, you read your story out loud. Then, we vote on which one is the best. By the way, since there's more of us playing now, you can't vote for yourself."

"I will go first," Cornelia V. volunteered. She looked around the room, making certain that she had everyone's attention before beginning. "The Peppermint, by Cornelia Ann V. Giraffing…"

Cornelia V.'s story was just okay, considering that it had probably taken her more than half of the time just to write her name. Nonetheless, I was a little relieved when she had finished her sermon about a peppermint king coming to terms with the destruction of his monarchy in the Candy Kingdom after the Great Gummy Bear Revolution. Next came Nadia's story, which was actually more of a poem. She had written about a clan of peppermint aliens who lived on Mars and tried to take over the Earth. The dialogue was pretty creative, especially how she rhymed 'I'll annihilate your planet' with 'sang a peppermint named Janet'. Although comparatively better than Cornelia's work, I still almost dozed off. When her story was over, it was my turn to read.

Really, I had no right to criticize the other stories because the one I wrote was by far the worst. To save you the agony, all I will say is this: peppermint candies are best when left alone, and should, under no circumstance, be adopted by hospitable families of walruses. It was obvious I was not the winner of that round.

Sandy was the last to share her story. It was without a doubt one of the most amazing things I had ever heard. I mean, it's not easy to write something even remotely interesting when it's about a decaying peppermint; or at least that's how I saw it. The way Sandy wrote, it seemed like much more. As she read, her words were so insightful, so honest, that it was almost like she didn't need to make up the story at all; that she was only observing the one we were too blind to see. After having read the last word on her page she looked up to find Nadia and me listening with our full attention. Cornelia V. sat generally expressionless, but you could tell that she was impressed.

"That was fantastic!" I complimented her once I had managed to scrape my jaw up off the floor.

"Thanks," she smiled.

When it was time to choose the winner of the game, the verdict was undisputed. Sandy had won.

Time after time, Sandy pulled one victory after another, humbly accepting each one. You could hear how much heart she put into each word she chose, carefully phrasing each piece of the story into place like a jigsaw puzzle. The way she wrote is hard to explain, but the passion and sincerity behind it made you believe every word. Her stories had hypnotized us.

After her third win in a row, Sandy decided to forfeit the game and give somebody else a chance. Seeing as watching three kids move a pencil from left to right isn't really a spectator's heaven, I excused myself from the contest as well. Together, we headed into the kitchen for some dessert. I whipped up some instant hot chocolate and after scouring around a bit, we managed to find the remains of what was once an overflowing platter of my dad's homemade biscotti.

By the time we had polished those off, plus the last of the caramel corn, the Drs. Giraffing were just standing up from the couch, thanking my mom and dad for inviting them over, and making promises of another get-together sometime soon. It wasn't long until they had collected a protesting Cornelia V. and overly-stuffed Sandy at their side, leading them into the foyer. I stood by the opened door, watching the Giraffings make their way out to their car after we had all said our reluctant good-byes. Everyone seemed exhausted from their outing, but I noticed that Sandy had a slight bounce in her step as she followed her family down the driveway.

She must have had a really good time, I thought to myself.

Completely unaware of how I emulated her stride, I closed the door and made my way upstairs.

chapter seven

I fought to open my eyes as the bedroom light flickered on, hopelessly attempting to drown out my mom's voice as she called Nadia and me downstairs to breakfast.

"Cara, I mean it, wake up now. Don't make me come up there!"

"I'm up mom, don't worry." Groaning, I rolled onto my side and buried my face in the pillow. Before I could change my mind, I pushed the lavender sheets off from my legs and stumbled out of bed. Eyes only halfway opened, I stumbled over to the curtain that separated my side of the room from Nadia's and shoved it aside.

"You up?" I asked to the empty room, realizing seconds too late that Nadia was nowhere to be found. In her place, a sloppily made bed and a mountain of stuffed animals had been left behind.

Jealous of her ability to cope with mornings, I dragged myself down the stairs, a tight grip on the railing my only prayer of staying upright. Upon entering the kitchen, the smell of self-sugared breakfast cereal led me straight to Nadia, who, as I had suspected, had already started eating. She was seated at the kitchen table with a Pop-Tart in one hand and a spoon in the other, munching her way through a bowl of Lucky Charms. I yawned in acknowledgement, and headed over to the cereal cupboard. After finding a half-eaten box of Froot Loops, I took my place at the kitchen table where a cereal bowl and a glass of grape juice had already been set out for me.

"Guhmornen," I grunted in-between bites. By that time, Nadia had her full attention on scraping the last spoonful of Lucky Charms into her mouth.

"GOOD MORNING, CAR—" she cried, stopping only once she saw the look on my face. "Someone got up on the wrong side of the bed," she mumbled after a minute, somehow still managing to sound cheerful. I couldn't help but to laugh, simultaneously wondering if maybe she should cut back on the sugar for awhile. We ate the rest of breakfast in silence; while I was trying my hardest to stay awake, Nadia was deeply involved with her food. Just as I was finishing my last few sips of juice, my mother rushed into the kitchen fully clothed and ready to go, uncomfortable looking pumps pounding against the tile as she made her way across the floor. Her eyes, though already bloodshot, somehow managed to distort themselves even further as she discovered that we were still eating our breakfasts.

"Girls!" she yelled, her voice cracking halfway through the word as a more panicked sound set in. She took a long swig of coffee, which had a very minimal effect in calming her, and then continued. "Do you know what time it is? You're going to be late for school! Quick—go, get ready!" She looked from my face to Nadia's, and then downed the rest of the coffee in her mug.

All week, my mom had been grading essays for her college class, and the pressure to finish was really stressing her out. Recognizing this dangerous mood, my sister and I knew better than to object. So, about as humanly possible as it is to hurry in the morning, Nadia and I were out of the kitchen as fast as it would take you to spell your own name (unless of course you're one of the Giraffings', in which case we were much faster).

Once we had reached the bedroom, Nadia, as perky as she was, threw on a pleated denim skirt with a long sleeved pink polka-dotted top that she had found in a ball on the floor. She crawled under the bed to get her white tennis shoes and attempted to brush her short, messy hair. A few moments later, she gave up, looking like a person who had been hit with a bolt of static electricity. Altogether forgetting to brush her teeth, she was in and out the bedroom door in a second, sporting a large juice moustache above her upper lip.

I had almost worn a skirt as well, but dismissed the idea when I remembered my leg. Although nearly two weeks had passed since the incident with Jawsie and the bite was no longer painful, the remaining bruises and scabs practically guaranteed unwanted questions. Settling on a pair of blue jeans was definitely the safer way to go.

I could hear the coffee maker downstairs, brewing what was undoubtedly a second pot for my mom. If there was a day to make her angry, this was not it. Missing the bus was simply not an option. Crunched for time, I pulled open my drawer and threw on the first top I saw—a t-shirt I had tie-dyed over the summer. After brushing my hair *and* teeth thoroughly, I squeezed into a pair of sneakers and ran downstairs, not bothering to lace them. Nadia was waiting for me at the front door, all ready to go with her coat and lunch bag, backpack hanging lopsided off her shoulder. She shot me a look of impatience, and I rushed to meet her.

It was nearly 7:45, so I figured that the bus was still a few stops away. Even so, Nadia was frantic about missing her ride, and had been ever since she had met the Giraffings. Cornelia V. was in the grade above Nadia and the bus rides to and from school were their only time to talk to one another on weekdays. Not wanting to deprive her of this occasion, I grabbed my lunch money off the kitchen counter and slung my bag over my shoulder, forgetting to take a coat. We yelled a quick goodbye to our parents before rushing out the door.

The autumn air flushed my cheeks and sent small shivers of pre-Halloween excitement through my body. Nadia read my thoughts and reminded me with a small Cornelia V.-like eye roll that Halloween was still over three weeks away.

"So what?" I smiled, letting my fantasy roll away from me almost as fast as the school bus was speeding down the road towards us.

"Oh, the bus is here!" my sister squealed with exaggerated excitement, pointing and waving her arms. Two seconds later and she was sprinting down the driveway to meet it, her tousled hair flying in all directions. I followed slowly behind. The bus came to a screeching halt in front of our house and the door began to fold back. Nadia, who had nearly been run over, forced her way through before they had opened all the way and ran down the aisle, hurling herself into a seat with Cornelia V. Flinching slightly from the dramatic entrance, Cornelia V. quickly resumed her perfect posture and greeted my sister as if she was acting quite normally.

It had taken her a few weeks, but Cornelia V. was finally getting used to Nadia's over-the-top exuberance.

Without further delay, the girls engaged themselves deep in conversation, whispering back and forth at a rapid pace, pausing only to giggle, or in Cornelia V.'s case, correct grammatical errors. A moment or so later, I made my way down the aisle and slid casually into a seat with Sandy.

"So, did your letter come back yet?" she asked eagerly, like she did every morning.

"Not yet," I replied, "but it should be coming sometime soon, maybe even today!" I focused all of my energy on being optimistic.

"That's good," Sandy shrugged, not sounding quite as positive. "Hey, how did you think the math homework was last night?" she changed the subject.

"What math homework?!"

We continued to talk until the bus dropped us off at school, pulling to a stop with a respectable three wheels still in the street. Only one had found its way up onto the sidewalk, but that was to be expected. Instinctively, I squeezed myself into the aisle, trying to beat the sea of bus-sick kids pushing and shoving to get out into the fresh air. I stepped over the curb and waited for Sandy so we could walk to class together.

School was usually painless, with the exception of my daily run-in with the 'flower twins' Rose and Violet. In truth, the chances are very slim that either one of them could contribute anything to society except one colossal headache. Since the second grade, they have passed their time in the Mapleview Public School System teaming up to play practical jokes on the unsuspecting passerby, which on more than one occasion, has been me. They never get caught, and they never get bored, but in-between their sessions of plotting and scheming, which I assume must be tiring, they resort to a relaxing day or two of irritation beyond belief.

In my homeroom class, Rose sits behind me and Violet sits in front (or at least that's what I think; I've never been quite able to tell them apart, nor, for that matter, have I been able to understand how one person could get so unlucky with the seating chart).

Lucky for me, on that day, Rose and Violet were feeling particularly social. They leaned in towards each other, which meant I was squished between them, and began whispering to one another at a rate so fast, all of their words seemed to slur together (not that this mattered anyway, since they still managed to finish each others sentences).

All class period, my ears were drowned in their murmuring, which paused only for them to face forward and give an angelic smile each time the teacher turned around from her place at the chalkboard asking that "whoever is talking, please quiet down." By the end of class, she must have got it in her head that it was me, and so I was reminded twice to 'control myself' and 'give it a rest with the talking so that *Rose and Violet could have a chance to learn, too*'.

Thankfully, Sandy sat next to me. It was merely her presence that was keeping me from picking a direction to turn and 'wilting' one of those flower twins. Under her silent surveillance, I remained poised, and soon homeroom was over. I rushed out of the room before the twins could provoke me any further.

It was strange for me to get so worked up over something harmless, but I suppose that waiting for my letter to come had set me a little on edge.

Even though Violet and Rose weren't in any of my other classes, that didn't exactly make the rest of my day a barrel of monkeys. I went from room to room following my everyday routine; copying notes, writing essays, taking tests, and raising my hand. It wasn't until Kenzie Bird's pet hamster escaped from her backpack and was running loose around the classroom that things got interesting. Other than that, I had a normal, boring day.

I was sitting alone on the bus ride home that day because Sandy and Cornelia V. were being driven home by a friend and Nadia was at her ballet class. Taking advantage of the quiet, I began studying for a geography quiz. I had gotten halfway through my study guide when the bus reached my street corner. A few moments too late, the front wheels came screeching to a standstill and the back ones went skidding to the right, sliding off the street just in time to knock the stop sign lopsided on its post. Unaffected, I slid the paper inside my book, stood up from my seat and made my way down the aisle, backpack dragging along behind me. I stepped down from the bus, and after leaving it much more space than necessary to pull back onto the road, reopened my notes. Once it had sped away, I was about to resume my studying when something caught my eye…the mail truck!

My heartbeat started up like an engine, sucking all the breath from my lungs with one pulsating beat. In that moment, hope turned me numb. I had no idea how tightly my hands were gripping my textbook until I saw the imprints my nails left in the cover later that day. I didn't remember that I had still neglected to tie my shoelaces from earlier that morning. I only realized that I was running across the street with my books after I had started, all senses dead except for the hope that the President's response was waiting for me at the other end.

Within a few seconds, I had reached the mailbox. Not bothering to catch my breath, I grasped the brass handle with my fingertips and gave it a good yank. I forced my hand inside and pulled out a tall stack of envelopes, magazines, ads, and newsletters. Slowly, I sifted through them. *Bill, bill, junk mail, Nadia, bill, Dad, coupon, junk mail, Mom, Mom, bill, magazine, junk mail, catalogue.* Nothing for me. Sighing, I shut the mailbox, eyes turned towards the ground. Staring back up at me was something incredible.

The White House
1600 Pennsylvania Avenue NW
Washington, D. C. 20500

Carefully, as if it were a newborn child, I knelt to pick up the letter. *Had I dropped it before?* A shiver ran down my spine. My nerves went from dead to painfully responsive within a single second, as if in place of blood, electricity was flowing through me.

This could only mean one thing.

Trembling, I turned the precious cream envelope over in my hands, and sure enough, my name and address were written on the front in elegant gold script. The Presidential seal was marked in the upper right-hand corner. It was enough to make me lightheaded. I couldn't think straight, which might explain why I dropped my bag and the rest of the mail in the street and madly sprinted down the block to Sandy's house.

I put on the brakes just before my nose squashed into her front door. Too stunned to worry about manners, I rang her doorbell about a thousand times, simultaneously knocking as loudly as I could. Hearing the sound of running feet, I briefly stopped my clamoring to step back. An anxious silence fell over the air, and then at last, came the sound of a door creaking open. A familiar face peered out through the crack.

"Sandy," I gasped, holding up the envelope to her widening eyes, "it's here."

chapter eight

Sandy's face practically lit up the doorway. In an instant, she was glowing. Without saying another word, she dashed back into her house, leaving me on the front steps with my letter. After mumbling a quick something to Cornelia V., she returned with a bent scrap of paper and scribbled a quick message to the rest of her family. I had trouble standing still as she taped her note to the door, and even Sandy, who was usually patient, looked restless.

After skimming the crumpled slip of paper one last time, she stepped out the door, closing it behind her. I watched as she stumbled down the driveway and onto the street, not bothering to check for oncoming traffic before crossing it.

"Come on, Cara, let's go!" she called to me, making her way back in the direction I had come. I did my best to keep up with her long strides, and we walked down the driveway and towards my house in silence. We arrived a few minutes later, still in quiet.

I loosened my grasp on the envelope and held it up to show my friend.

"I can't believe he wrote back." Her eyes were glued to the envelope, but her face still looked doubtful of its existence. Slowly, she took the paper into her own hands. Looking at her, you would think she had been just trusted to handle some precious antique.

We stayed glued to our spot on the pavement for a few lingering seconds, as if the initial shock of receiving the White House letter had permanently fixed us to the asphalt. As the surprise slowly wore off, excitement set in. Spellbound, I picked up my bag and the rest of the mail I had dropped earlier. After managing all but a few seconds of anxious laughter, we dashed up the driveway and through the open garage.

The door was unlocked so we let ourselves in, neither of us saying a word, but both knowing where we were running to. We were cutting through the family room when I collided with J.J., who was blocking the doorway. The mail and my backpack flew to the ground, landing in a pile at my feet.

"Sandy is over," I told her, just to make sure she had noticed. "She and I are just going to—"

"—Work on some homework!" Sandy exclaimed with a bit too much enthusiasm, finishing our feeble attempt of a cover-story while holding the President's letter casually behind her back.

Unconvinced, J.J. didn't budge. She stood almost catlike—arms folded across her chest, eyes uncharacteristically alert. Ready to pounce, she smiled smugly at her prey, no doubt feeling fortunate that two mice had just wandered into her trap. She opened her mouth to protest, but I cut her off before she could string together an actual sentence.

"We'll be upstairs if you need us. Check the guest bedroom. See ya!" With that, Sandy and I whizzed off to the guest bedroom closet, leaving J.J. in a state of confusion. As I ran, I could just picture the face of my babysitter behind me.

Once she realized what had happened she would open her mouth again. Not wanting to waste the energy it would take to navigate her way through the clutter of the second floor however, she would reconsider. Hopefully, it would be another hour before she realized that neither of us was carrying a backpack, and for the time being, she would resort to watching a soap opera with a bowl of pretzels.

"Come on," I urged once we had reached the top shelf of the closet. The tremor in my voice was apparent but I made no effort to stabilize it. "Let's open it."

Sandy leaned in closer to me, setting the letter onto my lap as if I was the one who should do the honor. It was only when my fingers were about to tear through the paper that she made another sound, inhaling sharply as if she had forgotten something important.

"Wait, Cara!" she hissed, her tone almost harsh. "Shouldn't we wait for Nadia? She's in her bedroom right?" She unfolded her legs from beneath her and turned to climb down the shelves. "I'll go get her."

"She's at her ballet class today," I informed her, the temptation of tearing open the letter building up inside of me like water collecting in a dam. I did my best to suppress my irritation. "She won't be home for a *long* time."

"Well, then *maybe* it would be alright. But you *have* to tell her as soon as she gets home." Sandy eyed me sharply. Seeing my face, she hesitated for a moment and I thought she might change her mind. I shot her a pleading look and she shrugged, pulling herself back up onto the shelf instead.

I did my best to wait for her, and when she gave a quick nod of consent, I began to open the envelope. As carefully as I could, I tore the back open with my thumbnail. With a deep breath, I pulled up the flap and slowly reached my fingers inside. They emerged again with a letter, stuck closed with the Presidential seal. I peeled off the sticker and read out loud:

Dear Ms. Greybird,

Thank you for writing to the White House! We sincerely appreciate your concern, and urge you to maintain involvement in government activities.

It is our pleasure to inform you that exclusive tours of the White House are now available, including illustrious areas such as the Blue Room and Entrance Hall, or if you prefer otherwise, a scenic viewing of the grounds. Regular hours are from 7:30 a.m. to 12:30 p.m. Tuesday thru Saturday, excluding all federal holidays. You are encouraged to reserve tickets as early as possible, as a limited number of tours are available. Reservations can be made up to six months in advance. All ticket requests must be made 15 days prior to your preferred tour date to be honored. Please understand that all White House tours are subject to be cancelled at any time.

All White House public tours are free of charge, but visitor requests must be submitted to your congressional representative before approval. Citizens of foreign countries interested in a tour can contact their embassy in Washington, D.C., for further assistance. The U.S. Secret Service reserves the right to prohibit any personal items from the White House premises, including cameras and video recording devices. For a complete list of prohibited items, please see our website or contact your congressional representative. Note that all guests aged 15 years and over will be required to present a valid form of government-issued identification upon arrival.

If you have any questions, comments, or concerns call (202) 555-0173 for more information. This is a tour worth taking, and on behalf of the White House staff, we would like to wish you the best possible experience during your trip.

Sincerely,

Lydia B. Spiders

Lydia B. Spiders

White House Tour Coordinator

At once, memories from the previous summer slunk into my mind. During my mother's senior year of college, she was invited to study abroad for a semester in Paris, France. She fell in love with the city, so much so in fact, that it would later become the namesake of my sister (Nadia *Paris* Greybird). Growing up, she loved to tell Nadia and me stories about her trip. Each tale would be a different adventure, but with always the same details. Even the air was different there, she'd say, like the flowers and the fresh bread and wine and cheese had become a permanent perfume of the atmosphere. She would tell us of the people, and the food, and the dancing and the lights. The city existed to us as a fairytale, beautiful and full of life. She would always tell us, that if it weren't for my father's career, we would all be living there, and at the end of each story, she would promise that we would visit Paris sometime soon.

Nadia in particular was enticed by these stories, and when the news came one summer that we would finally be traveling to the city, you couldn't imagine her excitement. For months prior to the vacation, Nadia insisted on being called by her middle name, bragging that it was as beautiful as the city which inspired it. To anyone who would listen (which became fewer by the day) she would boast about Paris being the finest city in the world, and how visiting it was sure to be the best experience of her life. Nearly every word that came out of her mouth had to do with 'poise' or 'elegance', or some of the 'the worlds most extraordinary things'. She was under a spell with excitement and confidence.

Soon, the time came when Nadia boarded the plane with me and the rest of my family, setting off for the trip of her dreams. When the plane landed, we did our best to hold off jetlag, climbing into a rental car so we could begin our sightseeing without delay. Somewhere along the way however, we took a wrong turn. The outdated map my mom brought for reference only added to the confusion. When we finally came to what was supposed to be the heart of the beautiful city, Nadia was shocked. She was standing in the midst of a dilapidated village possessing nothing remarkable whatsoever except for a thick dust, somehow managing to swirl through the motionless air. It was a dark and dirty place crowded with garbage and a scent that was anything but tolerable.

"Well, here we are," my mom smiled, eyeing the decrepit city as if it were an old friend.

Of course she was only joking. The small town was nothing more than a mistake, and within an hour's time, we had found our way to the *real* city of Paris. Nonetheless, Nadia, who was too young to sense her sarcasm, burst into tears. Until we could explain the truth, she was devastated. Her pride had been stripped from her and her hope had disappeared.

I had never felt that way up until the point when I opened my letter. Before that time, I hadn't experienced the transition from light to complete and total darkness. I didn't understand that the shift was fatal until it was too late to avoid, and I was unprepared for the feeling of worthlessness that settled in its place. Maybe I had never felt so weak because I had allowed my expectations to be strong. Perhaps it was true that the higher I built myself up, the farther I would fall. For the first time, I could understand the way my sister had felt. The only difference now was that in Nadia's case it had all been a mistake.

There was no way to correct what I had just seen.

And as soon as that pain hit me, tears began to well in my eyes. I tried not to cry, but I simply couldn't control the overwhelming disappointment. I shut my eyes and attempted to make the tears stop before they were noticed, but one managed to slip away. It landed with a soft thud onto the disheartening White House reply. Quickly, I wiped my eyes, now angry with myself for crying.

It was suddenly clear to me why the letter meant so much—losing my hope helped me to understand what I had been wishing for in the first place. I couldn't detect its presence inside of me, but now, the emptiness its absence left was anything but subtle. Remembering Sandy, I looked cautiously towards her, wondering how she was reacting. She was heavily focused on staring at her feet, pretending to be intensely interested in one of her highlighted shoelaces. Behind the curtain of hair covering her face however, I could see her eyes slowly becoming clouded. She ran her fingers over her forehead, exhaled deeply and composed herself.

"Cara, what happened?" she asked, speaking barely above a whisper. She looked me straight in the eye, her face full of genuine confusion.

"I don't know." I was surprised at the shock in my own voice. "I was so sure that he would write back. And the truth is…what I'm only just realizing now, is that I was positive that he wanted to know more about my opinions. Then maybe I could have made a difference…" My voice trailed off. I looked down towards the closet floor, talking more to myself than to Sandy. "It was never possible from the start. I should have known that."

I looked back at Sandy for support, but her expression was distant. She bit down on the corner of her lip and looked up to face me.

"Cara, you do realize that the President gets thousands of letters each day, don't you?" she asked, her eyes carrying the look of a parent telling their child that the tooth fairy doesn't exist. "He's a busy man."

Embarrassment set over me as I realized my mistake. I really wished I hadn't cried. "I guess I just didn't think about that," I murmured under my breath, considering the idea.

"I'm sure he would have loved to answer your letter if he only had the time," she added quietly. It was clear that neither of us fully believed this, but I nodded as if it were factual. I looked down at the letter still in my hand. As much as I wanted to let go of it, to set it aside where I wouldn't be reminded of words on the tear-stained page, I didn't allow myself to look away. Instead, I held the letter up to my face, forcing myself to accept what had just happened.

"I guess I should go home now," Sandy broke the silence. "It's almost 5:00 and I don't want to run into Jawsie."

I managed a weak smile.

"Cara, we *will* think of something you know. You'll finish your project, and maybe we can make a difference along the way. Just trust me, okay?" Although its message seemed impossible, Sandy's promise was heartfelt. I couldn't help but to believe her.

"Come on, let's go," I nodded my head in the direction of the door, mood considerably lighter. "I'll walk you home."

"Don't worry," she added with a small smile, beginning her climb towards the floor. "We'll find a way to fix this. You can only go as far as your imagination will allow." She paused, thinking over what she'd said. "I guess all I'm trying to say is, don't give up...at least not yet."

. . . .

The wind scraped against our bare arms as we shuffled out the door and towards the Giraffing house. Sandy seemed extra quiet on the way back, her eyes barely straying from the pavement.

"Gotta talk to them later," she mumbled after awhile, lost in thought.

"Talk to *who* later? Hey, lookout!" I grabbed her arm to steer her away from a mailbox she had nearly run into.

"What?" She raised an eyebrow, slowly returning to her senses. "Oh, nobody. I don't know what I was talking about."

"Whatever you say, Sandy." I rolled my eyes, unconvinced. "Just watch where you're going, okay?" Despite my curiosity, I dared not interrupt again to ask her what she was thinking about. In the few weeks that I had come to know Sandy, I already realized that there was no use questioning her. If she chose to fill me in, it would be on her own terms.

She looked up at me for the first time just before we reached her driveway, and when she did, it was clear that something in her expression had changed. Whatever conclusion she had come to in her mind had certainly been positive. Similar to the way she stumbled down them earlier, I watched as she made her way up the porch steps. She knocked on the door, and almost instantly, Cornelia V.'s head popped out from behind it. A second later it disappeared. Sandy stepped into the entryway, only turning to face me once she was already inside.

"Call you later!" she waved and departed.

The door shut closed, leaving me alone to wonder what was on her mind. It was no use playing the guessing game. I figured that I would find out sooner or later and so I shrugged to myself and headed home, considering Sandy's advice as I walked.

You can only go as far as your imagination will allow. *Don't give up.*

chapter nine

I didn't tell anyone about the letter, not even Nadia. Despite my promise to Sandy, I just couldn't find it in myself to confess that in spite of all my efforts, I had still managed to make an enormous mistake. I was embarrassed to admit I had failed, and so, instead of acknowledging my mistake, I avoided it altogether. Unsuspecting, my family kept up with its nightly routine, and the evening began with a fairly regular start. Nadia, now home from her ballet class, was absorbed in a picture book she had to read for her 'homework', my dad was pacing around the living room on his cell phone, trying to explain where the spare plates were kept to one of his restaurant employees, my mom, not yet recovered from grading those essays, was hard at work in the kitchen, trying to stop the chicken she was making from burning, and I was in my bedroom finishing up my math homework. That's when the phone rang.

"I'll get it!" Nadia yelled, abandoning the book she was holding and flinging herself down the hall as if she was taking cover from a bomb. She threw her arms out and grabbed for the telephone, picking it up on its second ring.

"Hello, Greybird residence, Nadia speaking, how may I help you?" Nadia recited, playing the role of the receptionist. There was a long pause while she listened to the voice on the other end of the line. "Alright," she said with a nod after a few seconds. "And who, may I ask, is calling?" Another brief pause. "Oh, it's you. Fine, I'll get her." Nadia sighed, now bored with her game and eager to move on. "CARA!" she hollered as if she wanted me to hear her on the other side of the world, much less the other side of the hallway. "SANDY'S ON THE PHONE, SHE WANTS TO TALK TO YO—". She was cut short of finishing her sentence because I had already run over to her and pried the phone from her baby-like grip.

Looking like she expected a tip for her services, Nadia remained at my side. I shooed her back into the bedroom before putting the phone to my ear.

"Cara!" Sandy was practically singing. "You will *never* believe the news I have for you!"

"What?"

"Guess."

"I don't know."

"Come on, guess."

"*I don't know!*"

"*Okay*, hold on, I'll tell you." I could just imagine the satisfaction on Sandy's face as she was talking, her smile practically screaming that she had a secret, but her eyes hinting that she might fill me in. I listened as she cleared her throat on the other line, loudly of course, to build up my suspense.

"Well," she began, as if she had rehearsed her dialogue before calling. "You know how my parents work at the Giraffing Children's Hospital, right?"

"Yes," I answered without pausing. I felt my fingers tighten around the phone and thought back to the mail I had received earlier that afternoon, wondering how much anxiety I could take in one day.

"Just recently they've started a new sort of therapy project where the patients work to create a garden around the hospital as a means of therapeutic treatment."

"Cool."

Realizing that I still had no idea where she was taking the conversation, she began to talk a little faster. "You see," she added, "to open this new garden to the public, there is going to be a ribbon cutting ceremony this upcoming

Sunday. After that, we're having a small party at the hospital to celebrate all of the patients and doctors who worked to make the project possible. I've already asked my parents if you could come along with us, and they said that it would be alright."

"Umm…That's great Sandy…Thanks." My voice trailed off. I waited a moment, wondering if there was more to the story. When nothing else came, I tried to act enthusiastic. "Thanks for inviting me…I'm so excited!" I managed weakly.

I could picture Sandy on the other end of the line now, smiling and rolling her eyes at my oblivion.

"Cara, do you know who the Guest of Honor will be at the ceremony?"

Suddenly, the news program I had watched the night I mailed my letter came flooding back to me. My body froze. I could feel my heart stop, and my lungs refusing to take in fresh oxygen. The phone slipped from my hand. I knew the answer to her question. The Guest of Honor would be none other than the President of the United States.

Defiance—the only time I'd felt it before was on my first-ever plane ride, right before I left the ground. In that moment, I was accomplished—limitless even—and a part of something special because *I had found a way to beat gravity*. I was in control. This feeling however, would be little in comparison to how I felt at that moment. Suddenly, I wasn't on a plane, but I myself was flying because I had defeated the force that was holding me down. The ground around me was disappearing and I was carelessly rising above it—invincible. I still had a chance to accomplish my goal. No, goal was the wrong word. It was more like a dream. Best of all, a dream I would get to fulfill in person!

Remembering that I had dropped it, I lunged for the phone. "Thank you!" I gasped, at a loss of what to say next. My mouth was opened but no sound could escape. Sandy seemed to understand.

"You're welcome, Cara," she giggled. "Tell me tomorrow at school if you can come. The hospital is about forty minutes away, but we would be happy to drive you."

"I'll ask my parents at dinner tonight!"

"Alright," she tried to disguise her laughter, knowing perfectly well that with or without approval, I had already made up my mind—I was going to that ceremony.

Pausing a second to breathe, I managed to take a few big gulps of air before continuing.

"Sandy?" I spoke into the phone hesitantly. "Thank you. You know how much this means to me."

"No problem. No problem at all."

After hanging up, I felt like a new person. I've heard the expression of a weight being lifted off from one's shoulders before, but it didn't seem to apply. It was almost as if something heavy had been placed over my chest instead, right on top of my heart. Only once it was removed could I feel it beating steadily again.

"Dinnertime—come on everyone!" My mom's voice alone was enough to send my heart rate climbing again. I sighed, pressing a hand to my chest. *It was nice while it lasted...*

Trying not to look overly-eager but doing a horrible job pretending, I ran downstairs, nearly knocking Nadia over as she tried to pass me in the hall. Reaching the kitchen, each of us took a plate from the counter and began to help ourselves to the food that had been laid out on the island. My mom must have given up trying to revive the burnt leftover chicken she planned on serving because the main course that night was a large platter of macaroni and cheese from my dad's restaurant. I spooned a heaping portion onto my plate, along with a small scoop of mashed potatoes, and helping of fruit salad. Knowing that my mom hated resorting to takeout, and deciding that I would need her to be in a good mood, I grabbed a stalk of broccoli as a second thought, setting it out visibly in the center of my plate. The night was turning out much better than I thought. After giving up on my attempt to wait for Nadia, who was busy picking apart the fruit salad, I headed into the dining room alone.

My parents were already seated at the table waiting for Nadia and me to join them. My dad looked as if he was going to dig into his food at any second, regardless of our absence, and my mom seemed on the verge of collapse from the day's exhaustion. Luckily, she was finished with the bulk of her work and was determined to get a decent amount of sleep that night. Nadia appeared in the doorway seconds later, her plate nothing but a mound of apples and potatoes. I poured myself a glass of milk from a red ceramic pitcher as she took her seat, not noticing that I had spilled most of it into my lap until I saw the look on her face. I wiped up the spill with a shaking hand, and we all began to eat.

From the moment I hung up the phone, I was dying to tell Nadia and my parents about my opportunity to meet the President. I knew however, that it would be best to wait. My eyes darted around the room and I watched as my family went about their own business, trying to get a few bites in before someone would pop the inevitable 'so how was your day?' question. Telling a good story was like going in on a hunt. I knew I couldn't advance too quickly. If I went in for the kill too soon, all would be lost. Waiting for this perfect moment made me nervous, and I found it difficult to swallow anything. Instead, I took to pushing my dinner restlessly around my plate with my fork.

My mom was the first to speak, starting off the conversation with a story about the essays she had finished reading, and comparing them to others she had graded in previous years. Everyone seemed interested, but to me, she might as well have been talking in another language. Within a few seconds, I found myself incapable of listening to anything she was saying. So, while the rest of my family was absorbed in 'the secret of getting through to students with short attention-spans', I was off in Cara-Land, concentrating on my food and waiting for the right time to interject.

I decided not to make my move until everyone was full and quiet. In the meantime, I churned my mashed potatoes around my dish until they were nothing but a watery mess of starch. Every once in awhile I would look up from my plate and nod thoughtfully, trying my hardest to convey a remote interest in whatever the current speaker was saying. Finally, after what seemed like an obscene amount of time to devote to a comedic anecdote involving a customer he had spoken to earlier that day, my dad finished his story and the dinner table grew quiet. It was my turn to speak.

"Everyone," I announced," I have something that I want to say."

"Go on," my mother urged, lifting her eyes from the tabletop to look at me.

"Well, you know about The America Project, right? I mean, they told you about it at the conferences last week, didn't they?" I started off tentatively.

"Of course," my dad replied, staring at his empty glass. My mother nodded like she was very interested while trying to pick something off of her spoon.

"Well, then you know how we're supposed to talk politics with someone and write a big report and stuff, right?" I looked up hopefully at my parents. They both nodded again.

"You want to speed it up a little, Cara?" Nadia cut in loudly. "I want to tell you what happened to Grover Finchy at recess today. Oh, it was the grossest thing—"

"Nadia!" my mother warned. "Be polite. Cara, you were saying?"

"Where was I? Oh, right, well…," I took a big breath. "The person I chose for the project is—," I swallowed hard, "—the President."

My father's face lit up, not bothering to swallow before giving his opinion. "Aw, what a great idea, Cara! I couldn't have made a better choice, myself! Uncle Marty will be so happy to hear that out of everyone here, you picked him to interview! You know how much pride he takes in being the President of the World Famous Rubber Cement Company! He'll be just—"

"Dad, wait," I interrupted him, raising my voice to be heard over Nadia's laughter. "I don't want to do my project with Uncle Marty. The person I chose to do this with is the President *of the United States*."

Silence. My parents exchanged *'Do you want to break it to her, or should I?'* glances. I quickly began to explain.

"No, really, it's okay—I've got it all figured out. See, I've already written a letter and—"

"Cara, I am sorry to tell you this," my mother interrupted, "but your letter will probably not be answered before the project is due, if it is answered at all. The President is far too busy to personally reply to all the mail he receives—why, he must get thousands of letters a day! Well, you saw how long it took me to grade just sixty-seven essays! Anyway, sweetie, the President might not even get the letter. All we can do is *hope* that it will be answered, but in the meantime, you should have a solid back-up option, just in case."

"Yes, I *know* that." I did my best to sound calm, although slightly annoyed that I hadn't gotten the chance to explain the details of my plan yet. "Yeah, it all started out as just a fun idea. Later, though, I realized that I am serious about getting my opinions out, and the whole idea of the project became something really important to me. And this afternoon, I got a reply from the White House."

Nadia was on her feet before I had a chance to realize what I said. "You got the letter back? Let me see it, let me see it!" she squealed.

"Shh! Cara hasn't finished her story yet, honey. Go on, Cara." Nadia narrowed her eyes and glared at my mother, but was quiet, all the same.

"Yes," I went on, "the letter did come back. And it turns out, all of you were right. Anything you write to the White House comes back as a universal, prewritten form letter, personalized with your name in the greeting, suggesting that you arrange a White House tour."

"Oh, I'm very sorry to hear that, dear," my father shook his head in expecting sympathy. "But, you know, there are always alternatives. Let's see…" He tapped his chin with his index finger. "Well, if you don't want to interview Uncle Marty, we could arrange something with one of your mother's students. And I'm sure J.J. would be more than willing to cooperate with you. You two will probably have some very different opinions to discuss…" I fought back the urge to roll my eyes.

"Thanks, Dad, but there's still more to the story. It gets better."

"COME ON, LET'S HEAR IT, THEN!" Nadia boomed from across the table, tired of waiting patiently and simply dying to tell us what happened to Grover. I shot her a look, already feeling a little less guilty about opening my letter without her. Although I knew that she was interested in the outcome of my adventure and extremely willing to help me along the way, Nadia would always be Nadia, and thus much more happily focused on herself.

"Alright, alright," I lifted my hands, as if surrendering. After receiving another look from my mother, Nadia closed her mouth and drew a finger across her lips, pretending to zip them shut. I couldn't help but enjoy her eagerness. I took a deep breath.

"Let's say that I just happened to come upon an invitation to a private garden party at the hospital where the President of the United States is coincidentally serving as the Guest of Honor." My voice faltered. "Would I be allowed to go?"

The room was dead quiet. A dinnertime first, I had the attention of six unblinking eyes and the respect of three dropped jaws. Nadia's hands were clamped over her mouth, like she was restraining some sort of dangerous animal. I could tell she was holding her breath so she wouldn't speak, as her face was nearly blue. My mom touched a hand to her forehead, overwhelmed. My dad was simply in shock. To clarify my plan, I filled them in on the conversation I had with Sandy earlier that evening, doing my best to leave nothing out. One 20-minute telephone call to the Drs. Giraffing later, and it was decided—I was going to meet Bob Deerun!

I could hardly wait.

The next day at school, Sandy and I went over all of the details for the trip. At lunch, she handed me a clean, typed schedule of the day that her parents had devised for us. I couldn't help but notice that the stationary had a slight grayish tint.

Garden Party Timetable of Events

```
6:23 a.m.— meet in car
6:25 a.m-6:29 a.m.— drive to Cara's house*
6:30 a.m.— pick up Cara
6:32 a.m.—7:12 a.m.— drive to the hospital.
7:12 a.m.—7:15 a.m.— park and walk inside
7:15 a.m.—8:56 a.m.— help set up,
        make final decorating touches
8:57 a.m.—   meet at garden entrance
8:58 a.m.-9:07 a.m.— greet guests
9:07 a.m.-9:27 a.m.— mingle with guests/eat
        hors d'oeuvres
9:28 a.m.— take seat in front row, left of aisle
9:30 a.m.— President arrives at back entrance
```

9:35 a.m.-10:30 a.m.— ribbon-cutting/recognition
    ceremony
10:31 a.m.-11:09 a.m.— walk around gardens
11:13 a.m.— report to hospital main cafeteria/make
    final decorating touches
11:25 a.m.— take seat at children's table
11:30 a.m.-12:45 p.m.— lunch is served
12:46 p.m.—2:45 p.m.— party (walk around/mingle)
2:46 p.m.— meet at hospital exit
2:47 p.m.-3:05 p.m.— say goodbye/give guests
    goodie bags
3:06 p.m.-4:00 p.m.— clean up
4:00 p.m.-4:03 p.m.— walk to car
4:03 p.m.-4:43 p.m.— drive to Cara's house
4:44 p.m.—drop Cara off
4:45 p.m.-4:49 p.m.— drive home*

Note that an * indicates that extra time has been
added in preparation for unforeseen delays/setbacks.

Just by the looks of the schedule, I could tell that in their own strange way, Sandy's parents were almost as excited as I was.

After what seemed like forever, the big day finally came around. At exactly 6:30 a.m., a familiar gray Corvette pulled into my driveway. Excitement had filled me with insomnia, and I had only managed to get four or five hours rest the previous night.

Regardless, the electric feeling had returned to my veins, and I was nearly bursting at the seams with energy. I smiled, quickly shutting the front door behind me and making my way down the front steps as if I was performing some sort of drill. Having practically memorized the day's agenda, I knew that I had only been allotted 2 minutes to reach the unnaturally clean vehicle before me. Not wanting to disappoint, I did my best to hurry, taking my last few steps at a run.

Dr. Giraffing (Sandy's dad) was driving the car and Dr. Giraffing (Sandy's mom) was sitting on the passenger's side, furiously dusting lint off of her gray wool suit jacket. Cornelia V. and I were sitting in the back seat together, with Sandy wedged in the middle, all silent in anticipation. I spent a great deal of the trip staring out the window. My family went out to West Liberty often on weekends and in the summer, as did many in New Castle, so I had traveled the route many times before. Today, however, I felt like I was going somewhere strange and far away.

It had been drizzling that morning, the faded yellow lines at the center of the road no more prominent than if drawn with chalk, washing away in the rain. We twisted our way forward with harvesting fields surrounding us on every side, stretching as far as the eye could see. Each gust of wind grazed the tall yellow grasses, swaying their stalks forward than back—waves in a massive ocean of grain. A lonely tree would appear every so often amongst them, standing out against the gold and brown like a head of lettuce in a candy store. A thick curtain of clouds hid the sun, blanketing the sky in a smoky blur, with flecks of white and pink beginning to break through down towards the horizon. Misty rain dusted itself across the windows, cool against my fingertips from the air brushing by.

"The timing of the rain is just splendid," Dr. Giraffing broke the silence, her hand nervously tapping against the car door.

"Why is that?" Sandy asked.

"Well, first of all, to make the plants in the garden look more presentable, and secondly, to get the rain out of the way so we won't have to worry about it later this afternoon," Cornelia V. answered with a smug expression, rolling her eyes as if this were the most obvious thing in the world. After that, the car was silent again. It remained that way until it pulled into the Giraffing Children's Hospital parking lot.

"Come on everyone, we have a lot of preparing to do before the guests arrive, so let's get to it," Dr. Giraffing announced as he pulled into a parking space near the front entrance labeled *CEO*. He reached into his pocket and pulled out the same gray itinerary that Sandy had given me the day before.

Eager to begin, I was out of the car in a second. Much to my dismay, the scar from Jawsie's bite had still not entirely faded, so I still had to stick with the long skirts and dresses.

It's strange to be able to say this from experience, but honestly, there's nothing that can hide a dog bite better than a floor-length gown. It was a faded pink with a simple cut, thin straps at the top, and a thick chestnut ribbon tied around the middle. Although definitely a little formal for a garden party (I had previously worn it as the flower-girl in my aunt's wedding), I didn't have many other options. Although elegant, it somehow managed not to look overdone. I hoped that it would leave the President with a nice opinion of me.

Sandy, who had not dug as deep as I had into the concept of first impressions, was wearing her sparkly chandelier earrings. In fact, when she stepped out of the car and they caught the light, their reflection nearly blinded me. It took more than a few seconds of blinking until I got my sight back. As if the earrings were not enough to stop traffic (or cause a car accident), she wore a sapphire dress that highly contrasted the color of her fiery hair. For a *much needed* splash of color, she threw in a pair of neon green kitten heels into the mix as well. I couldn't help but smile, knowing that the outfit was something only Sandy could have put together, much less look natural in.

Cornelia V. (who was, of course, gelled and pressed to perfection) was sporting a ginger jumper and matching argyle knee socks, with her hair pulled into two tight pigtail braids. The Drs.Giraffing were wearing the same stiff gray suits they had worn when I had first met them. However, Sandy's father had decided to go bold and experiment with a navy tie. I was proud.

Sandy's mom took a quick glance at her watch and then at another copy of the day's schedule, clutched tightly in her hand.

"Sandra Guinevere Vivian, Cornelia Ann Victoria, you know the way to the cafeteria, don't you?" She asked abruptly, realizing that we were no less than three minutes behind schedule.

"Yes," Sandy replied, "We've been there loads of times before." It had taken me up until then to realize that her comment was only directed towards two girls and not six.

"Good," her mother answered distractedly, fiddling with the short strand of pearls around her neck. "You girls can get going there right now. I would like you to set up place cards, blow up balloons, and help with whatever else needs assistance. We are running very late, so please do not dawdle, if at all possible."

"Alright," Sandy agreed, nodding to her parents. After exchanging anxious smiles with the Drs. Giraffing, the three of us walked across the pavement and through the hospital doors, with Sandy leading the way. I took a good look around, suddenly extremely aware that the President of the United States of America would be walking through the very same halls in just a matter of hours.

chapter ten

If you had asked me before I stepped into the room, I would have said that transforming a plain hospital cafeteria into an elegant party room would be an impossible task.

I was wrong.

By the time Sandy, Cornelia V., and I had reached the hospital cafeteria, it was 7:17. Despite the early morning time, it seemed like people had already been setting up for hours. Custodians were rushing here and there, carrying chairs, sweeping the white tile floor, and hanging streamers, balloons, and other ornaments from the ceiling. Party planners were frantically running around, fussing over place cards, decorations, table settings, centerpieces, food, and whatever else they could find that was not just right. In every direction, chefs were bustling about, carrying tray upon tray of elaborate appetizers, salads, entrees, side dishes, fruits, and dessert. My mouth started to water as a tall girl in a crisp white uniform came hurrying past, carrying a gigantic platter piled high with what had to be every kind of pastry ever invented.

Looking around, I noticed that the sterile walls gleamed unusually bright, as if they had recently been given a major scrub-down. The oversized windows sparkled in the dim morning light, crystal clear. All plastic chairs had been replaced with handsome wooden fold-up ones, similar to something you might see at an office meeting room in a hotel. Draped over the tables were silky golden tablecloths, on which silver flatware was set around cream-colored china. Deep burgundy napkins contained in thin gold rings sat neatly on each plate. Elegant glasses were placed to the right of each name card, which were written in fancy calligraphy and emblazoned with gold trim. In the center of each table lay a glass vase holding a simple bouquet of red roses, baby's breath, and small American flags. A big white piano had been brought in and stationed at the far corner of the room. Red, white, and blue balloons were festively set out in small clusters around a portable wood-planked dance floor. An enlarged photograph of all the kids who had worked on the garden was plastered onto a nearby wall. They were all smiling, holding up their garden tools like trophies, their faces smudged with dirt. Their arms were around each other like they were one big family. It was simply magical.

We stood awestruck in the doorway, thinking of all the effort put forth to make everything around us possible. However, our marveling lasted only a few seconds before we were put to work. Cornelia V. was using a diagramed seating chart to put the last of the place cards in their proper positions on each table. Sandy and I were ordered to Windex the already gleaming windows, push in chairs, and adjust the place settings. When we had finally finished our tasks, we each collapsed into the nearest chairs to take a well-deserved break. As soon as we sat, a frazzled woman in thick glasses and high heels came rushing over to us.

"What are you girls doing?" she demanded, madly waving her clipboard. Several strands of frizzy hair came loose from her tight bun. Before we could answer the lady, a loud beeping sounded from the walkie-talkie she had strapped to her belt. She pulled it out with an exasperated eye roll and listened to the fuzzy voice on the other end. "I don't care *what* it takes, Mitch, just make sure you can get it over here in time!" she screeched, panicked. "What do you mean you *can't?*" she gave a loud agitated sigh and walked off, still yelling and waving her arms. Just when we thought she had forgotten us, she called over her shoulder, "Go and blow up some balloons, girls! If you're not going to help, *please* go someplace else and stop wasting my time! Now, *Mitch…!*" Her hysterical shrieking trailed off as she stomped away, nearly tripping over a basket of flowers.

"Cara, meet Gertrude, my parents' personal assistant," Sandy whispered to me with a giggle as the three of us got up to find the helium machine.

"She sounds just lovely."

At 8:55, Cornelia V.'s watch alarm signaled us to start walking over to the garden entrance, where the ceremony was to take place. The first of the guests were starting to arrive when we met up with the Drs. Giraffing two minutes later. Sandy's mother stayed at the gate to greet the families of the patients and VIPs as they got out of their cars and Sandy's father stayed by the hospital doors to greet the patients as they exited the building and made their way toward the garden. By the time all of the guests had arrived, both of Sandy's parents looked like they would pass out if they had to shake one more hand. When everyone was settled, we took the seats reserved for us in the front row. The ceremony was about to begin.

"Do you see the President?" I asked Sandy, scanning the crowd.

Sandy took a look around and shook her head no. "He might be waiting for some sort of signal or something, you know? Like to say the coast is clear." I managed a nod "… Or, maybe he's just running late," Sandy quietly reassured me as she adjusted the collar on her sapphire dress.

"What if he doesn't come?" I asked, my voice wavering as my thoughts settled on the worst possible circumstances.

"He will come, I'm sure of that." A firm sort of finality was in her voice. She squeezed my hand.

I nodded. *Sandy is right,* I thought desperately to myself. *She just has to be. The plan can't go wrong now. All our hard work would go to nothing, it just wouldn't be fair. Yes, he's coming. He has to be.*

As I sat there waiting, I noticed that the sun was now visible in the sky and all traces of rain had vanished from sight. It was the perfect day. After taking a few moments to get settled, the noisy conversations shrunk down to whispers.

As soon as everyone was quiet, two children carrying index cards marched down the aisle towards the podium facing the crowd. The girl in front was using a walker. She looked like the older of the two, about twelve, maybe thirteen. Looking closer, I could see that there were small white scars everywhere along her arms, like little white spider webs. The boy, who I guessed to be around nine, was grinning from ear to ear. His head had been shaved, but it was growing back in uneven patches now, like bits of grass after a snowstorm. The girl was the first to speak.

"Hello. Thank you all for coming to the opening of the Giraffing Children's Hospital Therapeutic Garden." This was followed by a raging applause. When the clapping died down, the girl continued on.

"My name is Gwen Sharkey. I am one of the children who have been honored with the privilege of working on this garden. I cannot tell you all how lucky I feel to have done so. I was driving with my mom one night when a drunk driver ran a red light and hit our car. My spine and wrist were both broken. Glass from the windshield was stuck in my body everywhere. The doctors did everything they could to help me, but they still said the chances of me regaining full control of my legs were pretty low. I also needed intense therapy for my wrist.

"The first few weeks I was in the hospital, I was in a lot of pain. I was angry that I would never be able to do the things I could do before, like play softball or swim. It was then when I was invited to be a part of the garden project. After seeing the other kids' determination to get better, and watching them work so hard despite their disabilities, I was inspired to get my life back. I went to the garden everyday. I created new exercises to help heal my wrist and back. I met a bunch of new friends from all over the country, others from different parts of the world. The great improvements I saw in my condition gave me hope for my future. I was happy again.

"When I was finally allowed to leave the hospital, I still used gardening to help me get better. Today, it is one of my favorite pastimes. Now I am able to walk with a walker and my wrist is completely healed. And here's the best part; my doctor says that if I am to continue with my therapy, my legs will be completely back to normal in just six months!" Upon hearing this, the crowd burst into applause. "I would like to thank everyone who made this project possible. I hope that you all get as much enjoyment out of the gardens as I do." The ending of the girl's speech was met with more loud cheers. She smiled before stepping back to let the boy speak.

"Hi, everyone," he started, the smile never leaving his face. You could see the empty spaces in his mouth where his baby teeth fell out. "My name is Peter Catz. I'm a patient at the hospital right now because I have leukemia. I've had it for a long time and I've been in and out of the hospital for the past two years. I didn't really like coming here before because there were always a bunch of doctors, and machines and stuff. I was always being poked at and injected with treatments and I was never allowed to go anywhere because I had to stay in my bed. Two months ago, though, I needed a bone marrow transplant. They gave me my radiation and then I got the new cells. It was supposed to help me get better, but I didn't feel all that great right after my therapy. I was tired and nauseous all the time, so mainly I just slept and threw up." His audience didn't know whether or not to laugh. Peter continued with a small giggle, unfazed by the crowd.

"A few weeks later when I was feeling better, my doctors thought I should start getting active again. I tried playing sports with my friends, but I couldn't keep up with their game. My sisters just wanted to play dolls. When we told the doctor, he suggested that I become a part of the new garden project at the hospital. So I tried it. I met some of the other kids who are patients at the hospital too, just like me. Me and a kid named Trent became real good buddies, even though he's a year older than me in school. And I got to be outside, and not just locked up in a bed when I needed to stay overnight. It was fun playing around in the dirt. Much better than those old hospital board games, anyway. My dad thought that what I was doing here was really cool, and my mom said it was more productive than video games.

"It's impossible to enjoy a trip to the hospital, but after awhile, I stopped dreading my visits here because I really liked gardening and hanging out in the fresh air with my friends. I built up my strength and learned a lot of new stuff that I wouldn't have known otherwise. I'm even thinking of taking it up as a hobby. The gardens are a really nice place, and it was a great experience for us kids. It might even be because of these gardens that I am proud to say I am healthy again and cancer-free." An electrified applause followed this, and the boy beamed triumphantly before continuing. "I just want to say thanks for letting me be a part of it, and welcome to our garden!" He finished his last sentence with an even bigger grin holding out the microphone so that it was spaced evenly between himself and his fellow speaker.

"Thank you," the two children said in unison, closing their speeches. Everyone clapped and whistled. Before they went back to their chairs, a photographer knelt down and took their picture. When the children were seated, the Drs. Giraffing stood up and called the attention of the audience. They stepped up to the podium and turned to face the crowd.

"Let's give them another round of applause," Sandy's mother insisted, bending down to adjust the microphone to her own height. "Let's hear it for Gwen and Peter!" When the clapping had finally died down, the two doctors began their speech. It was about 10 times longer than both of the previous speeches combined, and to be honest, a little painful to sit through. Not because what they had to say was boring, of course. It was just that after a while, the whole thing seemed kind of repetitive, not to mention that the vocabularies that these people used were probably bigger than the dictionary's. Still, I knew that what they were talking about was important (even if I wasn't able to follow the majority of the stuff being said), so I tried my best not to zone out. You could tell that they had put a lot of effort into perfecting their deliverance, and neither of the doctors hesitated or stuttered once. They didn't even have notes to read from, which was pretty impressive. Nonetheless, their words still lacked the sincerity and emotion that the children had conveyed to their listeners.

After awhile, when I could no longer stop my anxiety from getting the best of me, I allowed my thoughts to wander away. Not wanting to disturb Sandy, who was deeply absorbed in her parents' words, I sat quietly in my chair daydreaming about meeting the President, and how the rest of the day would go. After what seemed like hours, I snapped out of it and glanced up at the Giraffings just as Sandy's mom was beginning to wrap-up their everlasting speech.

"Therefore, one can easily discern that the Giraffing Children's Hospital Therapeutic Garden has done much more than facilitate our patients; it has, indisputably, provided them with terrific life experience, endless opportunity, and auspicious futures. It is with great pride that I report this project as being an immense achievement. This revitalizing place has given our children a second chance at life. It is our dedicated ambition to see that all who were able to seek rehabilitation through horticulture are able to utilize their experience here to reach their full potential, not only now, but for the rest of their lives, carrying the wisdom they have gained here with them forever."

It took me a moment to realize that the speech had finally ended. Then, hurriedly, I began to applaud, clapping along with everyone else. I leaned over toward Sandy to tell her what an incredible job her parents had done. She was positively beaming with pride, but her expression was nothing compared to the smug look on Cornelia V.'s face.

As the flashing lights of the cameras became more and more sporadic and the hushed conversations of the crowd slowly resumed, it appeared that the ceremony was over. Instead of sitting back down in their chairs or dismissing everyone to the gardens however, the Drs. Giraffing remained behind the podium. When it was again quiet, Sandy's father stepped forward.

"Ladies and gentlemen," he addressed the crowd as calmly as he could, trying his best to hide his excitement, but failing miserably. "The moment we have all awaited for has arrived! It is my great pleasure to introduce the Guest of Honor we have all been so highly anticipating. He is one of the most prominent and influential figures in today's modern world, and we are incredibly fortunate to have him here in attendance. And so, without further ado, I present to you none other than the President of the United States of America!" He gestured with his hand to the very back row of chairs. All heads turned. And sure enough, as if it was all some sort of dream, there he was.

chapter eleven

Bob Deerun ambled casually up the aisle, shaking the hands of the hospital patients as he went. My heart felt swollen, as if it were taking up the majority of my chest, suffocating all of my other organs. He was actually here! Within a moment, the President had made it over to the place where Sandy's parents were standing. He shook each of their hands with a warm smile and the photographer snapped a few more shots. The admiring looks on the doctors' faces made me think that if the President told them to jump off a bridge, or even worse—wear an actual color; they would do it in a second. When they had finished greeting each other, Sandy's mother handed the President the microphone. Then, she and her husband dreamily took their seats.

The crowd was still clapping for the President as he prepared himself to speak, but unlike the previous two, this time, nobody was talking. All mouths were closed, every eye staring up at him, our hands moving as instinctively as a dog wagging its tail. The President actually had to talk over the ravenous applause to get started because after awhile, he saw that there was no chance of quieting the enthusiastic crowd. Before a full sentence could leave his mouth however, the group took the hint and obediently settled back into their seats.

Nevertheless, you could practically feel the excitement in the air. I couldn't help but follow the crowd as I leaned forward to listen more intently.

The speech was really something. He spoke so powerfully, his deep voice soothing, but every now and then sharp, keeping everyone attentive. The words he chose were so simple and easy to understand, but there was always something deeper buried behind his clever use of language, something profound and poetic. You could just tell it was all heartfelt. As he spoke, it seemed as if he were talking to me personally; like he saw worth in my understanding. I managed to pull my eyes away from him to glance behind, quickly realizing that I was hardly alone in my feelings—everyone else in the audience was staring back at the President as well, completely mesmerized.

I couldn't help but to be a little jealous of this power. I mean, not everyone can put their listeners in that sort of believing trance. Really—how lucky are you when people actually stop and listen to what you have to say? It was rare for just one person to open their mind to a message, but having that kind of control over a crowd put me in disbelief. Bob Deerun had the power to make a difference. If the afternoon went the way I planned, maybe I could too.

"Thank you all very much," he concluded. "Thank you for allowing me the pleasure of witnessing firsthand the magic that the Giraffing Children's Hospital Therapeutic Gardens has brought to our children. Thank you for believing in this worthy cause, and thank you for your work and your effort. You are truly an inspiration. It is with great happiness and extreme gratitude that I now invite all of you around to the front garden entrance, where I have been afforded the extreme privilege of leading the ribbon cutting ceremony and officially opening the gardens."

I was the first to give him a standing ovation and undoubtedly the loudest one cheering him on, too.

. . . .

Regardless of whether you're at a rock concert, a ballet, or a Presidential speaking engagement, there is always one crazy girl in the front row. The one who believes so much in a message that she would face her worst fear, or pay hundreds of dollars, or *get bitten by a giant dog*, just to be a part of its deliverance. This time, it was me—and I wasn't objecting. If what I felt then was insanity, then by all means, call me crazy.

When the applause had finally died down, the crowd stood (if they weren't already on their feet) and began walking across the lawn behind the podium to the winding stone paths that led around the gardens. Sandy, Cornelia V. and I squirmed our way through the mob until we were at its front, right next to the garden's entranceway. Between two young oak trees, a thick red ribbon was tied, blocking the way through. A boy with one arm heavily plastered and bandaged was waiting at its center, a pair of extra large scissors held out in front of him. The President was on one knee with a permanent marker, signing his cast.

"Thank you, sir," the boy's shirt had been pressed and his hair was gelled away from his face. It wasn't difficult to pick out his mother from the crowd, the flash on her camera practically in rapid-fire. "Now if you will please do the honors—" With great difficulty, the boy struggled to lift the oversized scissors into the President's hands.

"Ladies and gentlemen," the President began, lifting them parallel to the ground. "The Giraffing Children's Hospital Therapeutic Gardens are now officially opened!" A roar came from the crowd, sending a shiver up my spine. The President cut the ribbon with the scissors, and its pieces fell to either side of the pathway, leaving the people free to explore.

The crowd came alive almost at once, rushing like some sort of uncontainable force into the gardens—the grounds of which were completely covered in vegetation. Exotic flowers in every imaginable color, ivies, shrubbery, and even cacti spanned as far as the eye could see. In a place that had once been bare, I was surrounded by life, plants consuming any open space they could find and by way of some miracle, turning it green. The scene was breathtaking, although it was more than obvious that everything had been created by kids. Pinecones smeared with peanut butter and sunflower seeds hung from every low tree branch, while hand-painted birdhouses and feeders were placed randomly about. Hundreds of colorfully decorated name cards stuck out of the ground, labeling each plant in a careful print. A small tool shed had been built on the far side of the lawn, covered with the painted handprints of all the patients who had worked to create the gardens. A tire swing had been built next to the fishpond, and a cluster of picnic benches sat off to the side. Tiny white lights had been strung up through the treetops, and handmade kites of hospital linen were being passed out to children, their tails decorated with feathers and ribbon.

I wasn't sad, but I felt like crying. After just one look around, all I wanted to do was help out, to pick up a shovel and become a part of the project. Instead, I wandered my way through as a spectator, moving from one side of the garden to the other, then back again.

After we had all circled the gardens several times, my stomach reminded me that it was time to eat. I suppose that others had the same feeling because soon, I was following an awe-inspired crowd inside for lunch.

The cafeteria had hardly changed since the last time I had seen it. The only difference was that now, if it was even possible, there was *more* food set out upon the plates and platters, fresh and ready to be eaten. Most of the adults took to picking at the appetizers set out on the waiter trays but the majority of kids in the crowed went straight to the main course, grabbing their dishes and forming a cluster at the long buffet table, piling their plates with fancy-looking food. When Sandy and I finally reached the front of the line to the buffet table, both of us were amazed at what we saw. Next to each dish there was a familiar gold-trimmed card identifying the food and listing the main ingredients. I looked around eagerly, reading a few of the nearest labels.

Chicken
tenderized, grilled to a crisp perfection, marinated in a sweet
honey-mustard sauce with white wine, lightly glazed over with warm
capers and sun-dried tomatoes, topped with fresh basil from our gardens
Fish
salmon baked in our own original combination of olive oil, fresh minced
garlic, fresh rosemary, and red wine vinegar, evenly strewn with delicious
seasoning chosen by our head chef, served with a lemon slice

Pasta
penne pasta drizzled in an olive oil and chicken stock mixture,
topped with diced grilled chicken, fresh green scallions, fresh chopped garlic,
fresh parsley, sun-dried tomatoes, kalamata olives, grated pecorino
Romano cheese, and selected herb seasonings
Salad
homegrown romaine lettuce, cabbage, and spinach garnished with lemon
wedges, tossed with shallots, fresh sliced carrots, fresh green pepper,
fresh tomato, plump raisins, chickpeas, crunchy homemade croutons, feta
cheese, and sunflower seeds, served with a choice of creamy
peppercorn ranch, balsamic vinaigrette, or sweet Chinese plumb dressing

A message to all patients with dietary restrictions—
Please notify a chef or waiter of your particular nutritional concern, and at
your request, we will happily construct an original dish (or a version of one of the
above) to your nutritional specifications. If you are a patient who has pre-ordered
a meal, please inform one of our kitchen staff members, and your lunch will be
delivered to your table. Thank you!

I could already feel my mouth beginning to water. Unable to decide what I wanted to eat, I opted to take a small portion of everything, getting a taste of each dish. (Each and every one of them, by the way, was delicious.)

Dessert however was an entirely different story: my mind was set on having one thing and one thing only; a thick slice of triple-chocolate cake generously frosted with a homemade buttermilk icing and decorated with small sugary flowers. I helped myself to a slice and then sat back down at my table with Sandy, who was absorbed in chewing a large, strawberry tart.

"I'm so excited!" I turned to catch another look at the President, who was sitting a couple of tables away. "Just think! In a little while, you and I will be able to talk to him!" A small piece of cake flew off from the tip of my fork and onto Sandy's face as I waved it animatedly.

"Yeah," Sandy managed through mouthfuls of her dessert, wiping the cake off of her cheek. She swallowed, patted her lips with her napkin, and continued on. "Do you have some sort of a guideline as to what questions you want to ask him?"

"Yep," I answered, lowering the fork apologetically. I reached into the small change purse my mother had lent me, pulling out a folded piece of paper and a pen to take notes.

"Good," she gave a nod of approval and then went back to her tart.

Either Sandy and I ate the rest of our dessert incredibly quickly, or the adults were eating painfully slow. After we had licked our plates clean, the grown-ups were still at it, eating and blabbing away their usual nonsense.

"When is the party going to start?" I asked to nobody in particular after a long sub-conscious foot-tapping session. Cornelia V. appeared from behind me to answer my question.

"If you *must* know," she snapped curtly, as if I were a small child who had just asked '*Are we there yet?*' for the thousandth time on a long car trip, "the party will begin shortly. But I suppose you aren't paying attention to your surroundings, because if you were, you would notice that Gertrude is just about to make the announcement."

"Thanks," I muttered as timidly as I could, while Sandy shot me a sympathetic look.

Sure enough, almost as soon as Cornelia V. had finished speaking, Gertrude began loudly clearing her throat into the microphone, informing us all that the party was to begin momentarily. Her voice was high and nasally, carrying on in an efficient, monotonous drone. She never paused while speaking, as if stopping for something as silly as a breath would waste too much time. Now that she had calmed down, she seemed like the perfect assistant for the Drs. Giraffing.

By the time Gertrude had marched back to her table, people were already beginning to stand up and walk around. The doors leading outside to the garden were opened and a refreshment stand stocked with soda, punch, pretzels, and potato chips was wheeled out. The buffet table had been converted into a bar. A kids' DJ set up outside on the grass while a pianist began to play for the adults.

Looking around the room, I suddenly became aware of all the security there was to protect the President. Seeing as the man was the leader of our country, I should have assumed that they would be present, but to be honest, the thought had never crossed my mind until that moment. Looking around, I realized that the guards were everywhere, most of them only shadows pressed against the walls of the room, others stationed by doorways and windowsills. Each was armed and alert. Seeing all of them made me nervous, even though I knew I had done nothing wrong. It was sort of like the feeling I got when I was called to the principle's office back at school. Even though I knew I had done nothing to get in trouble, a tiny little voice in the back of my brain kept hinting otherwise.

The guards were silent, impassive faces pointed forward, but I couldn't shake the strange sensation that they were watching me. The directions of their eyes were masked behind tinted sunglasses, and the uncertainty made me uneasy. I frowned at the guard nearest me, not knowing whether or not he was looking back. For fear of being attacked by the Secret Service, I decided that it would be best not to move quickly towards the President. Instead, it was probably safer to ease my way over to where he was standing, now just a couple of yards away.

I was on a roller coaster. I had gotten on the moment I'd decided to write to him. Sure, along the way, there had been various ups and downs to the ride, but I had endured them. Now however, as I sat at the peak of its highest hill, I was terrified.

Sandy was finishing her dessert, and for all I knew, I was being watched by a million armed guards. The President was having a nice conversation with one of the hospital's doctors who had probably come down to the party during their break. It would be best to approach him later.

No, I thought to myself, *you don't have much time and you can't be afraid. Stalling will get you nowhere. What you need to do is go. Go to the President and do what you came to do. Now.*

I knew that time was of the essence. Opportunity waits for no one. Suddenly I was standing, taking a hold of Sandy's arm. Before I knew it, the two of us were making our way towards the most important man in the country. The wheels of the coaster began to inch over the edge of the hill. I held my breath, and went along for the ride.

chapter twelve

It always feels good to get something you've been waiting for, like the birthday present you'd known was hidden in the hall closet months prior to the day you would receive it, or simply the reply to a long-awaited letter. When finally confronted with your desire, a sense of accomplishment tends to follow suit, making your patience worthwhile. I had once considered myself no stranger to this feeling, but as I marched across the cafeteria, its satisfaction was stronger than anything else I had ever felt.

Every day since I'd had the idea to write to the President (well, *talk* to him, really), I had been eagerly awaiting the moment when we would finally meet. Of course I've wanted things before, *those shoes, that toy, this game,* but never had I wanted anything as badly as I wanted this. And now, as I approached him, I felt as if I'd just completed some sort of race. It had been a difficult run, but as I came within sight of the finish line, all that mattered was the trophy I'd get when I crossed it. As I confidently strode over to where he was standing, Sandy close at my side, I felt like singing. However, I decided to schedule the Cara-Concert for later, and concentrate on inching my feet over to my target, currently speaking with the Drs. Giraffing. Together, Sandy and I stood a yard or two behind them, pretending to be engaged in our own conversation, trying to hide our impatience as we waited for the adults' discussion to end.

"So Cara, how have things been going for you? I haven't seen you in ages." Sandy asked, speaking only so we might look like we had a purpose for standing near such an important person.

"Oh Sandy, how kind of you to ask!" I kept one eye on her and the other on the back of the President's head, hoping that any minute he might turn around, overcome with the sudden impulse to have a good talk with the friend of a redhead.

"Shall we nonchalantly move closer the President?"

"I believe we should." The two of us took another careful step closer to the adults, hoping that we might be the first to get his attention once their conversation was over.

After about ten minutes of waiting, I must say that I began to get a little annoyed. I mean, I had worked and waited for this moment longer than anyone (or at least it felt that way). For it to be so close, and at the same time so far away could only be described as agonizing.

When I had reached the point where I couldn't wait any longer, I silently expressed my irritation to Sandy. Thankfully, she took the hint. Without saying a word, she walked over to the big photo of the garden kids and peeled the top left corner from the wall so it sagged down across the picture. It was strange how a person dressed like Sandy could pull off something discreetly in broad daylight.

What are you doing? I mouthed to her cautiously. Sandy gave a nod my way, and flashed a proud smile. By the time she had jogged back to my side, I was still lost in confusion. *How could a fallen poster pry the Giraffings away from a deep conversation with the President?*

"Just watch," Sandy whispered, reading my mind with a grin that reminded me of a little kid on April Fool's Day, eagerly awaiting somebody to fall for the trick they had planned. Almost as soon as she had finished speaking, her eyes fell on Gertrude. She gestured for me to do the same. Sure enough, there she was, making her way across the room with a deliberate stride, right in our direction. I have to admit I was nervous, seeing as Sandy had just taken down a large portion of one of her decorations. Gertrude did not seem like someone I'd like to mess around with. Even so, the feeling was short-lived—vanishing within seconds. *It's not us she's heading towards*, I realized with a grin, *it's Sandy's parents!*

Without hesitation, Gertrude marched right up to the Drs. Giraffing, and stopped them mid-conversation with the President of the United States, as if she were interrupting something as trivial as a phone call to the local drug store.

"Excuse me, Mr. President," Gertrude said, a huge smile plastered across her face, "but I just need to borrow these two for *one* second. They'll be *right* back." And with that, Gertrude let out a high-pitched giggle and whisked Sandy's parents, who looked too confused to be angry, away into the crowd. I listened as she led them towards the photograph, mumbling away about buying some stronger tape.

"I think I just bought you an hour with the President," Sandy said with an amused expression on her face. "But just to be sure, I'll go do a little more… *redecorating*…just in case."

"Oh, thank you, Sandy!"

"Don't talk to me," she beamed pointing to the President, "Talk to him."

Sandy was off before I could say another word, loosening a large banner until it was noticeably tilted as she went.

I forced my legs forward. Sandy was right—it was now or never.

It was time for my first move.

"Excuse me, Mr. President, sir? Can I talk to you for a moment?"

When people are famous and powerful, they tend to get a little full of themselves. Bob Deerun was not one of those people.

"Sure you can talk to me!" he replied with a smile, quickly signaling for his guards to stop circling in on me. They backed off a few feet to let us speak, still lingering close by, just in case. "Come on, why don't you have a seat?" He gestured to the empty chair next to him.

I nodded, wondering if he too could hear my heart pounding in my chest, and sat down. Immediately, Bob Deerun cut to the chase.

"So, what's your name?" he asked me, extending his hand for a shake.

"Um…Cara…Cara Greybird," I stuttered. My hand felt like a brick in my lap, and it took an enormous amount of effort to lift it towards him.

"Well Cara Greybird, what is it you wanted to speak with me about today?"

"Well, you see Mr. President," I began, my voice nervous as I unfolded the crumpled paper from my change purse. "There was this project at school…"

I did my best to inform the President as much as I could about ONE Nation, MANY Opinions. I felt a little embarrassed to talk to the President about me wanting to be important and all that, so I just stuck to the basics and kept most of my personal motives to myself. That is, I told him I wanted to interview him for a school project.

Things seemed to be going well with our conversation on the surface, but it was lacking something important, and the overpowering satisfaction I had felt just moments ago had somehow slipped away. It was almost as if my words slid out soullessly, and I found myself hearing them as if they were from the mouth of another. My voice and my mind had become two separate bodies, and as my words dragged on, separately, my mind was racing. It began to analyze each alien word that escaped past my lips. Now, it seemed like I was telling my story from a different perspective, and it only took me a moment to realize who this viewpoint belonged to—Cornelia V. I was polite, I was pleasant, but in the end I was only there for an interview. Shocked, I listened to my own voice drone on, realizing why my pride had vanished so suddenly. Our conversation was missing something, and it was overwhelmingly clear what that something was.

The truth.

Our conversation was meaningless, like reading the first page of a book and then skipping to the end, passing over the plotline in the middle. What I had provided to the President hardly expressed the need for our conversation. There was more to the story, parts that only I could explain. As I heard my voice wind down in volume and speed, I discovered that I didn't care if the President thought of me as just a silly kid with a crazy dream. That would be *his* loss, but if I didn't tell him the truth now, then the loss would be mine.

"Yes, well, I've had a lot of fun talking to you, Cara. Thank you so much for choosing to do your report on me!" The President's expression was distant, distracted as he began to stand up. To my horror, I realized that we had gone through all of my guideline questions. In his eyes, we were finished, and I was about to miss my last chance.

"Wait! Mr. President!" I called, louder than I had intended. His attention turned back to me again.

"Yes, Cara."

"I have to tell you why I'm *really* here."

His eyes glimmered. "I thought there might have been something more to the story."

And so, I told the President the *whole* truth, leaving nothing out. I explained how it had all started as a school project, but then slowly evolved into something more important to me, something I realized I had wanted all along. How I desperately wanted to make a difference in the world, and have the chance to voice my opinions towards others. How one letter, a simple piece of paper, had never reached his hands. About how I met Sandy and how she had brought me to the party so that I could finally meet him. I told him about all of the failed attempts and sacrifices that had been made to get me where I was sitting right then. About how much I wanted to be there. And finally, I told him something I had never told anyone else.

"…And Mr. President, this means more to me than anything in the entire world. In all my wildest dreams, I never imagined I would be here, talking face-to-face with the President of the United States, the person with the power to make a difference, the person who can help me make my opinions, and those of other children, heard. *That's* what this is really all about." I finished in a sigh, relieved that someone finally knew how I felt.

My words felt genuine now. They had been stored up inside me for too long, and now that they had finally found a way out, I felt almost lighter. What I hadn't accounted for was that although this openness had lifted a weight from my shoulders, the empty space where the weight had once rested left me with nothing to hide behind.

For the next few moments, the President was completely silent. In fact, the more I thought about it, the more I realized that he hadn't said anything while I was talking to him, either. The seconds went by torturously slow, each one bringing a new fear with it. *Maybe the President thought I was nothing but a big joke, after all. Worse, what if he thought what I had said was actually amusing? What if he was about to break out into roaring laughter?*

The President broke his silence after an anxious eternity, his voice filled with the same confidence that I had so much admiration for during his speech in the gardens. I braced myself for the message they would bring.

"*I completely agree with you,*" he shrugged. My heart was practically in my throat, stomach having already dropped somewhere near my feet. Something in the back of my mind told me that he couldn't be serious, but his voice was filled with such a striking simplicity that I knew he must be telling the truth. *Could it be possible that he had been waiting for someone to bring up my concerns just as eagerly as I had been working to make them heard?* My heart knew the answer, but my brain was still unconvinced.

"WHAT?!" I was practically yelling, too overwhelmed to remember that I was supposed to be acting sophisticated. For future reference, screaming when you are supposed to be having a quiet conversation with the President is not a good thing to do. I learned this lesson quickly, because almost instantly, I was surrounded by security again. They grabbed my arms and yanked me up and out of my chair, away from President Deerun. The sea of black suits closed in around me so that he was blocked from my sight, their nearness making it very difficult to breathe. Looking concerned, but not quite as scared as I did, the President gave them another signal, and they were gone as swiftly as they had come. We seemed to be alone again, just as we had been before, only now I was a little more conscious of my actions, and a little more afraid.

"Sorry." I shrunk back into my seat, hoping that the President wouldn't reconsider what he had said earlier.

"Oh, don't worry." His expression softened. "They're a little overprotective." He smiled and I knew he understood. "Now, Cara. With all things forgiven, I'd like to continue on a more serious note. I have thought about this long and hard ever since I became President of the United States. It is my belief that if a child has ideas, especially good ones like yours, they should be able to express their opinions to people who will listen, just like every adult can. And if they are serious enough about their plans, I think that they should be able to carry on with them, free of obstacles regarding their age. It is wrong to hold back a fully qualified person from their potential. Who knows what a child is capable of accomplishing? Some day, one might even become President!"

"A kid...become President?" Even I found it hard to imagine.

"Yes, I believe so, if they are mature enough to handle it. I think that everyone should have that right."

"Wow!" I had never expected this to come up. A kid President... Just the thought was enough to leave me speechless.

"Actually, Cara," said the President, "I think you might have what it takes to do the job."

"*Me?*"

"Yes, *you,*" the President continued, deep in thought. "In fact, I should really be thanking you."

"But why?" I blurted out. "What did I do?"

"You are, in fact, the proof I have been waiting for." His eyes were practically glowing with excitement now, like a lawyer who had just come upon the piece of evidence that would win him his case. "For years, I've been preparing to do something like this, to show America the true capabilities of our youth." He lowered his voice, eye contact unwavering. "I've been aspiring to lead an underage rights movement, complete with a bill that gives *everyone* the opportunity to be heard."

Noticing that his tone had risen considerably with the mention of his bill, the President bit his lower lip. He had already said too much, too soon, and far too loud. I watched him sit in silence for a moment, as if substantially editing whatever realization had occurred to him. Only after his thoughts had been organized did he see it fit to continue again.

"All that matters for the moment is that I've thought out everything, each piece of my plan carefully constructed. Even so, I've never been ready to act—until now. Of course, I realize that it would be impossible to convince America of the abilities of our country's young people without a child to prove it to them." He was speaking faster now, his face still electrified with the breakthrough I was hearing only in scattered phrases. "For months now, I've been searching for the perfect child to help me, but no one was just right. I've gone to the most prestigious academies, rigorous academic events, national debate tournaments, all with the secret incentive of finding a child to show why the bil—" He was silent again, the pressure with which his teeth had clamped down on his lower lip now looking somewhat painful. "I really am sorry I can't disclose more, but this isn't the time..." he looked around, "isn't the place. What I *can* say is that I should have been looking here all along. The children I met before were filled with empty competition; they would work to succeed but their achievements were not fulfilling because they had no deeper meaning. *You* are the child I have been looking for, Cara. Without the child, after all, the plan is nothing! You believe in the cause and have the drive to promote it. This plan is capable of changing our country but it cannot go forward without you. Together, you and I can give everyone the power to make a difference." He leaned forward in his seat, taking a deep breath. "Will you help me?"

In a thousand daydreams leading up to that moment, I had imagined what it would be like to talk to the President. I had pictured the look on his face, creating a different dialogue between us each time. Every story played out differently, but in the end, all I could do was cling to the hope that he would respect my ideas.

Not even a thousand daydreams, a thousand different scenarios, could prepare me for the real thing. I had never expected something like this.

I was taken aback. Every instinct I had was screaming for me to grab at the opportunity, but my body was frozen solid, unable to act. It was almost too good to be true, and yet somehow, there it was, practically laid out in front of me. Still, the perfection of the offer felt strange—like I needed to find some fault in his words to make them valid. Until then, their proposition seemed intangible. I couldn't hold it in my hand, but rather, swipe at the shape their shadow cast against me, hoping to grasp onto something real from the empty air.

"So what you mean to say, Mr. President, is that—" I was cut off before I could finish my sentence.

"Cara, are you free these next two weeks?" he asked me, clearly making his mind up on some plan that was yet to be revealed.

I didn't bother to run through my schedule "Completely free! Well...I do have school, but that doesn't matter," I added as an afterthought. The President was quiet again. Realizing that down-talking the public education system in front of the President of the United States had probably not been my brightest idea, I silently kicked myself as I waited for him to speak again.

"Yes, school...," Bob Deerun was still thinking as he drew out the word. "Education is a very important thing, Cara." He smiled, "I think we *both* understand that. *However*, if you would just skip school for that time, and come to Washington with me, I can assure you that I will have no problem finding you a personal tutor."

It took me a moment to find the message hidden behind what had become an indirect invitation.

"Washington? Washington, *D.C.*? With *you*?" I was screaming again, the Secret Service probably just itching to drag me away. "But my parents...," I trailed off, suddenly remembering. I hunched over in my seat, convinced that they would not like this idea.

"Oh, don't worry about them, they are hardly an obstacle. You will receive a call tonight to confirm our plans anyway. I looked up for reassurance and his smile convinced me. I recognized it instantly as the look I had given him after his speech in the gardens. Now, the roles were reversed. He was the crazy one in the front row. I couldn't breathe. *He believed in me.* "Cara Greybird," he said, meeting my eyes. "Welcome to Washington, D.C."

chapter thirteen

Despite popular belief, there are not two types of shock—the surprised one, and then the electric one. *In truth, they feel exactly the same.* Even so, the worst thing about shock isn't the way it makes you feel—how it catches you off-guard, the numbness, the searing heat, the chills—it's the way you react *afterward.* Once shock takes a hold of a person, they can only do one of two things: a) become speechless, or b) babble like a complete idiot. After the President told me the news, I chose the second of these two options. Questions were coming out of my mouth so fast, *even I* wasn't sure of what I was saying.

"What? Wait, when? Today? But … for how long? Washington? But what about …? But my mom and…wow! *Are you sure?* Is this a joke? How is—?"

"Cara," the President held up a hand to silence me. "If this is going to work, no more nonsense can leave your mouth. You are a national political figure now, and although the people *want* to hear you, it would be a nice bonus if they could *understand* you, too."

"Alright," I whispered, my eyes wide. The term "national political figure" put me in a full daze.

"Now," the President replied softly, aware that I had been caught off guard.

"I know that this has been a big day for you. In fact, I feel exactly the same way. Why, I've got to call the press conference, prepare the speech, the idea must be introduced correctly or…" he cut himself off. "Never mind that, though," he decided, pushing whatever thought he'd had from his mind. "There is no time… but we must make the most of what we have and let this all sink in. Here, do you see that woman over there in the red suit?" The President pointed over to a small crowd of people next to the dance floor. I craned my neck, scanning the group until I caught sight of the woman he was describing.

"Yes," I answered, my eyes still following her.

"She is one of my private assistants. I'm going to need to get a hold of you somehow, so give her your contact information before you leave and she can record it for me. She will have my secretary call your family tonight at around 8:30 or nine to discuss the details of your trip to Washington."

"Thank you!" I exclaimed, having trouble steadying my voice. I held back the urge to jump up and hug him, deciding that the less the Secret Service attacks you in one day, the better. Once was more than plenty.

"The pleasure is all mine," he replied, smiling. He stood up to shake my hand and left to mingle with other party guests.

As soon as the President was gone, I collapsed back into my chair. The shock was slowly wearing away, but the disbelief remained. I didn't know what to do or where to go; I was just stuck in the past half hour, playing the scene over and over in my head like a song stuck on repeat in a CD player. Next thing I knew, I was making my way towards the woman in the red suit, clumsily relaying a tongue-tied version of the President's instructions to me. Apparently, he had already filled her in with a brief summary, and all the contact information she needed from me was my full name and phone number. I told her everything she wanted to know and then staggered back to my seat, still in a daze. After I had finally gotten over the initial astonishment, I remembered Sandy. I scanned the room for my friend, spotting her on the other side of the cafeteria, sitting with Cornelia V. and eating a peanut butter brownie.

"I'm telling you, Sandy; it is extremely impolite to eat *anything* without a plate or eating utensil! I know that it's just a small dessert, but table manners are a very important part of first impressions. Seriously, I'm almost embarrassed to—Oh! You think this is funny, don't you? Well, laugh now, but when the President goes back to Washington and tells everyone his afternoon was ruined by some little redhead from Pennsylvania who doesn't think she needs a plate or fork to eat a brownie, I don't think it will be quite as hysterica—"

"Sorry, Cornelia," I broke into the conversation, much too stunned to realize that my interruption would probably get me a very well-mannered scolding on the ride home. "I need to talk to Sandy for a minute." I pulled Sandy out of her chair and over toward the dance floor.

"V!" she shouted at us as we made our way across the room. "It's Cornelia V.!"

"Sandy!" I exclaimed, "I'm going to Washington, D.C.!"

"WHAT?" She grabbed me by the wrist, her feet merely a neon green kitten heel blur as she jumped up and down, making no visible effort to contain herself. I could just hear the Secret Service wondering how many times they could live through that reaction again, and so after receiving what I assumed to be an annoyed glare from a tall man in sunglasses, I led a hyperactive Sandy outside so we wouldn't be bothered.

"Tell me everything!" she squealed. I didn't know where to begin. All that had just happened was jumbled up in my mind like a tangled ball of yarn. Try as I might to sort out what I had just experienced, or at least get it in some sort of sequential order, the knots in the string refused to untwist, and I was left with nothing but a mess of memories. Sandy stopped jumping. I had been silent for longer than was acceptable. Seeing as her interest alone didn't seem to be earning her any answers, she changed tracks, taking me by the shoulder and practically throwing me into a folding chair lying out on the lawn.

"Spill," she demanded as if she were interrogating a criminal. Eyes wide with curiosity, she knelt down in the grass and leaned in closer to me.

I managed to laugh, though my mind was still working to loosen all the knots in the yarn that it could. Sensing Sandy's impatience, I decided to start talking, and maybe the ones that were too tight for me to unfurl would come undone on their own.

"It happened pretty much like this..." With a deep breath, I began to recount the story from where Sandy had last left off. With each word, the yarn unwound itself a little further. It wasn't long before all the details were back and my recollections would have been no clearer if I had taken notes as they occurred. I'm not sure how long the two of us were sitting there, me talking, and Sandy doing her best to take it all in, but by the time I was finished, everything had finally been rolled out straight.

"...And then after that, you pushed me into this chair, and I guess that brings you up-to-date." I finished talking, and looked down at Sandy for reassurance. Now *she* was the quiet one, staring up at me like I had performed some sort of impossible magic trick.

"Oh my gosh!" she whispered. Her smile began to fade.

"What?" I replied half-consciously, watching the hula-hoop contest the kids' DJ was leading out of the corner of my eye.

"Hey—you're teasing me, aren't you Cara?" she asked, raising her eyebrows. "Ha, ha, very funny." Rolling her eyes, she got up and started to walk inside.

"Wait, what? Teasing you? Sandy, what are you talking about?" I jumped out of the chair and ran to catch up with her.

"The President, Washington, D.C.—everything! What else?"

"It's the truth!" I nearly yelled, swatting the idea out of my head as if it were an annoying mosquito. She turned around and I lowered my voice. "You believe me don't you, Sandy? You know I wouldn't lie, right?" She looked into my eyes, evaluating my honesty. Gradually, as if returning in stages, her smile formed again.

"You're serious?! *The* President of the United States, personally invited you to Washington, D.C. to present your ideas?!"

"Positively serious," I said through a proud grin. "About everything, I swear."

"When are you leaving?" Sandy asked with a look of complete bemusement. She knew that I was telling the truth now, but the initial surprise of it all was apparently yet to soak in.

"This week." I watched as her face crumpled itself back into disbelief.

"You are *not* serious."

"Sandy!"

"Sorry, it's just an expression!" She laughed, raising her hands in surrender.

"Come on," I said, taking one last glance at the kids behind us. "We'd better go and find your family. They're probably looking for us."

"Oops." Sandy made a face. "Yeah, they've got enough to worry about today."

I followed her through the open door and into the cafeteria. Spotting an abandoned brownie on her way, she peeled it from its platter and casually popped the whole thing into her mouth, swallowing after one bite. "Like how many of these things I've eaten," she mumbled as an afterthought, licking her fingers.

The two of us were still laughing by the time we reached the Drs. Giraffing near the main entrance.

"Sandra Guinevere Vivian, Cara, over here!" Sandy's mom called, waving us in her direction. "So girls, how did you enjoy the event?"

"Words couldn't even begin to describe it!" I shot Sandy a sideways glance.

"Well, I'm glad that you had such a nice time. It's always rewarding to see your efforts pay off," she scanned the room, smiling. "After so much planning, I can't believe that all of the hard work is finally done."

"Definitely." I found myself nodding, thinking back to my conversation with the President. In my mind, I too had completed my goal. Considering all that I had already overcome, I found myself assuming that the rest would be downhill in comparison. "All of the hard work is done."

Little did I realize, pride had left me oblivious to the challenges that lay ahead.

Now was only just the beginning.

chapter fourteen

The party ended but Gertrude, the Giraffings and I stayed behind to help clean up. Time flies when you're having fun, and although providing free labor isn't exactly something known to make the seconds melt away, I was in such a state of euphoria that a similar effect was somehow achieved.

As we transported the chairs from the cafeteria to the parking lot for the rental truck to pick up, Sandy and I began to make up questions that the President might ask me when I was in Washington to help me prepare. Sandy did her best imitation of the President, asking me creative questions, evaluating my responses, and giving me advice on how to provide a better answer. This exercise ended up making us even more excited, almost to the point where we couldn't concentrate anymore. Towards the end, we were so animated that Sandy's questions hardly made any sense, and my answers got to be jumbled and incomplete.

When everything had finally been packed, scrubbed, and put away, it was precisely 4:00 p.m. and time for us to head home. Cornelia V. was jabbering away with her parents, and Gertrude was trailing close behind, interrupting every few seconds to provide an up-to-date report on the information spewing from her walkie-talkie. Sandy and I followed them to the car, taking care to keep our distance from the rest of the group.

"I can't believe it, Sandy. This afternoon, I mean, it's unbelievable!" I gushed in an electrified whisper. When I explained how vague and secretive the President had sounded when speaking about his rights movement, Sandy had decided that outside the two of us and my own family, it was best to keep the information quiet as well—for the time being. Still however, I was having trouble keeping my voice down. "Can you believe I'm leaving?"

Much to my surprise, Sandy didn't respond and continued to walk on, as if she hadn't heard me. Her focus had shifted towards the ground, arms folded defensively across her chest.

"Sandy!" I shouted. She kept walking. "SANDY!"

Finally, she slowed down. I ran to catch up with her and we continued to walk, Sandy still hiding behind her shield of strawberry hair.

"What's wrong?" I finally asked, after a few minutes of silence.

"Nothing," she sighed impatiently, "Just tired, I guess."

"Oh." I nodded as if this made sense, and stopped asking questions.

Cornelia V. had already called the 'same seats' rule, and so after her dad managed to pry a still-jabbering Gertrude away from his wife, Sandy slid into the car. The rest of us followed close behind, each reclaiming our pre-determined places before pulling out of the lot.

The ride home didn't seem nearly as long as the ride to the ceremony. The energy in the car itself had practically transformed, shifting from nervous tension to a peaceful excitement. In the front seats, Drs. Giraffing were involved in a deep discussion about how smoothly the event had gone, filled with the enthusiasm of a newly-wed couple just back from their honeymoon. After awhile, simply keeping up with their exchanges came to feel like following a professional tennis match. We turned our heads from left to right, and then left again as the compliments whizzed between them, watching the players volley their words with little hesitation or change in pace. Cornelia V. jumped into the conversation every so often, hanging on her parents' every word and periodically requesting switches between radio stations to see if there was any

Mozart, Tchaikovsky, Beethoven, or Bach pieces that she hadn't already heard. Once, she even suggested that we remain on a station playing Verstovsky, noting twice that '*mixing it up a little bit could sometimes be fun*'.

As for me, I sat back in content, just glad to relax. Nevertheless, when the scenery outside had finally grown familiar, I became tired of listening to the doctors' conversation and decided to talk to Sandy. She looked completely detached from everything going on around her, her head leaning against her shoulder as she stared solemnly out the window. I knew that something was wrong, but not wanting to force an answer out of her, I attempted to cheer her up in other ways.

"Sandy, you were really brilliant today."

"Thanks, Cara," she mumbled

"Sure. And, you know, I really like your outfit."

"Thanks, Cara."

"Cool shoes," I tried again.

"Thanks."

"And your hair looks great, too—"

"Cara?"

"Yeah?" I perked up.

"Silence is golden. Always remember that."

"Sorry. But I really do like your shoes today."

"*Cara.*"

After that, all car conversations came to a close. I sighed to myself, knowing that as much as I wanted to help Sandy, it would be impossible for me to do so. Like a splinter that's in too deep to pull out, when something really gets under your skin, not a word in the world can make it disappear. In those cases, it really is better to embrace the quiet. All you can do is wait for time to make things heal. I only wondered what had caused her mood, and while I tried to convince myself that exhaustion was purely to blame, something in the back of my mind kept wondering if I was somehow at fault instead. Whatever the catalyst was however, I left the matter alone, and soon the car pulled up onto my street. I told Sandy one last time how much I appreciated what she had done for me.

"Don't mention it," she said through a half-smile that looked like it was actually causing her pain. I smiled back, doing my best to disregard the way she was acting. After a few long moments of watching my house approach from the side window later, the car was coming to a slow stop in the driveway.

"Tell your parents we say hello, dear," Sandy's mother called as I reluctantly climbed out of their car.

"Thank you all so much for inviting me. I had such a great day. The event was amazing."

"Thanks, Cara. You're welcome to be our guest anytime." Sandy's father rolled down his window.

I smiled, looking towards the backseat. "Bye, Sandy!" I waved, hoping she would say something. Instead of responding, she pretended not to notice.

"Well, we should go," Dr. Giraffing announced, more to me than to the rest of his family, "We're way behind schedule." He shifted the car into reverse. "Say hello to your parents from us, will you?" I nodded.

"We're glad you had such a good time, Cara," Cornelia V. added. "See you later!"

The gray Corvette was waiting at the edge of the driveway when I reached the front door. I turned the knob to make sure it was unlocked, and then waved in its direction, signaling the Giraffings that I could get inside. I watched as the car turned into the street and sped away, having opted, no doubt, to take the longer route home for fear of passing the Hamstering house. I let myself in, smelling the junk food on the kitchen table before I saw it. Knowing that Nadia must be home alone, I didn't bother to announce my entry. Instead, I kicked off my shoes and ran up to our bedroom.

Everything inside of me was dying to tell my parents about my conversation with the President, but over the phone was not the right way to do it. I would tell them when they got home, but in the meantime, I would unload everything on Nadia. The door to my room was closed, but I ignored the knocking rule and rushed inside. Nadia was spread out on the carpet, working on a jigsaw puzzle and humming quietly to herself. It took her a moment to notice me.

"How was the party?" she asked without looking up, totally absorbed in her puzzle.

"Nadia, it was awesome!" I cried, unable to contain my emotions any longer. "You should have been there! And you'll never guess what happened. I met the President!"

"*The* President?" Nadia repeated, suddenly sitting up. "You mean of the United States? That President?" She jumped up and dove onto her comforter, as if the news was nothing more than a good bedtime story.

"Yeah, *that* President! And I haven't even told you the best part yet!"

"Really, there's more?" Nadia scooted over towards the edge of the bed, closer to where I was sitting on the floor. "Tell me!"

"The President thinks my ideas are really good, and he wants me to come to Washington, D.C. to help him! *I'm going to Washington, D.C., Nadia!*" I closed my eyes, still not used to stating the sentence as fact. "I am actually going out there to do something good for the world. I'm going to make a difference! It's all set!! Can you believe it, Nad?" I looked up at her. "Isn't it just too good to be true?"

Nadia was at my side before I could react, flinging her arms around me and pinning me flat against the floor. "I can't believe it! Well, yes I can. I mean, I knew you could—but I CAN'T BELIEVE IT!" she yelled through possibly the biggest hug I had ever received. I was laughing and so was she, both unsure of what was funny. "You've got to be, like, on top of the world!"

How could I not be? I thought as I twisted free, throwing myself onto the messy mountain of pillows, blankets and stuffed animals Nadia called her bed. I lay on my back with my hands behind my head, eyes staring up towards the ceiling. That really was how I felt; *on top of the world*. My heart beat like I was running, moving with no intention ever to stop.

I turned onto my side to face Nadia. The laughter had died down and now she looked kind of sad; a feeling that didn't seem to fit into the moment. It was like she was trying to be happy for me, but just couldn't seem to pull it off. It was the exact same face I had seen on Sandy during the car ride home.

I sat up. "Nadia," I murmured, back on a level with the rest of humanity for the first time all afternoon, "What's wrong?"

She sensed my concern and looked up, forcing a smile. "Nothing, I'm just really happy for you, that's all." I watched as she stood up and went back to her puzzle.

"Seriously, I know something's up, Nad. Please." I pushed my head over the edge of the bed, meeting her face at eye-level.

"Alright," she looked down towards the carpet, away from me. "Maybe I'm just a little jealous. I mean, I'm happy for you and all, I really am, but now everything's different. We used to all be in this together, me, you, and Sandy. And it really was fun. But now it's not just an idea anymore, or a game: now it's *real*. Now I'm not part of it anymore—none of us are, except for you. It's over for me and Sandy. I guess it's just a strange thing to realize—that things have moved on without you. But I know you," she smiled, "and you'll be great out there."

It should have made sense, but I couldn't understand. It had never occurred to me that she would feel like this, and in a way, I felt kind of bad. It was like I had done a huge school project with a group, but the teacher only recognized my hard work in the end. It wasn't fair that I was the only one getting credit, and I supposed that they had the right to be mad at me. On the other hand, I didn't *want* to leave Sandy and Nadia behind. It wasn't *my* decision—simply *my* time to shine. They should be happy for me…shouldn't they? Should I consider their jealousy a betrayal? I stared back at her in disbelief, unsure what to think or say. I waited for emotion to find me, *any emotion*, but none came.

I couldn't feel anything, and I wasn't sure if I wanted to. I tried to avoid looking back at Nadia so I could sort things out, but her gaze hit me with full force. Her eyes were weak and a little watery, yet so vibrant that it was almost hard to break away from them. That's the thing with Nadia. Just one look into her eyes and you can see right on through to her true emotions. It was like her physical form acted purely as a mirror into her soul. No matter what, the truth was always somewhere on their surface, and it only took a second of searching to realize why she was acting so sensitive. What she felt was sort of like when you hit your funny bone, and you don't know whether to laugh or cry. Of course she was glad that I was running fast, but she was also sad because she could no longer keep up. She was caught between her feelings just like me, the result being something of a bittersweet uncertainty. A melancholy pain.

"Sandy feels that way, too," I whispered, letting the realization float around in the open.

"You should call her," Nadia answered, smacking another piece firmly into the puzzle. I was surprised she had heard me.

"I wouldn't know what to say." I was talking more to myself than to Nadia. Everything always seemed so simple to her. She didn't understand that sometimes things were more complicated than that. Sometimes I wondered if they had to be that way.

"What do you mean, Cara? Last time I checked, you and her were best friends."

"No, Nad, it's not that," I answered. "I mean, sure, I could call her and we could talk, but I just can't cheer her up, believe me, I've already tried."

Nadia's eyes were smoldering, and I could tell she was hurt. I had said something wrong. Instinctively, I got off the bed and crawled to her side.

"You know what, Nadia, you're right. It's not like I don't know why you're so upset, and it's not like I can't fix this, because I can. *I know I can.*" I added, not sure which of us needed the reassurance more. "I don't want to leave you behind and I definitely don't want to do this alone. I need you. When I told you about my idea, you believed in me. It sounded impossible, but you had your faith, and we were in it as one. Now, nobody is dropping out. I won't let it happen. I don't know exactly where you two fit in with the President's plan yet, but I won't do this if I can't have you guys next to me. If all goes as planned, I'll talk to the President's secretary tonight, and if she doesn't understand, you know we can find another way. I couldn't do anything without your help."

I could see Nadia's face flood with relief. One second later, I had been tackled back to the ground. I was unsure about the previous one, but there was no arguing now; this was *definitely* the biggest hug anyone had ever given me.

"Hold up," she ordered after a moment as if I was the one calling the shots, repositioning herself so she was sitting comfortably on my stomach. "Did you say that the President's very own personal secretary is going to call *us? Tonight?*"

"Yup," I grunted proudly, pushing her off of me. I started to stand up, but she grabbed a hold of my wrist, yanking it towards her.

"Wait!" she called, her face glowing with curiosity. "Start over from the beginning. I want to hear *everything!*"

It felt really good to talk things over with Nadia, mainly because she was honest, and unafraid of giving her input. I was more than glad to have won back her full support. Nonetheless, as usual, Nadia eventually got bored of listening to me talk and returned to solving her puzzle.

"Hey, I'm really tired Nad. I think I'm going to go and watch some TV or something. Is it okay if I finish the rest of the story later?" It was a Sunday night, and my dad usually stayed later at work to help with the dinner rush. My mom however, who was no doubt off running errands, should be back sometime soon.

"Yeah, sure," Nadia was barely listening, focusing all of her energy on snapping another piece faithfully into the jigsaw.

Get real, Nadia, I thought as I stood up. *You're doing a puzzle, not inventing the wheel.* After closing the curtain that divided our room for privacy, I grabbed a cordless phone off the floor and brought it over to my bedside table. This way, I'd be the first one to answer if anyone from the White House decided to call a little early. Pulling my hair into a messy bun at the top of my head, I collapsed onto my bed and rolled over onto my side. When I opened my eyes, I found myself facing the same window I had climbed through just weeks before, beginning my adventure. Now, it had all seemed so long ago. I closed my eyes again. It felt good to rest after the long day, and my body seemed to sink into the mattress like it would into a hot bath.

Realizing that I was lying on something, I reached a hand beneath my back and pulled out the TV remote from under me. Sitting up a little, I clicked the 'on' button. I surfed through the channels thoughtlessly before settling on the five o'clock news report, a program I had been accustomed to watching during the past few weeks. I think they were talking about a pinkeye epidemic that had been sweeping the schools in the area, but luckily, I fell asleep before I saw too much of it.

. . . .

I had the strangest dream. *I was the President.* The first thing I could remember was speaking behind a tall podium, facing the hundreds of people who had gathered to see me. It was some sort of government-related deal, and I knew that I was doing a really good job with my deliverance. The address carried on and I read each line as it was written on my teleprompter, too excited to comprehend the meaning behind my words. A moment later, applause filled the room. I hadn't noticed that there were no words left on the screen until they were gone, and it took me a moment to understand that my speech was over. I hid my surprise with a smile and waved at the crowd, overcome by the sounds of their cheering.

Herds of newscasters surrounded me before I could react, begging for interviews and photographs. Their approval came as a shock, like I had achieved the impossible in earning it. Just as the mass of people had nearly closed in around me, I managed to notice one man standing towards the door, dressed in a crisp black suit and a pair of sunglasses that hid his face. Somehow, I knew that I was supposed to go over to him. As if in direct synchronization with my thoughts, the mob eagerly parted to let me through.

Only one person refused to move.

I was about to ask her to step aside, but stopped myself before I had the chance. There was something about this girl that distinguished her from the other reporters. Everyone around her looked at me in the same pleading way. They wanted to talk to me, but not because they cared. It was simply their job. This one was different. The look in her eyes alone made clear that she didn't want to talk to me for anyone else, just for herself. Her gaze was fixed firmly on me, carrying a strange mix of adoration and judgment. She didn't *want* me to talk to her, she *needed* it. I remember the emblem on the microphone she was holding; an orange circle with the letters SG written inside it in big white lettering.

In my dream, I knew that this girl represented some major news station, so I flashed her camerawoman a smile. My reflection in the lens made me do a double-take. It was my face, but something was different. I appeared much older. It wasn't that I was wrinkled or anything—I was still young. I had aged with knowledge and experience. The face I saw in the camera was more mature, but it also looked hard, like my past endurances had changed the texture of my skin.

"How is it for you?" the reporter asked after a long pause, tossing aside her thick red hair. "You're the President of the United States, and you got here all on your own." She held up a folded newspaper headlined *President Greybird's Approval Rates Skyrocket.*

I broke away from the reflection in the glass to take the paper into my own hands, staring down at it in disbelief. *Skyrocketing approval ratings? All on my own? What does all of this mean?* I thought to myself. Suddenly, I realized that neither Sandy, nor any of my family was in sight. The smaller woman behind the SG camera was motioning for me to turn back towards her so that she could continue shooting her footage, but I ignored her, moving to face the crowd.

"Um," I stuttered into the microphone, trying to sound composed. "It has definitely been a struggle getting to where I am today. All I ever wanted was to make a difference in the world. I've had to make more sacrifices to get here than you could ever imagine, some of which I truly regret. What I do not regret however, is where I am today. My goal has always been to help our country, and I thank you all, each and every one of you, for approving this mission so wholeheartedly, and for your continued support. Thank you."

The surrounding reporters cheered and burst out into a hearty applause. I smiled again and took the newspaper into my own hands, lifting it high above my head for everyone to see. All at once, the crowd closed in on me again, taking my picture, getting quotations, and asking questions. I stole a quick glance at the man in the corner, who signaled that it was alright for me to stay a little while longer. I smiled. Feeding on their interest in me, I talked and talked, speaking until everyone had eventually gone. Everyone that is, except for me. Me and the security guard who had been waiting to escort me outside since the end of my speech. I walked towards the man and he handed me a pair of sunglasses, identical to his own. I put them on quickly and he led me from the empty room.

I don't know what happened next because I woke up. From the place I had been longing most to be and back to the familiar shadows of my bedroom, the dream had stuck. I opened my eyes, noticing the drowsy smile stretched across my face. The message of the vision had eluded me, but as I tried to stand, it became clear, knocking me back to my mattress. Suddenly, I understood. In that moment, I knew how I could accomplish the difficult and tedious task that lay before me. *I had learned the secret to my own success.*

I can do this on my own, I thought to myself with a newly found confidence. *And nobody is going to stop me.*

chapter fifteen

It was after six o'clock when I heard the garage door opening. Two seconds later and I was flying down the stairs, rushing to tell whoever had come home the exciting news.

I should be happy for myself, I thought, skidding down the steps towards the front door. *Sandy's just being jealous, but I'm not going to let her ruin it for me. It's a once-in-a-lifetime chance, after all.* I got downstairs just as my mother was stepping out of her car. I was too excited to wait and tell her about the day's adventure—I had to let it out now or I'd explode. Catching her off-guard, I ran out into the garage to greet her. A purse was hanging over her shoulder and an overly-stuffed grocery bag was balanced in each arm. She looked tired, but still managed a small smile in my direction.

"Mom!" My voice escaped as an unfamiliar screech.

Running at a maniac pace towards her, I saw my mother's expression change from exhaustion to anxiety.

She set the bags down on the floor. "Cara honey, is everything alright?"

"MOM, THE PRESIDENT IS GOING TO CALL TONIGHT AND I'M GOING TO GO TO WASHINGTON, D.C. WITH HIM AND I'M GOING

TO TELL HIM MY OPINIONS AND GET THEM HEARD—I'M GOING TO HELP HIM MAKE A DIFFERENCE IN THE WAY PEOPLE THINK, AND I GUESS IT DOESN'T MATTER ANYMORE, BUT NOW I'VE TOTALLY ACED MY AMERICA PROJECT AND—"

For a second, I thought she was going to cry. I stopped talking and took a step towards her. There was fear in her face, and I couldn't understand why. My mom was hard to rock, and seeing her expression scared me. She looked as if I had just cut off my head and re-grown a new one. I wasn't sure what I had done, but I felt somehow responsible for the way she was acting. She shook her head and leaned her back against the car, all emotion draining from her face. She was in a trance-like state, staring at me as if she found what I was saying to be impossible, and at any moment now someone was going to pop out and tell her I was just kidding. That didn't happen. This was the real deal, and she spoke only after she realized that I was serious.

"Cara," she said, barely moving her lips as she spoke, "can you repeat all that? This time with punctuation, maybe?"

And so I did. I told her everything that had happened that day. Everything but two small little details: I left out the parts about Sandy and Nadia. After all, it wasn't important. I knew them; they'd get over it soon enough.

When I finished speaking, my mom was silent. She was looking back at me, but no longer looked afraid—just overwhelmed. It was a lot to take in.

"Cara...I am so proud of you." She was blinking hard. "To think—I discouraged this. I just didn't want you to get hurt..." She was back to crying now. Stumbling towards me, she pulled me into a weak hug. "But you did it. You followed your heart and you did it." She took a step back and rested her hands on my shoulders, her lips curling into a smile so strong with admiration for her daughter that it was almost painful to see. She wiped her eyes, taking a moment to regain control of her emotions before continuing.

"You know what?" she said through a tender smile. "We should really celebrate. How 'bout we go to your dad's restaurant for dinner tonight? If we're expecting the call from the White House tonight at 8:30 or nine, we really have to leave soon, but if we do go, we'd be back home with time to spare." She reached over affectionately and took her hand in mine. "I knew you could do it, Cara. Now, why don't you go tell your sister that we're going to leave in ten minutes and that she should be ready to go by then. I've got to go call your father and tell him the news!" With that thought in mind, she let go of my hand and hurried into the house to find a phone, leaving me alone in the garage with the groceries. My mother's reaction had besieged me with pride, but the thought of Sandy kept pushing its way back toward the front of my brain.

Maybe I should talk to her, I thought for the hundredth time that day. I had dumped the grocery bags onto the kitchen counter and was now heading up to my bedroom to alert Nadia about the change in our dinner plans. My mom, having reached my dad at work, could probably be heard down the block, recounting my story at such a volume that using a phone to relay the message was probably not necessary. *I could just send her a quick e-mail before we go.* I had half a mind to turn on the computer and do it right then, but my dream from earlier that afternoon held me back. *No. I don't need to talk to her—I didn't do anything wrong. It's just Sandy. Nadia will have to understand too, but at least she's doing her best to be supportive.* I nodded to myself. Satisfied with this argument, I made one final attempt to push all thoughts of Sandy from my mind, heading towards my dresser to pull out some more comfortable clothes. I slipped off my wrinkled dress and held it out in front of me, realizing that taking a nap in it had probably not been such a great treatment for the fabric. *Sorry Sandy, but you're just going to have to realize that this is MY big chance.*

Ten minutes later, I was giggling in the back seat of the car with Nadia, singing at the top of our lungs to a song on the radio. When we came to a stop in front of the Violet Turtle, Nadia and I jumped out of the van and into the gravel lot, racing each other into the restaurant. Once the doors were shut, my mom continued to drive around towards the back of the building, saving the front parking spaces for customers. Walking past the long line of people waiting to be seated, Nadia and I rushed to our favorite booth, knowing that our dad had reserved it for us. I climbed onto the violet seat cushions, the velvet material worn and soft under my fingertips. Closing my eyes, I settled into my seat, taking in the scents that filled the air. Over the years, this place had become something of a second home, always welcoming me back with warmth.

The restaurant was dimly lit, and soft accordion music was drifting off from somewhere in the distance. A faint purple tint given off by the lighting provided the room with a gentle artificial glow, and an aroma of exotic spices, oils and incense filled the space to its entirety. Most of the furnishings were made with dark, worn wood—from the carvings on the oversized booths to the wide beams on the ceiling. A sweet oil lamp burned atop each table, and small brass chandeliers swung from the ceiling, creaking every time a gust of wind flew in from the front door. I smiled, forgetting everything around me for the moment as my eyes climbed their way up the walls. My favorite part of the restaurant would always be the turtles.

When he bought the restaurant, my dad had ordered a unique, custom-made tank to go along with it. The tank was built into the wall toward the ceiling, about two feet tall, one foot deep, and ten feet from the ground. It wrapped itself around the whole restaurant, in one huge rectangle. Inside, swam exactly twenty-three turtles, each given a name by Nadia and me. This was definitely the perfect place for a celebration.

"Cara!" I turned to see my parents, walking towards me from the kitchen entrance. My dad was leading the way, dressed in his usual work outfit, a Violet Turtle t-shirt with jeans. Usually by the dinner rush, especially at the end of a busy weekend, my dad is exhausted and wants nothing more than to rest. Tonight was an obvious exception; he looked fit to run a marathon. There was a certain energy about him that he usually lacked after a hard day, and when I caught his eye, his smile was practically screaming with pride. He slid in next to me, and my mom took a seat next to Nadia. We all knew that we needed to keep my conversation with the President a secret, but everyone was having difficulty staying quiet. Without directly mentioning why they were being given, hugs and congratulations were sent my way until it was time to order.

Since it was a special occasion, Nadia and I were allowed to choose anything we wanted off the menu. Soups, salads, sandwiches, appetizers, stir fry, sushi, burgers, stew, steak, soda, filets, fish, fries, fruit, desserts, and the inevitable second helping was all fair game. If I was a bystander at a nearby table, I would have perceived it to be somebody's birthday, although in all honesty, that night was better than any previous celebration I'd ever lived through. You don't do anything to deserve a birthday; it just comes around on its own. I had worked for this night, and I had earned it. I had planned and dreamed of it. This was a time where I could finally enjoy myself.

The food tasted extra good that night and whether it was due to my imagination or not, I didn't care. I was having far too much fun to ruin it with that sort of thinking. Despite this, as I was slurping my way through a double-chocolate milkshake, I couldn't help but feel guilty about Sandy and Nadia again. This guilt, along with the 10 pounds I must have gained from dinner, both held their weight, bringing me back down to Earth with little difficulty. I inched in closer to my dad and took a look at his wristwatch. It was nearly 8:00—almost time for the President to call!

Pulling Nadia away from an ice cream sundae, and my mom from her coffee cake, I stood up and herded them out to the car. My dad had to stay behind at the restaurant because they were short on staff, but made me promise to fill him in on every detail once he got back. I couldn't bring myself to speak one word on the ride home. Nadia didn't seem to mind, and spent the entire drive belting a rousing solo version of 'God Bless America' that seemed to go on a bit longer than I remembered it being. We pulled onto our street just as Nadia began the chorus for the sixth time.

"God bless America, land that I love..."

I felt my stomach begin to stir. *I really shouldn't have eaten all of those fries,* I thought as I pressed a hand to my churning gut. As if I had just gotten on a ride at an amusement park, I felt such a strong combination of anxiety and apprehension that it was almost unbearable. My hands were shaking by the time we reached the driveway and I could feel tiny beads of sweat forming on my palms.

"What if *they* called while we were out?" I asked my mom, raising my voice so I could be heard over Nadia. There was no need to clarify that 'they' meant the White House. I could see her eyebrows furl in the review mirror.

"Stand beside her, and guide her. Thru the night with a light from above..."

"Don't worry honey," she reassured me, masking her concern. "If they did call early, I'm sure they would have left some way to contact them. And if not, they would definitely leave a message telling us when they would try again." She switched her focus to parking the car in the garage.

"Right," I sighed, half relieved, half not. I could tell my mother wasn't completely sure of what she was saying, but I forced myself to believe her. After all, I needed to rely on something or I'd definitely throw up.

To avoid any second thoughts, I tried to keep my eyes glued firmly to the ground, not daring to catch the uncertainty in my mom's eyes again.

"From the mountains, to the prairies, to the oceans, white with foam..."

I snuck a quick peak in the mirror. She looked tenser than before. Her back was stiff and she was gripping the wheel unnaturally tight.

This did not help to calm my nerves.

Nadia was getting louder, increasing volume as she went in for the dramatic last notes. *"Gggggodddd blesssss Ammmmeerrrriiiicaaaaaa..."*

I unbuckled my seatbelt.

"And thank God we're home!" I cried, shoving open the car door before we were parked.

"Hey!" yelled Nadia, upset that I had stolen her big finish. I was too focused on scrambling into the house to apologize. For my mother's sake, I kicked off my shoes before running into the kitchen to check the answering machine. A big flashing zero was floating on the screen. Before the uneasiness in my stomach could subside, I watched as that number disappeared and the words *'incoming call'* took its place. Within a moment, the phones started ringing. I snatched up the first one I could get my hands on and hastily pushed the 'talk' button. Hearing the ringing, Nadia and my mom bounded into the room, skidding to a stop at the doorway. Silently, I beckoned them closer. They quickly filed in and sat around the kitchen table like nervous kindergarteners on the first day of school, waiting for their teacher to speak. I took a deep breath.

"Hello?" I spoke as clearly as I could manage into the receiver, trying not to choke on my words. I didn't want to sound like a little kid, after all. I wanted to make it obvious that I was the best choice for the national project.

"Hey there, girl!" howled a nasal-y voice. "This is Alice from Advantica Satellite Service calling to check on your newly purchased equipment! Is your mother home?" My mouth twisted from an anxious smile to an irritated frown. This was not the call I had been waiting for.

"We don't own a satellite," I said stubbornly.

"That may be so," Alice replied in a deep southern accent, "but I'm sure y'all would still be interested in taking a quick little survey, wouldn't you, now?" I felt my face grow red.

"No, thank you." I pulled the phone away from my ear before hanging up. After tossing the phone back onto the counter, I looked up towards my puzzled family. Nadia's jaw was practically on the floor. My mother looked like, well, like I'd hung up on the personal secretary to the President of the United States. "Solicitors," I explained.

"Alright," my mother stood up and clasped her hands together. "There's no point in spending the evening staring into space and waiting for the phone to ring, so why don't we do something to pass the time?" I nodded in agreement. Anything that could take my mind off of the call for even a few seconds would be a real godsend. So, as my mom fiddled with the answering machine to try and get it to tape the Presidential phone call for my father, Nadia went upstairs to get a board game.

Just as she returned with Monopoly, the phone rang again.

I knew this was the one.

Instantly, my mother sat back down and Nadia came scooting back in with a small crash. They stared up at me, mesmerized. My hands were trembling slightly. I counted the rings on the phone. If I answered after one ring, it would sound like we had been waiting for the call all day and anything past four would seem rude. I answered it before the second ring had finished sounding, unable to help myself.

"Hello, Greybird residence, Cara speaking."

"Hello, Cara," said a women's voice on the other line. I'm glad I could catch you. This is Kate Muleson, the President's personal secretary."

"Hello, Ms. Muleson," I responded in my best imitation of a business woman. "It's a real pleasure to be speaking with you."

"Please, Cara, call me Kate," insisted the warm voice on the other end.

"Really? Wow, thanks!" I exclaimed, completely letting go of all self-control. "Uh, I mean, that's very nice of you," I stumbled, suddenly aware of my lapse of poise. So much for being composed and sophisticated.

"Oh, Cara, you sound so sweet!" She laughed. "It'll be so nice to have someone like you around here, for a change. President Deerun and his wife are two of the sweetest people you'll ever meet, but I'll tell you, he does get some peculiar house guests on occasion." She cleared her throat. "Anyway, let's get back to business. I'm calling, as you probably already know, about your trip down here to Washington, D.C."

"Yes, I know. My family and I are all very excited about it." I looked over at Nadia and my mom, smiling at my mention of them.

"That's just terrific, Cara. I'm glad you're so dedicated because you're going to have a lot of work to do."

"Really?" I asked a bit more nervously than I wanted to. "Good, well, that's what I'm coming over to do, right?"

Kate laughed, sensing my unease. "Oh, Cara, don't worry, it's nothing an old pro like you can't handle! Everything will be just fine while you're down here, you'll see. I've already got everything planned. Let's talk about school first. Your tutor is one of the best in the country, he's taught every President's child for the last 34 years, so I'm sure you'll find him satisfactory. I'm going to have him get in touch with your school, so he'll know exactly where you are in your studies by the time you get here. You should bring your school books when you come by the way, just so he can keep your lessons consistent with what you might be doing back at home.

"Everywhere you go you will be accompanied by a personal bodyguard, in addition to the protection of the President's Secret Service, when you are with him. These people are highly trained officials, the best protection anyone could ever offer you, so there's nothing to worry about as far as your safety is concerned.

"And lastly, in regards to where you will be staying Cara, you are one lucky kid, because as long as you're here, you will be living in the one and only White House!"

"What?" I gasped, nearly dropping the phone. "No way!" Nadia was ready to kill me, she looked so curious.

"You sure will be. The Queen's Bedroom is all set up for you on the second floor. It's one of the largest bedrooms we have, complete with its own bathroom, and I'm sure you'll find it quite accommodating."

"Wow," I whispered, completely in awe.

"Oh, Cara, it's nothing. We're delighted to have you. Now if I could just talk with your mom or dad, we can really seal the deal."

"Absolutely. It was really nice talking to you, Kate. Thanks!"

"Thank *you*, Cara. Bye."

Reluctant as I was, I surrendered the phone to my mother, now looking as if she had just been presented the key to the city. She stared at the receiver, a bit hesitant to speak, but after the first couple of minutes of talking with Kate, it was like she was on the phone with an old college roommate. Words came speeding from her mouth at a record pace, jabbering away like her life depended on it.

"What's happening?" I mouthed to my mom after what seemed like an eternity. Uncapping a nearby pen with her teeth, she grabbed for a piece of scrap paper and scribbled down a quick note, pushing me back towards the doorway.

"Mom, what's she saying?" I tried again. She held up an impatient finger, throwing her head back with an energetic laugh at something Kate had said. Knowing well enough that I wouldn't get any answers until she was done talking, I was left waiting for her to finish her conversation alone (Nadia had gotten bored and left to play herself in Monopoly ages ago). I stared up at the kitchen clock, the second hand moving with the urgency of a glob of molasses. Inch by agonizing inch, it slowly crawled across the numbers, and after half an hour of anxious waiting, I found myself in surrender. With a sigh, I stood to join Nadia in the living room. Two games of Pictionary, four rounds of 'go fish', and a 30 minute preview of Nadia's upcoming ballet recital later, Kate and my mom were still talking.

At last, they hung up with each other so Kate could send us some forms. I waited for my mom at the top of the steps, hoping to pry some information from her as she ran up towards the guest bedroom.

"Cara please, not now." She sprinted for the door, shutting it behind her. "Does anyone know where your dad keeps the fax machine in here?" she yelled after a moment.

"It's in-between Nadia's easel and the box for the inflatable—"

"Never mind, I found it!" From the hall, I could hear her knees as they settled at its side, fingertips wiping the dust from its keys. She pushed the on button and it sputtered its way back to life, probably for the first time in years. After a moment of warming up, the sound became something of a low hum. Ten or fifteen minutes later and I listened as the droning died down, followed by the sound of rustling papers. Having received her documents, I pressed my ear to the wall as my mom called up my dad at the restaurant, holding a considerably long phone conference with him, and later my aunt the attorney, to discuss and dissect each word of what I guessed to be some sort of contract.

The door opened again nearly an hour later.

"Cara, can you come here for a second pleas—oh," her eyes found me, sitting cross-legged two feet from the doorway. She smiled, opening the door to let me inside. "Come on in. We have some agreements to sign."

The thickness of the stack Kate sent had our hands cramping within moments, but we pressed on, faxing them back to the White House office only after a signature, date and initial accompanied each dotted line. Seconds later, Kate called back to confirm that she had received them. My mom practically dove for the phone, probably warm from overuse by this time, and they talked some more.

My dad pulled into the driveway just as Nadia fell asleep in her bed. If he was at all tired, he masked his feelings well. He burst through the door, and ran over to kiss my cheek and say hello, but that was just about all I saw of him. There was no time for us to talk further. Immediately, he grabbed a phone and spoke with Kate, too. Occasionally she would fax some more papers to our house, or point out some helpful websites to visit. The night crept on and on. I personally didn't understand what could take so long about such simple arrangements. I had thought my short two-minute conversation with Kate had covered all the bases, but apparently it had not. It was nearly midnight when everyone had finally hung up for good, and by that time I was sleeping on the living room couch. Before I knew what was happening, I was being shaken awake by my now phone-less mother, who had dragged a drowsy Nadia out of bed and to her side, next to my dad.

"Cara, honey, wake up." I felt my mom's arm brush my shoulder, nudging me to consciousness. I rolled over on the couch, trying to ignore her and go back to sleep. Unrelenting, she continued to prod and shake me, a little less tenderly each time, until I faced her with my eyes open. I realized that I should have allowed them to adjust to the light of the room only after it was already too late. Everywhere I looked it was now pouring in, its effect no more desirable than an electric shock.

"Come on, Cara…you're not going to believe this, but you need to get up."

"Wh-whaat?" I groaned, rubbing my eyes. "What time is it?"

"It's the middle of the night, sweetie," my mom replied. That was all I needed to hear. It was less than a second before my eyes were closed again and I was lying back on the couch. "But we need to get you all ready to go now," she insisted, shaking my arm again.

"Go? But…go where?" My mind was clouded and foggy. The only place I really wanted to go was back to sleep. I squinted and looked up towards my mom, whose attention was now turned back towards my father.

"Tell her," he mouthed, urging her to continue. Hoping they wouldn't notice, I shut my eyes again.

"Cara," my mom whispered. "You're going to Washington, D.C.!" If that couldn't get me fully awake, nothing would. Within a second I was sitting bolt upright, my body reacting before my eyes had a chance to open. My breath was uneven now, coming in sharp gasps. I pressed my palm to my pounding heart and then to my stomach, which had now clenched itself into knots so tight I feared that it might split in two. My eyes finally opened, but I couldn't find my voice to speak. My mom on the other hand, had enough to say for both of us.

"The President is leading a movement to pass a bill, and he needs your help! He believes that in government, the person best suited for the job should be the one to get it, regardless of age. He thinks that if you have an idea, nothing should stop you from getting it heard. Cara, he is going to lead an Underage Rights Movement to give every American an equal voice, and he wants you to help him! He thinks that you best demonstrate the movement—Cara, he thinks that with your help, the bill can be passed!"

"What? When do I leave? Where? How? Leave nothing out!"

"Your flight leaves at 7:00 a.m., which gives us almost no time to prepare," my mom answered, trying her best to stay calm. "We definitely have to be early to the airport for this one, so you're going to need to wake up at around 4:30 a.m. tomorrow—er, today, actually, seeing as it's past midnight."

I stood corrected. That was one detail I could have *happily* gone without.

"You'll be in Washington for two weeks," she continued, "so we need to get you packed. And you'll need to look presentable, dear, so I hate to tell you, but you're going to have to shower and do something with that hair of yours." I clutched the armrest on the couch for support, nodding. Excitement was practically flooding through my veins now, washing away all longings for sleep.

"As for the plane ride, I know you always like to wear sweatpants and comfy t-shirts, but today you'll have to wear something formal, so just keep that in mind. When you're all ready to go, we'd like you to eat a big breakfast, and then I'll drive you to the airport."

"Now, Nadia," my father knelt down and scooped her up into his lap. "I'm afraid you and I will have to stay home so we can get you to school and me to work. If you want, though, I'm sure Cara can wake you up before she leaves so that you two can say good-bye."

"Mmmmhm-hmm," Nadia murmured weakly, fighting with all her might to stay awake. Although you could tell she was totally excited, she was only seven, and was overpowered by exhaustion. Even so, she couldn't help but smile, making it quite clear that she was happy to sleep in.

"Nadia, after Cara leaves, I expect you to go right back to sleep," my mom instructed. "Sorry to say this, but you are not going to be excused from school tomorrow." Nadia gave a sleepy grunt.

"Anyway, Cara," she went on, "you and I are going to drive to the airport together. Kate has already faxed us your plane ticket. I'll hold on to it for now, but you'll need it tomorrow once we're at the airport, since I'm not allowed past the first security check without a ticket of my own. A flight attendant is going to meet you before I have to leave though, somewhere near the luggage check. He or she will have a big sign with your name on it, so you'll know who they are. That person will take care of you while you're in the airport and on the plane. Kate assured us that you will be shown exactly where to go, and get whatever assistance you might need. Everything else is all set. Kate gave me her phone number, as well as some other important numbers we should both have while you're away. In exchange, I gave her your cell phone number, so she can reach you in case there are any problems.

"Now, when you land, Kate offered to have an official Presidential car pick you up and take you to the White House! Doesn't that sound exciting? Once you get off the plane, the flight attendant will help you find a policeman to lead you to the visitors' area, where a chauffeur will be waiting for you. This driver has worked with the President for years, and Kate thinks you two will get along well. I don't think she mentioned their name, but whoever they are, they'll help you find your luggage and take you to the car. After that, they have agreed to drive you to the White House, and after a bit of security, you'll be inside!"

"And here's an exciting part!" my dad blurted, eagerly. "At the White House, you'll have your very own bodyguard! He's there for your security of course, but mostly just to make sure you have everything you need, and to help you around. He'll be with you wherever you go in Washington, doesn't that sound cool? It'll be like you're famous. I think Kate said his name was James." He looked over at my mom, who nodded quickly before cutting back into the conversation.

"On a more serious note, you'll be learning, studying and observing every second you're at the White House. On top of doing your school work, you'll be intensively trained in politics. You'll even get a personal political instructor who'll teach you all about political debates and speeches—even how to deliver them yourself! Then, most importantly, at the end of your two weeks of training, you're going to take part in one final debate to prove yourself to the public. You and a competitor are going have a televised one-on-one debate at the Deseo D.C. Coliseum in downtown Washington. You're going to get a debating topic, and you'll be able to express your opinions on it. Then, the audience is going to choose a winner of the debate. Kate told us that the debate will be a really big deal, and its going to generate a lot of publicity for the movement. The President is counting on you, and I don't care if you win or lose, but you have got to try as hard as you can, and really give it your best shot.

"You have a very important place in this Underage Rights Movement, and it is to show America why every person, regardless of age deserves to voice their opinions. They're really going to test you down there, and I just want you to know that it's not going to be all fun and games; it's going to be really hard work. The President has chosen you to represent the capabilities of the responsible underage American. I hate to say this, but there's going to be a lot of pressure on you. People are going to have opinions about you in Washington, and I wish it weren't true, but not all of them will be good. What the President wants you to do is amazing, but if you don't want to go through with this, that's totally you're choice. We can get you out of this whole thing right now, no proble—"

"No!" I cut her off. "Of course not! This is what I want." I swallowed hard, "I'm one hundred percent sure."

She smiled. "I was hoping you'd say that, but you know I had to ask." I nodded.

"On the plus side," my dad interrupted, "you're going to be a guest at the White House, Cara! Do you know what that means? You'll be spending tons of time with the President, and maybe even the First Lady! The Vice President is away on business, so you may not get to meet him, but you will get complete access to the White House and all it has to offer including the bowling alley, the movie theater and the swimming pool! But that's not even the best part!" I leaned in closer, dying to hear more. I was shaking with anticipation and desperate for details.

"Go on!" I said, a little louder than I had intended. Nadia stirred from where she had dozed off on my fathers lap and looked around edgily.

"Cara, it's what you've always wanted! Once you're properly trained up, the

President is going to have you do interviews with the public! Just think of all the important people you'll meet! You're going to be a real politician!" He carefully lifted Nadia off his lap and onto a chair to give me a hug. "I'm so proud of you, sweetie."

I nearly fainted. Be a real politician? It was a dream came true! I was finally going to be heard! I jumped up from off the couch, not knowing at all what to do. I was suddenly lightheaded, and my feet felt strangely unaffected by gravity, like they could lift off the floor with little effort. For a minute there, I was floating in midair.

I hadn't prepared for the violent landing only moments away, when a much heavier topic occurred to me.

"But what about clothes?" I asked to nobody in particular, suddenly panicked. "I don't have enough! I don't have anything appropriate! I can't be on national TV in too-small skirts and hand-me-down dresses, and we don't have time to shop! What are we going to do?"

"Cara, honey, don't worry," my mom reached over to pat my arm. "Kate and I have figured it all out. I gave her your approximate shoe and clothes sizes and she will give them to your personal stylist, who will bring you outfit choices to pick from for every interview you do, as well as any public appearance you make. She'll even do your hair and makeup, like a real star! Isn't that exciting?"

"All this from the President, Cara! He really wants you to come." My dad ruffled my hair. "I am honored and flattered that someone so important thinks so highly of my daughter. Kate said the President thinks you have real potential. He thinks you're the one who best represents all children capable of handling political positions. If your debate goes well, and I know you, Cara, you'll be fantastic, you would set a major example for the movement! Isn't this amazing, Cara! It's a once in a lifetime opportunity!"

A silence fell over us as we contemplated this. A once in a lifetime opportunity—it was simply overwhelming. I wanted to scream and jump and celebrate and let my emotions run wild, but I was working on controlling that instinct—mostly for the sake of the Secret Service. If I wanted all of this to happen, I needed to act mature. So I remained where I was, doing the best I could to restrain myself.

Suddenly, Nadia jolted, and with a violent snore, dragged us all down to reality again.

"Well, I'd better get this one to sleep," my mother whispered, bending over to pick up Nadia. "We've got so much to do, Cara, you'd better come with me." I nodded and stood up. The news from the phone call had changed me somehow, and I felt like a different person. It took a moment for my body to readjust to the new me. Although I might have looked the same on the surface, on the inside I had already gone from Cara—just an average kid from New Castle, to *Cara—the real U.S. politician*. I was one step closer to becoming the girl from my dream. Standing up just a little straighter than usual, I was about to follow my mother upstairs when I realized that this new Politician Cara had forgotten something.

"Sandy!" I exclaimed. She deserved to hear the news coming from me. "'Scuse me, Dad." I pushed him aside, determined to reach the phone. "I've *got* to go call her and tell her what's happening. She'll be so excited—"

"Oh, no you don't," my mother warned, snatching the phone away from me. Her tone was surprisingly harsh, and seeing my puzzled expression, she added, "Kate told us not to tell anyone about this project until the President officially announces it tomorrow."

I gazed up at her, still confused.

"See, Cara, if something we say gets misquoted or misunderstood, the whole thing could become really demoted in the public eye," my dad explained. "The President is going to describe his plan himself and doesn't want any other misleading ideas floating around until he's presented all the details clearly. He's called an emergency press conference for tomorrow at 7:30AM. This is when he will explain the details of the Underage Rights Movement to the public, and tell them all about you and how your debate exemplifies why his Underage Rights Movement Bill must be passed. This whole thing is mostly about the bill really, because if the bill is passed, the movement is a success."

"Well, what about school?" I pressed on. "I can't miss school without any reason and not get into any trouble."

"I asked about that," my dad answered. "Your absence will be completely excused. Kate said she would call tomorrow and explain as much as she can to the attendance office without giving anything away. As long as you're all caught up by the time you get back, I don't think there will be any problem. And remember, by tomorrow evening at the latest, everyone will know why you are in Washington. There's nothing to worry about."

"That's good," I smiled, feeling more awake than ever. Nadia let out another snore.

"Alright you, let's go upstairs," my mother said to Nadia with a sigh, motioning for me to come as well. Energy was biting at my body, and I tried to let it out as I ran to follow her. When we reached the top of the staircase she was still a stride or two in front of me—an especially impressive lead once you accounted for the 53 pounds of snoring Nadia still in her arms. Instead of putting her down in our room, we tucked Nadia into the guest bedroom across the hall so she wouldn't be disturbed.

"What should we do now?" I asked, careful to keep my voice down. I was only a few feet from the door now, making my way around a box of my dad's high school football trophies in the hopes of finding my way out of the clutter and into the hallway. My mom, with the same goal in mind, was not far behind. I turned to find her hopping over an old photo album.

"Cara, there's so much to do, and we don't have much time," she whispered back. "Right now, I think the best thing would be to pack." I agreed, just as I reached the doorknob. I turned the handle, and the work began.

Packing was a tough job, but the two of us managed. We figured that I should take only one suitcase and one carry-on bag, since I was the one who would have to lug it around with me during the trip. We dug through the clutter underneath my parents' bed until finally coming across the perfect luggage. The suitcase I would bring was my mom's, and though it was old, it was a good size and in perfect condition. As for my carry-on bag, we decided to use the miniature canvas backpack that I had once brought on a class trip. Not wanting all of my things to smell like mothballs, the two of us sprayed the insides of my bags with perfume before dragging them back into my bedroom. While she got to work on setting the alarm clocks, I began to pack.

Before long, my dad came to help. Together, we came up with a long list of things to bring, 'X'-ing off each item on the list as it was neatly piled into the suitcase. I tried my hardest not to over-pack, as I would not only have access to the White House washing machine, but I would also have some clothes given to me by my stylist. Despite this knowledge, my suitcase was stuffed to the brim within moments and it took almost all of my strength to force the zipper closed.

When we had finally finished, I was more excited than ever. It was as if each item in my suitcase was further proof that the next day's events existed at all. I needed tangible evidence of my Washington trip, or even I might have had trouble believing its reality. I read over the list one last time to make sure I had packed everything I needed.

Things to Pack (Suitcase)
X Toothbrush and Toothpaste
X Comb and hairbrush
X Shampoo and conditioner
X Hair stuff (spray, clips, bands, ties, bows)
X ChapStick and lip gloss
X Cleansers, moisturizers, and lotions
X Bathing suit (White House pool?)
Jackets
   X Light windbreaker
   X Warm fleece
   X Dressy jacket
   X Winter coat (just in case)
Pajamas
   X Slippers and bathrobe
   X 3 pairs of bottoms and 3 tops
X Stamps, envelopes, and stationary (for writing home)
X Socks (as many as possible)
X 2 pairs of tights, 2 pairs of stockings, 1 pair of leggings
X Comfortable walking shoes
X Dressy heels/flats (one black and one brown pair of each)

X Skirts (dump in the whole drawer)

X Underwear (ditto)

X Dressy tanks, tees and long-sleeved shirts (all of them)

X 3 or 4 Dresses

X Dressy pants (as many that fit)

X Accessories (belts, purses, jewelry, etc.)

X 1 casual outfit (not too casual)

X Journal to record the trip (not an option)

X School stuff for tutor

X Pens, pencils, highlighters, etc.

Carry-on Bag

X iPod

X Camera

Reading material

   X Book of choice

   X Magazine

Snacks

   X Healthy snack (apple)

   X Not-so-healthy snack (candy bar)

X Money for emergencies and souvenirs

X Cell phone (call home often!)

X More pencils and pens

X Notepad

"It's all in there," I announced to my parents once everything was ready and waiting by the door.

"Good." My mom stood up from where she had been crouched in the corner of my room, checking over what I had brought. She kissed my forehead and turned out the light. "Now go to bed."

I was on the verge of protesting when I realized how tired I really was. I had been so busy I hadn't noticed my own exhaustion, but once I had became aware of it, the effects were instantaneous.

"Goodnight," I yawned to my parents as they reached the hallway.

"Good*night,* Cara," my mom called back firmly.

"See ya in three hours," I whispered.

"See ya in three hours," my dad repeated.

After I was sure my parents were gone, I tiptoed into the bathroom to see if I had forgotten to pack anything that wasn't on the list. My spare toothbrush and toothpaste were laid out for me to use in the morning, along with Nadia's hairbrush and half-empty containers of extra shampoo and conditioner.

I felt like a little kid waiting for the tooth fairy. Everything was ready and in place, the tooth was under its pillow, and all that there was left to do was wait for the magic to come.

Still on tiptoe, I slipped back into my bedroom. I opened a near-empty drawer and took out the only clean set of pajamas that weren't already packed away. Not willing to break the sleepy silence, I crawled into my bed and pulled the blankets around my shoulders. I lifted my arm from beneath them to click off the lamp at my bedside table and then closed my eyes, finally at peace. The events of the hectic day were swimming in my head, and I fell asleep dreaming of the days even busier to come.

chapter sixteen

I awoke to the sound of my alarm clock. Barely conscious, I rolled over, swatting at the surrounding air until my limp hand connected with the snooze button. Still not fully aware of my surroundings, I squinted at the glowing digital numbers. *Four-thirty.* Shining with an annoying amount of intensity, the clock almost blinded me. I shut my eyes to shield them from the light, but couldn't shake the numbers from my head. In fact, the harder I tried to avoid them, the clearer they became—as if they had burnt themselves onto the insides of my eyelids.

"Whaat?" I mumbled to myself, disoriented. "It's not time for school yet." Having come to this realization, I reached towards the back of the clock and gave the extension cord a good tug, unplugging it. Smirking like I had defeated some sort of monster, I watched the glowing numbers fade.

Nadia probably did it, I thought as I rolled back onto my pillow, getting ready to fall back to sleep. *What a stupid prank. Wait, that can't be right…* I struggled to ward off sleep. *Nadia can't work this clock.* I rubbed my eyes. *But that would have to mean…OH MY GOSH!* My spine stiffened and then swung forward, pulling my body upright with unintended force. The blood went rushing from my head with this sudden change in position, and as my heart began fighting my stomach for space to pound, the rest of my body was overcome with dizziness. I leaned forward towards my lap, forehead resting in my outstretched palm.

I'm leaving today, I thought, slowly coming to terms with the idea. My fingers felt for my eyelids, pressing against their inner corners as the blood slowly returned behind them. *I'm going to Washington, D.C.! I'm going to meet the President!* My body came alive in an instant, finding some new source of energy that even I hadn't been aware of. *I've got to get up!*

With one frenzied motion, I somehow managed to both untangle myself from my sheets and thrust my feet over the edge of the bed. I didn't waste time in standing, and ignored the stiffness in my neck as I rushed for the door. The hall light was on before I reached it, meaning that my parents were already awake. I considered waking up Nadia too, but reconsidered within a moment, figuring that it was best to say goodbye right before I left. Trying not to make too much noise, although still not particularly light on my feet at 4:30 a.m., I reached the bathroom at a half-tiptoe, half-stagger.

Squinting, I made my way past the closets and the medicine cabinet to the shower. I cracked open the frosted glass door just wide enough to get my arm through, grabbed the faucet, and twisted its handle all the way to hot. Waiting for the water to heat up, I turned to shut the bathroom door behind me, and very slowly, raised the dimmer on the light switch to let my eyes adjust. I had waited too long to turn on the shower fan, and the next time I turned around, the mirror above the sink was coated in fog. I wiped its center with a washcloth and stepped closer to my reflection, curious to get a look at my face now that I was about to be more than just some kid.

In all honesty, I looked no different than I usually did, except for that morning's bonus of bloodshot eyes, my body's revenge for allowing it only three hours of sleep. I peered at my reflection disapprovingly. Hoping to wake myself up and cure my face from its current exhaustion, I switched the shower water to freezing cold and unwillingly forced myself inside.

With all reminders of sleep washed away, sinuses cleared, and mind shocked back to its usual self, I twisted the faucet to turn off the water and stepped out of the shower. I had forgotten to put down a bathmat, and nearly flooded the bathroom floor with wet footprints in an all-out sprint to the closet for a clean towel. I lunged for the first one I could find and wrapped it across my shoulders, more than ready to do away with the cold.

I began brushing by teeth only after they had stopped chattering, thinking of nothing but Washington and what it would be like. The city was a complete mystery to me—after all, I had never been there before. But it wasn't just the big things that were bothering me (like who I would meet, or what I would say)—I was worried about the little things, too. For example, was it really necessary to pack my own shampoo and soap, or was the White House like a hotel where it's already set out for you in little bottles and boxes? I just didn't know the answers, but was too afraid I'd sound silly if I asked.

I spit into the sink and rinsed out my mouth, catching another glance of myself in the mirror as I bent towards the glass. Unless I planned on meeting the President wearing a rather large hat, my hair, which had somehow begun to dry horizontally, demanded some immediate attention. Wincing, I grabbed Nadia's brush and got to work. A few bristles were lost in the battle, but after awhile, I managed to tame my tangled waves. After carefully spritzing my head with conditioner, I found our old dryer and blew my hair out straight, tying it back with an elastic band when I had finished. I checked my reflection one last time as I returned the blow-dryer to its drawer. The girl I saw staring back at me denied her relation to the previous two I had seen, and if I hadn't known better, I would have believed her. Satisfied, I headed back into my bedroom to get dressed.

As I walked through the door, I nearly stepped on the outfit I had laid out the night before. I had chosen to wear a gray pencil skirt that began high up on my waist and ended just above my knee. A thin white ribbon was strung through the belt loop, tied in a bow near where my hip would be. Tucked into this was a long-sleeved shirt, its faded pink fabric appearing almost white in the dark. I traced its v-neck with my hand, feeling the tiny fake pearls scattered along the collar as my fingers brushed over them. Lying off to the side was a pair of simple ballet flats. I smiled. It was perfect, but needed just one more thing. Scanning the room for anything that might complete my outfit, I spotted something silvery on top of my jewelry box. Recognizing it as my charm bracelet, I moved to put it on.

It didn't take long for me to notice that all of the tiny charms had been squished together to make way for a quarter-sized ornament of the White House, which was at its center. *Thanks*, I mouthed as I fastened the clasp, quietly acknowledging the early-morning efforts of none other than my own parents. The charm was undeniably worn, small scratches in the silver visible even in the dark, but I didn't mind at all. I wasn't sure where it had come from, but it was better than any gift I could have asked for. I finished getting dressed without bothering to turn on the light, and was ready to go within seconds.

Before I left the room, I poked my head around the curtain that divided it into two, expecting to see Nadia on the other end. I had forgotten that she had gone to sleep in the guest bedroom, and without her, this space too, looked empty. It seemed strange without Nadia, or my dirty laundry in a pile on the floor. I felt separated from it, like it was no longer *our* room, but just *a* room, and everything I saw before me belonged to somebody else. Adrenaline pushed this sadness from my mind. *Bye*, I thought to myself as I took one last look at the stranger's bedroom before closing the door. I was excited again from the moment I stepped into the hall.

Feeling more alive than I had ever thought possible before dawn, I headed down toward the kitchen, buzzing with the eager uncertainty of what was to come. As I turned the corner however, my old smile faded, making way for an even brighter one. My parents were busy bustling around, exerting more energy than I was accustomed to seeing from them at home during the workweek, preparing what seemed to be a breakfast for me.

"Hey there, sweetie," my mom called from the stove. "You look nice this morning."

"Just sit down right over there, Car. Your breakfast will be ready in a sec," my dad reported from the sink, motioning to a chair with a helium balloon reading '*congratulations!*' tied to it. A few minutes later I was confronted with a mountainous portion of food—a stack which seemingly defied the laws of physics in managing to stay upright, much less to fit on one plate. Looking more closely, I observed that it was actually an accumulation of scrambled eggs, French toast, and a side of hash browns, topped off with a large glass of orange juice and cup of fresh fruit. Doing all this cooking must have taken at least an hour, but despite red eyes and tired faces, their proud smiles from the night before were more intense than ever.

There were so many things I could have said to thank them for all they had done, but I found myself at a loss for words. My mom seemed to understand. She nodded and passed me a fork, pushing the plate closer towards me. Realizing that I had a restaurant chef waiting for feedback, I first attempted to make a dent in the pile of eggs, but I was so excited I could barely manage to swallow. The time being just after 5:00 a.m. didn't do much to fuel my appetite either.

"Eat," my mom encouraged me, as if I were an Olympic athlete who needed their strength for an upcoming event. Not wanting their efforts to go to waste, I eventually managed to gulp most everything down.

"All finished?" my father asked, glancing at my near-empty dish. I nodded appreciatively before pushing it over to him so he could finish the parts of my breakfast that were left.

"Ah-woo asa-eh o wuh?" he asked through a mouthful of toast. I stared back at him blankly, unsure what he meant. He held up his index finger, swallowed, cleared his throat, and repeated, "Are you excited or what?" He took another bite of toast.

"Yes!" Just one reminder of the day ahead was enough to make me jump out of my seat. My mom checked her watch.

"Cara, honey, if you're finished with breakfast, then we should really get going. Your father already brought your bags to the car, but it takes a while to get to the airport and we want to be on time." I choked a little on my juice.

"Let's go!" I whispered, getting up from my seat. "Oh, and by the way, I never really thanked you for the new charm, or the balloon or spending so much time on the phone with Kate last night. I really, really appreciate all of it."

"The charm used to be mine, you know. I collected them when I was about your age." My mom pulled me into a hug. "I know you'll take good care of it, and I hope you like it."

"All I can say is thank goodness for drugstores opened 24/7," my dad joked, letting a bit of exhaustion shine through in his eyes. I laughed before urging the two of them to get out of their seats, almost halfway to the door when I remembered Nadia.

Quickly, I disappeared up the stairs and into the guest bedroom. She was sound asleep, warm under her covers and snoring loudly, her face pressed down against her pillow.

"Nadia," I called, gently nudging her shoulder, "Nad..." She looked out of place without the two dozen Barbies and stuffed animals that usually surrounded her.

"Whattimeisit?" she groaned.

"Early," I replied truthfully, bending down so she could see my face.

"Cara?" she asked squinting, trying to find my outline in the dark.

"Uh-huh. I'm leaving now for the airport and I wanted to say goodbye before I left."

Before I could say another word, I felt two arms fling around my neck. It was meant to be a hug, although the actual gesture came off more like strangling.

"Nad, you're choking me." I was laughing even though I couldn't breathe.

"Sorry. I'm just gonna miss you." She gave me one more squeeze before letting go.

"On the plus side, I guess you're awake now," I smiled, kneeling down at her bedside. "And I'll miss you too."

"Good luck Cara. I'm rooting for you." She yawned, her eyes following me as I backed out of the room.

"Bye, Nad," I whispered back, closing the door. "Goodnight." Even if the only person with their full confidence in me was a little second-grader, it felt like more than enough. I was as empowered as ever.

When I got downstairs, my mom was waiting at the front door for me, holding out my coat.

"Sorry, Mom, I had to say goodbye to Nadia," I said as she rummaged through her purse for my plane ticket.

"Oh, don't apologize, Cara. She would have killed you if you left without waking her." I smiled a little, realizing that my mother had said this with all intended seriousness. "But you know," she sighed, "I'm really proud of you for being such a good sister. Over the past few weeks especially, you have been such a good role model for Nadia. She's just so proud of all you've done."

I guess I had never really noticed how much Nadia looked up to me.

"Alright, honey, I think it's time you left," my dad ran in from the kitchen to watch me go. Instead, I turned around to face him. I had never been nervous to leave home before. This time was different, and it was only then that I understood why.

It wasn't the leaving part that scared me—it was coming home—the idea that the life I was leaving behind now would continue on more or less the same without me. Nadia would have pushed through several new hobbies, my dad would be hard at work, my mom still flat-out exhausted, but I wouldn't be who I was before. *I* would be different. In a strange way, our lives had all blended together, seams interlocking like pieces in a puzzle. If I changed, maybe I would return to find that I no longer fit back into my old space. This was no average trip to a friend's house, and no session at an ordinary camp. It was something new—and undeniably permanent. For better or worse, there was no going back, and as much as my mind argued, I forced myself not to be scared. I couldn't be afraid.

"Cara, come on, let's move it," my dad instructed, motioning for me to turn around.

"Whoops." I could feel a shade of cherry-red embarrassment settling into my cheeks as I realized that I was blocking the doorway to the garage. Butterflies in my stomach, I stepped out the door, taking a moment to realize how cold it had become. Soundlessly, I pushed the small button on the wall next to the light switch, and watched as the garage door rumbled open. The cool gusts of wind pouring in slapped at my face, making it numb with chill.

"Cara, it's freezing!" my mom yelled, putting her hands to her shoulders and rubbing them to keep warm. She gave my dad a quick peck on the cheek before running to the car and climbing into the driver's seat, practically thrusting the key into the ignition so she could turn on the heat. Poking her head out the window as an afterthought, she reminded him to save some French toast for Nadia's breakfast and asked him to make sure she wore her coat. Then her eyes fell on me. "Cara, what are you waiting for? Come on, *let's go!*"

Without thinking, I ran up to my dad and buried myself in his arms. It was too early in the morning for my mom to honk the horn, and taking advantage of this common courtesy, my dad welcomed me in. I squeezed him as tight as I could, like I was trying to wring out my fears in him and leave them behind. I didn't know why I had to struggle to stop the tears that were welling up in my eyes from dripping down my frozen face. I couldn't understand what made me so unwilling to go. I wondered if he had the same fears too. If he didn't want to let me leave. If I was too small to change the world, and would instead be changed by it.

I stepped back, studying his face for any hesitation to let go of the hold his arms had around me. *Nadia has his eyes,* I thought. But looking deeper, I saw something more than a common Greybird facial feature. I saw his pride in me. And that's when the truth hit. He was always proud of me, and would always be proud of me. No matter how big or small my accomplishments were, whether I failed or succeeded. It didn't matter. I continued to stare, and through his pride I found a humble secret. He *knew* I would make it. And somehow, his unrelenting confidence awakened a part of me that knew this too.

"Bye Dad," I said, hoping that I could pass off the tremor in my voice as an effect of the cold.

"Good luck Cara," he replied, looking me straight in the eye. "Whatever you do, I'm proud—we all are."

I let go, unable to continue holding on to him as a safety blanket. "Thanks." I turned and headed back to the car. The passenger door slid open reluctantly, as if it were begging to stay in the security of the garage and would rather die than to venture into the early morning air. Despite its wishes, the gear was shifted into reverse, and we were soon rolling down the driveway. Sighing, I looked out at my house.

My dad hadn't moved.

Goodbye, I thought to myself. The next time I see you I could be a whole new person. We turned into the street and continued on towards Jawsie's den. Memories came flooding back to me, but somehow I could only smile— smile and wave back to my dad. I continued waving until the car turned, and everything I had left behind was nothing but a memory itself. Still, the grin never left my frigid face, and all I could think of was my destination.

chapter seventeen

The ride to the airport seemed shorter than usual. The heat in the car was cranked up to high but my teeth were still chattering, although whether this was due to excitement or the cold I couldn't be sure. My mind was focused on bigger things for the moment. We probed the parking garage, attempting to find the closest possible spot to the airport entrance. With no luck, we settled for an available space towards the back and then made a mad dash to the nearest door, practically sprinting to escape the cold. By the time we made it inside, I was out of breath, and my mom, who had gotten stuck carrying the luggage, was in an even worse state.

Inside, it was somehow more crowded than even the full garage outside had let on. My clock read only 5:43 a.m., and I was shocked to realize that some people had already been awake much longer than I had that morning. Everywhere you looked, droopy eyed security guards clutched onto their coffee mugs like a life support. Weary looking businessmen walked by with what looked like great effort, their eyes too tired and bloodshot to focus on anything in particular. I watched as they made their way past, grasping their briefcases and hobbling blindly through the airport crowd. Women were staggering along in their high heels as if the early morning could prevent them from walking, wishing that they could somehow trade them in for flats. A man dressed in a military uniform was leaning against a wall, whispering into his cell phone and smiling, his face filled with the anticipation of a return trip home. Some of the families passing by looked a bit lost, while others couldn't help but grin with familiarity. Children were dragging their feet, as well as their luggage across the ground like desert wanderers.

The dullness of the atmosphere washed me out. Nobody wanted to be there; everyone had someplace else they'd rather go, and somewhere they were trying to get to. They missed their families or their beds or the beach, and yet the New Castle Municipal Airport had brought them all here; to the bittersweet limbo in between home and work, daily life and the extraordinary, or perhaps the other way around.

There was so much opportunity that awaited us all at the end of our journey here, but although this sounded thrilling and bright, somehow everything looked gray. I shook the feeling off, managing to push out the melancholy around me and allow the excitement inside to surface. My mom, just having recovered from her run, grabbed a hold of my hand and led me to a long line of barely patient people waiting to check in their luggage.

"Alright, Cara," she said. "We'll check in your main bag, but keep the carry-on one for the flight. Inside you have your snacks, your book and magazine, your iPod, some money which you *are going to spend wisely*, and your phone, just in case you want to call home and tell us how you're doing." She paused and lowered her voice to a whisper. "I'm not sure if you'll have access to a television on the plane, but if you do, you can watch the President's big speech when he tells everyone about you!" I nodded, too excited to ask questions. After a few moments, we were next in line.

I fidgeted as my mother helped me to check in my luggage, unable to bear the fact that it was headed to Washington, D.C. Simply knowing that in just a matter of hours, my things would be delivered to the President's door didn't worry me, however. No, the part that made me nervous was that I would be going with it, and that meant saying the inevitable goodbye to the woman who was sending me. First though, we would have to find the guide who would help me get around the airport. My mom reminded me to look for a woman or man with a sign reading Cara. I nodded; hopefully, the activity would help me to forget my worries.

It wasn't long before we found her. She was easy to spot—being the only person grinning and waving at each traveler passing her by. We approached her, and she shot us a smile that gleamed like pearls. Her blue suit looked ironed and pressed to a level of almost uncomfortable perfection. Long blonde curls draped her face and hung at her shoulders. Her lips and nails were a matching shade of fiery red, a color which didn't seem to fit in with the cool autumn morning. She looked about 25, but her eyes held a certain maturity that seemed almost unfitting for her appearance. The unopened bottle of spring water she was holding stuck out amongst the coffee cups that otherwise engulfed the airport.

Somehow, this woman seemed oddly familiar to me, as if I had seen her before, but just couldn't place where or when. A moment later, I realized with a raw smile that I had only recognized her because of the unmistakable likeness she had to Nadia's stewardess Barbie at home.

"Hello," said the woman through her pearly-white teeth. "You must be Cara *Griebird*, right?"

"Greybird," I corrected politely, extending my arm out to shake her free hand. The woman was odd, but I decided that I liked her perkiness.

"Yes, that's right! Cara Greybird! How could I forget! I should have known that!" she exclaimed in a Cinderella voice. "The woman who recommended me to you, a Ms. Muleson or other, apparently couldn't stop raving about you in the fax she sent. So, it would seem you're going to Washington, huh?"

"Yes!" I beamed, reenergized by the smiling woman.

"My name is Lucille, and since you'll be traveling alone this morning, I am going to be here to make sure you find your way around and have everything you need to enjoy your flight."

"That sounds great. Thanks so much!"

Lucille reached into her pocket and came out with a small golden tube. She applied a fresh coat of her red lipstick before continuing.

"Well, we'd better get going now; we don't want to miss our flight." Lucille said as she gestured towards the first security check. "Why don't I save you a spot in the line while you two say your good-byes?" She looked over at my mother and me. I nodded in agreement, and Lucille turned towards the security table, leaving us alone.

I stared back at my mom for a moment, unable to find the words to explain what I was thinking. In haste, I dug into my swirling thoughts and quickly chose the most obvious one.

"Bye, Mom!" I said at last, moving in for a hug.

"Goodbye, Cara."

I rested my head on her shoulder. "I'll miss you." I waited a moment before backing away, preparing to join Lucille, who was now second in the line.

"Promise you'll call, write, e-mail, whatever works?"

"Of course. At least once a night." I recited with a trained smile.

"Good," my mother smiled. I could tell she was excited just like me, but also sad to see me go. I gave her one last hug and goodbye before turning and walking over to the security check. As much as I wanted to, I didn't turn around for awhile because I knew that if I did, I would become nervous and homesick again. Instead I concentrated on the future.

I passed through the metal detector slowly, every second fighting the urge to look back. It only took a few seconds for me to lose this battle, and before I knew it, I found myself turning to face my mom. My head hoped she was already gone, but my heart still wanted her there. I spotted her immediately, standing as if glued to the floor and smiling back at me. Instantly, my stomach punished me for my actions, twisting itself into a tight knot. I could only manage a small wave in her direction before forcing my body to turn toward Lucille, who had already gone on to the next security check. I moved rather quickly to catch up with her, seeing as the farther I went forward, the less I wanted to go back. Nevertheless, it took more than a few minutes for the pain in my stomach to subside.

There was barely a line for the rest of the security, and Lucille and I got through without any problems. When we reached our gate, she helped me to find a seat and then boarded the plane herself, making me promise not to leave the waiting area once she left. I told her that I was fine, but she insisted that she would check on me a couple of times during the flight anyway, just to make sure everything was going well. After she left, I sat quietly for awhile in my chair, soaking in my new surroundings. It was still early, but I felt much more awake. The seat Lucille had gotten me had gum stuck to both armrests and all of the other unoccupied ones felt strangely sticky, so I decided to stand while I waited to enter the aircraft, which wasn't long at all.

Since I was what they call an unaccompanied minor, I got to board the plane first. I looked down at my ticket for the first time—the White House had paid to get me first-class seats! *"Well, there's our tax dollars at work,"* I could just hear my mom mumbling, a devoted advocate on the behalf of coach seating. To tell you the truth, they could have shoved me in the baggage compartment for all I cared. The important thing was that I was on my way! I moved towards the tunnel which led to the airplane's door and handed my ticket to a woman at its entrance. She scanned the paper and then handed it back before showing me which way to go. I thanked her for the information even though there was only one way to walk in the passageway. It took every ounce of self-control left in me not to run, but before I knew it, I was entering the awaiting plane.

I had been on airplanes before for family trips and vacations but now that I was alone, it seemed as if I were entering a new world. In every direction I looked, there were attendants pointing me in the direction of my seat. They ushered me down a long narrow hallway crammed with coat racks and storage compartments before leading me through a small curtain and into my section.

Everything seemed comfortable and clean. The seats there were much more spacious than those behind them, and instead of the usual blue mystery fabric, they were covered in what looked like black leather. Earphones and a small cotton pillow were laid out across each armrest and a television was mounted on the back of every chair. After awhile of wandering, I found the space assigned to me. Quietly, I made myself comfortable, buckling my seatbelt, adjusting my seatback, and fiddling with my carry-on bag.

Once I had settled in, I looked around at the other passengers to pass the time. There were about eight other travelers, all spread about the section and pretending to be interested in their own affairs. Since it was a Monday, most of the people aboard looked as if they were flying on business, but one family composed of a mother, father, and a sleeping child sat about three rows ahead. I smiled; there was so much to be excited about but so little to do except daydream. The more I thought about it though, that didn't seem so bad. After all, it was daydreaming that had gotten me on the plane to Washington in the first place. After about ten more minutes, I decided that nobody would claim the seat next to me and so I took it as my own, sliding over in order to see out the window.

Given the free space, I placed my carry-on bag onto my original chair and began the task of tightening my new seatbelt, which was so large that if I were a triplet, we could all three fit into it. When I had finished I began to relax, much less nervous than I had been before. Somehow, I knew that if I could get this far in the day's plan, everything else would fall into place. I was about to take out my book when a voice, cheerful to the degree that it sounded almost like Nadia's, caught my attention.

"Hello, and welcome to Swifter Airlines— rated nationally as number one in customer service and relations by Blue Skies Magazine. It is a pleasure to be traveling with you today and on behalf of our entire company, I would like to thank you for your continued loyalty and business. My name is Lucille, and before we begin our flight this morning, I'm going to run through some safety instructions in the case of an emergency. Our plane is equipped with eight emergency exits, each denoted by a red sign above its window. If for any reason we should need to evacuate the plane, they can be opened and used as an alternative door. I would like you to take this time now to locate the emergency exit closest to you. Keep in mind that this exit may be behind you. If you are sitting in the seat nearest an emergency exit door and are either unfit or unwilling to perform the responsibilities required of you in an emergency situation, please notify one of our flight attendants as soon as possible and we would be happy to relocate you to somewhere else around the cabin. Now, in regard to your seatbelts…"

I looked down at my own buckled seatbelt, and seeing as I was already one step ahead, shifted my concentration to looking out the window. There wasn't much to see. It had become considerably lighter outside since my arrival at the airport, but the scenery was no more interesting than it had been before. I leaned slightly forward to check if there was anything interesting at a new angle. After discovering only a couple of trees standing far in the distance, I sighed and slowly turned back around to face Lucille, still addressing the plane through a small PA system.

I had heard her speech dozens of times before, and as I listened to the dull familiarity of her words, I felt strangely comforted. Shortly after the monologue was finished, Lucille approached me with a large rolling cart and asked me if I would like a snack. I took a package of sugar cookies, and began to eat them as we spoke.

"How are you doing so far?" she asked through a mouth filled with teeth that even an oyster would envy.

"Great," I replied through a mouth filled with half-chewed cookies

"Glad to hear it! I'll be back after we take off, but if you need anything at all, feel free to call for me." I thanked her, and she left to pass out the rest of the snacks.

As the hum of the plane's engine grew stronger, I swallowed the remaining cookie bits and turned to the window, only to find that we were slowly creeping towards the runway. We turned a blunt corner, and the aircraft began to increase speed. And with that speed came sound. What had once been the gentle purr of an engine, seemed now to be a roar of a crowd, multiplying so quickly in the plane I was half expecting it to burst at the seams. Nonetheless, as quickly as it had come, the moment soon passed. Within seconds, the sound had completely vanished. Nervous, especially for a person who had flown before, I glanced out the window, watching the ground disappear below as we climbed higher into the air.

See you in two weeks, I thought, taking one last look at New Castle before the plane broke through a veil of clouds. I pushed my palms, slightly sweaty from anxiety, against the glass. When I brought them back to my lap, a light, smudgy imprint of my hand stayed behind. I looked out over the horizon for awhile more, the beating of my heart becoming slightly less violent with every passing second. Once its pounding had become tolerable, I turned back to my baggage and pulled out my magazine, flipping open its cover and burying myself within its pages. I was quite content with my reading until I was interrupted by somebody moving into the seat nearest me. Confused, I looked over to see Lucille sliding into the chair, hurriedly shoving my carry-on bag beneath the seat.

Usually I would have taken her gesture as one of kindness but there was an urgent look in her eyes.

"Cara, you have got to see this!" she practically yelled, stirring the sleeping toddler three rows up.

"What?" I asked in a quieter version of her tone.

"Cara, you're on television!" she whispered, taking a hint from the child's mother, who turned around and shot her a look that said anything but 'happy customer'. "The President is talking about you, Cara! I'm not one for understanding Presidential speeches, but he says that you are a living example of why a responsible young adult should be able to hold a political position. He hasn't shown any pictures of you for your security probably, but he's mentioned your name, and I knew it had to be you!" Breathless, Lucille clicked on the television in front of me and turned it to the proper channel.

It was true! The President was speaking about the Underage Rights Movement, and he was telling everyone about me! He explained the idea to them like he was giving an important history lesson—filled with emotion, passion, and principle. When you heard the President as he spoke just then, even if you didn't agree with what he had to say, you couldn't help but to listen, and want to understand. As I watched him up on the podium, potentially making the greatest career mistake of all-time because of something he so strongly believed in, I saw the bravery in what he was doing, and knew that I couldn't disappoint him.

The speech came to an end but I was frozen in time. Just like the day I had received my White House letter, I was numb. I could no longer feel my pounding heartbeat, or my shaking hands. My body wanted so much to react to what I had seen, but the news could not register with my brain. I was unaware of time passing or anything that may have been going on around me, but I do know that eventually Lucille moved to turn off the television. The numbness slowly started to ease its hold on me, and I looked up to find that Lucille was still focused on the blank screen, looking as if she were begging it for more information.

Since there weren't any pictures shown for the speech, nobody on the plane but Lucille knew my destination in or beyond Washington, D.C. Nonetheless, even though everyone else onboard treated me just like a regular kid, I knew that *I* could never go back to who I used to be. Everything around me seemed so brimming with purpose now, and with this came the far more startling realization that within it all, I was finding my place.

Lucille and I had very little time to talk after the speech, because she was called on to help the other passengers. I think she felt a little changed by the news too though; kind of like when you're almost done reading a mystery book. You start to get comfortable with the story, thinking you know all the characters and can predict the ending. Then, before you know it, everything changes and something new is created—something better.

On my own again, all I could manage to do was sit back in my seat and stare transfixed at the world outside my window—the one that I was soon going to become apart of. After awhile, I felt a gentle hand tap me on the shoulder.

"Miss?" said a woman with such frizzy brown hair that it almost completely hid her face.

"Yes?"

"I'm sorry, Miss, but I'm going to have to ask you to re-buckle your seatbelt. The captain has turned out the fasten seatbelt sign in preparation for our descent, which should begin shortly."

I nodded and the woman continued down towards the back of the plane, asking the rest of the passengers to do the same.

Lucille came to sit with me for the last few moments of our landing, but once we were safely on the ground, she had to leave again in order to help the other guests. Although the airline normally required that she stay onboard until the last passenger left the plane, this was a special circumstance and she was allowed to walk me into the airport.

"I'm guessing that there will be police waiting at the gate exit for your security. All we have to do is tell one of them that you're the unaccompanied minor from flight 218," she explained, standing up from her seat. "They'll lead you straight to whomever it is that's taking you to the, um, well—you know."

"*The White House.*" I whispered. The words sent a wave of warmth through my body, like a magic spell. Even mention of them had power.

Eventually, a man's voice came over the audio speaker. "Good morning ladies and gentlemen. On behalf of Swifter Airlines, I would like to thank you once again for traveling with us this morning here to the Ronald Reagan Washington National Airport, where the local time is now 8:26 a.m. It looks like its going to be a chilly, but beautiful day here in Virginia, with temperatures dipping just below thirty-five degrees Fahrenheit, and predictions of sunny skies later this afternoon. For those of you planning on taking the forty minute drive to downtown Washington, D.C., we would like to remind you that the roads are a little slippery, and ask that you please travel carefully. There is a slight back-up here at the main terminal, and we ask that you remain seated while we make our way towards our assigned gate. At this time, the captain has just informed us that the use of electronic devices is now permitted. Thank you for your patience, and we hope that you enjoy your time her in Virginia, or wherever your final destination may be."

My phone had been turned off during the flight, and after awhile, I thought to check it to see if my parents had called. There were five new messages. The first one was from my mother, hysterically explaining to me that the President's speech had started. The second was from my dad, reporting that the whole press conference was amazing and he and my mom were proud. My mom had played it in front of all her students, and he had done the same for everyone at the restaurant. The rest were all from relatives; my Uncle Marty, my Aunt Lori and my grandparents in Arizona, their messages all more or less the same as the one my dad had left.

As soon as I ended the call with my voicemail, my fingers got started dialing my home number. It took until the third ring for me to realize that it was late Monday morning and nobody would be home, but I opted to leave a message anyway.

"Hi, Mom and Dad and Nadia. It's Cara."

All I could think to do was thank my parents for calling, say Lucille and I had gotten to watch the speech, and tell them that I was safe and couldn't wait to talk to them again.

"—and right now, I'm sitting in a first-class seat! Can you believe that?" I whispered into the receiver.

"Excuse me—are you the unaccompanied minor on board today?"

"Hold on a second." I told the answering machine, turning again to face brown-haired woman in the aisle. "Yes, that's me."

"Well, we're about to give the rest of the passengers the okay to leave their seats, but Lucille wanted me to give you a heads up beforehand. Whenever you're ready, you can start collecting your things and then meet her at the main cabin exit, back a few feet and to your immediate right."

"Thanks." I smiled, moving the phone back to my ear once she had gone.

"Well, we're about to head into the airport so I have to go now. But Nad, no bragging about this. I don't want you trying to sell things I've touched for a profit, or handing out signed yearbook pictures of me at the grocery store. That last part goes for you too, Mom," I added. "Love you all so much and can't wait to see you again. Bye!" I hung up and turned the phone back off.

Not wanting to waste any time that could be spent in Washington, D.C. stuck on an airplane, I gathered up my belongings, straightened my skirt, and headed towards the exit. I reached Lucille and the two of us began walking through the long tunnel leading out of the aircraft. I stepped into the gate, taking a much needed breath of un-recycled air. Shortly afterwards, we found a policeman who seemed happy enough to guide me towards the station where my party would be waiting.

"Follow me," he instructed, leaving no time for Lucille and I to say goodbye.

"Thanks for everything, Lucille," I was facing her sideways and inching backwards so I wouldn't get too far behind. "I'm not sure what I would have done without you being so nice to me today." She smiled, reapplying her lipstick for what seemed like the tenth time that morning and giving me a wave that would have made stewardess Barbie proud.

"I guess this is goodbye," I replied in a tone barely above a whisper. Lucille shook her head in disagreement and I stopped walking. Out of the corner of my eye, I watched as the policemen turned around, waiting for me a few yards off.

"Why not?" I asked her.

"I'm sure I'll be hearing great things from you for a long time to come," she replied, putting her teeth on display again in a melancholy smile.

I beamed back at her, hoping that what she said was true. "See you soon then." Turning, we headed off in our different directions.

"See you soon."

chapter eighteen

I followed the policeman only a short distance away from our gate before we reached a large open area near the baggage claim. My chaperone was easy to spot. He was standing in the exact center of the room, wearing dark suit pants, with a neon yellow dress shirt tucked loosely into them. Sunglasses were folded neatly into his front pocket and a black tie was tight around his neck. A dark piece of metal which I figured to be a telephone of sorts was wrapped around his ear. In his hands, he was holding a large white piece of poster paper where the flight number 218 was carefully printed in black marker and outlined in a pink highlighter. The President had already done his press conference, so it was a safe bet that there were people in the Washington, D.C. airport who knew my name. I supposed that he was identifying me by a number so I wouldn't be recognized. I indicated to the officer that this was the person who was to take me from the airport, and after thanking him, he disappeared into the jumble of tourists and suitcases. Slowly, I approached the man with the sign.

"Flight 218 from Pennsylvania?" he asked me, ignoring the need for a greeting.

"Yes," I answered

"Name?"

"Cara Greybird."

"Yes, of course you are!" The man was suddenly a different person, looking down to face me for the first time. "Sorry about the welcome—wasn't too warm, but I had to make sure it was you. After all, there would probably be a lot of unhappy people after me if I picked up the wrong kid!" He laughed at his own joke and shook my hand.

"I understand. It's very nice to meet you." I hesitated for a moment. "Are you the one who's going to take me to the White House?" I asked him finally, unsure if the man's bright appearance fit in with the description of an important person of the President's.

"Yes, yes I am! Well, we've got places to go and little time, so if you would just come with me to collect your luggage, we can be on our way! I checked ahead and all of your things should be at Area 6 there, directly to your left."

"Alright," I answered as I began to head towards the large motionless conveyor belt where our bags would soon be unloaded. I had almost reached the crowd of people waiting to collect their belongings when I heard a surprised gasp coming from behind me. I gave a small jump at the sound, turning around to realize that it had come from my chaperone.

"Sorry, Miss Greybird, I didn't mean to frighten you, I just remembered that I've forgotten to introduce myself, that's all."

"Oh," I replied, surprised that an adult was referring to me so formally.

"The name's Ray, that's what everyone calls me at least."

"It fits you," I blurted, not able to believe what I had just let slip from my mouth. Who could blame me—in a dull airport, this neon-clad man looked practically like a ray of 80's-inspired light beamed into the room. Amused rather than insulted, Ray touched a hand to his shirt, laughing again. The conveyor belt came to life, and bags started rolling out onto it. Looking for my own, I watched as they went by.

Black suitcase with black tag, red suitcase, black suitcase with pink tag, guitar case, black suitcase with green tag, black duffel with sticker...

"Alright, Miss Greybird, when you see your luggage, you just point it out to me, and I'll grab it for you."

"Thanks, Ray, but you really can call me Cara."

"Why thank you, Miss Greybird." I giggled. If this was what life at the White House was going to be like, I would have no troubles at all. I was trying to push past a group of tourists in Hawaiian print t-shirts when a static-y sounding announcement came on from an overhead speaker.

"Attention—flight AB218A from Pennsylvania, your baggage will now be unloaded at Area 7 *not* Area 6 as indicated. That's flight number 218. I repeat flight 218 from Pennsylvania your baggage will now be unloaded at Area 7 *not* Area 6. Flight 101 from Honolulu; please remain at Area 6 as you have been previously instructed. Your baggage is being unloaded there now. Flight 101 from Honolulu, your baggage has arrived on time and is being unloaded at Area 6. We apologize for any inconvenience this may have caused you, and thank you for your cooperation. Thanks again, and welcome to the Washington National Airport." A loud click ended the announcement, and half of the crowd formed around the conveyer belt left their spots around it, heading for the escalators.

"Miss Greybird?"

"Cara."

"Yes, of course, Miss Greybird. I believe that's your flight they've just called, so what do you say we go upstairs and collect your bags?" I nodded and together we headed towards the crowded escalator and towards Area 7. He was holding up his brightly colored 218 sign so we wouldn't be separated—as if anyone could ever lose track of a man in a neon yellow shirt. As soon as we reached the top of the escalator however, Ray took a sharp turn, and for a moment I had to do a double take of the room in order to find him.

"It's a good thing you look like a walking highlighter, or else you would be pretty hard to find," I mumbled to myself as I jogged over to Ray. I found him squeezing his way through a throng of people in order to be nearest the luggage carousel.

"Do you see your things?" he yelled to be heard over the surrounding noise. I pointed to my mom's old suitcase, nearly twice the size of all the neighboring bags. "Good!" he shouted. "Now you just stay right here and don't move. I'll go get it." Ray ran up to retrieve my luggage, and his space in the crowd was instantly filled by two businesswomen. I thought about moving away from the swarm of people but there was no point. The entire airport was packed—mostly with people that already knew my name. I hadn't even reached the White House, and already, I was unsure if things could get more exciting.

I moved to let a man in a suit cut in front of me, and my actions were met with a painful thud. I looked down to find something rather large settled on top of my foot.

"Ouch," I yelped, pulling away from the weight of the suitcase Ray had parked on my toes.

"Oh, I'm sorry, Miss Greybird, I didn't mean to harm you. In my defense though, you've got the heaviest bag I've ever carried for a person of your size." I forgot the throbbing for a moment in order to smile, forgiving him. "Well, now that we've got that all settled, this area over here is getting more jammed by the second, so I'm going to try and drag this suitcase out of here and you'll follow, I suppose. If for any reason we get separated, I'll be standing at the escalators, so you can meet me there." I nodded, and he began moving, struggling to walk with my bag.

After he turned from me, I bent down to inspect the damage done to my toe. Nothing looked broken, and so after carefully slipping it back into my shoe, I began to stand up. Something, however, caught my eye before I reached my full height. It was a five dollar bill! I bent back over to pick it up. The worn-down green of the airport carpet camouflaged it perfectly, and if I hadn't been bowed over as I was, I would have easily mistaken it for part of the flooring. Quickly, I picked it up and held it up to the light—it was real!

This has got to be a good omen! I thought as I folded the bill, placing it into a pocket on my backpack. *Washington is going to be perfect!*

By the time I had navigated my way through the crowd and towards my meeting place with Ray, he was already in a conversation with someone else.

"Yes. I just got her. We picked up her luggage and should be leaving the parking lot in about fifteen minutes." He paused for a moment. "Yes, of course. I'll get onto line two to speak with James once we're out of here." I smiled—Ray's earpiece wasn't just a phone—it was a White House security device! He was talking to someone inside the President's home right that minute…about me!

"Who is it?" I mouthed over to Ray, wondering if he was speaking with somebody I knew.

"Kate Muleson," he murmured back before returning to his conversation.

"Actually," he said, "Cara is right here with me. Would you like talk to her?" He nodded. "Great." I watched as he took out the earpiece, handing it over to me.

"Hello?" I said trying it out, speaking slower and louder than was probably necessary.

"Cara! Hi!" said the voice on the other end. "This is Kate Muleson. Are you enjoying your trip so far?"

"Yes, Ms. Muleson!" I answered. "I just want to thank you for all the trouble you took to get me here. I am so excited to finally meet you!"

"The feeling is mutual, Cara! So, how does it feel to be a national figure? Oh, I never asked, did you get a chance to see the speech? If you didn't, don't worry. There are plenty of copies we can get for you here."

"Thanks for thinking of me, that won't be necessary. I was actually lucky enough the view it on my plane ride. It was fantastic! I was absolutely stunned! You know, I have to tell you Kate, it's not even noon yet, and this is already the best experience of my entire life!"

"Aww, well that's very sweet of you. I look forward to meeting with you soon, but for now I think it would be best if we got you out of the airport before the crowd gets too large. Right now, there are people whose job it is to get information on you. School records, summer jobs, phone numbers, e-mail, and pictures especially. Luckily, nothing has surfaced yet, but the longer you hang around at the airport, your risk of being recognized is considerably raised."

"Good idea Ms. Muleson, you're probably right."

"We have your school picture from this year and are planning to leak it onto the internet once you're safely in the car. Ray will tell us when. Goodbye, Cara."

"Thanks again!" I heard a click similar to the one from before when the airport loudspeaker was turned off. Knowing that my conversation had come to a close, I handed the earpiece back to Ray.

The two of us agreed that it would be best to do as Ms. Muleson had suggested and leave the airport as quickly as we could. Ray rolled my bag along while I stuck to lugging my carry-on backpack. We were halfway to the door when a woman approached me with a camera.

My heart stopped beating. They had found pictures and I was being recognized. Instinctively, Ray jumped in front of me. The woman gave us a look.

"Sorry to bother you," she held out the camera. "I was just wondering if you could get a shot of us together." She turned around and gestured to a chubby man in a polo and golf visor. Her voice trailed off and I took my first breath in what felt like minutes. "We're about to leave on our honeymoon…"

Ray shot me a wide-eyed look of relief. "Congratulations," he managed. "I'd be happy to help you out."

The incident had been harmless, but we were both much more aware of the time as we hurried away. Together, we walked out of the airport and into the parking lot. I had packed my winter coat in my suitcase—something I completely regretted from the second we stepped outside. The wind nipped at my face and hands, and the cold drained all of the color from my skin. Damp and bitter, the air somehow managed to settle inside of my chest, chilling me from the inside out. Teeth chattering, I rushed ahead to Lot 8 of the airport, where Ray had parked the car. Although trying to remain professional, he had also forgotten a jacket and it wasn't long before the cold wore him down. Luggage and all, he ran to catch up with me, jogging by my side for the majority of the way.

"It's that large black one over there, Miss Cara." He slowed down, pointing to a huge limousine as casually as if it had been an old station wagon.

I momentarily forgot my frozen body to run up to the car. "Ray, this is a *limo!*" I couldn't help but state the obvious. "It's absolutely awesome!"

"I'm glad you like it, Miss Cara."

I bent my head down towards the back windshield to try and see if I could get a hint at its insides.

In that moment, my eyes did their best to take in every detail, but within seconds, I soon found that my vision was being clouded by none other than my own frozen breath, collecting on the window. I shrugged, stepping away from the foggy glass. Good thing I still had about ten others to choose from! Gasping, I ran from window to window, pushing my face to their darkened surfaces and trying to catch a glimpse of the world inside before my breath had a chance to ruin it. Lush leather upholstery in jet black taking up the length of the car, titanium white flooring and walls, silvery lights lining the ceiling and windows, televisions, fully stocked snack cases, and mini refrigerators all blurred past me as I ran, scurrying for even a peek at them. I felt as if I were a real star, being escorted into a luxurious car, and going off to see the President of the United States. Of course, all of this was true, but that only amazed me more.

"This is unbelievable!" I yelled over to Ray once I had finished my rounds of the car. He was fiddling with his key ring, looking each of them over in order to find which one unlocked the door.

"Take a look at the outside," he suggested. Both his voice and his body had begun to shake. "It's just been cleaned."

He was right about that. The sky was cloudy, but the car itself gleamed like it was directly under the sun. I took a step back for a better look, my image practically reflected back at me in the mirror-like hubcaps.

In the time that I had been examining the limousine, Ray had unlocked the car and was now loading my suitcase into its trunk. "If you'd like, Miss Greybird, you can set your carry-on bag in here, as well." He grunted as he pushed my bag in towards the back, making room for more. I shrugged and tossed it in on top of the 218 sign, having already given up on asking him to call me Cara.

Ray dove around to the other side of the car and hopped into the driver's seat. I could hear the sound of the engine and the blasting heat.

Having to jump in order to reach it, I grabbed a hold of the trunk top and pulled it closed myself. "Doors are all opened!" he called. I let myself in and took a seat in the back, which had already become a few degrees warmer than it was outside.

"Welcome to a Presidential limo, Miss Greybird. It's missing the usual Presidential seal, as well as the flags, to make us less conspicuous for security reasons, but it's Deerun's car all the same." He smiled, looking back at me through his rearview window. "Not only is this one of the cleanest cars you'll probably ever ride in, it's also the safest. She can drive up to 200 miles per hour then stop on a dime, she's bulletproof, and—" he held up a finger, "she's got seatbelts too. So, if you would just strap yours on, we'll get started."

I buckled myself in, and we began to drive.

As soon as we left the parking lot, I stopped marveling at the car and resorted to staring out the window. The landscape was beautiful. The roads that I was used to seeing at home were paved with cement, sometimes featuring dying shrubbery planted in rows across the curb. Here, there was emerald green grass, covered in sparkling beads of dew and surrounded by patches of colorful wild flowers. There were houses as well, most colonial in style and all with manicured lawns. Forests, woods and fields decorated the sides of the road, each with more vivid colorings than the last. Shades of amber, fiery red, rich purple, ginger, and hazel flashed past us as we drove. Once or twice during the ride I even saw some fountains, all constructed of polished stone and dripping with clear water. Ms. Muleson had later explained to me that it was her idea for us to take the more scenic route to the White House. I couldn't have been more pleased with her decision.

After a couple minutes of riding in silence, Ray turned on the radio and rolled down the windows. The cold air felt as if it were blowing through my skin. Within moments, it had turned my face red and my fingers blue, but I was too excited to care. I was finally there… finally in Washington, D.C…going to see the President. The idea alone brought shivers up my spine. I was so absorbed in this thought that I forgot to look out my window, and the next thing I knew, the car was jerking to a stop. The sound of my door being opened brought me back to reality. Surprised, I looked up to find Ray, standing on a long driveway. We had arrived in front of a certain *big white house.* I tried to remain calm, but my body wouldn't allow it. I felt weak in the knees and couldn't move from my seat. My eyes widened.

"I can't believe it!" I swallowed hard, attempting to stand. My legs were trembling, and I was worried they might give out on me. "The White House!"

Ray nodded, smiling before he headed around to the back of the car. "Wait here, Miss Greybird. I'll go get your bags." He disappeared from view, leaving me standing alone on the White House driveway. Either the air outside had just warmed up thirty degrees, or the weather no longer bothered me.

"Excuse me—Miss." The voice I heard didn't belong to Ray. Unwillingly, I turned my eyes from the White House and over in the direction of the sound. Two figures were approaching. Both were men, dressed in dark, identical suits. Their faces were straight and their muscles were stiff, as if they were frozen. I was reminded again of the weather.

"Name?" the taller one asked me, staring directly into my eyes without breaking contact. I assumed that they were policeman for the President and so I answered.

"Cara Greybird." Nodding, he whispered something into his earpiece before asking me to stand still while he did a check to see if I was carrying anything hazardous. He took a small device resembling a miniature paddle, and waved it over me. The small metal detector showed that I possessed nothing dangerous, and so the shorter man with the big sunglasses spoke.

"Cara, are you in possession of a firearm or weapon?"

"No sir."

"Are there any poisons, toxic materials, or otherwise harmful substances on your person?"

"No sir."

"Good." His voice was brisk. "It's nice to meet you Miss Greybird. My name is James and I'm going to take you inside the White House while my friend here searches your bags. It is just a standard security rule, nothing to worry about."

On the surface, the man's words were polite, even hospitable, but there was still a certain air about him that made me nervous. Nonetheless, I had heard him say 'take you inside the White House,' and so I ignored my other feelings. Anyone who could get me through the door of 1600 Pennsylvania Avenue was an automatic friend.

"Great. Thank you!" I followed James closer towards the most famous house in America. As we neared the steps to the entryway, I heard the sound of an engine and turned just in time to watch the black limousine heading down the drive. The windows were too dark to see in from the outside, but a neon-yellow arm stuck out from the opened window to wave in my direction before pulling out onto the street. I waved back to Ray as I reached the top of the North Portico, the front door now only yards away. Standing on either side of it were two policemen, but seeing my escort, they pulled open the doors to the White House without any questions. I couldn't wait any longer.

"You first," mumbled James after I had already run inside.

Barely able to breathe, I took my first steps into the White House.

Before I had arrived where my feet then stood, rooted to the ground, I had promised myself not to act like a little kid in a candy store. I had reminded myself over and over, that when I was to enter the building I would keep my legs moving, my jaw up, my eyes in their sockets, and inevitably, my foot in my mouth. I had sworn that no matter how gorgeous, or dazzling, or astounding my first sights of the White House would be, I would under no condition, ever act like a tourist. Once I got inside, however, I just couldn't help myself.

Sparkling crystal chandeliers decorated nearly the entire ceiling, blanketing it with light. The floor was marble, alternating between shades of ivory-colored tiles in a checkered pattern. Red carpeting with golden embroidery was placed neatly under my feet, leading straight into the next hall and encircling the edges of the room like a narrow moat. Velvet curtains with golden fringe draped the immense window space. Paintings and large mirrors filled the walls, their frames just as beautiful as the works inside of them. On both sides of the door were dark marble statuettes, each figure crafted delicately and cradling a gleaming candelabrum. The walls were the color of rich cream, and large pillars stood at the sides of every doorway. Above the main entrance were layers upon layers of detailed molding, all leading up to a half-moon window at their peak. Fragile looking chairs were set out in clusters across the floor, and a bouquet of fresh flowers was placed on nearly every table. It looked to me as if every inch of the room was dusted, polished, and scrubbed every fifteen minutes—there wasn't a spot or a smudge to be seen.

"This is the Entrance Hall. You may look around if you like," James offered, not bothering to take off his sunglasses. I watched as he retreated to the back of the room, muttering into his earpiece with his eyes still on me. Ignoring his gaze, I did as I was told and breathlessly examined the rest of the room, unable to stop until I had studied every table, chair, plate, embroidery, and pattern. As much as I tried to resist, my eyes were thirsty for each detail, and I savored everything I saw. I was just finishing up when a woman dressed in a beige pantsuit marched into the room, nearly knocking me over.

"Cara Greybird, I presume?" she asked, straightening the short string of pearls that hung around her neck.

"Yes, nice to meet you. Are you Ms. Muleson?"

"No, but I am here on her business, delivering this message on her behalf. You see, the President is very busy, given all the crazy media that comes with a speech like the one he gave today. So, he apologizes about not being able to greet you upon your arrival. However, we have just received word that he will arrive back here in time for lunch with you around noon. He insists that you should make yourself comfortable while you wait, so I'm going to take you into one of the more relaxing rooms of the White House."

"Alright," I shrugged, still in a daze.

"Good then," the woman smiled, "Now, if you'll just follow me. Oh!" she added pointing to the man in the corner, "I think it would be best if you came along with her as well." James nodded, stepping away from the wall, and the three of us started walking. We stayed close behind the woman, moving past a row of pillars and through a hall narrower than the first before stopping.

"This, Cara is the Green Room," she explained once we had reached its doorway. "I think you'll find yourself quite content in here. It has been a sort of lodging room for past Presidents and their guests since about the year 1800. If you'll notice, the walls are covered in an emerald fabric composed of watered-silk, chosen by Mrs. Kennedy herself. The drapes were added in the late 1900's and if you care to look carefully there are stripes of taupe and crimson mixed in with the mint color you see here. Atop these drapes is a large golden valance, above which you can see an eagle statuette with its wings spread, as if in flight. As you may already know, this eagle is a symbol of the United States itself. The Oriental rug which sits in the center of the room was hand-made and has been added just recently. All the furniture is authentic, so although you are welcome to sit anywhere you like, I must remind you to be careful. There is an older looking showcase against the far wall. If you care to open it, you'll find a wonderful collection of books inside, and you may read one if you choose to. Your guard over there," she motioned over to the man in sunglasses, "has been assigned to you for the day and so he will remain here with you. I really must go now, but I hope you enjoy your time in the Green Room. If you have any problems, feel free to call, but I wouldn't recommend any further exploring until after your lunch with the President. Enjoy your stay."

I was about to mention that the woman had never given me her name, or a location where I could find her, but she had left the room before I could say a thing. Slightly confused, I sat down in a red armchair next to the mantle and tried to decide how I would spend the next hour or so of my time. I thought of calling my family but my phone had been left for the security crew to inspect and the thought of walking back outside into the cold to retrieve it did not agree with me. Besides, the woman, whoever she was, had told me in so many words that I shouldn't leave the room until the President arrived. The only thing she had really mentioned for me to do was read one of the books in the room. Silently, I tried to locate the display cabinet that had been pointed out to me earlier.

It was small, but took only a moment to find. My security man was having a quiet conversation with somebody on his earpiece, and I tried not to disturb him as I stood. The wood of the antique showcase looked brittle, so I took time in opening its swinging glass doors. Behind them were three stout shelves, lined with books. They were all leather bound, and most of them looked like they hadn't been read in years—if they had ever been read at all. Squinting, I read the titles of the books out loud. *George Washington, The Electoral Process, A Brief Take on America, Stars and Stripes Forever...* None of the books caught my eye but they were all I had to work with, and so I decided to take the least dusty of the collection. If it had been read the most, it would probably make good use of my time as prisoner in the room. With this reasoning, I scanned the shelf again, choosing a book called *White House History*. I smiled, turning it over in my hand. I had almost missed it before because of its thin size, but it might help me to learn my way around.

I pulled it from the shelf and held it out to examine. It had the air of something old. The binding was done completely in leather and the paper inside was thick and uneven, like bits of hand-cut parchment. Its title and author were imprinted on the cover in small golden lettering. Unlike those around it, there were deep creases in the spine. I fanned through the pages, surprised by how well they had been maintained. Not daring to touch it again, I left the showcase open and carried the book back to my chair.

From the very first page and on, it was fantastic! The book started off like a tour, bringing you through the front door of the White House and taking you past the various rooms. I didn't have a watch but judged the time by the expression on James' face, which was looking more and more bored by the minute as he listened to security updates on his earpiece. I asked if he wanted to get a book as well, but he just shook his head 'no' and so I went back to my reading, looking back in his direction a few minutes later. His sunglasses hid his eyes, but I was almost sure he'd fallen asleep.

It wasn't until I had reached the last page of the book that I looked up again, but it wasn't because I had finished. Someone very important had arrived.

Before I knew it, I found myself in the company of the President. Of course about ten security guards came through the door first, but after that, there he was. Immediately, James stood up at my side. Trying to be polite, I did the same, placing the book aside on a nearby table.

It was not yet one o'clock in the afternoon, but you could see that the President was already tired. Nonetheless, his eyes held a remarkable amount of energy, as if there was some power inside of him that even a hard day couldn't seize away.

"Cara!" he exclaimed, navigating his way through the sea of security before he reached me.

"President Deerun! It's great to see you again!" I cried, running to shake his hand. "I loved your speech, and I'm so excited for this program, and I just want to thank you so much for this opportunity, and the airline tickets too, and letting me come to stay here, and…"

"Cara, slow down!" laughed the President. I pointed my chin down, feeling like a dog who just wanted to please their master but was doing something wrong. "If you don't, we'll have nothing to talk about over lunch!" I giggled. "Are you hungry?" he asked me. I hadn't thought about it until then, but once the idea came around, my stomach wouldn't let me forget it.

"Yes," I answered. "Very."

"Great! Why don't we go and have ourselves some lunch then. I didn't know what your taste was, so I asked them to prepare us a simple salad. Is that alright with you?"

"Perfect!" I smiled as he led me out of the Green Room.

"I thought that you might like to eat in the Family Dining Room today, so that's where we'll be headed."

The two of us were walking side by side through a hallway styled much like the room I had first seen when I entered the White House. The book I had just read was fresh in my mind, and I searched my memory for information on it.

The chandeliers were made in eighteenth-century London, and the marble walls were added at request of the Truman administration. During Buchanan's term, the tradition of hanging Presidential portraits on the wall was begun, and is still continued today...

With a small smile I remembered the name. This was the Cross Hall.

"The Family Dining Room sounds great!" I agreed, walking a little faster in order to keep up with him.

"It is more of a formal room, but I thought that since it was your first day in Washington, we could eat there as a treat."

"Thanks!" Nearing the end of the corridor, the President turned into a shorter hallway. We reached the dining area a moment later.

The walls were a striking shade of yellow. They were warm, but very pale, and it took me a moment to decide whether the color was more similar to white or gold. Most of the dark wooden paneling on the floor was covered up by a large throw rug, eggshell white and covered in a blue, china-like pattern. The chandelier was unlit, but its crystals shone as it captured the light flooding in from the window. Sitting directly below was a small round table, barely reaching four feet in diameter. It was set with only two chairs, positioned directly across from one another. A long lace tablecloth stretched nearly to the floor, and was layered over a shorter gold one. Serving as the table's centerpiece was a bouquet of pink and yellow roses. Although the little table was clearly meant to act as the focal point of the room, I couldn't help but notice the little things too. Potted green plants were placed atop the surrounding furniture. Paintings covered the walls and a golden light fixture was mounted in every corner. A fire had been started in the mantle at the far end of the room. After just one look, I couldn't help but to feel at home.

"This is one of my favorite rooms in the White House," he explained, stepping towards the center of the room. "Please, make yourself comfortable."

I didn't know much about how to act around a President, but I learned a lot about royalty in history class and I figured that the same social rules applied. You should always remain standing until the King is seated, and so I waited until my host took his place at the table before joining him.

Almost immediately, two men in navy suits appeared in the doorway. The President gave a nod in their direction and they advanced towards the table, asking us if we would like anything to drink. The older man took the President's order first.

"I'll have the usual iced tea, please—unsweetened, if possible."

"Absolutely, sir."

The younger man turned to face me. "And for you?" he asked.

"May I have some water, please?"

"Sure, sparkling or still?"

"Still please."

"Sure, bottled, tap or mineral?"

"Bottled please."

"Sure, Swedish, Canadian, or spring?"

"On the other hand, tap water is fine."

"Sure. Would you like a lemon slice with that?"

"Sounds great."

"Yes ma'am."

The two men backed out of the room, returning seconds later with our beverages. I hoped that these were the usual White House waiters so that they would remember my drink order because I wasn't about to repeat that process again any time soon.

"Enjoy." They murmured once they were through. "Your meals will be ready shortly."

We folded our napkins in our laps, and the President began to speak again.

"So, Cara..." He looked rather calm for having made a speech that would be played on every news station in the world before eleven that night. "I've been thinking a lot, and I've decided that we really haven't gotten to get to know each other before the Underage Rights campaign as much as I would have liked."

It was true, I thought, looking back at him. In fact, all the information we had exchanged until that point had been squeezed into a half hour conversation at a hospital garden party.

"I guess a longer introductory period wouldn't have hurt."

"Cara, you are a national figure now. I would have liked to have taken the time before your trip down to Washington to ask you more about your political strengths and weaknesses. Once you inspired me however, I knew that I had to start the movement without delay. So, let me ask you now, are you good at making public speeches? How well can you persuade a crowd?" I thought about it for awhile. I couldn't say no, but then again I couldn't say yes either. The reality was that I had never really made a speech before, and the thought of what would be needed in the upcoming debate made my stomach turn.

"The truth is Mr. President, sir, I would really like to say yes, but I can't. I've never done it before, you see."

"Well, that's a straightforward answer. Very sincere, Cara, very good. Your limited experience is nothing to be worried about; you will be taking classes during your time here to help you improve in those areas, anyway. The good thing is you are obviously not afraid to speak your mind, and you know that there is an honest and fair way to do it. You are friendly, you are determined, and you have a point of view. That is why you're really here, Cara, not for your speech-making talent, but for those qualities."

"Is that why you want to pass the bill?" I asked him, noticing for the first time that it wasn't just the President's eyes on me, but four other pairs as well. The security men lining the walls were facing me too, all looking more or less interested in hearing a response.

The President paused for a moment, as if he knew the answer but had to think in order to convey what he really wanted.

"Yes," he said after a moment, "that is exactly why I want the bill to be passed. I really do think you, and many other underage peoples in America have what it takes to make it here in Washington. If my bill is passed, you being here to accomplish your goals and help others would be accepted simply because of your intentions. I do not believe that age should play such a defined role in our society today. A number should not tell us who is qualified for a job, but our abilities should. If my bill is passed, all anyone would need to get here would be skill and talent. I'm not saying that possessing experience isn't important—I don't mean that at all. All I'm trying to say is that if a person has a message that they believe in, then they should have the right to deliver it. Age shouldn't keep a person from voicing their opinions and sharing their ideas."

"Wow," I whispered. "It all makes so much sense, and I'd never thought to define it like that before."

"That is exactly what I am trying to make people understand Cara!" the President cried, obviously glad that *someone* supported his bill in a time of such political confusion. "I believe that it is in our country's best interest to pass this bill. It states that underage people in America can hold political positions *if* they are best suited for the job. Now, of course this wouldn't mean that we would have an eight-year-old running our country. What it *could* mean however, is that a smart, sensible, boy or girl mature enough to handle adult situations would be able to accept a government or political occupation. Maybe it will never happen! My bill doesn't say it has to. Maybe a child better suited than an adult for one such job will never come around. But *they need to have the option to share their beliefs*. It is their *right* to have that option. That's what my bill really means. Everyone should have the ability to be heard." He paused. "Regardless of age."

"It sounds brilliant!" I exclaimed. President Deerun looked as if he were about to add something else, but before he had the chance, a portly woman dressed in a crisp white uniform walked into the room.

"Lunch is served," she announced, approaching the table with a large platter in her arms. She kept the tray balanced on her right shoulder, keeping it steady with one hand while unloading it with the other. It wasn't long before a plate of salad and a small pitcher of dressing had been laid out in front of each of us.

"Enjoy your meals!" she said before turning towards the exit.

We began to eat a few moments after she left our sight.

"This is not going to be easy you know; passing this bill," the President said quietly after he had swallowed his first bite of food.

"I know," I replied, taking a sip from my china water glass "but I'm willing to do whatever it takes."

"Good!" he smiled, pleased with my answer. "I knew this little luncheon of ours would bring us progress." We ate in silence for a long time after he spoke—enjoying each others company of course, but just happy to eat our lunches. It was only after the President and I had finished our last forkfuls of salad and our plates were cleared that I broke the quiet.

"That was an amazing meal. Thank you so much."

"Yes it was, and you are certainly welcome." The President leaned back in his chair. "In fact, that was one of the best meals I've had in a long time. Nobody was trying to force a story out of me, or search for meaningless conversation. I feel like I've just had a good meeting with an old friend." I tried to hide my smile—*the President had referred to me as his friend!* "Now, it's not easy for me to say this," he continued, "but I'm going to have to leave. I would love to stay longer, but there is a conference that I need to attend."

"I understand, sir."

"Great. I do hope to see you later in the day though. As for this afternoon, Ms. Muleson has planned a very exciting day for you. After I go, James, your security guard, will lead you to Kate's office—Kate Muleson, that is. I've talked to her personally, and she says she is happy to help you get settled. Afterwards, she plans on giving you a tour of the White House. There isn't much scheduled activity for the rest of your day, and so you may want to spend it getting to know your way around the building, or exploring it if you wish. As sorry as I am that I can't be with you, I am sure you are going to have a lot of fun this afternoon, and hopefully learn a thing or two as well."

"Thank you so much," I stood up from the table. The President did the same, straightening his suit before walking towards the door. His security men followed after him like ducklings to their mother, leaving me with James as my only company.

"So, should we head over to Ms. Muleson's office then?" I asked him once we were alone.

"Yes, follow me." As a Secret Service agent for the President, his face was naturally a hard one to read. Still, I hoped he was warming up to me.

"There are no tours on Monday or Sunday, so we didn't have any problems today, but the rest of the week, from around 7:30 a.m. until half past noon, I like to avoid the more commercial rooms of the White House," he said, ducking behind a closed door. I was trying my hardest to keep up, but the deeper he led me into the maze of staircases and hallways, the more my feet started to hurt. "Getting caught off-guard by a bunch of tourists probably wouldn't be such a good publicity move for you right now."

I agreed. "So, I guess this means no lounging around in the Blue Room with my pajamas on tomorrow, right?" It took him a moment to realize I was joking.

"Exactly." After awhile of walking, the rooms we passed began to decrease in grandeur, becoming more office-like. I stopped in a narrow hallway, branching out into a series of small rooms. Most of their doors were closed, but the open ones revealed various people in meetings or on the phone.

"This way," James called to me, taking a sharp right turn that brought him into an open workplace area. There wasn't much to the room, but whoever it belonged to was indisputably dedicated to keeping it clean. In its center was a large wooden desk, shaped like a semi-circle. Its outer rim was built upwards like a fence, as if to keep the area inside private. I craned my neck in order to see who was inside of the massive desk, only to find a trim woman seated in an office chair. She was talking on the telephone and typing furiously on her computer, pausing occasionally to click on something with the mouse. I listened as she spoke, her voice a more impatient version of the one I had talked to on the phone.

"That's her," James whispered. "Ms. Kate Muleson." I looked back at him for guidance. "She's busy, but just let her know you're here," he added. The woman grew quiet, and I figured she had finished making her call. Being in the White House was kind of like visiting the Emerald City. The President was the Wizard, but Kate looked like the woman behind the curtain.

Cautiously, I stepped up to the desk, trying not to disturb her. As soon as I was within an arm's length of the counter, she abandoned her work at the computer and resorted to sorting through a stack of mail.

"Hello?" I tried to get the woman's attention, unsure if she could hear me or not.

"No, no, *no!*" she answered. "Yellow ribbon is *not* alright! I was distinctly told that the ambassador was coming for a dinner party, not a luncheon or breakfast, and therefore, it would just be inappropriate—especially considering the season! I *cannot* use any pastel shades for this meal, the color pallet must be suitable for an evening event!" I jumped back. Apparently, she was still on the phone. Not wanting to interrupt, I waited for her to finish her conversation. "Yes, midnight blue; in silk if at all possible. Fine, go check. Uh huh, uh huh. Yes, I'll hold." She sighed, still with no clue that I was in the room.

"Hello!" I tried a second time, slightly louder than before. The woman's eyes darted down towards me.

"Cara!" she cried, covering her hand over the phone receiver to muffle the sound. Her voice had gone back to the way I remembered it. "Hello!" Hearing something on the other line, she motioned for me to wait and went back to her conversation.

"Linda? Linda, are you still there? Yes, it's me, who else would it be? What do you *mean* I sound different? Well, did you check? Great! I am so sorry, but I have to go. Will you call me back with the estimate? Good, then…yes, it was nice talking to you too, Linda…Alright, goodbye." She hung up the phone to face me again.

"Cara, it's you!" she announced, standing up for a better look. "I've been waiting to finally meet you, and now here you are! This is spectacular! How was your trip over here?"

"It was grea—" I started to answer, but the woman hurriedly cut me off.

"Enjoyable, I presume. Well, that's wonderful! Oh my, I haven't introduced myself in person yet, have I?" I began to shake my head 'no', but she didn't acknowledge it. "I'm Kate Muleson!"

"Nice to finally meet you," I cut in as we shook hands. Kate left her desk, and walked around to where I was standing.

"So, Cara," she said. "Today I am going to give you a little tour of the White House so you'll be able to find your way around on your own. I would ask you where you'd like to start, but first, I bet you're *dying* to see your bedroom for the next couple of weeks, aren't you?"

"Yes!" my response came without much thought.

She turned to face James. "I have Cara now, so you don't have to tag along. If we need you later, I won't hesitate to call. Thank you so much for looking after her over the last couple of hours."

"No problem," he mumbled, adjusting his dark sunglasses and slipping out of the room.

"Come along now," she instructed, waving me back in the direction of the smaller offices. The walk to my bedroom was relatively short. Every so often Kate would stop to tell me the history of a piece of furniture, where the phone was located, or where the bathrooms were, but besides that we moved pretty quickly.

"You will be sleeping in the Queen's bedroom during your stay here," Kate reminded me as we made our way down what she called the Central Hall. "I picked it out for you myself. It isn't too far from my office so if you ever need help, feel free to come and find me. The President and I both think that your bedroom will be your favorite part of the White House. Royalty of Europe has slept there on past visits, so you can only imagine how elegantly it's furnished. I also picked it for you because it has its own telephone. That way you can call home whenever you like. It's also on the White House main line so you can dial the extension numbers of other phones in the building, say, if you need to reach me in my office. Usually, children who visit the White House stay in one of the smaller bedrooms, but President Deerun is so glad that you could come and help with his bill that he decided you should get the very best the White House has to offer!"

"That was very nice of you both," I thanked her. "Everyone has treated me so well since I got here. It's an honor that I was invited to come." Kate nodded, and then turned to face a large wooden door. I stopped walking.

"It's just through here," she announced before I could ask any more questions. Carefully, I touched my hand to the knob, twisting it slowly to the right. Once the door was wide enough for the two of us to slip through, I took a deep breath and made my way into the room. Kate found the switch and flicked on the light.

"It's breathtaking," I sighed open-mouthed, staring in awe at my new bedroom. It was quite large, probably bigger than my living room at home. The entire floor space was covered in an oversized oriental rug, with only the corners revealing the original wood flooring. Everything looked so antique and fragile that I almost felt scared to examine it. Portraits, fading with age and bordered by delicate golden frames were hung along walls the color of pink limestone. There was a couch and an armchair placed in the center of the room, facing the wall nearest me. They were each covered in the same fabric, striped with pale shades of olive, pearl, gold, and salmon.

At the end of the room was a fireplace, made from what looked like one huge slab of white marble. It was long, but only protruded a few inches from the wall, and had tiny floral patterns carved along its outer edges. On both sides of its ledge sat a large white candlestick in an elaborate silver holder and above those, a polished rectangular mirror was hung. Against the far wall sat a bookcase with a narrow board of wood attached to the front so that it could double as a writing desk. Most of its shelves were lined with aged volumes, but some of them were taken up by small silver ornaments or dainty-looking china. In the corner of the room next to the desk was a grand armoire, probably wider than I was tall, and completely empty except for its beige velvet lining. To my surprise, I also found my suitcase sitting propped up against the wall, looking just as it had when I left it.

The room looked old and gave off the scent of a heavy perfume. Of course it was beautiful, but I felt odd to think of it as my own.

"Cara, have you seen the bed yet?" Kate asked, using the tip of her shoe to rub out a tiny scuff mark that her heel had made on the floor. She looked up only once she had finished her cleaning. "Go on, it's to your right." I turned around.

It was perfect.

The mattress was probably king-sized, but looked much larger with all of its blankets and pillows. Its platform, hidden by a long dust ruffle, was of equal width, raising it nearly two feet above the floor. Draped over all of this was the comforter. If you looked closely, you could see that it was white, although intricate jade embroidery caused it to appear green from far away. A ribbon of silky trim was sewn across its edges, and near the headboard lay a long cylindrical pillow, covered by four smaller square ones. The best part however, hung over the bed in the form a huge canopy, made of the same fabric as the couches. I couldn't help but picture the queen herself as I saw it crowning the bed, looking extravagant and proud.

Dizzied by the appearance of the room, and even more flustered with the knowledge that it was my own, I rested my hand on a nearby table.

"Wow," I managed after a moment's silence. "This is amazing." I scanned the bedroom again, and the shock on my face began to contour itself into a smile.

"I knew you'd like it," Kate smiled. "When I brought the Queen of England here last month, she told me that it was '*just lovely and would accommodate her for the time being*'. Your reaction was a lot more fun to watch. They brought your suitcase and backpack up here if you haven't seen them yet, and besides that, everything else is ready for you. Through the door to your right is your own bathroom, complete with its own beautiful little sitting room, and the phone is on the bedside table. It hasn't been brought in yet, but somebody should be delivering a laundry basket up here for you too. Just leave your dirty clothes inside and they'll be cleaned and returned to you, usually by the next day. Before I forget, when I was talking to your parents the other night, they mentioned that you might be sending some letters home. We at the White House would be happy to mail them for you if you'd like. Just leave them on your bedside table in their addressed and stamped envelopes, and we'll be sure they're sent.

"I'll give you awhile to get settled, unpack your things, or rest a little while if you like. The bed is a Siberian down, and from what I hear, it's the most comfortable in the White House. When you're finished, you can head back to my office, and I'll give you the rest of your tour. If you get lost, dial my extension number, and I'll come to get you. I wrote it on that slip of paper next to the telephone before you came. Oh, and by the way, we may go outside to see the gardens so bring a jacket, if you want to." I thanked Kate again, but she was gone before I could say another word, leaving me alone in the stunning space. It amazed me that I had to share a room in my own home, but already had one to myself in the White House.

Before anything else, the first thing I did was try out the bed. I dove onto it headfirst, landing mangled amongst the once perfectly aligned pillows. I took a deep breath and melted into the comforter. Prior to my arrival, I had worried about not being able to fall asleep in the White House, but now I had no doubts whatsoever. Reluctantly, I fought myself to get back on my feet. I unzipped my suitcase and unpacked most of my things into the empty dressers, bringing my toothbrush and hair gear into the bathroom, as well. Once I was finished, I placed my empty suitcase under the bed, not wanting to ruin the historical look of the room with my mom's old luggage. Before closing it, I tossed my backpack into the armoire and stood back to admire my work. Everything looked exactly as it had been when I found it except for the bed, whose sheets were hanging slightly off to one side, and whose pillows were somewhat crooked. Deciding that it was neat enough, I grabbed my jacket from where I had stowed it in the dresser, clicked off the light, and left to go find Ms. Muleson, closing the door behind me as I went.

I found her office without much trouble, having taken a wrong turn only once. Right away, we got started on the tour. I saw the swimming pool, the tennis courts, the Library, the Map Room, the East Room, and the Truman Balcony. We even got to take a look at the Oval Office! Afterwards, she led me outside through both the Rose, and the Kennedy Gardens. For the rest of the world, it was early autumn, but to the grounds of 1600 Pennsylvania Avenue, it was springtime.

Being inside the White House was like visiting a city in some sort of parallel universe—a town that functioned independently from the rest of the world. Each portrait, flower, and book fortunate enough to land a spot there had a history behind it, and a reason for being where it was. When I told this to Kate, she merely smiled. "The same goes for people in the White House, Cara. Why, you're the perfect example!"

In a city where everything and everybody has its own purpose, I'd found mine in a pretty good neighborhood.

When the tour was over, Kate and I headed back inside through the Palm Room door in the West Wing, and then turned into the Center Hall. I followed her through a small doorway on the left and nearly bumped into James, who was waiting for us near the elevator. Ms. Muleson explained to me that there was some business she needed to attend to back in her office, and so James would be looking after me until seven, when I would be joining the President and First Lady for dinner in the Family Dining Room. The dress for dinner would be more formal, so she advised that I change into a dress sometime before then.

"You can never be too overdressed for a dinner with the President," she reminded me. "I'd suggest something really nice, floor-length even, if that's possible." I managed to smile. It took awhile, but my bite from Jawsie had finally healed into a faint enough scar that it wouldn't draw any attention from strangers. That night, I had been excited to select an outfit unrestricted by the indentations that a dog's teeth can leave behind in a person's leg. Now, this didn't look as if it would happen after all—not that it mattered in the slightest. A formal dinner with the President was well worth a minor wardrobe disappointment.

Kate reached over James' shoulder and pushed the 'up' button on the elevator. Realizing that she had to leave, I thanked her profusely; careful to mention how much fun I had had over the past few hours with her. She said the same to me, and promised that I would see her later in the week. The doors of the elevator opened and Kate found her way inside them, ready to get back to work. The next thing I knew, Ms. Muleson was on her way back to her fortress of a desk, and I was on my own again with James.

"What would you like to do now?" he asked, a few moments after Kate had disappeared.

"What do you mean?" I turned to face him. For some reason, after the tour, I had assumed that my day would be suspended until dinner. Apparently I was wrong.

"We still have a little bit of time until you need to be on your way." He looked stiff, and you could tell he hadn't had much experience talking to kids. Still, it was apparent that he was trying his hardest to be nice, and I appreciated his effort. "It's five o'clock now, and dinner is at seven so we have about one hour of free time. I decided that you might like the other hour to get ready for your dinner. You've been touring all day so how about we have a little fun?"

"Sounds great!" I had really enjoyed my day at the White House so far, but was eager to release some of my energy. "What did you have in mind?"

"Why don't we go to the bowling alley? I can't usually play down there myself, but sometimes I do manage to sneak in a game or two with the other employees. I must admit, I've gotten pretty good over my past few years here."

"Alright," I agreed, thoroughly convinced. James nodded before motioning for me to follow him back into the Center Hall. He led the way as we walked; pointing out the name of each room we passed on our way. In-between the offices of the Secret Service and the curator, we took the North Hall straight down to the Basement Hall, until we were standing in front of two white double doors.

"This is it," he announced, opening the door into the alley.

Inside, I was surprised at what I saw. I had pictured a large open space with a rental shoe counter and a snack shop. Somehow it had gotten into my mind that everything would be made of dark wood, with granite countertops, and crystal chandeliers hanging from the ceiling. The pins would be painted with gold and silver instead of the traditional white and red. The bowling balls would be extravagant as well, polished to the point where you could see your reflection in them.

What I saw now was an entirely different story. It looked no different from the bowling alley I had gone to back home, but on a much smaller scale. There was only one lane, and you could tell that the room had been intended for private use. A mural of three large bowling pins had been painted on two of the four taupe-colored walls. The carpet was a dark burgundy, and the ceilings were moderately low. There were two different machines where the bowling balls were brought back up to the players after being used. To my right was a series of small cubbies where the different sized bowling shoes were stored. On top of the cubbies was a large leather book, opened to a page located in about its center. The lane itself was made of a waxy, light colored wood. Hanging behind it, on the wall farthest from where I stood, was a screen meant for recording the scores of the game. A matching monitor, complete with a keypad to type the names of the players, was sitting a few feet behind the lane, near the back of the room. Above the pins, in the center of the far wall was a painting of the White House. I have to admit that it was a pretty amazing thing to be bowling in the President's personal alley, and although I had never been much of a bowler, I was excited to begin the game.

Almost at once, James led me over to the corner of the room near the cubbies. An older woman was standing there, leaning against the wall and flipping through the pages of a magazine. Long brown hair hung over her face, looking as if it had been previously used as a grease rag at a gas station. Just as I had failed to notice her until then, she didn't seem to realize that we had entered the room. James coughed into his fist to get her attention, and as if someone had pushed the play button on a movie, the woman instantly sprang to life.

"Oh, good, it's you, Sunglasses," she looked up, throwing the magazine aside. Her voice sounded surprisingly feminine. "So you decided to come down here after all. I was hoping you would. Oh, and hello, Miss Cara. It's a pleasure to meet you."

"You too," I replied quickly, eager to get started. I wondered if everyone called my chaperone Sunglasses, and I almost laughed out loud when I thought about what a fitting name it was.

"Would you like some shoes?" she asked me. Her tone was relatively flat.

"What?" I answered, making sure I had heard her correctly.

"Bowling shoes," she explained, bending down to get a good look at my feet. "You look like maybe a size six or seven. I'll go for a seven. Yes, that looks about right." I watched her mop of hair shake as she reached into one of the cubbies and pulled out a pair of beige and black bowling shoes. "How about these?" she asked, holding them up. "Do you think they'll fit?"

"They look great." *Nicer than any pair of bowling shoes I had ever seen, anyway.* The woman shrugged, modestly acknowledging her talent for recognizing shoe sizes before handing them off to me. I accepted them quickly, rushing to lace them up on my feet. Sunglasses took his shoes from the woman and tied them on as well. Mine fit a little big and looked strange with my outfit, but I suppose all bowling shoes do.

"There's just one thing we have to do before getting started," he explained, pointing towards the thick leather volume I had noticed earlier. "It's an old White House tradition. Anyone who plays down here, when invited of course, signs their name in this book, and before they leave they have to add their score." I smiled at the idea of documenting my trip to Washington for the first time, and neatly printed my full name in the books' next available space, right under the ambassador to Spain with a 90 and Julie Andrews with a 72. I noticed the Queen of England at the top of the page with a 215 but I was guessing that her game had been fixed.

"Cara, why don't you head over to that screen near the door and add our names into the scoreboard so we can play. I'm going to get another size in these shoes."

"Alright," I answered as I walked over to the machine. Quickly, I typed my own name next to the 'player one' space on the keypad and then began to add in James'. I had been thinking about his nickname as I did so, however, and accidentally wrote '*Sunglasses*' instead. The woman working the alley came around to ask me if I needed any help, and saw what I had typed. She burst out laughing, but I somehow found a way to delete the letters and type '*James*' in their place before anyone else got a chance to see them. When I was finished, I moved over to the ball-return area and picked out a light-weight green one that reminded me somewhat of an oversized marble. I grabbed it with my right hand, using my left to secure it from underneath as I headed back to meet James. He was standing near the center of the room with a heavy looking ball in his hands.

"You go first," he insisted, stepping aside from the lane and giving me a clear view of the other end. I nodded and stepped up to the front of the alley. I had only bowled on a couple of past occasions and was eager to see if I would do well with so little practice.

Carefully, I placed my toe in the middle of the lane and looked towards the pins. As my eyes focused in on them, I could tell that they were brand new, much unlike the chipped ones at the bowling alleys I remembered from home. After a moment, I took two swift steps forward and flung the ball in the direction of the pins. Initially, it began to travel straight, but spun to the right once its speed wore off. I watched it roll lazily into the gutter.

"It's alright," Sunglasses gave an effort to cheer me on. "You've still got one more try left." He handed me a turquoise ball from the ball return machine and I began again. I placed my toe on the center of the lane and took two steps forward before releasing the ball. Another gutter-ball left me with a tentative score of zero.

"The first game is always the hardest," James reassured me, stepping up for his turn. He got a strike with what looked like minimal effort, putting him in the lead. I got a little bit better after my first couple of turns, but not by much, and our game followed in roughly about the same pattern as our first frame. When it was all over, I was left with a score of 28 while Sunglasses had managed a humble total of 216. Just one more than the Queen.

"Good game, *Sunglasses,*" I congratulated him, setting my ball back on its rack after I had been annihilated.

"You too," he offered with a smile. As I was unlacing my bowling shoes, James took a look at his watch. "Cara, I'm so sorry, but I lost track of the time. We are a little bit behind schedule and if you don't want to be late for dinner, we're really going to need to hurry." James headed for the door, beckoning for me to follow him. Relieved that he had forgotten about adding my pitiful score to the book, I slipped on my own shoes and jogged towards the bowling alley's exit. Before we left, I thanked the woman next to the cubbies. Having gone back to her magazine, she managed a wave without lifting her head from her reading.

"Nice meeting you, Cara. Bye, Sunglasses!" she murmured, flipping to a fresh page.

Walking at a faster pace than usual, the two of us scurried towards the elevator on the ground floor. Its doors were opened, and then quickly closed again. James pushed the button for the second floor and we were let out in a room near the Central Hall. Because I had navigated through it on my own, I knew the second floor relatively well and was able to lead the way back to my bedroom. We reached the wooden door at a run. I was almost out of breath but James looked unaffected by the exercise. He explained that he had just received an urgent message on his earpiece and was needed downstairs. Chances were good that he would be missing for awhile and that I would need to get to the dining room by myself.

"Once you're ready to go, all you have to do is find the same elevator we just left and take it down to the first floor. You'll find yourself right in the hallway leading up to the Family Dining Room, which is where you'll be eating tonight."

"That sounds simple enough." I thanked him one last time before opening the door. "Thanks for the game by the way—I had a lot of fun!" I closed it behind me once he started down the hall. As Sunglasses had already pointed out, I was late and couldn't afford to waste time.

The first thing I did was open my wardrobe and select an outfit for the evening. I only had two long dresses, and seeing as one of them was wrinkled beyond repair after I had fallen asleep in it the day before, I wasn't left with much of a choice. I reached out my arms to pull my selection off the hanger. It was a shade of dark green, and the last time I had worn it was to the fifteen-year anniversary celebration of my dad's restaurant. That had been almost two years ago, but there were no other alternatives. I had to hold my breath, but eventually got it to zip. The dress was strapless, and so I pulled a shawl over my shoulders in order to make it a little more suitable for the evening.

Almost finished, I crouched down to the side of my bed where all of my shoes were lined up. I had grown since my last time wearing the dress and the heels that matched it would now make it too short. Trying to be resourceful, I chose a pair of flats instead. They were dark brown, almost the same color as my shawl. A small strip of the material stretched over the front part of my foot and an even smaller one was tied at my ankle to fasten the shoe. They caused my dress to drag across the floor a little, but I would rather that happen then wear pumps and look like I was getting ready for a flood. With my outfit completed, all that was left was to fix my hair.

I took out my hair band and raked my fingers through the surrounding knots, too concerned with the time to be gentle. My eyes found a digital clock as I ran to the mirror. The numbers read 6:57 p.m..

There are lists of both acceptable and unforgivable actions that are etched into everyone's mind. Offering a set of guidelines as to what one can and shouldn't do, this list helps to filter our potential actions. It varies from person to person of course, but there are certain things that usually find their way to a universal side. Being late to a private dinner party of the President of the United States was easily on the inexcusable one—probably in the top ten. I had three minutes to make it—no exceptions.

I turned out the light and threw open the door. I was running, which was quite difficult since I had only a little idea as to where I was going. Desperate, I tried to remember the instructions that James had given me before he left. The quickest way to go would be to find the elevator I had taken on the second floor. Focused on saving as much time as possible, I ran across the stair landing and down the Central Hall to the room where the elevator was located. As if sensing that I was in a hurry, the doors opened without much delay and I practically lunged inside. I hit the first floor button, but my mind went blank as I tried to recall the remaining instructions.

As it turned out, I didn't need to remember. The elevator stopped at my floor and I found myself standing in a very small hallway. I found the dining room almost at once. The door was closed but the four security guards standing outside of it gave the President's location away.

"Am I late?" I asked one of the guards, rushing in his direction. He looked just like a guy I had seen in a spy movie two weeks before.

"No," he answered, "but you had better hurry."

Kate told me that I would be dining alone with the President and his wife, but those plans had apparently been changed. As I got closer, I heard laughter coming from what sounded like three or four different people. One carried a high-pitched tone, while the others were much deeper.

I reached the door, and the guard I had spoken to pulled it open for me, announcing my presence into his earpiece. I slowed down just before I became visible to the waiting diners, attempting to look confident in my timeliness.

As I entered, everyone stood up to shake my hand for what felt like the hundredth time that day. It was almost a reflex—something that came naturally to adults. I wondered if my arms would be sore in the morning.

I smiled, moving closer towards them. The President was there, along with Liz Deerun, the First Lady, but there were two other men, as well. I recognized one of them to be the Vice President, Kent Eagles. I didn't know the other man in the room, but trying to be polite, I shook his hand along with the others. When we had all greeted each other, I took the only empty seat at the table, which was between the First Lady and the man I still could not place.

"Oh, Cara, forgive me for not introducing you," President Deerun said, pointing towards the man at his left. "This is Aaron Owls, the President of Egypt. He arrived here earlier this week, and I thought it would be nice for him to join us for dinner before he departs for home. I hope you don't mind."

"Not at all, sir," I answered, doing my best to be polite. "It's a pleasure to meet you, President Owls. I'm sorry for not recognizing you initially. We were just studying you in school and you look a bit different in person than you did in the pictures I saw. Please accept my apologies, and know that it's a real honor for me to be able to meet you here."

"Thank you," the man replied curtly before turning to face the mantle. I did my best to hide my disappointment in the apparent coldness of the President Owl's personality.

"So, Cara, are you enjoying your stay here?" the First Lady asked, trying to make conversation. I wondered if it were possible *not* to enjoy a stay at the White House, but after looking at the expression on President Owls' face, I figured that it might be doable.

"It's amazing! I absolutely love everything about it. I haven't had a chance to thank you in person for sending me here, but I know that you must believe in President Deerun's bill too. I just want to thank you for helping to make this trip possible. It really is a fantastic opportunity, and I've already learned so much.

Hopefully, if everything goes as planned, we could be making a huge change in the way people see the underage members of not only our country, but maybe even our *world*."

"Well, that's great, *honey*," she said as if I were in kindergarten again. I tried not to show my irritation.

"I'm glad you had a good day, as well," the President cut in as if I had just arrived home from school with a painted picture of a bunny in my arms. I nodded politely, but inside, I couldn't hide my confusion. The President had never treated me like this. He had always seemed a bit superior, but he had spoken to me like an equal up until that point. Somewhat hurt, I pretended to be busy folding my napkin across my lap, hoping the action would somehow hide me from the rest of the dinner party. It didn't seem to work.

"Cara, did you realize that I've returned early from a very important trip?" asked Vice President Eagles. "I plan on staying for tonight only, because the President and I really needed to work out the details of his bill in person. I am resuming my travels tomorrow," he explained. My parents were impartial, but so far, I wasn't a big fan of the President's right-hand man.

"That's a really dedicated thing for you to do on behalf of the bill, sir," I somehow managed to sound polite. "I really appreciate all you're work and efforts. It must have been difficult to put your traveling aside to come back to the White House, and I'm sure that going along with this bill hasn't been an easy career decision to make. I just want you to know that I think what you're doing here is amazing. Today alone has been one of the most exciting of my entire life! It's—"

He didn't wait for me to finish, carrying on in the same condescending tone as before. "The President and I are sorry to say this, but tomorrow won't be as *fun* as today. You are going to give an open interview with the press in the morning which will carry on well into the afternoon, and from two thirty to six thirty you will have a political training course. If you don't know what that is, it is a class where you will learn political secrets, like how to speak properly in front of others, debate, etcetera. On normal days, when you don't have an interview, you will have to take a tutoring course from seven-thirty in the morning until two o'clock. However, since that time will be taken up by the interview tomorrow, you will have your tutoring at a special time. It will be shorter than usual and run from seven to eight at night."

"That sounds fantastic, actually!" I exclaimed, trying desperately to prove myself to the adults. The First Lady didn't react. Instead, she signaled that the meal should begin, raising her pointer finger in the direction of the door. Instantly, three waiters entered the room. Our drink orders were taken and served moments later. Just after my water had been poured, five new waiters in titanium white jackets approached the table. Each was carrying a bowl of steaming red soup, which they then placed in front of us. The woman who had brought the President and me our lunch was last to appear, balancing a tray of five identical dishes.

"Thanks," I muttered as she set one in front of me. It looked like a salad, but contained no lettuce—just a pile of vegetables mixed with dressing.

I was just about to dig in when I noticed that nobody had begun to eat yet. The four adults were staring down at the food as if it were a dying flower arrangement. They weren't avoiding it of course, just taking care not to acknowledge its presence directly. After what seemed like forever, President Deerun began to speak.

His question was not directed towards me.

"Aaron, is the economy finally beginning to stabilize in Cairo? For your sake, I do hope that you will be creating a plan to alleviate it. We don't want it to have the consequences of the 1967 trade and industry collapse, that's for sure!" This comment seemed to ignite a fire of conversation among the two Presidents, as well as Vice President Eagles and the First Lady. Having no idea as to what the four were talking about, I did my best to sit quietly until they were finished.

The President took a spoonful of soup and everyone else followed, continuing on with what had now become a tasteful economic argument. I sunk into my chair. Everyone was ignoring me anyway, so there was no use in hiding my bad posture. *Would this be my future in Washington, D.C.?* I wondered to myself, trying to tune out the laughter around me. *Why was everyone treating me like such a little kid? Hadn't I proved myself worthy of being with them? Even if I didn't, when would they give me a chance?* I continued to pity myself until I could no longer ignore the burning I felt behind my eyes. Knowing that I was on the verge of crying, I bent over to hide my face, pretending to have lost my napkin. The adults didn't seem to notice. I tried to hold back my tears, but it was becoming increasingly difficult as the dinner progressed.

Why would they be treating me like this?

I had wallowed through the entire soup course of the meal, and by now we were halfway through with our salads.

I could accept the behavior of the First Lady, Kent Eagles, and even Aaron Owls, but it was hard to believe that President Deerun was a part of it. Just yesterday, he had believed in me enough to send me to Washington!

How had this happened? It just didn't seem realistic that his mind could change so quickly…maybe it hadn't after all! My eyes widened.

"I found what I was looking for!" I blurted, sitting up. Despite what the adults may have thought, I wasn't talking about my dropped napkin.

It was all a test! The President and the rest of his dinner party must have wanted to put me in a tough situation to see how I would react. Of course people who opposed the Underage Rights Movement would want to treat me like a child! *They* still believed in me, but plenty of others wouldn't. There was no change of heart among them; only a curiosity to see how I would respond when faced with those who didn't support the President's bill! I was in Washington now—everyone had an opinion about me, and I would have to face even the most hostile ones.

I picked up my fork—*there was more to the test as well.* They had purposefully chosen to discuss topics that were unfamiliar to me, wanting to see if I would find a way to join in.

Since the dinner party was nothing more than a controlled simulation of political opposition, President Owls was obviously in on it too. The adults must have wanted to know how I acted around unfamiliar people, and if I would be able to convince them that there is more to wisdom than age.

If it is all a trick, 'President Owls' must not be who he says he is. Would that mean that he works for President Deerun? But who could he be—?

The answer came to me before I could finish my thought. President Owls was no President at all—he was my political trainer! That would explain why I didn't recognize him from his picture; he was a fake!

They may think that I'm failing their test, but not for long! I had been sitting idly as I watched them continually lower my grade, but this was my chance—I still had an opportunity to prove myself to them!

Ending the existing conversation at the table, I said the first thing that popped into my mind.

"So sorry to interrupt, but I was just wondering if you were enjoying *your* stay at the White House, *President Owls?*

"Yes," he answered, not bothering to look at me. Assuming that I would soon give up on talking to him, he began to take another bite of his salad. I stopped him before he could swallow.

"So, are you here on official business, or just visiting?" I asked again, making sure to keep in direct eye contact with him.

"Both." His voice was cool but his attempts to avoid my gaze had now become obvious.

"And what would that be?" By this point, my smile was practically teeming with suspicion. When he didn't answer, I simply fed more to the question. I was playing with the idea of the test, dancing along the borderline between acting obvious, and letting him know I had stolen the answer key. He couldn't read me, and it was making him sweat. "I mean you *could* be here to, I don't know, let's say, discuss some trading issues. But, *maybe* you're here for something else." I paused. "*Political training*, maybe?"

The imposter looked up to see if what I had said was just ironic for the situation, or if the exam was over. His eye caught mine for perhaps the first time all evening, and within an instant, he knew that I had seen behind his disguise. He looked towards the President, silently asking him if he should offer an explanation for his fake identity. I watched him break into a smile, encouraging the man to go on.

"*Alright, already!*" he flung his napkin onto the table in defeat. "I am your political trainer!" I nodded as if I had known the truth all night. "I must apologize for all that we put you through this evening, Cara—you should know that this was all my idea. I just needed to test your limits before allowing the public and the media to speak with you tomorrow. Through this little experiment, I get to see how you react in a situation where you are treated like someone undeserving of political power and not given a fair chance to prove or explain yourself. I am sorry to say that tonight is not the last time you will be faced with this situation. It will happen again—for real next time, as it does with the figurehead behind every other bill. I also wanted to see how you interact and involve yourself on subjects you aren't so clear on, like that economic business the four of us were chatting about."

I blushed, realizing that although I had seen through the man's scheme, the rest of the evening hadn't been handled quite as professionally.

"Not to worry though," he quickly added. "You may not have done well on the test, Cara, but I'm pleased with your results. You're smart—quick to observe, wise to think your actions through, and determined to resolve the problems you are faced with. It's like I always say—I can teach you politics and facts. I can give you directions, or offer you advice, but I cannot teach cleverness. For that, I am glad you have come with the skills you did. I think it's safe to say that you have officially earned your spot at the White House."

I was more than willing to accept this news along with the adults' apologies. The beginning of the evening was behind us, but one question still lingered in my mind.

"Sir," I turned towards my new political trainer, "if you aren't really President Aaron Owls, what *is* your name?"

"How rude of me not to say earlier!" he exclaimed. "I may not be President Aaron Owls, but quite similar. My name is Arthur Owls." I shook Arthur Owls' hand for the second time that night.

"Well," the First Lady announced, lifting her glass. "Now that everything has been sorted out, I think it's time we all begin to enjoy ourselves!" She nodded to a blonde waitress in the corner of the room. The woman gave the same nod back, disappearing behind the main entrance and down towards the kitchen. A moment later, four other girls followed her back into the room, each carrying a small plate of what looked like chicken placed over dark colored pasta. The blonde woman reached us first, balancing a china tea set in her arms.

"Enjoy your entrées," she smiled, setting it down carefully at the center of the table.

After being at the White House for only a few hours, I had already learned a major rule—the President is always first. It wasn't written or spoken of, but understood all the same. When it's your birthday, you get the first slice of cake. The same rule applies when you're the leader of the free world, but its privileges are much more extensive. So, after the President took his first bite, I helped myself to a cup of tea, and our third course began.

The conversation carried on unbroken for the next hour, long after our plates had been cleared away. Mr. Eagles told jokes, and Mr. Owls even taught me a little bit about politics! Plus, President Deerun was able to give me more details about the interview I would give the following morning. He thought that allowing America to get to know me better would be great for his bill's publicity. I wouldn't need any training because the interview would be mostly basic opinionated and personal questions, nothing that anyone could really research or prepare for. Most of the meal however, was spent on the subject of the Underage Rights Movement—which we decided to nickname the U.R.M. for short.

I found myself wishing that the night would never end just seconds before Mr. Owl's brought it to a close.

"I am so sorry," he apologized, beginning to stand up, "but I really must go. I need to prepare for Cara's lesson tomorrow, if that's alright." President Deerun excused him without objection.

"We should all really be going," added the First Lady. Everyone but me seemed to think that this was best, slowly rising to their feet. "Tomorrow is going to be a big day *for all of us.*"

After thanking the President and his wife for their dinner invitation, we headed out the door to go our separate ways. Not knowing any other way to get back to my floor, I walked back towards the elevator outside the Family Dining Room. Although it was dark outside, the White House itself was very well lit, and I found my way back to my bedroom with no trouble at all. Finally alone, I took a deep breath. It had been an amazing, but *very long* day. The morning seemed like a distant memory to me now, like something that had taken place weeks ago. It was hard to believe that I had not yet been away from home for 24 hours.

Thinking about the week's worth of events that had been squeezed into a day helped me to become conscious of how tired I was. As if a plug had been pulled, the electricity in my veins disappeared, and my energy drained away with it. Instead of blood, anesthesia returned in its place.

I needed to sit down. Yawning, I hobbled over to my bed and fell towards the comforter. The temptation to fall asleep right then and there was almost overwhelming, but I couldn't afford to lose another dress that way. Instead, I forced myself upright, and tried to pry off my shoes. I managed to unfasten their buckles with a wearisome amount of effort and slid them beside my bed, in line with the others. Once I felt up to it, I dragged myself into the bathroom and got out an elastic band, pulling my hair back into a loose bun. I was thrilled to wear it up and out of my face again, but even happier when I could take off my dress, exchanging it for a pair of pajamas and worn moccasin slippers. To the side of my armoire, I found the laundry basket Kate had told me about earlier. I tossed my outfit from the airplane and the green dress inside, also adding my pink dress to the pile in the hopes that somebody might be able to get the wrinkles out.

The weight of my eyelids was becoming almost too much for me to handle. Groggy, I sifted through the contents of my suitcase until I found the stationary I had brought. I lifted a piece onto the writing desk next to my dresser, and then sorted through the rest of my belongings until I found a pen, an envelope, and a stamp. I placed these at the desk as well, pulling over a nearby chair before taking a seat at their side. I had sworn to write my family every day I was in Washington, and didn't want to disappoint them. I had also promised my mom that I would record each day of my trip in a journal for myself, but figured she wouldn't mind if I opted to get some sleep instead. Not wanting to fall behind, I would catch up the following day by completing two entries—both the one I would normally owe plus the one I missed.

I yawned again. By this point I could barely see straight, and so it was probably best not to get ahead of myself. Switching focus to the task at hand, I grabbed for the pen and began my letter.

Dear Mom, Dad, and Nadia,
    Hi, it's me, Cara. Washington is amazing. I had a lot of fun today. The plane ride was good, and I got to watch the President's press conference speech. I explored the White House, went bowling, and was even invited to a Presidential dinner party! Extremely tired. More tomorrow—I promise. Tell Sandy (and anyone else you feel necessary) that I say hi.
    Love You,
    Cara
    P.S. Big interview tomorrow. Check TV listings!
    P.S.S. Sorry about the letter. I'll give you more info tomorrow. Really, really tired.
    P.S.S.S. Ms. Muleson probably has a copy of my day-to-day schedules, and I'm sure she'd be more than happy to e-mail them to you if you ask.

Once I was finished, I held the paper up to my eyes and looked it over, only half-satisfied with what I saw but not particularly caring enough to make any changes. I put a stamp onto the blank envelope and then addressed it to my house, sticking my letter inside before licking it closed. As Ms. Muleson had suggested, I set the note onto my bedside table so that it could be mailed the next day. With my work done, I collapsed back into the bed, instantly being swallowed up by the warmth of the covers. I was asleep before I remembered to turn off the lights.

chapter nineteen

The next morning, I awoke to a pleasant voice.

"Cara....Cara..." The sound could barely penetrate through my dreams, and was muted by my unconscious mind. *I was imagining it.* Ignoring the voice, I continued to sleep.

"Cara....Cara...," it continued, a bit louder. This time, it woke me. I forced my eyes to open, just enough so that they could filter in the light. Nobody was there. Relieved, I turned onto my side,

I almost jumped out of my skin when I saw a woman standing hunched over my bed.

"Oh good, you're awake." Her voice sounded sweet and she appeared not to have noticed my fear upon seeing her. I recognized her vaguely as the blonde waitress from last night's dinner, which lessened my original shock, but still didn't help me understand what she was doing in my room.

"Huh?" I grunted in return, managing the most complete response I could for the moment.

"Everything's fine, Miss Cara," she laughed, stepping back to pick up a large silver platter from a cart I figured she had rolled into the room. "I received a special order from the President to serve you breakfast in here today. This is a real special treat you know, especially since you're going to be eating over the fanciest bed in Washington, D.C. No pressure, but try not to spill. All I heard was that he felt especially bad for putting you through Mr. Owl's test yesterday and wanted to make it up to you. I suppose that this is both an apology and his repayment."

Slowly, I pushed myself upright. He was definitely forgiven. Once I was sitting up, the woman handed me the tray in her arms and lifted the silver cover that was placed over the plate. I looked over its contents as I adjusted it in my lap. There was a large bowl of fruit piled high with berries, banana slices, pieces of kiwi, and pear wedges. They were drizzled in a sweet sauce that smelled like a mix between mango and milk chocolate, and lightly sprinkled with powdered sugar. A large plate of scrambled eggs sat on the side of the platter, along with slices of toast and jam, half of a bagel, and a tall glass brimming with orange juice. A canvas napkin was wrapped around my silverware in the corner of the tray.

Not willing to risk dropping it, I set the juice aside next to the telephone on the bedside table. I felt my mouth begin to water—despite my three course dinner the night before, I somehow still managed to be hungry.

"I hate to rush you, Cara," the blonde woman smiled as she began to roll her cart away from my bed, "but you're going to have to eat quickly today. I hear you have an interview coming up, and you must be adequately prepared for it. This will be the first time the press has heard from you in person. They don't quite know who you are right now, and so I suppose they'll be eager to get any information they can. You're a big news story, Cara Greybird. I'm pretty into politics myself, but I would bet that by the time this is over, there won't be a soul in the United States that doesn't know your name!" Humbled, my eyes shifted towards my lap.

Her face was still visible as I looked down, reflected onto my silver tray. At first glance, she appeared to be deep in thought, but the look in her eyes didn't suggest that her mind was present. They seemed far away—as if she were searching for something, her lips pursed in a lopsided smile.

It took me a moment to decipher her emotion. She was *hopeful*. She couldn't believe that the U.R.M. was taking place so soon, but she had hope – and she desperately wanted it to pass.

I didn't know what to say. The silence was stretching on, and I felt obligated to say something wise. My mind instantly searched for quotes, and things I had heard in the movies, but none of them seemed fitting for the moment. Above all, what I really wanted to do was thank her for believing in me, but I couldn't find my voice to speak.

After a moment, the woman snapped out of her trance. Quickly, she masked her feelings, speaking as if none of the thoughts racing through her mind had ever been conceived.

"Eat," she whispered in the same soothing voice as before. If I hadn't recognized the look in her eyes, I would have guessed she had been staring at a scratch she noticed on the floor. I gave the best understanding smile a person could possibly manage after they have been woken up in the morning, and the woman continued on.

"When you're finished, set your tray down on the bedside table. I've already taken your letter to be mailed and your laundry to be washed, so you don't have to worry about that. Then, you need to head down to the East Sitting Hall. It's directly outside the front door of your room—all you must do to get there is take an immediate turn to your left. I was told that a woman will be waiting there for you. Don't bother changing out of your pajamas to meet her. She's the stylist for the First Lady, and Mrs. Deerun thinks you'll really like her work. She's going to help you pick out something to wear, and then she's going to do your hair and makeup for the interview."

"Is this going to happen every day?" I asked her, even though she probably had no idea what the answer was.

"Only for public events, I suppose." She shrugged, wheeling her cart towards the door. "The press and the people are going to be all over this interview, so good luck! The phone extension number for the main kitchen is 37. Call if you need anything. My name is Sandra, by the way."

I ignored the coincidence.

Without giving me time to reply or thank her for breakfast, the woman was making her way into the hall, shutting the door behind her as she left.

Looking down into my lap, I realized that I had been left alone with a rather large plate of expensive looking food and silverware.

"Thank you!" I called loudly, hoping that the sound of my voice would somehow pass through the door and down the hallway to the blonde woman. There was no answer back, and so I began to eat.

Half a bagel, the crust from a piece of toast, a bite of eggs, and a fruit cup later, I was finished with my breakfast. My plate of food was almost empty, but I scattered some of the eggs around on the tray to make it look like I hadn't been too full to indulge in them.

Stuffed, I wiped the corners of my mouth with my napkin one last time, and set the remainder of my breakfast in the spot where I had been instructed to leave it.

I had eaten pretty quickly but was still in a hurry, slipping a bathrobe over my pajamas and hurrying out the door in search of my stylist.

I found her. Like Ray, let's just say that she wasn't very hard to spot. In fact, it would be pretty difficult to miss her. For starters, she was wearing a purple trench coat so long in the back that it dragged wedding-train style across the floor for several feet. On the off-chance that this didn't catch your eye, there was more that gave her away as not your average White House guest.

Around her neck, she wore a thick golden chain with a string of plastic looking jewels dangling down from its center. It reminded me of something Nadia might like if she was going to be a princess for Halloween. On her wrists were a few dozen mismatched bracelets. Some were gold, others were silver, and a few were painted with bright colors and patterns. However different they looked, each one still managed to give off an annoyingly loud jingling sound each time she moved her wrists. Her nails were painted with a deep red polish and each one extended about an inch past her fingertips.

The woman herself stood out to me, as well. Aside from her broad shoulders and solid build, she had to be at least six feet tall—and that was *without* her heels. You could tell that her hair had originally been brown like mine, but she had covered it up with a yellow dye that reminded me somewhat of a goldfinch. Despite all her oddities, the strange thing was that she was actually sort of pretty.

"Hello, you must be my stylist. I'm Car—."

"Cara! I must say I am delighted to meet you!" the woman bellowed through a fake-sounding British accent.

"The pleasure is all mine," I replied, navigating my fingertips in-between the woman's nails to shake her hand.

"Well, I'm sorry we can't chat, but we really must get you ready. Why don't we head into your room and see what we have to work with for this interview?" I was about to agree, but the woman had already decided the answer for herself. It didn't take a whole lot of effort for her to push past me, dragging a large black suitcase behind her as she went. Before I could object, she had already made herself comfortable on the sofa inside my bedroom; her luggage set right beside her.

I could hardly think of what to do. I suppose she had been working with White House personal for so long that she assumed *I* knew what was coming next. Not knowing where to go, I stood in my doorway for a moment, waiting for the woman to acknowledge me, or provide further instruction. It didn't take long.

"Cara!" she patted the couch cushion next to her. "Come on, let's get to work!"

What does she mean by work? I wondered, trying to hide my hesitation as I took my seat.

I had no time to ask.

Almost at once, the woman began to empty the contents of her suitcase onto my bedroom floor. I was surprised at how much she had fit in there. Most of the suitcase was occupied by clothing, all covered in long fabric bags to keep them safe. The rest of the space was taken up by a makeup carrier that could have easily doubled for a beach bag. I began to have second thoughts about letting her do my makeup for my first public appearance.

"Ma'am?" I said quietly as she began to arrange the items in rows along my floor. "I'm not sure I caught your name."

"Why, I am the great *Genevieve!*" she cried with a smile. This time though, she had spoken with what appeared to be an attempt at a French accent.

"Oh, yes that's right!" I said, pretending to recognize her name. "Well it's nice to meet you…again." Genevieve smiled.

"En your ewn wourds, Cara, ze pleasure is all mine," she answered, her French accent having become noticeably thicker within the last ten seconds. "And now," she continued, "We muzt get down to business. Your hair iz a mess, by ze way." I shot her an insulted look that was anything but discreet, but she seemed not to notice. Or maybe she just didn't care.

Instead she studied me—eyes wide, and nails tapping on the top of her suitcase as if she were deep in thought.

"Blue is your color," she said after awhile, holding up a dress wrapped in a clear plastic covering. "No, maybe pink," she argued with herself, picking up another dress that was a bit shorter than the last and holding it up next to my body. "It'd better be blue," she decided, tossing the first dress into my hands. "Now gew into ze bathroom and try eet on." Not daring to argue, I did as I was told.

The top half of the dress was simple, with a crew neck, narrow sleeves, and satin that clung tight against my skin. A bow was stitched on towards my hip with a silvery rhinestone fastened at its center where the knot should have been, cut in such a way that it looked almost diamond-like. After the bow, the dress's fabric became thicker and began to move away from my body. A ruffled layer of crinoline was sewn in underneath the skirt to give it more volume, stopping just an inch or so above my knee. I zipped up the back. It fit perfectly, and I was surprised that my mom had guessed my sizes so well. Hoping she would like it, I headed back to the couch to show Genevieve.

"Egzellent!" She clapped her hands, speaking through a thick accent I didn't recognize. "Ez very formal, but modern too, no? To me, et louks pervect for a virst interview. I ave just the shoez you need for it, too." She pointed towards the foot of my bed where an assortment of silvery flats were laid out. My favorites were a pair of metallic looking ballet slippers. Besides the color, they looked almost identical to the ones I had worn on the plane ride to Washington—the only other difference being that they lacked a bow on their tips.

"How about these?" I asked, setting them in front of me. They slid onto my feet with little strain.

"Good Choize." Genevieve nodded at my selection and then beckoned me over to my desk chair so she could do my hair and makeup.

Even now, it would be too painful for me to explain what went on during that portion of my morning.

I *can* tell you that the process involved a whole lot of brushing, straightening, curling, hairspray, cutting, clipping, glitter, painting, and on my part, *a whole lot of wincing*. My less-than-admirable level of pain tolerance earned me a lot of 'Ztand still Cara's!' as well.

When Genevieve had finally finished, she placed my hand into the strong grip of her own, and led me over to my bathroom mirror so that I could get one final look at myself.

All of my previous pain had almost been worth it. *Almost*. I looked very natural; my hair had been detangled and separated into loose, controlled waves. Genevieve's makeup job had a very strange effect on me as well. Something about my face had changed. I didn't look older, like I was trying to be admitted into a film I wasn't old enough to see. The thing was though, that I didn't look younger either, like a 17 year old kid trying to buy a child's movie ticket for the discount. I still looked like Cara, just a different version of her. I'm not sure how Genevieve did it, but slowly, I understood how she had come to work at the White House. She had made me look more mature, more understanding even. Something in my expression had softened and the angles in my face were suddenly less severe. I was someone you could trust and believe. Somebody that you can rely on. In just two days, I had become the girl from my dream. *Somebody important.*

"Wow." I stepped away from the mirror to examine my dress again. "Thank you so much, this is fantasti—"

"Yez, of courze, you like it. I am *ze* Genevieve, am I not?" Genevieve cut me off, somehow managing to come off both pompous and kind at the same time. I smiled, stepping up to the mirror again. It was strange, but I wasn't able to believe that the girl I saw in the mirror was me. I felt more like I was observing somebody else through a large window rather than looking at my own reflection.

"Carrra, stop admiring yourselv and get downstairs for your interview! I was told that the President will be meeting you in the Entrance Hall. He will be speaking to the press vith you, in case you need some help on you first interview. You vill be talking out on ze Vite Houze lawn, zo I vill be able to vatch you from ze vindows!"

"Great." Knowing that the President would be with me was the only thing that kept my voice steady. "Thanks so much Genevie—"

"Chop, chop!"

There were certain people in the White House I was constantly trying not to get on the bad side of. The Secret Service was one of them. Genevieve was another. She was exactly the type of person you don't want angry, and so after thanking her again and sneaking one last glance of myself in the mirror, I left my bedroom and headed down to the Entrance Hall on the first floor. I found it quickly, the Entrance Hall being the first room I saw inside the White House. Besides my own bedroom, it was probably my favorite space in the building, and one of the most elegant as well. The President was already waiting for me, surrounded by the usual security guards.

He spotted me within a moment and stood from his place at an expensive looking armchair. Together, we walked in the direction of the front door.

"Are you excited for your first interview, Cara?" the President asked, sounding stronger than I would have expected.

"Very," I answered in a tone that was more nervous than excited.

"Good. Before we go out there though, there are some things you need to know. The first one is to try and sound as confident as you can. If you sound unsure, or anxious, the people won't listen to your message. You have to have faith in yourself before anyone else will even consider believing in you.

"Secondly, if you don't know the answer to a question, *do not* make one up. If you get confused, give me some sort of signal, like moving your hands behind your back. If you do that, I'll come in and give my input on the question, answering it myself. If they still ask for your opinion, repeat my response, rephrasing it to make it your own. Those two things shouldn't be much trouble.

"Another thought to keep in mind is that you do not have to answer every question you're asked. If you feel that a question makes you uncomfortable, politely reply that you will not provide a comment on that issue—there's no reason to tell them why. After a couple of seconds, somebody else will pitch a different question which you may answer if you like. I must ask you to try not to skip *too* many of them or the press may see you as uninformed or vague.

"The fourth piece of advice I have to give you is that you must think through everything you say—and Cara, I can't stress that enough. Especially at this stage, it's very important for the bill that you keep the meanings of your words as obvious as possible. You are new to the media, and so people are looking to get information on you—as much as they can. Try to say things that are very up-front and clear. If you don't, they could be misinterpreted and everyone might think that you said something you really didn't mean. Some reporters are going to try to twist your words, but you can't give them the opportunity." He straightened his tie. "Don't worry about that though. If for some reason I ever need you to drop a subject, I'll interrupt you and begin speaking, signaling you to wait until the next question before you talk again. Do you have all that?"

I swallowed hard and nodded. My face felt hot and I realized that I wasn't just anxious for the interview…I was *scared*. I closed my eyes in a desperate attempt to calm myself, hoping that it might make the feelings go away. Instead, new fears began to materialize from the darkness, closing in on me. *What if I didn't know the answers to any of the questions they asked me? What if the press thinks I'm just a big political joke?* The President saw me worrying, and began to speak again. This time, his tone was more soothing than rushed.

"Don't worry about it. I always get nervous before a big public appearance, too, but after the first couple of questions you'll start getting the hang of it. And besides, I bet you that you'll understand every bit of what they say to you. This really isn't a tough interview or a debate—they'll probably just be asking for some basic information. They're going to want to know where you go to school, your favorite subject, and the names of your parents and sister. They'll probably want to hear your thoughts on the U.R.M. Bill too. I'm sorry if I scared you

before, but you should always be prepared just in case the press has a couple
tricks up their sleeves, which they often do."

I smiled at the President and the color slowly returned to my face. Sure, my
stomach still felt like it was going to explode, but I concentrated on hiding my
panic. The President wanted this bill passed more than anything, and he had
chosen me to support it, even though I had no previous political experience.
He picked me to be an example, and I couldn't let him down. I *wouldn't* let him
down.

The President looked into my eyes, and it took every ounce of willpower
I had to smile back at him. "I'm glad you feel better. There really is nothing
to worry about. The interview will be held right on the White House Lawn,
and the press has already gathered out there. I never like to keep them waiting
long. It's a little trick I've learned—if I can help it, I like to make most of my
announcements in the morning. The longer the reporters and journalists are
given to make their deadlines, the happier they'll be and the more they'll like
you. Are you ready?"

"What are we waiting for? Let's go!" As much as the sentence pained my
nervous insides, I knew I couldn't let the President in on my worries. I locked
my jaw into a grin and put on a happy face. He sighed, and I could just imagine
him thinking, '*thank goodness I picked the right kid*'.

A least one of us was convinced.

"Well, if you're sure you're ready then…"

Two guards swung open the front doors to the White House. Looking
like a true American politician, I stepped outside, the President right behind
me. Before I knew it, we were surrounded by reporters, photographers, and
a security team who didn't appear quite as in control as I would have hoped.
Everything was bright, and lively and filled with light and purely terrifying. My
mind went blank except for the idea that the President was right—*nothing could
have prepared me for my first interview*. I found myself unable to read deeper
into what I saw, or comprehend it to any other degree than what brilliancy
flashed past my captivated eyes. Everything in the past was gone, and the future
was unknown.

In just one moment, everything in my life had become backwards. I was living in a present that I couldn't understand. I was in a state of pure euphoria, but in the same way, more afraid than I had ever been. The warmth of the moment had left me frozen, my emotions torn between *over* and *empowerment*, each tugging at me from its own faraway pole. The combinations of opposites left me dizzy, and my heart no longer seemed to beat, but flutter—refusing to give out so that it might enjoy the scene a little longer.

Keeping the illusion of confidence with me in every step, I strode down the front steps of the White House and onto the driveway. It was quite difficult to see because of all the flashbulbs and cameras, but I did my best to pretend that they didn't affect me. My eyes were watering, burning from the flashing light, and I struggled to keep them opened. The President had fooled me into thinking I was ready for this moment, and I had tricked him into believing I could handle it. Now, all we had to do was persuade the rest of the world that we had no doubts.

I slowed down as I neared the bottom of the stairs, waiting for the President to catch up with me. He made it to my side just as the flashing from the cameras had become temporarily blinding. I began to blink, feeling the blood rushing behind my eyelids as I tried to erase the lights from my vision. It was no use—all I could see was the white blur of the flashbulbs, layering themselves over my eyes like snowflakes piling onto a rooftop.

It was sightlessly that I led the President to the head of the large mob of people gathered on the lawn. I stopped before I reached the sounds of the crowd, taking care to keep a considerable amount of distance between the press and myself. They had been invited here, but something in the back of my mind told me that behind the lure of their smiles and shouting voices was something quite dangerous.

Everything began all at once. At the beginning, my interview was anything but organized. While the photographers snapped away with their cameras, numerous men and women yelled their questions to me, each voice louder than the last. President Deerun had warned me that this might happen, and so I simply waited for a question I wanted to answer. It concerned the U.R.M Bill, and I talked for nearly five minutes straight on it. Eyesight returning gradually, I glanced back at the President numerous times as I spoke to make sure I was representing him well. Each time I found his blurry outline nodding me on, encouraging me to continue.

After my first response, things seemed to settle down. I was asked a little about politics, but most of the questions were related to simple opinionated matters. I answered each one of the reporters honestly, looking back for the President's response after every one. He smiled a lot.

I had assumed that there would be at least one unfriendly question, and wasn't at all surprised when they came around. Remembering from the President's dinner experiment that I shouldn't feel hurt, I took extra care with their answers. I tried to be as clear as possible, arguing without getting angry and quickly explaining my point of view before moving on. The President never needed to take over a question for me, but did choose to answer some of them on his own—each of them having something to do with budgeting issues or finer government statistics. As the interview went on, the things I was asked became increasingly lighter. Questions about my future goals, role models, hobbies, family and even a few hypothetical situations were all given and covered.

It was only when the President began to thank the press for coming and make some final concluding points that I realized that I was no longer nervous. By pretending to enjoy myself, I had forgotten to think about how afraid I really was. The fear I was trying to hide had evolved into something much better—I was actually having fun!

I heard the voices of the crowd raise to a roar in the hopes for more information, and turned to see that President Deerun had already begun to walk inside. I took a step back, waving and thanking the crowd before following him back up to the White House. The screaming behind me was relentless, and it seemed to grow louder as we moved away from it instead of the other way around. The front doors opened quickly, and I slipped through them back into the Entrance Hall. Even inside, the sounds of the mob were no softer, pleading for just one more response. As if it were instinct, the President moved towards a corner of the room where he couldn't be seen from the windows.

"Well done, Cara!" He praised me as soon as I caught up with him. "Now, that wasn't so bad, was it?"

"Not at all." It was strange to think that I was being honest. "I thought it was fun!"

"You should know that the people responded very well to you, Cara. There were a few who were obviously very against the bill, too, but all in all, most of them really liked you. I consider it a job well done! Things went much more smoothly than I had expected, and you were better up there than I hoped you would be."

"Thank you!" I exclaimed, proud to have made a positive first impression on a good chunk of the world. As I began to think about all the people who would be hearing my name on television and reading it in the paper, I couldn't help but wonder how I had forgotten to be nervous. Listening to my heart still hammering away in my ear, I decided that this might not have been altogether true.

Before I had time to congratulate the President on a job well done, a man in a black suit ran in from the adjoining hall and pulled him aside. They argued quietly with one another for awhile, until having reached some sort of conclusion, the President moved back towards the door.

"I'm so sorry, Cara," he said, preparing himself to step outside again. "The crowd is simply demanding more information. We don't want them to wrongly interpret you or any of your concepts, so I must go back out. The most important thing is to show we have nothing to hide—it won't take long, I'm sure." He smiled. "Try to think of it like an encore. Besides, I suppose it's a good thing that they're so interested in you. That must mean that you did a good job with them."

"Should I come back outside with you?" I asked him as headed over to the door.

"Not necessarily. You can't miss your tutoring, or your political training course either. It's important that we keep you up with your schoolwork, and we need you to be prepared for your big debate. It's only two weeks away, you know. I think it would be better if I go out to speak with the press and you go to your classes. Somebody has already paged James to come and lead you to your first lesson, so don't worry about getting lost. Since there wasn't a real classroom available for you, Mr. Owls has agreed to let you use his old office."

"Thank you, sir! Good luck!" I'm not sure exactly what I wished him good luck for, but he seemed to appreciate my gesture, nonetheless. Giving one last smile, he and a couple of his bodyguards disappeared out the door and into the screaming mass.

I listened to their cries amplify at the mere sight of him. It was like my presence was empty, ghostlike. No matter who was watching me, their hearts would always lie with the President. Their attention would always lie with the President. Could I ever unite a crowd as he could? I listened to the voices of the mob rise as if in unison, shouting a single word over and over. Could I ever get a country to focus like that?

It only took me a moment to realize the answer.

When the President walked outside, it was my name they screamed.

. . . .

The rest of the day was a daze to me in comparison to the interview. Sunglasses came and led me to my political training course. Mr. Owls was pretty strict, but his lessons had some interesting points. During his class we talked about presenting ideas and sounding serious, but also full of emotion. We even did a little practice debating, and I was told that I would prepare my own argument on a surprise subject the following day, just to see how well I had grasped his lesson. I hadn't been watching the clock, and was surprised when class was over. It was about six thirty at the time, and instead of stopping by the kitchen for dinner as Mr. Owls had suggested, I ran upstairs to my bedroom to collect the school textbooks and supplies I had brought with me from home. It turned out that I didn't need them all that much, because by the time I had finally lugged them all down to the White House 'classroom,' a new stack of them awaited me, along with a middle-aged woman named Mrs. Eelini.

This woman, who later introduced herself to be my tutor, had short graying hair and what I would soon find to be a nonexistent personality. Although class had been shortened to only an hour for that day, I found my eyes drifting towards the clock more often than not as she tested me on reading proficiency. Sensing my boredom as I droned on through an excerpt of War and Peace, I was promised that we would have the time to do more the following day. This didn't make me feel much better, especially after she presented me a list of homework that held an unsettling resemblance to the novel I had just read from. By the time class was over, I was exhausted and ready for bed, but I knew that my night was still far from finished.

Carrying twice the amount of books I had come with, I said goodbye to my teacher and began to shuffle out into the hallway. I was using my carry-on bag from the airplane as a backpack and could only hope that the seams would hold out, surviving long enough to make the trip home

Before I knew where my feet were taking me, I was headed downstairs to get something to eat—I had forgotten to have lunch that afternoon and my stomach wasn't letting me forget it. Since I wasn't meeting anyone for dinner, I figured I should probably get my food from the kitchen, rather than one of the dining rooms. Kate had shown me where to find its main entrance on the ground floor, and although it was my first time walking there alone, I hardly had any trouble finding my way.

The White House was crowded with workers, especially for so late at night. Many of them smiled at me as I passed, but others just shot me looks of confusion. For the first time all night, I became conscious of the fact that I was still wearing my dress from the interview. Feeling a little silly that I had forgotten to change, I set my backpack down in the corner of the Center Hall and headed into the kitchen. To my surprise, the cook had already prepared something for me...pizza! In all my life, I don't think I have ever been so happy to receive a microwave meal—it was the first time I would be able to eat something I recognized from home at the White House. After thanking the chef, I carried the pizza up to my bedroom on a paper plate, dragging my backpack along as well. Careful not to spill grease anywhere in the antique room, I set my food and books carefully at my writing desk. Every muscle in my body felt as if it had already given out, and I wasn't sure what had survived the day to keep me running. I finished up my homework while I ate dinner, yet again forgetting to take off my dress. When I was done, I grabbed a piece of paper from my suitcase and began to write another letter to my family.

Dear Mom, Dad, and Nadia,
　　Hi, it's Cara again. I got breakfast in bed today and new clothes for my interview. I did well so check the news. I'm having a good time, and am learning a lot. It's around midnight right now and I'm really tired because I had to wake up early this morning. Love you!
　　xoxo,
　　Cara
　　P.S. tomorrow I promise promise promise that I'll write something good. Really, I will. Yes, I know I said that yesterday.

When I was finished with my excuse for a letter, I jammed it into an envelope and quickly scribbled my home address down on top of it. I set a stamp in the corner and then laid it down on my bedside table so that it could be mailed. Heading into the bathroom, I then attempted to remove all of the makeup Genevieve had applied for me earlier that morning. It stuck like glue. One miniature bar of soap and about two hundred splashes of water later, I was only halfway done. By the time I had managed to scrape away about two thirds of it, my face had grown red and so I decided to leave the rest until morning. Quickly, I changed into pajamas and set my dress and shoes near the front door to my room, in case anybody wanted them back. I had been told by Mrs. Eelini that tutoring would begin at its normal time the next morning, 7:30 a.m., and that I wasn't to be late. She advised that I set my alarm for around six so that I would have time for breakfast, and although it would only allow me a few hours sleep, I did as I was told. It only occurred to me once I was safe in bed that I had forgotten to record the day's events in my journal again and that if I waited until the next day, I would have three entries to post. I however, was so tired that I could hardly care. I fell asleep with the lights on again.

chapter twenty

The next day wasn't much different from my previous one at the White House, except I didn't do an interview and I got more homework. The rest however, pretty much stayed the same (hard work, hurting shoes, microwave pizza for dinner, and yes, more work). James asked me if I wanted to play a round of bowling, but I had to turn him down. I was up until the middle of the night working with no breaks, as it was. My letters got shorter and shorter until finally, I just stopped writing them, and instead, left brief messages on my home answering machine, clarifying that I was fine and having 'fun'. I now owed my journal more entries than I could count. The inbox on my cell phone was full, but I never deleted or returned my missed calls. Nothing really changed until about a week later.

As usual, I woke up at 6:00 a.m. sharp. My eyes were burning the second I opened them, back aching before I rolled out of bed. Every ounce of energy in my body had been long drained away, but somehow, my will kept me going. Strong as a wall of concrete, it refused to consider me a prisoner of my own wish, forcing me to awaken and dress each morning. After managing to squeeze my schoolbooks inside my backpack, I dragged myself downstairs to the kitchen where I was expecting my usual freezer-burned waffle. Instead, I found President Deerun.

He insisted that we should eat breakfast together that morning since we had barely seen one another since the interview. I agreed; in the past couple of days, he had been busy working for the U.R.M Bill and it was rare to catch me looking up from my books. The only place we had seen each other lately was on the news.

Together, we headed up the kitchen stairs and towards the Family Dining Room. As if he had been sitting by the door waiting for us to arrive, a tall lanky chef whom I had never seen before entered the room with our breakfasts. In front of each of us, he placed a large bowl of some mushy oat cereal that looked utterly disgusting, a plate of fruit, and a small glass of orange juice. I couldn't help but miss the bowl of Froot Loops sitting in my closet at home as I choked down the meal.

Trying to appear cheerful, I asked the President how things with the U.R.M Bill were going. A spark managed to leak past his tired eyes as he began to explain. If it was to be, the President believed that the bill would be passed in a matter of months, weeks even. I tried to read the papers and follow up on the movement when I got a chance, but I always thought that it was better to get information straight from the source. The President also told me that among many others, most young people were really getting into the campaign for underage rights and couldn't wait to see the bill pass.

"Great!" I smiled, trying to carry on the conversation as long as possible. This was partly because I was totally interested and excited in what he had to say, and partly because I really didn't want to take another bite of the cereal. When breakfast was over, I thanked President Deerun and headed down to my lesson, homework in hand.

Tutoring was not exactly what you would call a great time. After forgetting to write the last paragraph of my science essay, I sat through the third consecutive 'Be Prepared' lecture since my arrival. When that was over, we reviewed the rest of my homework, and began to move on to some new material. I worked through my lunch period, and had almost finished a history report on the Civil War when Mr. Owls entered the room to begin his class. This was usually about the time of day when I regretted not eating lunch, but from the moment my teacher walked in, my mind was far from food. Somehow, I knew this day would be different. They had taught me to imagine the inconceivable in Washington, but I was still unready for the change that one day can bring.

Anyway, I was sitting in a large blue swivel chair closing up my schoolbooks when he arrived. He walked in with a smile on his face, which for him, was pretty rare. Instead of wearing his usual sport jacket, he was dressed in a full suit. It was all pretty out-of-the-ordinary, but he began to explain himself before I had time to ask any questions.

"Cara!" he cried, a grin still clinging to his face. "The time has finally come!"

"For what?" I asked him, curiosity beginning to build over my exhaustion.

"Well, do you remember when the President told you that at the end of your two weeks here at the White House, you would take part in a big political debate as sort of a way to prove your age group to the voters of America?"

"Yes, I remember but—"

"We must begin working on it! Time is running out."

"How could you say that, sir? I asked him, sitting up in my chair. "I've only been here for a week."

"A week and a half," he corrected me. "It is now the time to prepare. The debate will be international. People will be watching it on television and listening to it on the radio, not to mention the 3,000 people in the public audience where you will be debating. By the way, we have already arranged for your immediate family to be joining you at this event. We have set this up as any usual debate, and as is common for these sorts of things, you will be going up against an adult with a high reputation in our society. The both of you will have exactly from today until the day of the debate to work. The event is on Monday, which leaves you with three days to prepare including today—four, if you count the actual day of the debate. Because you both have such a short time until the big day, we have decided that you will not be required to take any more classes here, mine included."

I was too shocked to comment. Taking my pause as a cue, my teacher continued on. "Cara, the rules of the debate are as follows: you are to have one person to help you with this, and one person only. They may be the adult or child of your choosing. If this person is out-of-state, you have permission to bring them to the White House, where the President is allowing them to stay while helping you prepare. You will be accountable for any time lost if this person cannot come immediately. Besides that, you have unlimited nonliving resources. You will be given 1,000 dollars to spend on any aspect of the debate, but I must caution you to use it wisely. Are we clear on that?" He looked at me for a moment as if waiting for some sort of response. Slowly, one came.

"Mr. Owls, I don't mean to be rude, but what is the debate on? What am I going to argue about? Who am I going to argue with? I know we've practiced long and hard for this, but am I really ready?"

"Quite, Cara! There is no need to worry. I know that it feels like you don't have much time, but you can do it. We all have faith in you. Would you be here if we didn't? As for the topic of your debate, you will be speaking on a subject of the utmost importance. You see, every year, the government gets a certain amount of money which they divide amongst hundreds of different causes like homeless shelters, scientists trying to find the cure to different diseases, etcetera. I am sure you already know that about the government budget, but recently an issue has been brought up which questions the current distribution of its funds. Certain people argue that one of the places the government gives to—animal shelters— are not a just cause for our tax dollars to go towards. What do you think?"

"Well, I know that it should—" I was cut off yet again.

"Shhh! This is not for me to know. I will not be the one you are debating against, after all. All I can say is that you must research the subject thoroughly. Find out where you stand and know why. Be able to back up your opinions." He stopped speaking for a moment, as if he was deciding whether he should spoil the ending of a movie to me or not. After thinking it through, he opened his mouth again. "That is very important, Cara, what I just told you. *Know Why.* I have been informed that your opponent, who is to remain nameless for the time being, believes that the funding should be spent on a cause other than the shelters. If you agree with this opinion, you may pick any alternate cause that the money should go towards as well, assuming that it be very specific. Otherwise, you are to argue that the money should remain with the shelters. I would like to thank you for all of your hard work during our class, Cara, but I'm afraid that I can no longer be of any help to you. You need to do this on your own. When you decide what you want to spend your money on and who you want to help you, tell Ms. Muleson, and she will arrange for whatever or whoever you want to be brought to the White House. Good luck, Cara."

I could tell he had meant all that he said with profound sincerity, and for a moment, I was too overwhelmed to reply.

"Thank you," I finally managed. "You've been such a fantastic teacher. Really, I mean that. Without you, there would be no debate."

"See you on Monday." His smile was a faded version of what it had been before. I watched as he took a step towards the doorway, leaving the office that had become my temporary school place. "Class is dismissed." He turned into the hall, his voice clouded with mystery.

I was overwhelmed. *I had four days.* My future and the future of my country depended on me. I had worked hard to deserve this opportunity, but then why did I still feel like I was about to let everybody down? I had a lot of work to do.

. . . .

I have to admit that I was totally excited to begin my work on the debate. I brought a bowl of macaroni and cheese into my 'classroom', and spent the next few hours of my afternoon researching about animal shelters and how they run from the encyclopedia. When I had first heard about the debate topic, I knew instantly that I wanted the government funding to stay with the animal shelters. The only problem was that I had no idea what had caused me to think that way. When the topic was mentioned, something inside of me just made the decision—I was still unsure why.

Why should the animals get the money? I thought to myself, leaning back a little in my chair. There were so many other worthy causes in the world… why animal shelters? I had no clue as to what I should do or say. Looking for some sort of sign, I scanned the room for an idea. The carpet was a faded blue color and the walls were a pasty white. There wasn't much detail to the room except for the dark wooden desk where I sat in its center. I turned towards the doorway for inspiration. A few potted plants were set out at the corner table, but they didn't seem to spark any thoughts for me. The moldings at the top of the walls were worn-down to the extent that I couldn't make out any design they might have otherwise shown. A small window towards the top of the wall was only just large enough to let in light, much less provide me a look at the outside scenery. Papers were scattered all around me, along with a few manila folders whose contents had spilled out amongst the surrounding clutter long ago. The computer seemed to be the only new thing in the room. It sat in the middle of the desk, its screen blank.

Having no other ideas, I shrugged and pressed the power button to turn it on. Mr. Owls said that I could have as many non-living resources as I wanted, and so using the computer had to be alright. For hours, I searched for information on government funded animal shelters, reading as much as I could from online sites, textbooks, and magazines. When I found something I liked, I wrote it down on a bulleted list to support my side in the debate. Two more bowls of macaroni and a soda later, I hadn't made much progress. It was nearly eleven o' clock at night, and I only had about 30 bullet points. My brow furrowed as I read over what I had written. It was the same sort of face you make when you spill ketchup all over your new white blouse just before you get your yearbook picture taken.

My eyes crept their way towards the bottom of the page, expression doing little to improve. I frowned. It wasn't that the points on my list were bad, because they weren't. *They were boring.* The most important step in convincing a person of something you believe in is to get their attention, but as I read over the list a second time, I could feel my own eyelids beginning to droop. I definitely needed some help.

Frustrated, I sighed and clicked into another animal shelter webpage. *It was no use*—I quickly closed out of the site and shut down the computer. Standing up, I began to gather my materials from the table, placing them into one of the empty manila folders from the desk. My eyes began to blur as I put down the one page of results I had gathered from a day of research. Without warning, I began to panic.

It's alright, I thought as I tried to calm myself down. *You'll get more tomorrow, it'll be easy. You have three days left. You'll be done in no time.* I managed a small smile. Still, I couldn't shake my doubt.

You'll never win this unless you have the answers. They won't go easy on you just because you're a kid. One question you don't know the answer to, and you'll lose, just like that. I tried to shake the clammy feeling that was creeping its way into my chest, but I knew that everything I had just considered was true.

Then the tears came, leaking past my eyelids as I ran up the White House stairs and into my bedroom. They continued as I brushed my teeth and changed into pajamas. Even as I sat alone on my bed, clutching my debate folder tightly to my chest, they never failed to silently fall from my eyes and stain my cheeks with the salty streak of a trail they left behind. I sat there crying quietly until my eyes were red, and tired from blinking.

Feeling a little better but a lot weaker, I dragged myself over to the corner of my room and turned out the lights. The darkness came over me, and it seemed to have a soothing effect. For a moment I believed that I would be able to fall asleep. Instead, I stayed awake for hours, flat against my covers with my mind feeding me ghost story after ghost story in the form of a political debate.

If you don't know one answer, you'll lose for sure. If you don't know one answer, you'll lose for sure.

My mind repeated this sequence over and over, like a talking children's toy that can only say one phrase. Each time I thought about it, the idea settled into my brain a little more. This didn't necessarily make it less painful, however—it just deepened the wound.

That is what I thought about as I lay awake in bed, and finally, that is what I thought about as I fell into an uneasy sleep.

chapter twenty one

My eyes fluttered open, suddenly alert. I had just been awakened, but not by a noise or light. I glanced over at the alarm clock sitting at the corner of my bedside table. It was ten minutes past three in the morning, and there wasn't much going on outside my mind. Yet, within its boarders, something was becoming so blatantly clear that I had somehow forced myself to consciousness. Suddenly, I understood what was going on around me, and for a moment, everything made sense. I should have realized it from the very beginning. I myself couldn't believe I had forgotten. I shook the thoughts away. None of that mattered anymore. *I knew a solution.* There was a person who could make me think. Somebody who would help me win.

I was strangely refreshed as the new idea traveled about my body, sending a ripple of warmth up my spine. Fresh adrenaline began to flow through my veins, washing away all of my previous doubt.

I could feel the energy pulsing through my body now and I widened my eyes, waiting for them to adjust to the surrounding black. Once the shadows around my room had sharpened into the distant outlines of furniture, I sat upright against my headboard, reaching out for the telephone. My hand found its surface and I pulled my face forward, squinting as I tried to locate its buttons. After a long while of impatient staring, my eyes finally focused in on the numbers. Without wasting time, I punched in the digits to the Giraffing's home phone, hitting the wrong keys twice because my fingers were shaking. It was only after I had dialed correctly that I realized what I had done.

Hang up—it's three in the morning! A voice inside my head screamed.

I could no longer hear a dial tone. Someone picked up on the other line.

"Heeelloo…," moaned a low groggy voice, sounding like that of a hospital patient who had just come off of anesthesia. The pit of my stomach lurched forward when I realized it was Dr. Giraffing who had answered the phone. Thinking that he might be mad if he knew I was calling struck me silent. *Why hadn't I dialed her cell?* The quiet that followed felt like when someone pauses a movie at its climax…agonizing and suspenseful.

"Hello?" he repeated. "Who is this?" I could hear the cold anger building up in his tone. Not knowing quite what to do, I stuttered at the other end of the line, trying to find the right words (or any words at all for that matter) to say.

After a couple seconds, I finally thought to hang up. Not daring to speak, I slammed the phone down into its cradle.

Hope had turned me numb again, but I felt alive for the first time all week. My heart was racing, but the early hour prevented me from carrying out my plan any further. There was nothing to do but wait. I settled myself back onto my mattress, buried my face under its pillows, and with eyes wide opened, silently waited for morning to come.

Three hours of off-and-on dozing later, I rolled over in bed to the sound of my alarm, excited, although not entirely awake. The thought that I would need to be completely finished with my debate information in less than 72 hours time was enough to quickly bring me to my feet.

Leaving my pajama shirt on, I pulled on a pair of blue jeans, snatched the information I had gathered for my debate from the bedside table, and ran downstairs towards the kitchen. The President was at a meeting to promote U.R.M. that day, and so not caring one bit that I was still partially in my nightclothes, I walked into the kitchen's main entrance and grabbed a granola bar from the storeroom pantry. I was just about to think up an excuse for not doing my tutoring homework when I remembered that it had been cancelled and I was to work on my debate all day. I had nothing against Mrs. Eelini, but the thought that I wouldn't ever have to see her again wasn't really something to cry about. Smiling, I took a bite of my breakfast and steered myself back upstairs to the White House 'classroom'.

The door was opened and I let myself in, surprised to see Mr. Owls waiting for me inside.

Assuming I was late for something, I prepared myself to apologize.

"Cara!" he called my name before I could manage a word. "You're not late," he added, sensing my confusion. Mr. Owls usually had very little sympathy when it came to tardiness. "Sit down," he ordered, motioning to a smaller chair next to his desk. His expression looked solemn and a little uninviting, but not angry. I did as I was told, and took a seat next to my teacher. Soon after I had settled myself into the chair, I pulled out my list of bullets from my folder and smoothed it out on the desktop. Once it looked presentable, I casually explained to him that I had taken some notes the night before in order to prepare myself for the debate. As I did this however, he only seemed more displeased.

"Cara, I am not here to see your work. Remember, I can no longer help you."

"Oh, that's right. Sorry," my voice sounded shaky, like a child who had just been caught doing something mischievous.

"Don't worry about it. Listen, the real reason I came here was to ask you something. I know you have been working very hard on this debate, and I know the kind of stress you must be under to complete a task like this one, but I have to ask you one little question before you get back to work."

"Go ahead." I put my note sheet back into its folder.

"Well, I just happened to be talking to Ms. Muleson this morning, and she told me that you haven't come to her yet to tell her who you want to help you with this debate. Although I'm sure you've been thinking very hard about this, I hate to tell you, but you're getting close to crunch time here. I have to admit that I was a little concerned, and so I came down to ask you if you've decided yet."

"As a matter of fact, I have." I paused, hearing the finality in my tone. "The only thing is that she doesn't really live near the White House, or anywhere close to Washington, D.C., for that matter. In fact, she's more like an hour and a half plane ride away. She's my best friend from home, you see. Her name is Sandra Giraffing."

It felt a little weird to say Sandy's full name out loud, but for some odd reason, I felt as if it should be formally introduced to the White House.

"Anyway," I continued, "she knows me really well, and we have a lot of the same ideas. She's not afraid to speak her mind, and besides all that, she's really smart. Plus she's a fantastic writer, which could help me out a lot for the debate. I did a lot of thinking last night, and I know she's the best person for the job."

I took a deep breath, embarrassment that I was still in a pajama top growing with each second I waited for a response.

"That shouldn't be a problem," Mr. Owls answered after a moment of torturous silence. "I'll just need to make a few phone calls, and she should be here before noon. All you have to do is write down her name, address, and phone number. I can take care of the rest."

"Thanks, sir!" I felt as if my heart was climbing its way into my throat. I had to swallow hard to push it back down, and it landed with an unsettling thud on what felt like my stomach. I grabbed a pen and scribbled Sandy's contact information onto a piece of scrap paper. "This is really unbelievable! She's going to be thrilled when she finds out!"

"Oh, I don't need your thanks, Cara; it's really not a problem at all. I'm going to inform Kate of your choice, and she'll make all the necessary arrangements for your friend's arrival. You just get back to work. However, before I leave, I just want to make sure that this 'Sandra' girl really is the best for the job. I only want you bringing here if you believe she is best suited to help you win. I'm sorry to say, but if this is just about friendship, I'm going to need you to pick a new helper."

I shook my head. "No! I wouldn't do that to any of you at the White House! I realize that this debate is serious, and I *really* think that Sandy is the only one who can help me win." I wasn't lying. As of three o'clock that morning, she was my only hope.

Mr. Owls understood. "Good, I'm glad to hear that. Best of luck to you

Cara." He stood up from his desk and walked out of the room, heading in the direction of Ms. Muleson's office.

Everything ran smoothly as planned, and within 45 minutes, my best friend was on her way to Washington, D.C.! Ms. Muleson dialed the extension for my office phone, calling to share the news and fill me in on the details. As it turned out, she had quickly spoken with Sandy's parents and then faxed them all of the papers that they would need to sign. They returned them within a few minutes, the necessary signatures included. After everything had been made official, Kate sent a plane ticket over to their house as well. Sandy was told to leave as soon as she could, and that the White House would pay for her parents to mail over all of her clothes after she had gone in order to save time. It was explained that somebody from the airport would be helping Sandy find her way, like Lucille had done for me. Once her flight landed, Ray would be picking her up from the airport and bringing her directly over to the White House.

It seemed that Sandy's parents were ecstatic when they got the call from the White House, and so was Cornelia V., whom Ms. Muleson had described as 'a tad on the eccentric side'. It was nearly an hour later before I got to know how Sandy herself felt about the whole ordeal.

I had just gone upstairs to change out of my pajama top in preparation for Sandy's arrival when I heard my cell phone ringing from my backpack. There had been many messages left on it since I had come to Washington, most of which I purposely didn't answer. This time, curiosity got the best of me and I decided to see who was calling. The bag was a mess because I had used it for tutoring. It was only after a little bit of searching that I flipped open the phone and began to speak.

"Hello?" I said into the receiver, wondering if the person on the other end of the line had hung up before I had a chance to answer the call.

"Cara?"

"Yes, this is Cara."

"Hi, it's Sandy."

Sandy. The one person I wanted to talk to! I gave myself a small pat on the back for answering the call.

"Sandy! Look, I've never really thanked you for all you've done for me. You're basically the reason why I made it this far. And I just *had* to have an ego, and I ignored you. And now I understand why you were mad at me. I would have been mad at me too if I were you. Hey, if I were you, I would probably never talk to me again. After you did so much for me, I went off to the White House without a single thanks or goodbye! And the worst part is I never called, or wrote. Even sending an e-mail would have been a halfway-decent thing to do, but of course I never did that either. What I'm trying to say is that I realize I was wrong, and you still might be mad, but this is my way of making everything up to you. You're the only person who can help me win this debate, and I want you to be here with me."

The speech tumbled out of my mouth like an avalanche of words that had been waiting to fall for a long time. Sandy didn't reply, so I continued to ramble, trying to win back my best friend. "Sandy, I really need you. I can't handle everything by myself, and I know that you'll be able to do it. Together we can win this debate. I can't do it alone. Please forgive me." I could envision Sandy on the other line, searching for exactly the right words to say. It was only when she finally found them that she spoke. Her patience was an admirable quality, but one that I clearly didn't possess.

"Cara…I'm the farthest thing *from* being mad at you. I *forgive* you! I know you feel bad about leaving me behind—I'm here to help."

I felt whole again for the first time in the past two weeks. Sandy had forgiven me, and put my neglect behind her. Somehow, everything might work out after all. I smiled to myself—she even seemed excited to be coming! I opened my mouth to speak, but a sound from the other line entered my ears first.

"Flight 112 to Washington, D.C., your plane is now boarding. May we have all families with young children, persons requiring assistance or the use of a wheelchair, and unaccompanied minors board the plane at this time, along with our first class members. I repeat, flight 112 to Washington, D.C., your plane is now boarding. May we have all families with young children, persons requiring assistance or the use of a wheelchair, and unaccompanied minors board the plane at this time, along with our first class members. If you have just been called, please step up to the front desk with your tickets ready. Thank you, and have a great flight."

"Um, Cara," Sandy cut in. "I have to go. I'm at the airport right now—my plane is boarding."

"Alright Sandy, see you at the White House!" She laughed. For the first time during my trip, something inside my chest wound its way into homesickness for my friends and family. Somehow, the pain triggered a smile on my face.

"See you at the White House," she repeated. After that, the signal went dead. Sandy was really coming. Things could only get better.

I flipped the phone closed and tossed it into my backpack before heading down the hall towards my borrowed workspace, ready to continue with my debate research. On the way, I stopped by Kate's office to let her know that I appreciated her help with getting Sandy to Washington so quickly. I stepped up to the counter of her desk and peered over its edge, surprised to see that there were two people behind it. Ms. Muleson was talking on the phone and taking notes down on a legal pad, muttering something about finalizing Sandy's security plans as she went along. Mr. Owls had pulled up a chair at her side, manning the computer as he sorted out some last-minute details of Sandy's arrival.

"It's no problem at all—I'm just happy you finally found somebody to help you," Ms. Muleson managed to look up from her papers after I had finished thanking her, smiling before burying herself beneath them again.

"Same goes for me!" Mr. Owls chimed in during a break in his conversation with the airport police. "We've got everything under control here, but we'll call if we need you. In the meantime, I think you have a debate to prepare for."

"Thanks again!" I was out the door and on my way to the White House 'classroom' before he could remind me again. It was time to get back to work.

Hunching over the keyboard, I continued to read up on animal shelters from the internet, adding any important points I found to my bullet list along with their sources. After about an hour, my eyes had become tired from staring at the screen, but instead of stopping, I strained them to keep on reading. Another two hours later and they had begun to sting. I tried to ignore them but there was no use, and with much hesitation, I shut the computer down. With the blank screen occupying most of my line of vision and an uninteresting office space to serve as my surroundings, there wasn't much to do, or even look at.

The room wasn't much of a relaxing getaway, but I was in need of a break. I leaned back in my chair and shut my eyes as if I were applying a band-aid, shielding the ache under the darkness of my lids. For the time being, it would have to do.

It wasn't long before I heard a noise coming from the hall. It was the same quiet voice I had remembered from weeks ago on the bus ride home.

"So, I heard you needed some help."

A million possible reactions flooded my mind. They swarmed around me, each pleading to choose my words and actions. My brain couldn't decide between them. Suddenly, there was so much to do—so much I should have done. Yet, all I seemed capable of was smiling. A delirious sort of grin hanging on my face, I spun around quickly in my chair, nearly tipping it over at the thought of finally catching sight of my friend—spray painted shoes and all. I rose to my feet and ran over to Sandy. She was standing near the front of the room, leaning against the White House wall as if unaffected by the fact that it was one of the most important buildings in the country.

"I'm so glad you're here!" I shouted, pulling her into a hug. She laughed and adjusted the bangles that were taking up most of her left arm.

In an instant, my mind went from feeling blank to bursting with activity.

"Sandy!" I cried, grasping her bangle-less arm as I spoke. "There is *soo* much that I need to show you. You just *have* to see the rest of the White House. It's amazing! Well, first there are the gardens and the pool, of course…Oh! You're going to love the movie theater… and the bowling alley, too! And if you think that's cool, just wait until you go out on the porch! You can see almost all of the monuments in Washington! Come on, I'll show you everything!" I tightened my grip on her arm and pulled her gently towards the door.

"Hold on!" She dug her feet into the carpet, nails burrowing into the chair rail to keep herself from following me. "Cara, we have *a lot* of work to do." Her voice was as stern as it was final.

She loosened my grip on her and tied her strawberry hair into a bun, giving me a look as if to say *'we both know that this is going to take awhile'*. Not bothering to wait for a response, she gracefully pushed past me and let herself into the office. I watched as she pulled up a seat for herself at my desk. Seeing as it had gone a little astray when I first turned around to see her, she rolled her eyes and pushed in my chair as well. With the air of some sort of expert, she turned on the computer and waited for a picture to appear on the screen.

Not only had Sandy arrived, but she had also made herself comfortable. With her at my side, I realized that we were going to get my work done whether I liked it or not. She would make sure of that.

Knowing that an all-access tour of the White House would have to wait until later, I sighed, dragging my feet back towards the desk.

Sandy was right—*what else was new?*

I took my seat next to her. She was already sorting through the messy blanket of clutter that covered the desk, wanting to see what I had done so far. A moment later, she had finally located my debate folder amongst the surrounding half-finished sodas and crumpled papers. She tossed it into her lap, pushing everything else out of her way before setting it back down. If there was any uncertainty before, I now had no questions whatsoever as to who was in charge.

"And now," she whispered, unfolding the contents of my file, "let's get to work."

chapter twenty two

I'd never thought of the ability to teach as a talent. Some people are natural artists, some can sing, some can cook, and others can dance, but never had I considered teaching to be a gift among them. It didn't take long for Sandy to prove me wrong. She took charge from the moment we were seated, and to tell you the truth, I didn't mind one bit. Sandy had a reason for everything she said and did. Better yet, she could explain, argue, and even prove the logic and truth behind her point. Every figure that came out of her mouth was factual, and every idea carefully thought out.

The way that she presented information was so professional that I found myself asking her if she wanted to take my place in the debate.

"I can't do that, Cara," she turned to face me. "The President would never let me. I'm a stranger to the press and public. Plus, if I took your place, people would think it was because you couldn't do your job. That would do some serious damage to the U.R.M. and I don't think either of us wants that." She sighed, knowing that I still wasn't convinced. "Besides, although I may speak well in front of you, I'm no good at talking in front of a crowd. It's best that we keep with the jobs we have." I was about to object, but I knew that I couldn't change her mind. Her words were like cement—once they were left out in the air, they became something solid and unchangeable. There was no use trying to break them up or remold the principles behind them.

I could only hope that the rest of America had a little more faith in me than I did at the moment.

As much as I wanted to reconnect after my time away, Sandy was just as eager to get to work. The first thing we did was add more information to my bullet list. I scribbled down the points on a sheet of notebook paper first, and after narrowing down my sources to eliminate the unqualified ones, Sandy recopied the remaining facts in a more readable, less crumpled form.

Once we had created a sizable list, Sandy began asking me why each of its points was a good reason to continue giving the money to the shelters. The object of the exercise was to answer each question confidently and without hesitation. I had to present my information in a form that made me seem so sure of myself, that people would *have* to believe me. To say the least, I needed quite a bit of practice at this part. Unwilling to cut corners, Sandy had me reread every piece of information I had gathered until I found the answer to her question, plus some additional information to back it up. If there was no information, emotion, or story to back up the reason, we searched the internet until we found one.

"You've known from the start that whoever you're going up against for the debate is going to be a professional politician. I saw your interview, last week, and you're a fantastic public speaker, but our biggest threat right now is the experience of your opponent. The only way *I* can think of to combat that is to make sure you can defend your points like something you really believe in," Sandy explained, eyes shifting between me and the screen.

That part wasn't *too* hard.

By the time we had worked through all 314 bullets on my list it was already past dinnertime.

I took this as an excuse to walk over to the kitchen for a meal, but Sandy stood her ground. We were both starving, but she insisted that we weren't to eat anything until we had found and recorded at least 100 more good strong points, and gathered at least 200 more facts and figures to go along with them. After a moment of arguing, I took my seat again, both of us determined to finish.

If I got one lesson out of the hour that followed, it was that hunger and time are both very powerful things. It gnawed at us as we pushed through our agonizing silent work, interrupted only by the occasional growl of a stomach. We were only halfway to our goal when Sandy finally cracked.

"Maybe just a little snack," she called as I was already halfway out the door. "But don't even think about getting dessert!"

Relieved that I would finally be eating, although somewhat disappointed by Sandy's dessert statement, the two of us left our work for a moment and ran down to the kitchen for a quick dinner.

We ended up finishing our meals over the computer that night, seeing as Sandy was disinclined to spend more than fifteen minutes away from our work. Her first dinner at the White House was nothing at all like my own, but she seemed happy regardless.

After taking our seats back in the office, Sandy and I took turns reading information aloud from the computer until our throats were dry from speaking and our fingers were tired of recording fact after fact down onto paper. When we had finally finished, we had four hundred and sixteen points recorded on our list, plus another six hundred and eight facts to help me persuade my audience.

The worst was yet to come.

"Alright!" Sandy exclaimed. "I think we're finally prepared with our information."

"Are we done?" I asked her, rubbing my eyes and leaning back in my chair. Her laugh only made me feel worse.

"Done?" she repeated. "Oh Cara, you're funny. We're nowhere near it! There's still so much to do!"

"Like what?"

She snorted, piling all of our fact lists into a stack. "Like memorizing these," she answered, plopping them in my lap.

It was another one of those moments when you don't know whether to laugh or cry. Sandy regarded my silence with a shrug, continuing on with her teaching.

"My goal for today is to have all of these facts and points memorized. I see these types of debates all the time on TV. You need to be able to answer any question they give you or you're done for."

"But there's so much to know!" I shot back. "What if they ask me a question that we haven't covered?"

"I thought about that too," Sandy smiled as she began to tidy up the desk. "If you don't know an answer, try to give a response to the question anyway. I'm not telling you to lie—that would be the worst possible thing to do. Since this isn't an interview, you can't skip the question or simply say 'no comment' either. Instead, your response should answer the question in a different way, or give information on a related subject. For example, let's say you were asked why Alaska isn't part of Canada. If you didn't know the answer to that, or enough facts to give a well thought-out and descriptive reply, you could instead say something about how friendly Alaska and Canada are to each other. Assuming that you're very well-informed on their relationship, you could throw out any facts you want on the subject, plus any other information that seems fitting for the two places. It's not exactly the answer they had hoped for, but it's a true one, and it's better than saying nothing at all. As long as you tie it in with the point you're trying to make, and if your message is clear, the audience will forget all about the original question. Politicians do it all the time. Do you get it?"

"Yep," I replied, taking a look around the room, and for the first time, realizing how late it really was. I was sure everyone in the surrounding offices had already left their workspaces for the night. Their absence didn't settle with me, and I felt as if I was trespassing, lurking somewhere I shouldn't be and violating their territory. The small window at the top corner of the wall looked like somebody had spray painted it black.

"Cara!" Sandy snapped, bringing my attention from the darkened window to the annoyance on her face. "You have got to pay attention! I'm begging you here!" she pleaded, her expression becoming soft.

"Sorry," I mumbled, planting my feet firmly into the floor to keep myself from wandering.

"Alright then," Sandy nodded, following my example as she tunneled her toes into the carpet. She set the list out in front of her, using her arm to block it from my view. "Let's begin, then. How many animal shelters in the United States are non-profit, and how many of those shelters receive government funding?"

"Will you be mad if I have no idea?" I asked her; barely able to remember what I had eaten for dinner that night, let alone something I had jotted down hours ago.

"Most likely." Her voice was flat and her stare was blank. I could tell that she was in no mood for an educated guess. Having no idea what the real answer was however, I decided to give it my best shot.

"Umm…," I began. She shot me another look and I assumed that she didn't find my stalling any more humorous. "I think that 657 shelters are non-profit in the United States and over 80% of them are government funded. Right?"

"Nowhere near," she said with a dim smile. "Do you want to look over the list one more time before I test you?" I knew that she was serious, but I could still catch the wit in her voice.

"Sure." I sighed, taking the papers into my own hands. My eyes skimmed over the points, all in Sandy's neat handwriting. Somehow, most of them found their way back into my memory quiet easily. Others however, I could hardly remember writing at all.

I looked at the list for a long time, my fingers moving over the words and numbers as I read them quietly under my breath. Through all of this, Sandy sat patiently, tapping her nails against the desk to keep herself occupied.

Finally feeling confident in my knowledge of its information, I handed the list back to Sandy.

"You're finished? That was quicker than I thought." She set the papers carefully down on the desk before speaking again. "Are you ready for a test?" I looked over at the stack and Sandy covered the papers with her arm again. It didn't matter anyway—from where I was sitting, our notes looked more like zebra-print. I couldn't tell whether the paper was black with white margins or white with black letters; reading it would be nothing short of impossible.

"Drill me."

I had forgotten to take into account that the test would contain a total compilation of over 1,000 points, facts, figures, and sources. Needless to say, it took much longer than I had originally expected. I got through the section listing the important benefits of giving money to animal shelters, but struggled on many of the statistic-based questions. When I started to miss consecutive points in a row, Sandy took to marking down a red X next to the information I couldn't remember. After going through the list for the first time, this turned out to be around half of them. So, she quizzed me again, this time only going over the questions I had gotten wrong. When I gave an incorrect answer during this round, she added a second red X next to it. We repeated this process several more times, going over the missed questions from the previous round with Sandy marking her X's as we went. No question ever had more than ten markings at its side.

"We're done!" I cried as Sandy set down the papers, shuffling them into a pile. She looked just about ready to collapse.

Remembering that it was late, I lowered my voice to a whisper. "I can't believe we did this all in one day!"

"Actually, it's been two days," she corrected me, pointing to a small watch hidden beneath her bangles. "It's four o'clock in the morning."

I pressed my palms to my eyes as I leaned back in my seat, more grateful for caffeine than I had ever been. Sleep deprivation hadn't turned me into a walking zombie just yet, but I had a feeling that I couldn't escape its effects much longer.

"Can I assume that we're done for now then?" I asked her jokingly. She shrugged, her weary eyes focusing slowly upon my own.

"You know all your facts and you know all your points," she replied. "I think it's fair to say we deserve to get some sleep. After all, I've been told we should wake up at six."

"Can't wait," I mocked her, forcing a smile. "By the way, do you know where your room is?"

"Yeah, a Kate Muleson showed it to me before I came to see you. It's pretty close to where you're staying, I think."

"And where would that be?"

"The East Bedroom. Apparently, that's where a lot of past Presidents' kids have slept. It's a pretty big room, and it has its own bathroom too. Kate walked me past it on my way up here and it's really nice. I think I can find my way back—hope I can, anyway. My bags should have arrived a few hours ago via some favor that UPS owed the White House, and she said that somebody would bring them up after security is finished checking them."

"That's great!" I focused my remaining energy on standing up from my chair. Sandy did the same. Her flawless skin looked papery now, and a deadbeat expression hung over her face.

"Here," she managed through half-closed lips, handing me the list of bullets we had created. "Look these over before you go to bed, and then again when you wake up. We won't be practicing them together anymore because there are a lot of other things we need to do in order to get you prepared. Since it is technically morning, the debate *is* tomorrow. We only have a day and a half left to prepare, and I don't want you to forget one thing that we've researched."

"Don't worry." I watched a tired Sandy make her way towards the front door of the office, her bracelets weighing down her arm like a prisoner's chains.

"Want to walk out with me?" she asked with a voice that said she didn't care about anything I did as long as she got some sleep. In the time before I could respond, she was already inching her way into the hall.

"No," I decided, sitting back down at the desk. "You go ahead. I need to study in here. I know that I'm going to fall asleep the second I get into my bedroom, and the last thing I want to do is have to relearn what's on this list. I might as well look it over in the area where I'm least likely to pass out."

She nodded, and with a smile that said *good choice, and good luck with that*, disappeared down the dark hallway. "Goodnight!" she called, her hair illuminating the hall like a torch in a dark chamber.

"Yeah, whatever!" I mumbled back, knowing that the sound had no chance of reaching her. When there was no reply, I turned to face the desk. I looked over half of the points on the list, and remembered almost all of them, but there were one or two that I had already forgotten. Figuring that everything would come back to me after I slept, I grabbed the list from the desk, tucked the papers into my folder, and headed upstairs.

Aside from security, it appeared as if everyone in the White House was already asleep. I dragged my feet like blocks of lead as I walked, but their sound traveled as nothing but an indistinct echo. The corridors I passed were intentionally constructed to have poor acoustics so that whispered political conversations wouldn't carry to unwelcome ears, and I was suddenly very thankful for their architect. I thought of stopping by Sandy's bedroom on my way, but its door was closed and I didn't want to risk waking her.

As was predicted, I rose to a new level of exhaustion the second I entered my bedroom. All of a sudden, my muscles felt weak. Even the slightest movement of a limb seemed to tire me. I turned to close the door, realizing that my shoulders were sore from hunching over my work, and my throat was aching as if I had swallowed a mouthful of hot sand. My eyes felt like I had been staring directly at the sun, stinging every time I closed them to blink. Each of my senses were painfully on edge, but my mind could no longer process thought. All I wanted was to rest. I set my debate information on top of the desk, placing a small glass paperweight on top of the pile so that there was no chance of anything falling out of the folder or going astray. More unconscious than awake, I changed from my day clothes into a fresh set of pajamas.

Unable to stand against the rising pain and fatigue, I shuffled my way towards the bed and became lost beneath its sheets. I would have turned off the light, but it seemed to me that it wouldn't make a difference—seeing as the sun had already begun to rise on the corner of the cranberry horizon. I knew that I should be setting my alarm to wake up in thirty minutes, but my body was unresponsive. The second I closed my eyes, I was out cold.

I was in such a deep sleep in fact, that I didn't notice when Sandy came in, or when she left. I didn't notice when the sun went from barely visible, to directly overhead in the sky. In the end, it was only my stomach that woke me. It gave a rather large growl, and with a groan, I opened my eyes to find the source of the noise. When I realized what had made the sound, I turned over in my bed, holding my stomach as if signaling for it to quiet down. I was surprised when I saw my alarm, reading that it was 11:36 in the morning. I knew that I needed to get up, but it took a moment for the message to reach my legs. With much reluctance, they swung themselves over to the edge of my bed. My arms pushed off against my mattress and helped them to reach the floor.

Knowing that Sandy would undoubtedly be angry with my tardiness, I pulled my hair back into a bun, brushed my teeth, and changed into the most casual clothes I had packed with me, not caring whether or not they were clean. Still wearing my slippers, I grabbed my overstuffed folder of debate information and hurried towards the door. I reached for the knob, but found that something else was caught in my grip. Seeing that what I had snatched was a small paper card bound to the doorknob, I carefully peeled off the tape that was helping it to stick, and held the paper up to my face. It was a note, written in Sandy's perfect handwriting. I read the card out loud.

Dear Cara,

Great job setting the alarm today! (Don't worry, I'm not too mad.) I was going to let you sleep in a little anyway. We're probably going to be up late tonight again, and tomorrow being your big day and all, it's good that you won't be living on only a couple hour's rest. I came in around seven to get you up, but you looked so tired that I figured I'd give you the morning off. By the way, you were snoring really loud.

When you first get this message, I want you to get out the lists we made yesterday and look over them one last time. You are going to need to have them memorized. If you studied last night, this shouldn't be too much of a problem. If you didn't, well, good luck... Whenever you're done, meet me in Mr. Owl's office for a little working on the debate. I planned something really cool—it's a surprise!

~Sandy

P.S. don't bother getting breakfast. I already told the kitchen staff that you aren't allowed to eat until we're finished. ☺

I held my stomach. So far, the day hadn't gotten off to a terrific start. I shoved the card into my pocket and headed down the hall, Sandy's torturous postscript in mind. As promised, she was already waiting for me when I arrived in Mr. Owls' office, sitting at the desk chair and tapping her spray painted shoes rhythmically against the carpet.

"G'morning, Cara. Did you have a nice rest?" she asked, wearing a smile that said she enjoyed being in charge.

"Good morning," I answered, avoiding her question.

"We have a ton of things to do today, so we should get started right away." She stood up. "Don't bother taking a seat, but set your debate folder down here on the desk. You won't need it. Today, I decided that we are going to do a practice debate on your topic. I am going to be the person you are debating against, and the one asking the questions too. You just concentrate on winning. I'm going to be holding the list, and using it to my advantage, so I hope that you know your information."

"I hope so too," I added quietly, remembering that I hadn't looked over the list twice as Sandy had suggested.

Sandy ignored my last comment. "Why don't you go over near the window and get yourself ready. I'm going to be standing across from you for this exercise, but first I need to go and get something from the hall." She disappeared behind the doorway, returning a few moments later dragging a black leather suitcase. It was probably large enough for me to fit comfortably inside, with space left over.

"This is my distraction suitcase," she announced, unzipping its largest pocket. "I brought it here all the way from home for one purpose. Right now, this office is a pretty good place to think, but tomorrow, you can bet that the Deseo D.C. Coliseum won't be. Stillness and quiet are luxuries you surely won't be afforded, and the things in this bag are here to help you learn to concentrate under those circumstances. Don't acknowledge anything but your own thoughts—okay?"

"Seems easy enough," I managed a smile.

"It wasn't a picnic to get this over here, but I'm glad you approve. I'm probably on a permanent UPS blacklist for asking to have this thing shipped," Sandy laughed, turning the suitcase onto its side. I watched as she began to unzip its various compartments, unpacking the items contained in them.

The first thing I saw was a large orange flashlight. The lit bulb on the inside was considerably duller than the color of the plastic around it, but it was still enough to get my attention. Sandy tossed it into the corner of the room. Against the wall closest to me, she placed a portable DVD player. After popping a disk inside and setting the volume to low, one of the Harry Potter films started up on the screen. Next she brought out two tape recorders. The first one she turned on was playing the sound of a barking dog. The other seemed to be taken from a crowded room, probably our school cafeteria. She laid these down on either side of the desk. Dumping out the rest of the contents of her bag, she scattered different colored beach balls and stuffed animals all around the room. Now, instead of looking like a work room, Mr. Owls' office looked like someone had recently thrown a party and had forgotten to clean up. Sandy picked up a glass bottle of perfume from her desk, and without warning, sent a few sprays in my direction.

"Quit it—this stuff smells horrible!" The mist found its way into my open mouth. "And it tastes even worse!" I gagged, trying to swat the scent away.

"Sorry about that. I found it sitting out in the East Bedroom and I thought it might be....well, *distracting*." She glanced back in my direction. "Looks like I was right."

"Congratulations," I choked, rolling my eyes.

"Oh, I'm not finished yet." She was smiling again as she vanished into the hallway.

When she came back I could hardly believe my eyes.

"It's probably going to be very bright where you're standing for the debate, with the lights and the cameras and everything else. So, I decided to bring up this spotlight. It's important to get you comfortable with everything that will go on tomorrow so that you can focus on the more important things. We don't need any surprises." She grunted, dropping the huge light directly in front of me and plugging its extension cord into a wall outlet.

Instinctively, I put a hand over my face to shield myself from the light.

"Get used to it," mumbled Sandy. She had picked up my debate folder from the desk and was flipping through its pages. "Your eyes will adjust." I turned back to face the spotlight, surprised to find that its initial blinding effect was already wearing off.

"Wait a second," I asked her as I became used to the brightness. "You said you *brought up* a spotlight. Brought it up from where?"

"You know, the movie theater is very nice. Tons of high-quality equipment, too. You should really check it out," she shrugged.

"Sandy, this is the *White House*! You're not allowed to run around stealing spotlights!" I yelled, realizing all too late that what I had said was the kind of thing that should be whispered.

"Don't worry," she giggled as she began to retreat towards her side of the room. "I asked Ms. Muleson, and she said that it would be alright, as long as we got it back by the end of the day. No problems."

There was nothing I could say. I should have known better than to argue with Sandy.

"Should we start the debate then?" I asked her as she settled into the only corner of the room untouched by the spotlight.

"If you're ready," she replied.

We both drew in a long breath, and the debate began.

"Miss Greybird," she posed. "Name three negative affects which would follow if the animal shelters were denied their government funding."

"Well, the evidence itself is undeniable," I began without hesitation. Sandy had explained that my statements would appear more powerful if they were aimed at the people rather than my opponent, and I attempted to keep my eye contact with the crowd of stuffed animals that represented our audience. "Of the five million animal shelters in the United States, half of them are funded with government money. Without this government funding, these shelters won't be able to be run, increasing the number of homeless animals on the streets by 2.5 million! Undoubtedly, this overflow of stray animals would be harmful to humans, bringing disease, damaged property, injury, and etcetera."

I looked over at Sandy only after I had made my point. "I have to wonder, though, Ms. Giraffing, what would you plan to do with the funding if it was not given to the shelters?"

We went on like this for hours, unwilling to stop until we had finally asked and answered every question on our sheet. I have to admit, that although I remembered most of the questions, there were at least 100 things on the list that I had forgotten. Sandy handed me my debate information, and after another hour of studying, the answers came back to me without much work.

Sandy held out on her smile until the last question had been answered up to her standards.

"Great, Cara!" she cried when we had finished. "You know everything. I have to say that the distractions hardly seemed to bother you, or at least that's what it looked like—they were driving me crazy the whole time. I think you have a chance tomorrow, I really do. Even though you did well today, don't think I don't know that you didn't study this morning. I wouldn't be surprised if you didn't study last night either. You might want to do that tonight. If you don't remember one hundred things on the day of the debate, we may be in for some trouble. You've got to know this stuff like the back of your own hand."

"Don't worry," I countered. "I won't forget anything." I was about to say something more, but was interrupted by another loud growl from my stomach.

"Oh, that's right, you haven't eaten yet!" Sandy laughed. "Sorry to starve you, I lost track of the time. Why don't you go grab something from the kitchen while I finish cleaning up? I don't think your political training teacher will be very happy if he walks into his own office and sees a giant spotlight, and a stuffed kangaroo."

"*Or,* maybe we could both get some lunch and then clean up together afterwards?" I offered.

I was surprised when Sandy didn't argue. "Sounds good," she nodded, leaving our list at the desk as she made her way towards the door. Figuring that we would have to eat eventually, the chef prepared Sandy and me a large pot of soup. All he had to do was heat it up again, and as soon as we knew it, our lunch was ready. The soup was poured into two ceramic bowls, each with a silver spoon half-submerged in it. Its smell alone was enough to make my mouth water. The base was thick, white and creamy, looking like some type of exotic chowder. Flecks of deep green, earthy brown, and rich red seasonings were sprinkled into the mix as well, sending up a scent so strong it flushed all previous traces of Sandy's 'distraction perfume' from my sinuses.

It struck me as just the sort of thing my father would serve at his restaurant. I took the bowl into my hands, homesickness twisting my stomach into an unsettling melancholy.

"This looks great," Sandy thanked the chef before taking her lunch. "So, Cara, where should we eat this?"

Both of us knew the correct response. Of course, we should go straight back to Mr. Owls' room and keep working as we ate. We had both silently accepted this answer, but neither one of us could bring ourselves to verify it aloud. I looked up at my friend and understood why.

Sandy had come for the sole purpose of helping me. She knew nothing more of the White House than its offices and the East Bedroom, and yet, she had never once complained. The only meals she had eaten here were consumed while sitting in an office chair, eyes fixed on a computer screen. She needed a little reward.

And then, suddenly, I had an idea.

"I know just the place," I answered, motioning for her to follow me.

Leading the way, I took Sandy down the long red carpet of the Central Hall. The walls were decorated with sandstone tiles, and the floors were a cream-colored marble. Lantern-like chandeliers lit the corridor. Every couple of steps there would be a fern in a golden pot or a china vase, and all furniture in the hall was a deep mahogany wood. Although usually a highly-trafficked area for tourists, it was too late in the afternoon to find any wandering visitors, and the hall was deserted. It seemed like the perfect place to sit down and enjoy a meal. I guess Sandy thought so too, because she stopped walking the second we saw a bench, as if waiting for me to declare that this was her big surprise.

"Aren't we going to eat here?" she asked after a moment of silence.

"No," I shook my head. "This place reminds me too much of a museum. Come on."

Knowing that I had no intention of giving away our destination before we reached it, I took Sandy up the wide Central Hall Stairs at the end of the corridor. Once we had climbed our way to the top, we found ourselves standing in a small landing area. Directly to the left was the Entrance Hall, and the Entrance Hall Staircase was directly to our right.

"Up here," I motioned as Sandy climbed the last of the stairs to join me in the small walkway. I waited until she came within a few feet of me before taking a quick turn to the right and continuing up the steps.

"How high up are we going to go?" Sandy yelled, struggling to keep up with her brimming bowl of soup.

"You'll have to wait and see!" I called down to her, continuing to rush ahead.

I stopped at the top of the stairs to wait for my friend. She reached me only seconds later, looking winded. Strawberry hair was floating around her face in wispy strands and a few stubborn pieces were sticking to her forehead.

"Any more stairs?" she asked in-between breaths.

"No," I answered, "but we have a ways to walk."

"This had better be worth it, Cara," she muttered, moving to my side as we walked through the second floor's stair landing and into the Treaty Room. This was a place to pass through carefully, as it didn't exactly possess the kind of décor that might match with a chowder stain. In fact, it was one of the most delicate in the White House, with faded oriental rugs, fragile yellowing portraits, and aging wooden furniture. Multiple chairs, some of which bore the Presidential emblem on their backs, were scattered throughout the room. The room was generously furnished and complete with a large chandelier—fixed to the high ceiling with a copper chain. Small spheres of blown glass hung below, shining like oversized pearls when lit. Beneath the gleaming glass hung an assortment of identical crystal pieces, diamond-cut to refract light, and dangling down on golden strings thin as a single strand of a spider web.

I remembered Kate telling me that this was a room used frequently by the President, and so I took care not to bump into the large writing desk placed at its center.

Sandy clutched her bowl closer to her chest. Mine was in a death-grip, as if I were instead holding a lighter and walking ankle-deep in a gasoline spill. This was not the place for a picnic.

Without spill or accident, we somehow managed to reach the other side of the Treaty Room. I let out a sigh of relief. Our lunch place was now only a few feet away.

"This is it!" I explained. "It's right behind this door."

"Oh, is that what it is? Looks to me more like the size of a one car garage."

I ignored her, slowly turning the knob.

We were met with sunlight.

"What is this place?" Sandy no longer seemed conscious of the bowl in her hands. She took a step into the autumn air.

"The Truman Balcony." I followed behind her, entering the terrace and closing the door behind me.

It was even more beautiful than I had last remembered. The air was clear and the lawn below stretched out for miles. To either side, we were surrounded by trees, their leaves streaked with crimson and ginger. In the distance, the silhouette of the Washington Monument stood out against the sky. I was only a floor above the South Portico, but it felt like the peak of Mt. Everest.

For just a moment, everything was perfect. I forgot about all the expectations and promises. Maybe it was the elevation, or perhaps the fresh air alone. Maybe it was the smell of the red roses, potted everywhere in sight. Maybe I was delirious with hunger. It didn't matter. All that seemed important was that I was looking over the city like a snow globe, standing on the burgundy marble tile of a White House balcony with my best friend. Outside, I was dangerously exposed, but at the same time, felt safer than I had ever been. I was home.

It was then that I realized why I *needed* to win the debate. There were thousands of kids out in the world who were dying to witness what I was seeing, and it was up to me to make it possible for them. Everyone deserved an equal chance to tower over the world on the Truman Balcony. Everyone had a right to try and make it there.

"I've got to hand it to you, Cara. You were right about this one—much better view than the one we get from Mr. Owls' mail-slit of a window." Sandy had already begun eating, leaning back in a cream colored lawn chair and staring out in the direction of the trees. I took a seat next to her and examined my meal, mixing it around with my spoon to try and help it cool down. Steam swirled from my bowl and drifted up into the air, rising until it became completely translucent. I lifted a small spoonful to my mouth, closing my eyes as I let its warmth take over my body.

It took me a long time to realize that I was shivering.

We were both shivering, in fact, but neither of us had seemed to take any notice. The day was cool, and the soft breeze had nestled its way into my bones. I looked down to find my feet a ghostly white with chill. Taking my slippers off in Mr. Owls' office had turned out to be a very regrettable mistake. Sandy's bare feet were even paler than mine, and on their way to developing a sort of bluish tint.

"Sandy, it's freezing out here!" I nudged her forearm, grabbing my empty bowl with my free hand as I stood up. We had both been lost in the landscape around us, but my statement seemed to catch her attention. As if I had broken her trance, she departed from her previous state of mind rather quickly, and turned to face me. Her arms instantly shot up in an attempt to warm her shaking shoulders.

She laughed. "It's so strange—I didn't realize it earlier. Let's go inside!" I was already one step ahead, waiting at the entrance to the Treaty Room. "You go first—the last thing we need is for you to get sick," she added, picking up the dish from her lap. That wasn't something I needed to hear twice. Within a moment, I had already scurried into the warmth of the White House.

Sandy was at my tail before long, shutting the door behind her. I took in several deep breaths, feeling the cold rushing from my frozen lungs and warm air entering to thaw them out.

Still shaking, the two of us attempted to warm up by running all the way down to the kitchen. We deposited our dishes in the sink and then headed back to work in Mr. Owl's office.

"So, you finally got to experience the White House!" I whispered once our bodies had reached a normal temperature. Sandy nodded.

"That was fantastic! Being up there—it's like everything else just falls into perspective for you, you know? Thanks for showing me." We had begun to clean up all of the distractions from our mock debate, but I didn't have to look up to catch her sincerity. "I still feel like an icicle, though," she added after a moment. I smiled back at her, dumping the last handful of distractions back into her suitcase. The only thing left now was the spotlight. Neither Sandy nor I felt like we had the strength to carry it all the way down to the movie theatre and so we simply turned it off and pulled it into the corner of the office, deciding that we would return it later.

Sandy waited until everything had been cleaned up and we were sitting back at the working desk until she spoke again.

"Cara," she began slowly. "I think that you're pretty much prepared for your debate. You know what to do, you know what to say, *and* you know that you are going to look over all of our bullet points tonight so you don't forget any of them."

"That's right," I chanted sarcastically.

"There's one more thing, though." Her voice was softer this time. "I think we should have discussed it earlier, but got kind of sidetracked. Not that it's a problem at all," she added before I had a chance to worry. "If we can decide what to do today, we should be all set"

"And what is it that we have to decide on exactly?" I asked her, now confused.

"Well, Mr. Owls told you that you would have one thousand dollars to spend on props or examples for your debate, right?"

"Yes."

"Well it only took around four hundred of those dollars to get me and my things to Washington. That means you still have approximately six hundred dollars left. We should spend it on something, and choose what that something is as soon as possible. You don't have to use it all, of course, but I don't want you to be unprepared."

"Definitely not," I somehow managed through mounting shock, "but what should we buy?"

"That's up to you," she answered. "Why don't we search the internet and see if anything sparks your mind?"

I agreed. Sandy and I browsed on the computer for some sort of example as to why the United States of America should give their money to homeless animals. Everything we saw seemed to support the cause, but there was nothing I was willing to settle on. I wanted something personal—something that I would be able to relate to and have feelings towards.

The only problem was that I just couldn't think about what that was. My mind was blank, and even the slightest of things seemed to upset and distract me. The bite on my leg was one of them. Although it was hardly visible anymore and was now only a light scar, the cold had somehow irritated it. Compared to the rest of my skin, it felt icy and swollen.

"See anything you like yet?" Sandy asked me, moving her eyes away from the screen.

"No, I can't concentrate." My voice was acidic. "It's this stupid dog bite on my leg. I don't understand why anyone would want to save a dog like Jawsie!"

"Cara, you don't mean that!" Sandy was taken aback. "Jawsie is actually really great now. He took some obedience classes while you were gone, and now he's perfectly normal. He's actually kind of cute...Hey, wait a second, did you say *save?*"

"Yeah," I explained, still clueless. "The Hamsterings' got him at an animal shelter last year...AN ANIMAL SHELTER!" I couldn't understand how I had missed something so important that had been right in front of my eyes.

I had been doing that a lot lately.

"Sandy, Jawsie is the perfect example!" I can use my money to send him over here. This is great! He was in an animal shelter and nobody wanted him, but somebody had faith in him, loved him, and accepted him into their home. He made a difference in their lives and in all of our lives. He may have been a *little* rough around the edges, but now, he's a great pet! If there had been no shelter to take care of Jawsie, he would have continued to be a potentially harmful dog on the streets, and he could have really hurt somebody, or himself. The animal shelter gave Jawsie a second chance, and it gave the Hamsterings' and everyone in the neighborhood a friend! Sandy," I couldn't help but repeat myself, "this is perfect!"

"So," she said, smiling as she leaned back in her chair. "I guess Jawsie is coming to Washington, D.C.?"

I could hardly believe what I was hearing. The dog who had once caused me to jump through a window during a rainstorm was now repaying me in a bigger way than I had ever imagined. "Yep, Jawsie is coming to Washington, D.C."

chapter twenty three

It was time to pay Ms. Muleson a visit.

Sandy and I headed out into the hall, dizzy with the thought of what we would now have to plan and prepare. There were a lot of things to be excited about, but just as many new worries to accompany them. Kate was the one handling our budget money, and I figured she'd be happy to receive the details of her newest task. We reached her office within moments. She was, as I had predicted, sitting at her desk and working on eight different things all at the same time.

The moment she saw me, all of her work came to a crashing halt.

"Cara!" she shrieked, seconds before I approached her desk. "What brings you here?"

I looked up towards her workspace. The papers which had once been carefully organized were sitting in jumbled mounds, and even her outfit looked as if she had thrown it on in a hurry. In fact, everything about her appearance, from her collared dress shirt down to her pencil skirt looked wrinkled and thoughtless. Even the surface of the desk looked in need of a good dusting.

Every one of my instincts told me that this was not the real Kate Muleson, for she would never allow a list to be read that wasn't in alphabetical order, much less the memo box on her office phone to be overflowing with 63 unheard messages. There was definitely something wrong.

"What's the matter, Ms. Muleson?" Sandy blurted, motioning to the unorganized office as if she had read my mind.

Kate shrugged, straightening the unusually loose collar on her shirt and fixing the string of pearls around her neck so that they were no longer hanging off more to one side. "I guess I've just been nervous," she answered after a long pause. "I don't mean to worry you, but tomorrow, whatever it is that happens, is going to change America, change the world, maybe. And I know I'm not able to really help you, but I just want everything to go…well, smoothly. I want everything to be perfect."

That definitely didn't worry me.

"Well, although we're very grateful for it, there's no real reason for your concern," Sandy cut in, trying to cover the fear that was forming in my face. "Cara has decided on what she wants to spend the rest of her budget money on."

"That's fantastic!" Kate nearly jumped out of her seat. Instantly, all of the anxiety I had gathered from the President's secretary seemed to melt away. She really cared about my debate—maybe a little *too* much, but I appreciated the support regardless. "So, what's the big decision?" she asked.

I had never seen Kate act quite like this before. She was usually such a natural leader, so calm under pressure, always in charge. Now, I thought I could hear her voice shaking.

Again, seeing as I had gone too long with no response, Sandy answered my question for me.

"Cara has decided to bring in a real shelter dog from our neighborhood as an example," she answered with a sideways glance towards me.

"That's great!" She turned to her right and began rummaging through some papers in a blue legal file. After a moment, she pulled out a single typewritten document and pushed it towards me across the counter of her desk.

"I thought that you might be bringing in a live animal for your example, and composed this sheet for you just in case my hunch was right." She slapped a ballpoint pen down on top of the form. "Bringing a live animal here, especially one of private ownership is a much more difficult task than simply purchasing an item, and I wanted to be prepared. I'm going to need you to fill out everything that you know about the animal and its owner on this sheet. If you don't have the answer to a question, simply leave it blank. I will be arranging for the pickup and delivery of the dog for you, so you won't have to worry about technicalities very much. What we have to concentrate on now is getting this dog to the White House as soon as possible. It's going to be very expensive to ship an animal over here, and the longer we wait, the more transportation will cost. In the case where I have any additional questions, I will contact you by way of either your bedroom telephone, or Mr. Owls' office extension number. You got all that?"

Now *that* was the Kate I knew.

"Yes, Ms. Muleson, I understand." I took the paper and pen from the top of her desk. "Thank you."

"No problem, Cara," she murmured, already having gone back to work. Sandy and I gave her one last wave of thanks before leaving her office and heading back down to Mr. Owls'. Together, we completed Kate's paperwork. I read over each question out-loud and then dictated its answer to Sandy, who seeing as she had better handwriting, wrote down what I said. When we were finished, the form looked pretty much like this:

Animal's name: Jausie Hamstering
Name of animal's owner: Gina Hamstering
Breed of animal: Husky / Rottweiler Mix (Dog)
Estimation of animal's height and weight: About 150 pounds and 2½ ft tall (on all fours)
Full address of animal's owner: 6479 West Oak Street, New Castle, Pennsylvania, 16102
Phone number of animal's owner: (724) 555-0147 — You might want to look that one up. I'm not completely sure that I'm right.

To verify it, call (724) 555-0195 (Cara's home phone.) Her parents can give you the right number.

Does this animal show any violent or aggressive behavior?: Not anymore ☺

What is the estimated age of this animal?: Around Five Years Old

What is the gender of this animal?: Male

Do you have any special requests for the transportation, care, grooming, etc. of this animal?: Yes. This dog is what I will be spending the remainder of my budget on. Be sure to give him the nicest possible accommodations for the trip. Also, if possible, thank Mrs. Hamstering 1 billion times for being soooooooo cooperative. She really loves her dog and so you must assure her that Jawsie will be adequately cared for during his stay. If I have money left over, I would also like Jawsie to be groomed upon his arrival. Thanks, Ms. Muleson. I really appreciate all you have done for me.

It was nearly five o'clock by the time we had finished filling out all of the information on the sheet. Sandy needed to take the spotlight back down to the movie theatre at that time, and so I volunteered to bring the completed form to Ms. Muleson's office alone. She agreed, and after a few minutes of walking, I was standing at the foot of Kate's oversized desk.

I peered up over the counter. Although her general manner seemed back to its normal in-charge self, something about her still looked apprehensive.

"Hi, Ms. Muleson." The moment she saw me, a new dosage of color seemed to flush into her face.

"Have you finished what I gave you?" she asked, making a last-minute change to the e-mail she was typing before looking up at me. Her voice sounded worried.

"Finished." I held up the paper for her to see. She took it from my hands, pulling it closer to herself as if I had returned some type of treasured family photograph.

"Perfect," she murmured, scanning over what I had written. "I'll make it my first priority to call this Mrs. Hamstering, and see if we can borrow her dog for a day or two. Like I said, I'll contact you if I have any questions, or to let you know when everything is set. And if things don't work out, we'll just go with your backup plan."

"What backup plan?" I caught myself looking as if I had just smelled a skunk.

"Well, you *must* have a backup plan! What if the dog can't make it?" she answered, obviously amused, her eyes never leaving the page.

I'm sure if she did happen to look up, see the terror in my eyes, and realize that I never thought to have a backup plan, then none of what I had just said would have come off quite so funny. Nevertheless, she saw nothing, and the childish smirk remained on her face.

Not wanting to seem unprepared, I laughed along with her. Even with all the effort I put into it, my giggle still sounded more like a dry cough.

"Well, it's good we have nothing to worry about," I lied.

"I can always count on you, Cara."

I swallowed hard, concentrating on finding enough oxygen to satisfy my racing heart. No matter how much I took in, I felt like I was suffocating. Finally, I found the energy to nod at Kate, managing a smile that resembled more of a grimace.

Suddenly, I felt myself walking out of the office.

I needed to find Sandy.

"Whatever the results are, we'll be in touch tonight!" Kate called out to me. I rounded the corner and headed for the door.

"Bye, Ms. Muleson."

"Best of luck tomorrow!" she yelled. "I'm sure you'll do great!" My heartbeat was louder than my footsteps.

"I can only hope you're right," I said under my breath.

chapter twenty four

When I finally found Sandy, she was near the elevator on her way up from returning the spotlight. I met her at a run. Nearly out of breath, I relayed my conversation with Ms. Muleson. As I spoke, I expected her eyes to widen with each word. I was counting on her face going pale, and any expression leaving her eyes. In the end, all of my predictions were dead wrong.

She laughed.

"Sandy!" I screamed, to shocked to realize that half of the White House would be able to hear me. "What exactly do you think is so funny?"

This only made her laugh harder. I felt my cheeks grow hot. "Sandy!"

She had to take several deep breaths to calm herself before speaking.

"Cara," she finally answered, "You can't think like that! You have to believe that your plan is going to work out. Don't lose faith in yourself now. Look, if it's not to be, we can always bring in another dog, but right now, that's not even an issue. You have nothing to worry about. Trust me on this one Cara, you've got to!"

I wasn't convinced.

"Look," she sighed. "If this isn't going to happen, you'll know by tonight, and then we'll be able to think of a backup plan. But right now, we've got more important things to do."

I realized I could breathe again. Sandy never ceased to amaze me.

"Like what?" I asked.

"Well, for starters, we have to figure out how you are going to incorporate Jawsie into your debate. He will probably only be with you for a small part of the event, and maybe for the other part, I'll take care of him. When you want him to come up for your example, just give me some sort of cue. A wave or a specific gesture will be just fine."

"Or I can invite you and Jawsie onstage," I thought aloud. "It would probably be more polite. Plus you'd get on TV, which would be a nice bonus."

"You can do that too," she smiled.

Late afternoon soon became night. Through it all, Sandy and I worked to find facts and memorize important points about shelter dogs that I could present when it was time to bring out my example.

I memorized them all, too excited to remember that our whole plan still had a very good chance to backfire. The hours flew by like seconds, but no call ever came. All we could do was wait. By then, it was about 8:00, but neither of us was very hungry from the filling soup we had eaten for lunch. So, in order to stay productive, Sandy and I ran another mock debate, this time without the distractions. Instead, before she asked me a question, I would be given a number of seconds or minutes I had to provide an answer. My responses for the debate would be timed, and Sandy thought it would be a good idea to practice conveying my thoughts with a time restriction. I managed to catch on after awhile, and we had skimmed through the entire contents of my debate folder within an hour and a half.

"What should we do now?" I asked her with a yawn once we were finished.

"I think that you should get to sleep," she answered. My jaw dropped—Sandy was usually never one to retire early. She thrived on practice.

"We both deserve some rest," she explained, sensing my surprise. "You know everything there is to know—plus, there's no way I'm letting you sleep in again. And besides, it's going to be a big day tomorrow. I have the feeling that everything will run just as we hope it will."

"Whatever you say, Boss." Sandy handed me the list of all our facts and figures, now several pages longer than it had been that morning. I turned out the light and the two of us headed in the direction of our bedrooms.

"Thanks again Sandy, for everything, I mean." I added quietly as we continued to walk. "You know that I never would have been able to do this, any of this, without you, right? I don't think I've given you as much credit as you deserve. If it weren't for you, I wouldn't be here. And if for some strange reason I did get to the White House, I never would have finished the debate in time." There was a long pause as we reached the stair landing. We were nearing the Queen's Bedroom.

"There's really nothing else to say," I whispered. "I just wanted to make sure that you know how thankful I am. No matter what happens tomorrow."

"Happy to help," she beamed, twirling a piece of strawberry hair around her pointer finger. I stopped at my door, but Sandy continued on.

"Goodnight!" she called after awhile. Judging by the sound of her spray painted shoes clomping across the floor, she had made it about halfway down the carpeted hall.

"See you in the morning!"

"Look over your facts again tonight!" she responded loudly. There was nothing I could say. The next thing I heard was the closing of a door, and I knew that Sandy had made it inside the East Bedroom.

As usual, Sandy was right. I sat down at my writing desk and began to study. Knowing that the debate would be the following day made me extra cautious, and I took my time reading over each word, double-checking every source and point. I finished in a little under two hours, and then tested myself again, just to make sure I hadn't missed anything. This time, I went through my folder with no mistakes. It hadn't been easy to finish, but when I did, confidence triumphed over my drowsiness and I no longer felt sluggish.

I knew that I would need sleep, but was not at all tired. And so, in a strange new state of awareness, I searched the room for anything that might help me prepare for my debate.

I figured that Genevieve would be coming to help me dress for the event, and so there was no need to bother with picking out clothes. Instead, I dug through my dresser until I found my last clean pair of pajamas.

I was in no hurry to pull them on, and took my time brushing my teeth. It was with reluctance that I finally climbed into bed, and even then, I had trouble situating myself. I threw the pillows to the foot of my bed and pulled the comforter up to my waist, then my shoulders, and finally my neck. Restless, I kicked off the covers and tried again, this time lying on my side, then my stomach, and after that, my back.

It took me a few moments after this to realize that I had forgotten to turn out my light, but only seconds to recognize the task as an opportunity to stall. I made my way over to the switch and then leisurely back to my bed, repeating the process of making myself comfortable all over again.

The sound of the telephone had me sitting back up within seconds. Already knowing who was on the other line, I managed to grasp it after the first ring.

"Hello, Ms. Muleson?" I began, my heart racing with such fierceness that I wondered if Kate could hear it too.

"Hello, Cara. I'm sorry to be calling so late—I hope I didn't wake you. I meant to contact you earlier, but the President called with some very important last-minute business and I've been trapped on the phone for hours. How are you?" I frowned. This was not a good time for casual chatting.

"I'm a little anxious, now that you mention it," I let slip.

"Anxious?" said the voice on the other line, "Why would you be an—Oh! I bet you've been wondering about Jawsie, haven't you?"

I didn't respond in the hopes that it would save time. After a brief silence, Kate continued.

"Well, I'm pleased to say that as far as Jawsie Hamstering is concerned, I have some very good news! Jawsie is coming to Washington! We are sending him straight over to the Deseo D.C. Coliseum, which is the location of your debate, and he will be taken care of during the hours prior to your arrival. I have been told that he will be fed and groomed there, so there is no need to worry about any of that."

I let out a deep breath, but for some reason, my heart was still pounding.

"Thank you so much, Ms. Muleson!" I breathed, laying my head back against the mattress.

"As always, Cara, you're very welcome. Can't wait to see you and Jawsie tomorrow for the big day!"

The line went dead before I had a chance to respond, and once again, I was left in silence.

Sandy and Kate are right, I thought to myself with closed eyes as I waited for sleep to come. *It is going to be a big day tomorrow.*

However prepared I felt that night in the darkness of my bedroom and the quiet of my thoughts, I was unaware that what would be awaiting me in just 24 hours time was beyond anything I had ever imagined.

'Big' was an understatement.

chapter twenty five

I don't remember falling asleep that night, but the next thing I knew, light was streaming into the room like liquid sun.

"Wake up!" I could hear Sandy's voice, and then her footsteps, as she entered the room.

"I'm awake! I'm awake!" I whispered.

"Wake up!" She tried again, shaking my shoulder in an attempt to get her words to register.

"I'm awake!"

The shaking continued, pausing just long enough for Sandy to grab a pillow and smack it down onto my stomach. "Rise and shine!"

I snapped up from bed like a child's toy that had just been wound. "I-am-awwwakkkkeee."

"Sorry," she giggled, dropping the pillow. "Guess you're up now."

"You got that right." She took a step back and my eyes struggled to adjust to the surrounding light. I squinted, unable to believe them—Sandy was wearing a formal gown, spray painted shoes absent from the picture. *Obviously the work of Genevieve.*

The dress was possibly the simplest thing I had ever seen her wear, violet strapless silk that flowed down to about an inch above her knees. The material hung close to her body without looking tight, and I was reminded of the lanky girl on the bus who I worried might blow away. Draped around her otherwise bare shoulders was a black satin shawl, so thin that it was almost translucent. The loose ends of the wrap were dangling gracefully at her sides. Her hair had been straightened, and she smelled like perfume. It was a side of Sandy I had never seen before, and yet somehow, she still looked exactly like herself.

"Sandy, you look fantastic! Oh! And Jawsie can come to the debate!" I exclaimed as she waited for me to stand.

"Uh-huh," she answered in a voice that said she already knew both things to be true. Apparently, Kate had called more than one person last night. "Before I forget, Cara, don't worry about your debate folder. I just brought it down to the place where we'll be practicing today—it's not missing."

I nodded, rubbing my eyes before getting out of bed. A feverish knock came from the door almost the second I was upright. After about half a second with no response, whoever it was let themselves in.

I was hardly surprised to see Genevieve. She was standing at the entranceway to my bedroom with the air of somebody in the royal family.

"Hello," Sandy and I chorused. I waited for Genevieve to come further into the room, but when that didn't happen, I walked quickly over to her side. To my relief, we didn't have to shake hands this time. (This was because she dropped her trunk of clothes on my foot, but I hardly minded.)

"Are yew alrightee?" she squealed in a Dutch accent, bending over to retrieve her fallen bag. "I broote a little morre clothing thees time because I knoo your size. Pluz I think I know your taste now zo I broot some clozing zat iz more *you*—more fazionable iv you will," she explained, pushing the suitcase off of my toes. She quickly unzipped it, searching its contents for awhile before coming up with a dress. It was made of red satin and had what looked like a feather boa sewn around the collar.

"Now for ze shoes!" she cried triumphantly, pulling them from the trunk, as well. They looked as if they were made from the same material as a disco ball, and with all of the sunlight around, they nearly blinded me.

"I thenk they geve ze outfit a little zomething extra. Down't you?" She smiled, waiting for a nod of approval.

I looked back at Sandy for help. Her expression was blank, staring back at me like she was watching an entertaining movie.

I drew in a deep breath. "Um, I think it may not be formal enough."

It was the nicest way I could possibly tell her that there was no way I would ever wear the dress in public, and I hoped she would get the message.

"No?" she asked as she began to fold the dress, returning it to the suitcase. It was only when I shook my head again that she spoke. "I thought that you might zay zat. Luckilly I ave a something a little more fanzy. Let uz try it!"

She reached into her bag again, this time surfacing with what looked like a wedding gown. It was large and puffy with layer upon layer of frill and lace stitched onto the sleeves and skirt. If I had tried it on, it would have reached to about my ankles. At least there wasn't a train attached.

I turned to Sandy for support again, but I didn't get it. She was now seated cross-legged on my bed, smiling innocently at me as if she seriously wanted to know if the dress was suitable or not. *At least one person in the room was enjoying themselves.*

"I'm not sure…," I began, starting to tell Genevieve that I wanted to look at another dress. "I think that maybe…"

She cut me off.

"Of courze you aren't sure! Looke, you aven't zeen ze hat yet!" She reached back into her suitcase and dug out the ugliest hat I had ever seen. It was pine green and had a wider brim than I had ever thought possible. There was a large dome at the top, and pinned onto the side was an assortment of plastic flowers.

"Wow, you were right, that hat really completes the look!" Sandy exclaimed with that same innocent grin. I shot her a look, but she just smiled back at me with a '*what did I ever do wrong?*' sort of expression.

I didn't speak for some time after that.

"Zo, Cara, do you loike it?" Genevieve asked with another fake muddled accent.

"Yeah, Cara, do you?" Sandy countered, now holding back laughter.

"Well," I stuttered, not wanting to hurt Genevieve's feelings. "Um, well—"

"I think what Cara is trying to say is that the hat really completes the look, but she doesn't feel that it's appropriate for her to wear during the debate, because it might detract from what she says," Sandy came in just in time, once again on my side. I owed her for that one.

"Vaht you say about this hat iz true," Genevieve mumbled after a moment, struggling to squeeze the outfit back into her trunk. "Now ze problem iz that I only ave one more dress for you in thiz suitcase. I don't know vuy I brought it, zough. It iz vay too plain for a *debate*. Zo, why don't you waight here while I go get my other suitcaze from ze car."

I stopped her—the word *plain* had an entirely different meaning by Genevieve's standards. "Wait!" I cried. "Can I see the other dress? *Just in case?*"

"Iv you vant." She shrugged, pulling it out from a dress-bag at the bottom of the trunk.

It was perfect.

I held the fabric up to my body. "Genevieve, I love it!"

"Are you sure that you don't vant to see my other dresses?" she asked, obviously confused.

"Thanks for the offer, but yes, I'm sure."

"Vine then," she handed me a pair of black leather pumps. "And take zese matching shoes. Go try it on."

I did just that. The dress was a charcoal black with straps about three-quarters of an inch in width. It had a nearly corset-like fit at the very top, with a thick strap of silvery colored lace cutting across my waist. A couple layers of crinoline were sewed beneath this, causing the fabric to frill slightly outwards as it drifted towards my knee and ended in a lace trim the same color as the dress's sash. With the dress came a cropped cashmere sweater. It was just a shade darker than the lace at my hips, with small black buttons, and sleeves that reached a little below my elbow. The shoes I was given were easy to walk in, with a small heel and an opening at the very top for my toes.

When I walked out to show Genevieve and Sandy, I found that they were already busy with something else.

"Genevieve thinks you need a bracelet or necklace of some sort," Sandy explained as I entered the bedroom. "Maybe something silver to match your dress."

That gave me an idea.

"I have just the thing!" I ran over to my drawer and pulled out the charm bracelet I had worn on my very first day in Washington. "How about it?" I asked.

"I think it's perfect!" Sandy decided, reaching over to help me clasp it.

Genevieve made a face "You do not vant anyzing more… *funky*?"

"I think this is just fine," Sandy smiled, stepping back to admire my outfit.

"Well, if dat iz what you vant, than I suppoze you can vear it," Genevieve surrendered, leading me over to the desk where she had set out her makeup.

"Now, why don't you take off zat dress and change into zome normal cloze. Ze debate starts at six o'clock but you vill have to leave before zen, zo maybe you should get ready around four. Owever, Cara, I zink I am going to do your makeup now, just so that we can experiment a little—maybe try zomething more fun. This vay, we can do it later for the debate iv you don't like it. I vill do your hair the same vay I did it for your interview unless you vould like to try one of my different styles, but ve can figure that out later. Zandy, you can change, too." She tossed a pair of what looked like six-inch stilettos in her direction. "Here are ze shoes for your dress. Mayve you ought to vear them a little vile so zat you can get used to zeir height. For now, change, and meet me back here ven you are done."

"Alright."

"Sandy, you can go first," I called to her as she headed towards my bathroom. "I have to find some clean clothes in my dresser."

"Okay," she yelled back. When she had finished changing into an oversized t-shirt, dress pants, more necklaces than a manikin in a cheap jewelry store would ever be displaying, and the heels that made her well over six feet tall, I stepped into the bathroom. My mom had only allowed me to pack one casual outfit, and seeing as it was dirty, I got stuck wearing an old itchy sweater and a gray polyester skirt that was much too large for my body frame.

Genevieve was waiting for me when I returned. The two of us had to try several different looks before we found one that fit. At first, Genevieve thought it suitable to give me the most sparkly eye shadow ever made. I begged and pleaded, but she powdered the stuff on like a four-year-old putting makeup on her Barbie, which is what I looked like when it was finished. As if that wasn't enough, after a couple of blinks, the shadow found its way into my eyes.

"Beauty takes pain!" Genevieve recited in an accent all of her own, hoping that this might change my mind about washing off the makeup. "Don't be a baby!"

"But this stuff is blinding me!" I nearly yelled back, both hands pressed over my right eye.

"Vine then, vash it off. We'll just have to start all over again then," Genevieve pouted.

And thus began round two of our makeup session. It didn't work out too well, either.

Two coats of liquid-y lipstick in a shade Lucille might find suitable were painted onto my lips followed by layer upon layer of black eyeliner. After the first application, I looked half-alright, but when we got to the seventh, I looked more like a raccoon than a thirteen-year-old.

"Cara, you like it?" Genevieve asked. Her voice was confident as she took a step back to admire her work. "I muzt caution you, zough. You can *not* –"

Frustrated, I cut her off, mid-sentence.

"Genevieve, I think that this is a little too much. We need to tone it down!" I buried my head in my hands, and irritated, let my fingers slide down my face. I heard a gasp.

"…touch your face! *You can not touch your face!* The makeup ez still vet and takes ten minutes to dry."

I looked down at my fingertips only to see streaks of black and red across them. My face was in a fashion very similar. I sighed. Sandy laughed. Genevieve rolled her eyes.

"Vash it off, Cara," she mumbled. "I vill give you more common look, iv you really want." By common, of course, I knew she meant makeup more widely accepted by the American public. We were nearing a breakthrough.

"Thanks, Genevieve," I called on my way to the bathroom. Once my face was clear of gooey smudges, I returned back into the bedroom for round three of my makeup.

At last, we had success.

This time, eyeliner was absent from the picture. Instead, I was given a shimmer-y eye shadow with just a hint of metallic pigment to bring out the silver in my dress. My lips were covered in a natural peach gloss, and once again, all the harsh angles and lines in my face seemed to melt away.

When I looked in the mirror, I couldn't help but smile. I was the trustworthy girl from my dream again, but no longer her exact replica. I wasn't on my own anymore, and it showed in my eyes.

This was a better look for me.

"Do you like it?" I asked to nobody in particular, admiring my reflection in the mirror over the fireplace.

"It's perfect," answered Sandy, who had been reading a magazine on my bed, bored ever since Genevieve had stopped getting creative with my makeup. I agreed.

"Good then. Iv you like et, zen ve are done for now," Genevieve nodded, giving us the okay to leave.

"Why don't we all go down for breakfast?" Sandy suggested, returning the magazine to my suitcase. "I'm starved!" I accepted the offer, but our stylist declined, seeing as she had already eaten that morning.

"Vhatever you do, do not eat fish!" she yelled as we were halfway down the hall. "If you get food poisoning and vhrow up all over your dress tonight, I vont be the vone cleaning it up...And reapply your lip glozz ven you are done eating. The *last* ving we vant today is vor you to ave dry lipz!"

At least her priorities were in order.

"Don't worry!" I called back. "Thank you again for all your help, Genevieve. I couldn't have asked for anyone to do a better job. See you tonight!"

"Zee you tonight!" she roared back, seemingly unaware that distance between us was five yards as opposed to five miles.

When Genevieve spoke this way, I wasn't sure whether I wanted to draw myself nearer to her, or run away as fast as I could in the opposite direction.

Unable to decide, I thought it best to play it safe and kept my distance, waving goodbye before heading down to the kitchen. Sandy, still wearing the high heeled shoes that Genevieve had given her in an effort to break them in, was struggling down the long carpeted staircase when it struck me.

I had forgotten about Nadia.

She was young, but my little sister, regardless, and I had promised to involve her.

A good politician never breaks their promises.

I stood frozen on the steps, thinking. It wasn't long before I had an idea.

"Sandy!" I called to where my friend was wobbling to catch up with me. She looked too concentrated on not spraining an ankle to answer, and so I continued. "Sandy, I have to make a phone call. I'll be right back."

"Take your time!" she hollered back, grabbing onto the banister for support as she adjusted the straps on her right shoe.

I smiled, sprinting down the rest of the stairs and into the Green Room, where the usual guard was standing next to a table with an old-fashioned telephone. His expression was weary as I approached him.

"May I please use the phone?" I asked politely. The man said nothing, nodding once he made up his mind. After another stretch of time, he moved aside, leaving me a clear path to the device. With only a quick 'thanks' in return, I rushed over to the telephone, picking up the receiver and pressing it close to my skin. The brass and copper that lined the earpiece felt cold on my face.

I dialed my home phone number. The White House had arranged for my family to fly out for my debate, but that wasn't until later in the afternoon. If all went well, I figured that I might be able to catch Nadia before she left for school. Sure enough, it was she who answered the phone, as energetic and cheery as usual.

"Hello! This is Nadia Greybird. Who are you?"

"Nadia," I laughed, "It's me—"

"Cara!" she exclaimed, testing out the name as if it was the first time she'd said it in awhile. I was even guiltier to realize how happy she sounded. "What's going on? We haven't heard from you in such a long time! No, worse, you haven't heard from *me* in such a long time! Grover Finchy ate a bug, and

I finally beat Cornelia V. at checkers! She said she let me win, but I bet she's just jealous. You've missed so much here—ever since you left, reporters have been calling our house every day! Mom makes me say 'no comment' like they do in the movies, but sometimes when she's at work I manage to squeeze in an interview—those people just *love* to talk! Oh! And I wrote you a letter. Did you get it yet? Plus, guess where we're going tonight?" She didn't wait for a response. "We're going to Washington DeCey to see your *DEBTE!*"

"That's *debate*, Nad." I corrected her gingerly, realizing that I missed the sound of her voice.

"Yeah, that, too," Nadia sighed, dismissing the subject. I took a deep breath. I would need something big to get my little sister's attention. Something explosive. A simple spark wasn't enough this time—I needed a full-blown fire.

"Nadia, wait!" I cried dramatically. The guard at my side shot me a bemused glare. I ignored him—what I was about to do would take my full focus. "I need to tell you something important!" I whispered, adding a touch of mystery to my voice.

"What?" she asked impatiently. When I didn't answer, she lowered her tone, now desperate to hear what I had to say. "*What?*"

"Well," I began, pausing to twist the long telephone cord around my pointer finger. "I *need* your help." There was an electrified silence on the other end of the line. "Please!" I fake-begged, knowing that she had already made up her mind on the subject weeks ago. "Remember how you *promised* that you would help me?"

"Yes!" she answered eagerly. I didn't have much time left until Nadia's school bus would arrive, and I knew I would have to please my sister quickly.

"Nadia, I need you to tell everyone at your school to watch the *debate* on television tonight. The more viewers the better. Maybe you could even make an announcement about it at the morning assembly. In fact, do you know what would be really spectacular?"

"What?"

"If you told them to spread the news. We want everyone to watch this debate tonight. Just think—*you* are helping to pass a bill, Nadia! I could never do this without you!"

"I know!" she yelled back. "That's the best part!" I didn't have to see her face to know that her eyes were glowing—practically illuminating the room with spirit. "This is going to be great, Cara! We're such a great team!"

"Yes, we are," I agreed. "Now don't forget what I said. Oh, and tell Mom and Dad I called. Tell them I can't wait to see you all tonight."

"Sure," she replied, drawing out the word in a '*you totally owe me*' sort of voice. It was quiet on the other line and I could tell that, for once, Nadia was struggling to choose her words. "Thanks, Cara," she added after a moment.

"My pleasure."

"Bus is here. Love you—Bye!" Nadia didn't give me the opportunity to say more, hanging up within a second and leaving me listening to a dial tone. I stood still for a moment, clutching the phone to my ear.

"I'm glad I got to talk to you, Nad," I murmured to myself.

"*Please hang up and try again. If you need help, press one for more options…*" The operator's voice rung in my ears.

"Alright, alright." I put down the phone, smile wider than it had been all day. I bet that at home, Nadia was looking the same way.

I had finally fulfilled all of my promises.

Feeling better than I had in a long time, I headed down for breakfast.

chapter twenty six

"Why are you so *happy*?" Sandy vented. She was seated against the kitchen door, rubbing her feet. I could tell that her new shoes had not worked out too well.

"Oh, it's nothing," I replied quickly, trying to hide my smile. She didn't look convinced. "I just followed through on a promise I made to Nadia."

"Whatever," she shrugged, crunching down half of a breakfast bar in one bite. She chewed and I watched the fierceness drain from her face. I sat down next to her. "Here," she said through a mouth full of food, tossing one of the bars into my lap. "I got one for you."

"Where is President Deerun?" I asked her, too excited to eat anything at the moment. It went silent. Sandy swallowed hard before speaking.

"He's at a meeting for U.R.M."

She covered up her secretive smile by taking another large bite of the breakfast bar, sending little granola crumbs all over her shirt. Casually, she brushed them off onto the floor, like there was some invisible dog down there to lap them up.

"So," Sandy changed the subject, "do you want to practice some more for the debate?" I watched her lick the excess granola bits off her fingers. There was no way she was going to tell me anything more about the President's whereabouts, so I didn't ask again. Instead, I looked around the hall, weighing my options. Deciding that practicing for the debate was the most mature thing to do, I agreed.

Together we stood up and walked back out into the Center Hall. I opened my breakfast bar, and took a small bite.

"Finish it. We didn't have dinner last night and you need your energy," Sandy reminded me. I noticed that she was barefoot, and wondered what she had done with her shoes.

I decided I would rather not know.

Instinctively, I started walking in the direction of Mr. Owl's office, but Sandy grabbed my arm and pulled me in the opposite direction.

"Come on!" she called, her bare feet making strange sounds on the marble floors. "I have a better idea of where to practice."

Playing along, I only shrugged before following her.

Strangely, Sandy knew her way around the White House quite well, especially for someone who had only been there for a couple of days.

I myself, had no idea where we were going, and so I followed her blindly along, watching for any hint that might tell me where I was being taken.

After a few minutes of walking, we came to the end of the hall and found ourselves in the Visitors' Foyer. The floor was made of glossy ceramic tiles and the walls were such a stark white that the effect they had on your eyes was similar to looking at the sun for an extended period of time. Since the President wasn't home to have guests and there were no tours on Mondays, the room was empty. At my left, I could see the East Colonnade hallway, and on the right was a large door. Sandy pushed it open and led me inside.

It was only then that I realized where she had taken me.

The President's movie theatre.

"Stand up there," she instructed, pointing to the stage in front of the movie screen. I was awestruck, walking down the aisle and up to the corner of the stage Sandy had indicated. A small microphone had been set up for me there, along with another at the other side of the stage for Sandy. I looked out over the red vinyl seats of the theatre, trying to imagine a face in each one, and hoping I was ready for what lay ahead. Sandy was going to have another mock debate with me.

"You picked a pretty good spot." I could hear my voice echoing off the theatre walls as I waited for her to join me.

"I don't deserve all the credit," she answered modestly, fiddling with a large box in the back of the room. She inserted a CD into a slot towards its back, but neglected to push play. "Residents at the White House use this room all the time for practicing speeches. President Deerun did it just this morning."

"But you said he was at a meeting," I replied. "Why does he need a speech for a meeting?" Sandy bit her tongue. She knew she had said too much.

Instead of speaking again however, she started up the projector machine and an image instantly appeared on the screen behind me. I recognized it to be a commercial for an iPod. Curious, I looked over my shoulder, watching as different celebrities were shown listening and dancing to the kind of music they liked. Once the screen was set, Sandy turned a knob, cranking the volume so that it filled the room with noise. Country, then classical, rap, hip-hop, rock, and jazz were all pounding in my ears at once, all blending into one blasting frequency. As much as I wanted to get away from the speakers, I did my best to be patient, waiting to see what my friend would do next and praying that the room was soundproof.

Without warning, Sandy walked over to the spotlight box, and adjusted the bright light so that it shone directly into my face. I felt like a book that she was trying to read in the dark.

"*What are you doing*?" I finally asked, one hand trying to cover my ears from the music, while the other attempted to shield my eyes from the light.

"I figured you would need a bigger distraction," she shrugged, heading towards her microphone on the stage. I noticed that she was holding our list under her arm, while her hands were grasping another stack of papers that I couldn't recognize.

Our debate began, and it didn't take me long to realize that the pile contained a secret weapon.

New questions. Questions we hadn't looked up, or even covered in the smallest form of detail. I found myself speechless, and not knowing what to say. An icy sweat began to trickle down the back of my neck, despite the hot light in my face. The iPod commercial was beginning to irritate me, and the asking of each new question became increasingly frustrating.

I was unprepared, and I knew it.

. . . .

"How could I have *lost?*" I spat out the last word as if it was foul compared to the rest of the sentence. The mock debate was over and I was standing in Mr. Owls' office with Sandy. I was beginning to get nervous.

"How could I have lost?" I repeated. Nothing was right anymore—my face felt hot, the air was stiff and my sweater was itchy.

"Listen," said Sandy, who was not the sulking type. "You lost. Believe it. You lost. You lost. You lost. You lost. You los—," I shot her an edgy look and she stopped mid-sentence. "Anyway," she continued, "you lost...*as I mentioned before*, and we need to do something about it. Not even trying to correct your mistake is just going to make you look bad on international television. The President is counting on you, and you can't let him down."

I knew she was right.

"Cara," she tried again, her voice more encouraging this time, "you know a lot. We've worked harder than ever before over these past few days, and you memorized more facts in one day than I thought you would be able to remember at all. There is a very slim chance that your opponent will even be asking you any of the questions you didn't know today. I just want you to be prepared. There is so much to know, and the worst part is, not having the answers in a debate can cost you."

Her version of a pep talk had no effect and I continued to whine. "Sandy you beat me. And no offense, but you aren't even an expert. The person I'm going up against tonight does this sort of thing every day. I stand no chance." I collapsed into the office chair behind me and tried my best to blink back tears.

My efforts added up to that of a fish attempting to herd back a shark...hopeless. Tears flooded my eyes and rolled down my cheeks, each leaving a dark, trail of wet mascara to mark its path as it went.

"Hey," Sandy looked uncomfortable, as if she didn't quite know how to act in the situation. "I want to show you something."

"What is it?" My voice cracked as I looked up towards her, hands shielding my face. I wiped my eyes with my sleeve, realizing that my makeup was probably too far gone for me to be concerned with preserving it.

"Look." Sandy reached out from behind the computer and pulled a stack of papers towards her, all bound carefully together with scotch tape. The pages had been adjoined to one another so precisely that I mistook them for a script or official document of sorts. Without saying a word, Sandy flailed the stack of papers to its full length, thrashing all but the top sheet to ground. Even when held at her shoulder, they could easily reach the ground.

My eyes were irritated from being rubbed, and I couldn't make out the words on the pages.

"What does it say?" I whispered, craning my neck to get a better look.

"It's our list."

I stopped fidgeting. With her opposite hand, she ran her pointer finger down every figure and bullet, folding each paper back into the stack once she had scanned it.

"Look at all we've accomplished." She spoke softly, setting the stack onto my lap. "We've done so much, but we can always try just a *little* harder. We can always accomplish a little bit more. The only reason you lost back in the theatre was because you were caught off-guard. If I'd told you what to expect, there were tons of strategies you could have used to answer my questions with the facts from our list. You would have won if you had a little more faith in yourself—I have no doubt. Now, what do you say we memorize a few more things before the debate?"

I wanted to agree, but something held me back.

"Sandy, we've already visited every site for animal shelters on the internet— all the credible ones at least. There is nothing more to look up...right?"

"That's right, we did." Sandy nodded as if this was no big deal. "That means we have to research our subject under a different name." She turned on the computer and brought it up to Google, preparing herself to explain.

"It's kind of like finding a recipe for a marble cake in an alphabetized cook book. It could be under D for Desserts, but it could also be under M for Marble cake, C for Cake, or even S for Special occasions. You have to check all those different names before you can find what you want, and in this case, we want information for the debate. All this time, we've been searching for information about animal shelters, but there is still more to check. For example we could look at *United States government funding.*" She stretched out her last word as she typed her topic into the search box. Within a moment, the results for 'government funding' were already listed on the screen.

"Feeling better now?" She didn't wait for a response, clicking on the first related site and beginning to read.

"Much," I moved in towards the monitor so that I could follow along. "Thanks." I dried my eyes and the work began.

We sat for what felt like forever, our eyes stuck to the screen like gum attached to the underside of a desk. The seconds slowly turned into minutes which gradually changed into hours, but the clock to us was nothing but time running out. The only sound was that of our pencils, quickly jotting down fresh facts, followed by the occasional quiz of everything we had just learned. I began to feel slightly more positive, and slowly regained the confidence I had woken up with that morning. We had been searching relentlessly, looking up our information under a different topic name every hour or so. Nonetheless, after awhile, the only facts we were reading were ones that we had already learned.

Without warning, Sandy clicked the x button on the screen and stretched back in her seat, recapturing her posture. I felt like a kid whose mother had just turned off the television because it was past their bedtime.

"Why did you do that?" I asked innocently, motioning towards the blank screen.

"You've known everything on those sites for the last half-hour." She sat up straight, glancing towards the doorway and into the hall. "You're finished."

"No," I argued, unsure. "There's still so much more to find. You said so yourself."

"No." Sandy's tone was as flat as it was final. She wasn't going to argue.

"That's crazy," I sighed, figuring I should give it one more try. "We only checked a couple of sites, and we only got a few more points."

"Forty-eight sites, and one hundred-eighty-two new points," she countered, daring me to respond. She held out the list of new questions she had used against me in our debate. "I've been checking these questions off as we learned the answers and we've found all of them, plus more." I ignored her.

"There are tons of other pages with things we don't know," I finished, voice sounding weak. She rolled her eyes.

"Cara, you're overworking yourself. You're letting your anxiety get the best of you." I did my best to look unaffected by this comment, but Sandy saw right through me. "Let's take a break." She stood and began to walk out of the room, her bare feet thumping against the thin carpeting each time she took a step. "I'm going to get some lunch," she announced, grabbing our debate information before turning the corner into the hall, and with that, thumping her way out of sight.

"Sandy, come back!" My words came out as more of a plea than a command. I waited for a reply, but a solid silence was all that followed.

Giving in, I jogged towards the kitchen in her pursuit, arms folded dutifully across my chest.

No Sandy.

It took awhile for me to find her in the Family Dining Room. I had always thought that you needed a special invitation to eat there, but apparently, I was incorrect.

As was characteristic, Sandy was already seated at the table, napkin folded across her lap as if she owned the place.

"Sit down," she smiled as I came through the doorway. "I ordered for us both already." Of course, she knew I would come.

"Listen Sandy." Anger was beginning to rise in my voice. "Why can't we study some more? Maybe we did check a couple of websites and encyclopedia articles, but what about books? I'm sure that the White House Library has tons of great references and facts. Plus, we've hardly even checked any catalogs, or magazines. We really don't have much information to go on at all! It's true that we can't know everything, but we might as well try to do as best we can!"

Sandy got a far away look in her eyes, pretending to ponder what I had said before telling me to sit down again.

Coldly, I did as I was told.

"Here," she murmured, handing me a napkin.

"Thanks," I snapped back, meaning nothing of the sort.

Neither one of us spoke for awhile after this, and as time progressed, my anger towards Sandy slowly simmered down. In the quiet that followed, I absentmindedly arranged the napkin on my lap. Sometime later, the blonde waitress who I had met on the morning of my first interview appeared with our lunches.

Our meals were served on china dishes with small lilacs painted around their outer rims. In the center of each plate was an overly-buttered, overly-toasted grilled-cheese sandwich. Two tall cups of frosted glass were positioned at our right-hand sides, and in between them, a pitcher of icy milk was set.

The waitress acknowledged our soft-spoken thanks, and was gone from the room as soon as she had come. Not another word was spoken.

I worked up the nerve to pour myself a drink.

It wasn't until I had taken my first sip, letting the cool creamy liquid settle inside my mouth, that I dared to question Sandy again.

If her mind was anything, it was practical. She had a reason for everything she did, and when I say this, I mean it in the true sense of the word. *Everything.* She picks up a dropped pencil with her right hand so that she can continue writing immediately after she retrieves it. Her alarm clock at home is set out in the hallway so that if she ignores it, Cornelia V. will wake her within the next minute, running in to inform her that the noise is disturbing her and asking that she kindly turn it off. Despite this, you can usually figure out *why* Sandy does what she does. There must be some logical reason behind her actions, and usually, it isn't too difficult to figure them out. What bothers me most is when she leaves you completely clueless.

"Why are you doing this?" I did my best to sound bold. When no answer came, I resorted to ripping off the crusts of my bread.

"We only have two hours left until your debate," she clarified, taking a delicate bite out of the corner of her sandwich. She swallowed. "You know everything that is important. And besides, I've already checked the White House Library—no updated books that mention animal shelters besides the encyclopedia you've already read. Plus, we must have studied at least twenty newspaper articles online, not to mention the thirty-some that came from magazines. You know more than you think, Cara. It's good for your ego, I suppose, but not so much for your self-assurance." I found myself nodding.

"Sorry," I admitted. My voice sounded much more tender than I had anticipated.

"It's not *all* your fault," she joked. "There has been a lot to handle these past few days. I would act just the same way if I were in your shoes."

I took a big bite of my sandwich, knowing that I had been forgiven.

"Speaking of shoes, Sandy, what happened to yours?"

We kept the conversation light throughout the rest of our meal, laughing and talking to relieve the stress we had both felt earlier that day.

"I wonder where President Deerun is," I thought out loud as we placed our crumb-filled plates and empty glasses on a counter in the kitchen. As we headed back down towards the movie theatre, I realized that I had seen the President very little over the last couple days.

"Hey Sandy, any ideas as to where he might be?"

"Not a clue," she shrugged. I was about to ask again but found that she was no longer walking at my side. I turned to find her staring at a framed painting on the wall. "Come here, you've got to look at this."

It was a field. Small golden stalks were growing everywhere, looking like some sort of grain. Scattered between them were small burgundy flowers, most of their roots exposed from the soil, swaying with a powerful breeze. In the center stood a single tree, positioned as if it were dominant over the rest of the landscape. Its structure made it seem like a willow, but none of its branches appeared wilted or lifeless. Instead, they either grew parallel to the ground or straight up into the sky, like the flames of a fire. Leaves of emerald green sprouted from each one, stretching and curving around to cover nearly the entire backdrop of the canvas. Its trunk arched against the wind, and although its bark was worn in spots, none of it was damaged or torn. A small nameplate under the painting titled it as 'Motto'. The artist was not listed.

The painting was beautiful, but neither Sandy nor I allowed ourselves the time to understand it. Within a moment, our attention had been turned back to reaching the downstairs theatre.

"Do you think that the President will be back in time for my debate?" I asked Sandy, beginning to worry all over again once we had reached the Center Hall.

"Of course!" she reassured me, her words coming almost too quickly. "You still have a lot of time to go until then. He'll definitely make it."

I tried to believe her, but when that didn't work, I simply forced the thought from my mind. By the time we neared the Visitors' Foyer in the East Wing, I was nearly successful, and once I had taken my place at the theatre stage, the idea had been completely pushed from my head.

As if practicing for an international debate had become routine for us, I turned on my microphone and waited for Sandy to get her iPod commercial and spotlight full-go. Once the noise and light had been cranked to their peak level of annoyingness, she stumbled up the side steps of our practice area.

Sandy was right—there really was nothing to worry about.

I had trouble remembering two or three statistics, but besides that, everything went perfectly. I don't mean to brag, but I had all the answers and counter-questions down pat.

Time went much faster than I had expected, and it wasn't long before I had finally triumphed over Sandy's last question. With a confident smile, she admitted that I had won.

It was almost time to go.

chapter twenty seven

Together, we ran upstairs to my bedroom. Genevieve was waiting next-door for us in the East Sitting Hall.

"Quickly!" she yelled as she first caught sight of us. "Time to do hair and retouch makeup!" Sandy and I exchanged a look, as if we were proud parents shocked at how quickly our child had become an adult—Genevieve's accent had sounded almost American.

Once we got closer however, her feelings towards me were anything but reciprocated.

"VHAT AVE YOU DONE?" she screeched in reference to my smeared makeup. I couldn't help but laugh. Genevieve must have missed the humor.

"Urry now," she yelled as if we had a choice, taking Sandy and me into her claw-like hands and pulling us into the bedroom. "Zere is vork to be done!

"Oh, and I ope you don't mind but I let myself in a vew minutes ago to zet up my needed materials," she added, leading us over to the writing desk. I looked around—apparently, she had also taken it upon herself to open the curtains. Sunlight was streaming in through the window like water slipping through a cupped hand.

Since Sandy had *not* ruined her makeup, Genevieve insisted that she get her touch-up before me. I was asked to change into my debate clothes while I waited. Predicting that whatever frustrations I caused her would be released when she untangled my hair, I knew better than to argue. Once I was finished, I sat down on my bed to watch her work. It was the first time I was able to take a good look at what she was wearing.

Her top looked like a hot pink tuxedo—or it would, at least, if the train of a tuxedo reached to the floor and had patches of yellow feathers sewn around its hem and collar. Its buttons were lined vertically downwards, starting about an inch or two below the lapel, and each one was a different color. The one near her waist was a traffic-cone orange, the one that followed a speckled shade of tortoiseshell, and beneath that was a button looking as if it had been made of hardened blue cotton candy. A large slit was cut at the side of the jacket's matching skirt, but had been filled in with what looked like yellow velvet.

I wondered where she bought her clothes.

Since Sandy had not been as careless as I had that morning, she looked almost exactly the same when Genevieve was finished with her. The only thing that had changed was her strawberry hair, now twisted up into an elaborate bun, held in place with purple barrettes.

"Pearvect!" Genevieve smiled. "No go and get into your dress vile I get to vork retouching vat Cara here has undoubtedly ruined zince tis morning."

I sat down at my desk chair, and let the pain begin.

Once we had finished, I unfurled my cowering body to reveal somebody that, for a moment, I didn't realize was myself. Genevieve held out a mirror for me, and I stared back at the girl reflected on the other side—I hoped that she would stick around.

"Thanks. You did a great job," I admitted, running my fingers through my hair. Despite her pleading, I had asked Genevieve to do my hair as it had been for my first interview, this time clipping back the pieces in the front with Bobbi Pins so that they would stay out of my eyes.

"Don't vorry about it!" cried Genevieve, obviously proud of her work. "I vill be zeeing you in your debate today. You arre going to be vantaztic, I just kno it!"

Although I had more than enough reason to believe that Genevieve had no idea what the word *debate* even meant, her praise gave me confidence.

"Yep. Thanks again! It's been great!" called Sandy, who had managed to make her way towards the door. A fake smile was plastered to her face, and I noticed that she was now wearing her spray painted shoes. "Hope to see you soon then. Come on Cara, let's get going now…"

Genevieve caught her at the last moment.

"STOP!" she bellowed, her tone no less gentle than a rock slide. "*Vere* are your shoes?"

"Right here." Sandy pointed meekly downwards towards her feet.

"You *lozt* ze onez I gave to you?" Genevieve asked.

"You could say that…," Sandy began, her eyes searching desperately for help.

"Good." Genevieve backed into one of her suitcases and stuck her hand into its front pocket. "*Because I found them!*" She pulled out the stilettos from behind her tuxedo jacket. I bit back laughter as I waited for Sandy's response. Genevieve however, continued to speak. "Yez I found them vor you! Zey were in a *cupboard* in ze kitchen! One of ze cooks vound zem, and zank goodness, she returned them to me in time! Iz it not very strange of them to end up zere?"

"Imagine that," murmured Sandy. Defeated, she moved to retrieve the heels. Genevieve checked her watch.

"Ay, it'z nearly five o'clock!" she yelled, flinging the stilettos in Sandy's direction. "Ve vere supposed to be finished ten minutes ago. I ave to stay and clean up, but you two must urry." Sandy was leaning against my bed, working to fasten the straps on her shoes.

"Hurry where?" she asked.

"Vuy to ze debate, ov course! James ze security guard should be vaiting for you already at ze Entrance Hall. A car vill be stationed outside to pick you up."

That was all I needed to hear.

"Sounds great. Thanks again!" I was out the door before we had time to shake hands.

Sandy managed to pass me after only a few minutes. "Come on Cara, hurry!" she yelled, making a substantial effort to run in her heels. My debate would be held in the Deseo D.C. Coliseum, and although not very far away, it was in the middle of the city so we could bet that there would be traffic. Understanding our need to rush, I did my best to catch up, racing down the staircase and into the Entrance Hall.

Sunglasses was already waiting for us. Clearly bored, we found him pacing across a throw rug near the door.

"You're late." His voice sounded angry but his expression was soft.

"I'm really sorry," I apologized, pushing the subject aside as quickly as I could manage.

"If it's any consolation, at least you aren't stuck in these shoes." An out-of-breath Sandy pointed towards her feet.

A small smile escaped from the corner of his mouth. "You're forgiven—now let's get going." He whispered something into his earpiece before opening the door; the sun reflecting off the tips of his sunglasses like it would a mirror. Blankly, I stepped back from the light, eyes squinted and hands blocking the rays from reaching my face. I hadn't been outside in the sun for awhile, and the day was brighter than my body could easily adjust to.

Sandy on the other hand, looked positively thrilled to be outside the White House walls. With an expression that said she had put the issue of her shoes behind her, she hobbled down the steps and out from under the shade of the North Portico. I watched as she lifted her face in direction of the sun, her skin doing its best to soak in the warmth that settled upon it.

James headed down the stairs in the opposite direction, towards a long black limo parked underneath the portico at the top of the driveway.

I stood alone, still at the door. It was late October by then, the 27th to be exact, and even the White House flowers and shrubbery were beginning to grow pale. They appeared to have withered since I had last seen them, and now looked prepared for an overnight frost. The sun was shining and the air was warm, but the wind felt cold against me. In an attempt to block out the chill, I wrapped my sweater more snugly around myself before rushing down to the car.

"Come on now, we can't be late!' I could hear James' call from behind the front passenger's door.

"Sorry," I apologized, letting myself inside. Sandy wasn't far behind, tottering back up the driveway and to my side.

"Alright then, let's get going," I could hear a voice murmur from the front of the car. I turned in its direction, surprised to see Ray in the driver's seat, sitting behind the steering wheel in his infamous neon dress shirt. He appeared to be involved in some sort of argument with James, who was in the chair directly to his right. I couldn't quite figure out what they were saying, but the seriousness in their tones wasn't at all difficult to pick up. They seemed to have reached some sort of conclusion just as Ray began to pull out of the drive.

"Miss Cara, James has some news for you," Ray reported, accelerating as he reached the street.

James pretended to focus on the road ahead, not bothering to turn around. All I could see of him was his sunglasses, peaking up at us through the rear-view mirror.

"The President called Ms. Muleson's office about five minutes ago with a message," he informed us. "Although he was planning on driving down to the Deseo with you, his meeting is running a little late and he'll have to meet us there. He sends his apologies."

An icy insecure feeling rushed over my skin. The air turned cold, thrashing around me in such tight circles that I soon found myself struggling for breath. The President had motivated me through everything—everything leading up to that moment. To imagine myself without him didn't seem right.

James twisted his body around in his seat, glancing back to see how I was taking the news. He cringed, the expression behind his dark sunglasses almost readable.

"Cara, there is no need to worry," he tried to reassure me. "The President *will* be at your debate, he just couldn't make the car ride."

I sighed, my uncertainties disappearing as quickly as they had come. *Everything is going to go just fine,* I told myself, leaning back against my seat.

James let out a deep breath, looking like a first-time babysitter who had somehow managed to stop a little kid from crying. He wasn't sure what he had done right, but whatever it was, he was glad that it worked. I watched as he took off his sunglasses, nervously beginning to clean them.

It was the first time I saw his eyes—a swirling mess of deep browns, screaming with expression. His face was impassive, but they gave him away.

They told me the truth.

The air grew solid, ripping through my lungs like concrete as their message spread throughout my body.

James didn't believe a word he had said…and neither did I.

chapter twenty eight

The car ride to the Deseo D.C. Coliseum was anything but relaxing. In fact, I spent its majority trying to avoid a panic attack.

Of course the President will be at the debate. It's such an important event for him—he said so himself. He wouldn't miss it...he can't miss it, I thought, trying to seal my mind away from any thoughts which might tell me otherwise. My efforts were barely successful.

Sandy couldn't stand the silence, but the car remained relatively quiet despite her attempts to start up a conversation. She gave up her cause reluctantly, and after what felt like a slow, traffic-jammed eternity, the car pulled to a stop.

Directly in front of us was a large white building. Lines of cars surrounded it, newscasters and cameramen rushing out to cover the sidewalk like a swarm of insects. Men and women whom I had never seen before were making their way past the media, dressed to satisfy anyone's definition of formal. Their faces weren't as easy to read as those of the reporters, but you could tell that they were excited. In tight secluded groups, they made their way up the walkway as one mechanical body.

A violent tremor shook my stomach as I realized who all of the strangers were talking about: *me.*

"This is it," Sunglasses announced. "The Deseo D.C. Coliseum—the largest public political gathering place in Washington." He gestured towards the colossal building out our window. "Why don't we get out here before Ray pulls around towards the VIP lot?"

"Come on!" Sandy nodded, thrilled to be talking again. She pushed open the door of the limo and gracefully strode into the parking lot. I followed close behind, Sunglasses moving to my side.

I looked out with Sandy in the direction of the coliseum. It reminded me of some famous monument, chiseled from marble and towering over the rest of the surrounding world. The structure itself was rectangular in shape with a large dome set at its peak. A narrow red carpet directed our way to its base, where a few dozen sets of polished stairs led up to an expansive balcony some fifty feet above the ground. A full portico stretched over the terrace, supported from below with the help of five huge columns. At its center, a tiled walkway guided crowds towards the lobby. Behind all of this, a circle of rich green ferns had been planted, looking almost too lively for the weather to permit.

"Built in 1864 at the request of our sixteenth President, this building is arguably one of the most historically significant in Washington, second to only the White House. The outside is made entirely of Carrara marble; that's what the ancient Romans used to design their statues. It was originally created as a public facility for political debate, and acted as a sort of a gathering place for people of the time to stay informed about national events or issues. Anyone was welcome to come and discuss their opinions and beliefs on that stage back then. In 1956 the building went under a series of renovations, including a seventeen million dollar expansion project, which enlarged the coliseum to the size you see today. So many people have made it in politics— have thrived in Washington, because of what they said on the stage right through those doors. So many dreams have been realized here. Even now, at least two nights a week, the coliseum is open for public use to serve just that purpose. In fact, the name of the coliseum itself, Deseo D.C., means D.C. dream, or wish, in Spanish," Sunglasses recited breathlessly, his eyes fixed on the oversized dome.

My feet were rooted to the ground, my eyes seeing nothing but the Deseo, focused on nothing but the Wish. For a moment, I was lost. Everything was quiet and everything was calm. My hopes were no longer just thoughts and the fire was no longer just something in my mind. Now it was real, and it was standing right before me. It had a place in the world. My wish was suddenly attainable. Staring at the Deseo, I was pulled down into a new kind of dream—one where the quiet could last forever and no one could wake me up. Then again, I'd never met anyone quite like Sandy.

"Let's go in!" she cried, tugging on my arm in hopes that I would budge.

"Alright!" I managed, freeing myself from her hold on me as my mind gained one on reality. It seemed too daunting a task to walk up the stairs alone, kind of like climbing a mountain without someone on belay. With Sandy and James at my side, I was glad I would never have to.

The front entrance to the Deseo was set up more like a party than a government function, and any tension between the different sides of the debate was hardly noticeable. Aside from the scattered fake smiles and sounds of forced laughter, things were pretty uneventful. Only a few media representatives had been allowed up to the veranda, and I smiled for one or two of the photographers before walking inside.

There were more people in the lobby than I had expected to see. Some were seated on the large chairs and sofas scattered throughout the room, but most remained standing. Waiters circled around the crowd, offering drinks and bite-sized appetizers on silver trays. Two couples standing nearby were speaking louder than the others, arguing about some speech that had been given earlier in the afternoon.

"Cara!" I heard a voice call. The crowd grew silent upon hearing my name. In an instant, one hundred pairs of eyes were darting around the room, all searching to find me. "Cara, come with me!" the voice repeated. This time, I recognized it as belonging to Sunglasses. I scanned the room in the direction of the sound, and spotted him standing under a large wooden archway.

Heads turned as Sandy and I moved to reach him, trying to ignore the crowd's low whispers. I could catch my name in almost all of them.

"Look!" a man with a large gray moustache murmured to his wife. "There she is! *That's* Cara Greybird!"

"She's much shorter than I would have imagined, don't you think, dear?" noted a middle-aged woman to the man standing next to her.

"Back up, Hilda, give the girl some space!" a kindly-looking woman urged her daughter.

I smiled, trying my best to appear comfortable with the attention. "Thank you all for coming." I waved at the crowd. "We'll be debating on a very worthy topic tonight, and I look forward to discussing my position with all of you!" Sandy smiled as we took our last few steps toward Sunglasses.

"Follow me, girls," he muttered, herding us under the archway. A man in a black security uniform opened the door he had been guarding and we rushed through to the other side, leaving the crowd behind.

"I am so sorry for putting you in that situation, Cara." James' breathing was steady, but his voice was uneven. "I didn't realize that you had been stopped by a photographer on the balcony, and by the time I got inside, you were nowhere to be seen. I couldn't help but panic."

"No problem—it wasn't your fault." I looked around. The three of us were standing in a hallway so wide that the entire mob from the lobby could have formed a horizontal line inside without ever touching an end wall. The floor had been laid with sand-colored tiles but shone gold under the light of the overhead chandeliers.

"Thanks," he shrugged. "Now how would you like to head down to the most important room of the Deseo?" Smiling, Sunglasses led Sandy and me through the rest of the hall and into a high-ceilinged room. Row-upon-row of theater seats stretched as far as the eye could see, each fixed to the dark wooden floor and upholstered in burgundy velvet. A long red carpet laced with golden trim had been rolled out between each of the four or five aisles separating the chairs. At the front of the room, about ten feet of open space was all that divided the last line of chairs from the colossal platform serving as the stage. It was probably six feet in height and four times that in width, composed of a wood so dark it appeared black from far away. On either side of the platform, a gilded staircase led up to the top half of the stage. Attached against the longest part of its base, a red, white, and blue striped banner was pinned to face the audience, fastened at its edges so that it hung in the shape of an upside-down rainbow. The walls were a faded china-blue, giving way to a tall marble pillar every couple of yards.

"Cara, look up there!" Sandy pointed towards the ceiling. Suspended at its center was the largest chandelier I had ever seen, nearly filling up the entire dome with its small prism-like crystals. Even alone, it was more than enough to make up for the lack of natural lighting—practically drowning the room in glowing golden shadows.

The room was empty aside from the few people still setting up for the event. I figured that the public spectators wouldn't be allowed into the debate room for another half-hour or so. It was hard to imagine that each seat before me would soon be occupied.

"Come on," Sunglasses led us deeper into the heart of the coliseum. "Feel free to look around. I'm going to go run a few security checks with the other guards here, just to make sure we're on the same page. I'll be right back here if you need me."

Neither Sandy nor I needed much of an invitation. Within a moment, the two of us were racing down the incline of the aisle, up the gold staircase and onto its platform. I had seen that stage many times before on television, heard it mentioned in *Newsweek* and *Time*, but never before had I cared to know all of the remarkable things that had taken place there. That night would be my first time witnessing them.

The stage floor was covered in wooden planks the same color of its base, with a podium for speaking on either side. A small microphone was perched atop each stand, fixed to the wood with a wiry coil so that its height could be adjusted. About an inch behind this was a wooden block meant to act as a stool so that you could be seen by your audience when speaking at the pedestal. Three modern-looking chairs had been lined up at the back end of the stage, each one built with the same stiff, metal back. My guess was that they were meant for us to sit in during breaks. Parallel to the rows of audience chairs was a low, narrow table covered in a white cloth. Another one of the metal chairs had been tucked into its center, facing opposite the audience. This was undoubtedly the seat of the debate moderator, the one who would be asking the questions to my opponent and me.

"Cara, hey, snap out of it!" Sandy nudged my arm, interrupting my thoughts. "Why is *she* here?" I watched her point towards a slim woman with short blonde hair, quickly approaching the stage. Within a second, I recognized the woman to be Kate Muleson.

"Not sure," I whispered back, fearing she would come within earshot if I said anymore.

"Girls!" She was smiling, but alarm was evident in her eyes. Kate marched over with her arms outstretched, as if she was going to pull us into a hug. Instead, she grabbed Sandy and me each by the shoulder, pushing us with an intended force into two of the metal chairs.

She looks out of place away from her office, I thought to myself as she began to speak.

"Listen," she whispered, taking seat in-between Sandy and me. Her tone was strangely rough. "I—"

"Hold on a second." Ms. Muleson looked more than irritated at being cut off. "Sorry to interrupt," I added, "but why are you—"

"I know," she smiled as if reading my mind. "I really shouldn't be back here right now. I'm actually coming to the debate later tonight, but there was just something I had to tell you.

"These debates, there's a certain thing about them. It's hard to describe because it is something that can't be told, but rather felt. The discussions that take place here in Washington, D.C. aren't just organized arguments, nor are they friendly. They are battles, Cara. I realize that you may not understand, but in order to win this, you've got to know what you're up against." I glanced towards Sandy for her reaction on what had become nothing less than an urgent warning. She looked just as confused as I was.

"I'm sorry," Kate sighed, "that came out wrong. I don't mean to scare either of you, and I'm not asking you to proceed with caution. I just came to offer some advice." She took a deep breath. "Never show defeat—I guess that's the just of it.

Never show defeat. *Even if you are defeated.* The only things that will determine the real winner tonight are your actions. I believe in you, Cara."

Sandy was still for a moment, letting the suggestion explain itself.

The both of us knew that Kate's reassurance was as unclear as Genevieve's accent choices would be for the following day, but I decided to take it gratefully.

"Thanks." I smiled as Ms. Muleson stood up from her chair. "That means a lot to me."

"Just remember what I told you. Oh, and by the way, Jawsie is being held outside near the entrance stairway. I was told that you may collect him whenever you like," she added, disappearing down the staircase and away from the platform with one final look in our direction. "Good luck tonight!"

I watched as Kate made her way out of the room, surprised to see that she now had to travel against a steady swarm of people spilling into it. The crowd was much quieter than they had been in the lobby, all displaying a more serious face than the one they had entered with. They briskly shook hands with one another and then hurried to their seats. Every eye carried weight and most were fixed heavily on me.

The attention caught me off-guard. In something I attempted to pass off as a purposeful manner, I averted my eyes to the unoccupied sections of the room.

I looked over towards Sandy, now readjusting the straps on her pumps. Giving an anxious smile in her direction, I turned back to face the far corner of the stage.

There was a woman standing next to me. I fought back the urge to jump out of my chair. Her presence was unexpected, and closer than made me comfortable. Worse, she was staring right at me, as if waiting to be noticed.

"Hello—." My voice trailed off as I inched away from her shadow. The woman's hair was dark brown, but it seemed to take on a leaded tint when she stood under the stage lights. Her eyes looked grey, and her eyebrows were archless, as if tilted into a permanent angry slant. A thick gold chain was hanging from her neck, and a pair of wide, flat-soled shoes had been laced on her feet. Her body was solidly built, with broad shoulders and a thick waist. The dress she wore was simple: black polyester with thin straps and a high neck. The fabric hung off her body like a paper bag, stopping just a few inches above her ankles. She did not appear to be wearing any makeup, nor did she appear to care. I frowned. Ms. Muleson was right about this debate.

It was going to be a battle.

But I was prepared to fight.

chapter twenty nine

"*Carol*," the woman sneered, examining her nails.

"*Cara*," I corrected her, forcing a smile as pleasant as I could manage.

She ignored the attempt.

"*I* am Winifred Tigers," she announced. I was half-expecting an 'and I approve this message' to follow it, but no such words ever came. She rolled her eyes instead. "But I'm sure you've heard of me."

"Yes, of course." It took an overwhelming amount of effort to sound sincere, even though I had truthfully never known or heard of a Winifred Tigers in my life. As she smiled back at me, clicking the gum she had been chewing, I wished I had never met a Winifred Tigers either. I swallowed hard.

"Well, of course you've heard of me, haven't you?" she replied in an '*I know something you don't know*' kind of voice. "I'm up against you in the debate!"

"Oh, well that's *fantastic!*" I turned back towards Sandy for help. She shot me a look as if to say '*Well, I never guessed that you'd get to debate with the Queen of the Universe! Lucky you.*'

Like she were breathing out smoke from a pipe, Winifred formed her lips into a thin 'o' and slowly exhaled. I could feel her breath against the top of my head.

"Don't think you knew that, did you, dear? I can tell from the shock on your face. It was decided that since I don't know your style of debating, then you shouldn't know mine. Since you can find information about the way I speak online, in the newspapers, on television, and of course from most everyone else in Washington, they kept my whole identity a secret from you."

I gave a small nod of agreement, but said nothing. Winifred took a step closer, enveloping me in her shadow.

"I really should be going now," she whispered, a glossy look in her eyes. She never did give a justified reason for leaving, but I didn't mind too much. Happy to see Winifred go, I stood to shake her hand.

"It was nice meeting you," I murmured through clenched teeth as I extended my arm. She looked down at my fingertips and smiled to herself like she knew some sort of secret.

"Goodbye, *Carol*," she turned on her heel and began strutting her way towards the opposite side of the stage, having completely disregarded my effort to shake her hand. She reached the other side of the platform within seconds, shooting one last glance towards Sandy and me before disappearing down the stairs and into the crowd.

I wanted to burst. Her eyes were dead as marbles, flat like a soda that had been sitting out for too long. Yet, she had looked down at me like some sort of unfortunate animal, her lifeless expression somehow brimming with arrogant pity. Her smile hinted that the whole idea of the debate was humorous to her. Like she had already won. As if I was some sort of subhuman species, an alien, an ignorant child undeserving of her respect. I shrugged to myself, it made no difference.

She looked at me like a child, and *that is what I was*. I was hurt, but knew that I couldn't show defeat. The battle had begun, and we were in open fire. She had gone in for a deadly shot I had only just narrowly dodged. I couldn't run out of ammunition just yet. I was a kid, and only time could make me older no matter what I did. Winifred made her way up onto the stage again, and something gave me the confidence to return her glare.

I remembered the words of the President's secretary. Your actions will determine the winner. *Not your age, but your actions.*

Suddenly, I knew what I had to do.

I could never change my age, but I would change the look in Winifred's eyes. I was sure of it.

chapter thirty

Sandy was making a face like she had just been force-fed a very unpleasant tasting vegetable.

"I *cannot* believe that Winifred woman," she whispered, her voice stiff as the air around us. "I mean, really, how you can go around treating people like subordinates— like we're nothing. No offense Cara, but she acted like you were dirt. Hey, I guess that's not too bad though, because she didn't even bother to acknowledge me!" She took a deep breath. "Just a simple 'hi Sandy' would have been fine. But then again, how could I expect her to know my name when apparently, she doesn't even know yours! Unbelievable…"

"I know," I whispered back. "But this is war! She'll never win if we don't give her the satisfaction."

Sandy laughed, the sourness already gone from her face.

"You're right."

For the first time in minutes, I looked out towards the audience.

Nearly all of the people were settled into their seats, waiting for the debate to begin.

"Cara!" Sandy exclaimed, now aware of the crowded room. "Cara, I have to go and get Jawsie! I remember where he is, don't worry. When you want to bring him onstage, just call me up. I'll take him up to you and hand over the leash. Got it?"

She rose from her seat, combing through the crowd with her eyes as if trying to pick out someone in particular. Completely overwhelmed, I hardly took notice of her frown. Beads of sweat were forming on my forehead quicker than I could dab them away with my sweater sleeve. The air in the room felt hot and thick, burning my throat as I struggled to gulp it down.

War is a horrifying concept. You never know just what you're getting into until it's too late to back out.

It wasn't long before Sandy noticed my anxiety.

"Breathe, Cara." The order was soft-spoken. "You'll be fantastic," she reassured me. "We both know that."

"Thanks." I forced myself to believe her. Sandy was already moving down towards the front of the stage, in the direction of the staircase. "Good luck!" She waved before climbing down into the crowd below.

Seconds after Sandy had disappeared from view, the overhead lights were dimmed, and the ones pointed towards the stage became brighter. My head was spinning, searching for a memory that might help me to appear calm. I took a deep breath—I was back at the President's movie theatre with Sandy, and the audience didn't exist. The sounds I heard were nothing more than an iPod commercial and I knew just what to do. I stood to approach my podium, and Winifred did the same.

I was still alone in the President's theatre, but as I moved towards the front of the stage, it became increasingly difficult to pretend. At the speaker's platform, I overlooked everything and everybody in the room.

There must have been thousands of people staring up at me, but somehow, Sandy still managed to catch my attention. She was standing at the corner of the room next to a dark furry shadow that I assumed was Jawsie. Not bothering to be discrete, she pointed animatedly towards something in the crowd. My eyes followed in the direction of her finger, wondering what she had wanted me to see. It didn't take long for me to find the answer.

For a second I forgot where I was. I couldn't remember that I was on international television or that the eyes of millions were fixed upon my face. All I could see were my parents, swelling with pride and staring up at me from the second row with a childlike mix of wonder and astonishment. Each of them was doing their best to restrain the overpowering parental instincts that urged them to snap a picture. Nadia sat in-between them, staring straight up at the chandelier as if it had just performed some sort of magic trick. I couldn't help but smile. Short attention span put aside, she was still my biggest supporter.

I scanned over the room again. My eyes had adjusted to the new lighting and it was no longer difficult to distinguish James from the cluster of guards near the door, nor was it hard to find Ms. Muleson, sitting in the center of the fifth row. Ray had never been very tricky to spot, and I found him near the back of the aisle. Mr. Owls and Mrs. Eelini were sitting side-by-side near the fourth row, whispering excitedly to one another. I looked downwards and saw Genevieve, who appeared to be sneaking licorice candies out of her purse and into her mouth when she thought nobody was looking.

It took all these observations to build up my confidence, but only one to tear it back down. My knees went weak before I could react, nearly giving out beneath me. Within a few seconds I had gone from a star on a stage to an ant under a magnifying glass, the overhead lights burning my skin to ash. I stopped smiling.

It wasn't what I saw that scared me.

It was what I didn't see

The President!

Frantic, I looked over my audience, desperate to find him. As I had suspected, he was nowhere to be seen. We had always stood by one another until that point. He had given me a lifetime opportunity, the encouragement to speak my mind, and taught me more than I had ever dreamed of learning. I had repaid his kindness by striving to meet our goals, working to spread his message. All of our efforts had led up to the present—a moment with me, alone on a stage and facing a battle I may not have been armed for. Now the President, my teammate, had not shown up. The soldier who had promised to fight by my side had abandoned me.

"Cara Greybird and Winifred Tigers?" I heard my name being called and momentarily left my state of panic to see who had wanted my attention. It was a small, portly man sitting at the upstage table.

"Present, sir," I answered as clearly as I could manage into my microphone. Winifred merely nodded.

"Hello, I am Jeremy Foxwell," the man introduced himself. His suit was made of gray polyester, and a pattern resembling alligator skin had been stamped into his necktie. The top of his head was bare except for a small tuft of hair in its center which had been combed and matted so that it spread down towards the nape of his neck. The lights shone directly onto his forehead, which was already beginning to show traces of sweat. His cologne was thick in the air. There was no doubt that he fidgeted when nervous, as he was constantly pushing his thick tortoiseshell glasses up towards the narrow bridge of his nose, only for them to slide back down again moments later.

Jeremy Foxwell wrung his hands together before he continued to speak, his voice strangely high-pitched. "The pertinent issue addressed during tonight's debate deals with whether or not we should continue to give a portion of government revenue for the funding and upkeep of animal shelters, or if we should adopt an alternate cause for the budget money. Ms. Greybird, to the right of those facing her, believes that we should continue with our previous approach, while Ms. Tigers, to the left of those facing her argues that the money should be put towards an alternate usage. Shall we begin with the debate?"

Winifred and I both nodded.

"Yes? Well, let us start then." Mr. Foxwell stuttered.

He took a deep breath, and then began.

. . . .

It had been decided that the debate would cover a series of fifty direct questions, each of which would be unknown to Winifred and I until they were asked. Mr. Foxwell would give us the time limit we had to spend on each response, and when time was up, we would move on to the next topic. The order in which we were to answer alternated with each question. As was determined by the flipping of a coin, I went first on odd numbered questions, while Winifred started off for the even ones.

"Question one: how would giving to your cause be better for our future? You have two minutes each. Cara, please begin…Question four: what good would your cause do for the average citizen? You have one minute each. Winifred, please begin…Question nine: why do you support this cause and not that of your opponent? You each have 45 seconds. Cara, please begin." Mr. Foxwell squeaked out question after question, each of which Winifred would relate back to the model replica she had manufactured with her $1,000 budget.

My opponent argued that the United States government should use the funding to flatten out the land on main streets and highways. The roads would then be smoothed down and repaved, resulting in what she called 'an easier, highly economical, and more convenient driving experience.' Over and over, she stressed that Americans would save gas money by driving on her leveled streets because they wouldn't be burning up excess fuel by traveling uphill. She claimed that all money saved through the use of this cost-effective means of travel would go straight to the pocket of the American consumer, and when spent, would improve local economic conditions. Winifred was also sure to point out that the roads would be safer and easier to drive on.

The example she had brought to prove her point was a small racing roadway with toy cars hooked onto it. There were two tracks on the roadway and each one was going in the exact same direction. The only difference was that the roadway for one of the cars was very hilly and scattered with rocks, while the track for the other was flat and smooth. She explained that after pushing a button on her example, the cars would move around the track one time. A small electrical instrument attached to each lane of the track provided an estimate of how many gallons of gasoline the cars would be using if they were built to size, with one lap around the track representing one hundred miles on a real road. In the end, the car with the flattened, smooth road was quicker and used up less gasoline as it traveled. The impressive display set her apart from me quickly, but I was confident that she would soon run out of fire. It was only when I sensed her weakness that I planned to bring out Jawsie as my secret weapon.

By the thirtieth question, Winifred and I had each defended our positions well and had put up good rebuttals to make our points clear. As I soon learned, Winifred was a much more difficult opponent than Sandy, often trying to trick me by using long and confusing terms of speech. Nonetheless, I responded as I had been trained to do, quickly transitioning into something I felt more comfortable answering. If I made a strong point, the audience forgot about Winifred's dispute and took on my new argument, as if I had brought up something more important.

I was concentrated on only our fight for the next hour or so. As the battle raged on, I forgot that my palms were sweating and my face felt clammy. I had learned to ignore my pounding heartbeat and to speak without tremor. It was unclear who was winning and who was loosing ground, but all I could do was follow my plan of attack and hope to finish up strong.

The only thing I had trouble disregarding was the light at my face. It was blinding—having reached a level of intensity not even the President's movie theatre spotlight could have prepared me for. By question number forty-five, I had to look down at the base of my podium for a good portion of my response because my eyes had begun to water. A few moments later, the debate reached its 90th continuous minute of progression. Jeremy received a signal from a cameraman backstage, and stopped the debate to make an announcement.

"We will now be taking a five minute commercial break," he announced once I had answered his question. Our audience is encouraged to remain in their seats, while our contestants are not permitted to leave the stage area. Communication between a debater and audience member at this time is strictly prohibited. Our program tonight will resume shortly." He pushed the microphone away from his mouth and moved to wipe his brow. "Thank you."

Almost at once, the spotlights were shut off, and the chandelier was turned back on.

It was nothing short of a miracle.

With the resolution that I would finally be able to rest my feet, I turned towards the row of chairs at the back of the stage. Winifred, torn between standing and having to sit next to me, eventually gave in to the demands of her feet and took the chair to my right. Jeremy appeared a few moments later, dabbing at his forehead with a handkerchief and offering each of us a warm cup of water. After many apologies about 'the lack of attainable refrigeration on the historic premises', he moved back to the moderator's section at the front of the stage, leaving Winifred and I to sit in silence. No member of the audience was permitted to join us, so while the crowd below chatted quietly and stretched their once dormant legs, my eyes began to search the room for something to do. I blinked a couple of times to get the translucent yellow speck of once vivid spotlight cleared from my vision.

The seconds continued to tick by, each one seeming like an eternity. I glanced sideways over at Winifred. To my dismay, she had already found something to occupy herself with, and was staring straight back at me. I met her gaze and her eyes turned sour, shooting me one final look before she shifted her body in the other direction.

It was a look I had never received from an adult before and it took more than a moment to find the proof in her face—she had been wrong about me. I was no longer just a kid, but her competitor. Now, she didn't seem to care who I was. The only facts that continued to matter were that I was still fighting and that I was in her way of getting what she wanted. To say she thought of me as a superior was a bit extreme, but somewhere in her mind, I was considered an equal—maybe even a threat.

I was an equal with The Great Winifred Tigers, and by default, I guess that made me co-Queen of the Universe, too. I hoped Winifred wouldn't mind sharing the title, but regardless, I had no intention of relinquishing it.

The crowd below was settling back into their seats as I considered this, getting ready for what lay ahead. Assuming that there wasn't much time left for recuperation, I gulped down the rest of the water in my glass, letting it wash over my stinging throat. Returning back to my place at the podium, I allowed myself one last hopeful search for the President. It wasn't easy, but this time, I forced myself to accept his absence. I was no longer sorry and nervous for my own sake, but this time, on the behalf of President Deerun.

What if something bad happened to him? I thought to myself, feeling guilty for thinking so selfishly beforehand. Images flashed through my mind faster than I could process them, each one depicting a possible scenario of what might have gone wrong. The chandelier was slowly dimming, and I knew that the return of the spotlight would be next.

No. I tried to persuade myself otherwise. *It's impossible. I would know if something happened to the President, everyone would. Someone would have informed us. He must be running a little later than expected, that's all. Don't worry.* The spotlight returned, and I knew that I couldn't carry on two debates simultaneously. Desperate, I made one last attempt to settle the current one.

Please, I found myself pleading, *Cara, don't worry.*

It was a cold night in Washington, D.C., yet, the room was a sauna.

I flexed my fingers and rubbed the sweat from my palms onto the sides of my dress, bracing myself for the near future. Mr. Foxwell's voice filled the room once more and the organs beneath my heart moved aside, sending it crashing down through my chest.

"At this time, I request for our audience to abstain from conversing as we resume our debate. It is expected that everyone who has not already taken their seats do so now," he squeaked into his microphone.

Stragglers wrapped up their whispered conversations mid-word and soundlessly found their chairs. After all but a few seconds, the room was silent again.

"Thank you all for your cooperation. Now, Ms. Tigers, are you ready to begin?"

"Yes," she answered without allowing for a pause in-between the question and response. I turned my head to see where her voice had come from, and found that she too, was waiting at her podium.

"Miss Greybird?" Jeremy's voice cracked as he said my name. He cleared his throat. "Are you ready to begin?"

"Yes," I responded, sounding slightly more composed than I would have expected. I smiled at Mr. Foxwell and he nodded in my direction.

"These last five questions will be permitted much longer replies, but are considerably more difficult. With this in mind, if both of our competitors are ready, let the second round of our debate begin."

With either new found courage or a newly realized fear of loss, Winifred and I sped through the next four questions. Each topic, although difficult to address, was dealt with quickly, in a much more sophisticated manner than I had imagined myself capable of.

Winifred concluded her response for question number forty-nine, and time came to a crashing halt. The room was still—waiting.

There was only one more question left. Ready or not, it was time to bring out my secret weapon.

"Alright," Jeremy screeched into the microphone. "We have reached the final question." A series of low whispers electrified the crowd, and Mr. Foxwell waited until the hum of voices died down before he continued to speak. "Now, when the fiftieth question has been answered, I will call upon you, the audience, to take part in a vote. This election will determine the party whose viewpoint is most favored by the public's unbiased, political opinion. I know that some of you have never been to one of these debates before...," he paused to take an unnecessarily long glance at my family, "but I urge you not to base your vote on nepotism. That is to say, do not vote for a candidate solely because...," he paused, searching for the right words to use. "...Because of personal ties. Yes, personal ties, that's it!" Jeremy sat up a bit straighter in his chair and turned to face the crowd behind him. "Everyone, this is legal business and we need it to be fair. Nonetheless, as an added precaution, both Winifred and Cara were allowed the same number of tickets for their guests and families. However, Deseo regulations prohibit anyone under the legal voting age from taking part in this final event."

My heart sunk as I thought of Sandy. She had worked so hard for the debate, and now she wouldn't be able to have a say in the results. I heard an exasperated sigh in the audience, undoubtedly coming from Nadia. Half of the crowd laughed, while the others pretended they hadn't heard her. Apparently, she wanted a vote, too.

Encouragement found me when I least expected it, and I was no longer upset. At least I was there, up on that podium. At least *one of us* was there. That was a start. If all went well, even without the support of Sandy and Nadia—if the world continued at the rate it was going, at the speed it was changing, then they would have the freedom to vote for me next time. And I knew that they would use it.

Mr. Foxwell began to speak again. "For all voters, I must add that underneath each one of your seats there is a laminated rubric with a grading scale, if you will, on proper debating. If you wish, you may use this rubric to determine who you will be voting for." He cleared his throat with a high-pitched cough. "Are there any further questions or objections from the audience? If so, they will be taken at this time." Mr. Foxwell cupped his hand over his forehead like the brim of a visor, shielding his eyes from the light as his eyes scanned the crowd.

From the corner of my eye I could see Nadia's hand shoot up from in-between my parents. The impatience on her face told me that she had a word to say about not being able to vote. "Nadia!" My mom turned and swatted it back down. I covered up my laughter with an unconvincing fake sneeze. Nadia may have been small, but she sure knew how to stand up for herself.

Mr. Foxwell appeared to not have noticed Nadia's outburst, and continued to scan the crowd. He straightened his tie—no other hands were raised.

"Good then." Jeremy sighed before turning to address Winifred and me once more. He cleared his throat and adjusted his tortoiseshell glasses one last time. "As you two may know, the fiftieth question will be a sort of reflection on your general position, and will conclude the debate. You will have fifteen minutes each for this question and it is highly advised, although not required, that you utilize as much of this time as you can. Again, Winifred argues the funding should go towards our public roads and highways while Cara believes it should remain with the animal shelters. Your final question is: *who benefits from your cause?* Winifred, since Cara started us off on the last question, you may begin when you are ready.

I turned my head to face Winifred, an action that earned me a monstrous glance.

"Well," she began, her voice louder than necessary. "If this money was put towards the construction of more fuel-efficient and transportation-friendly U.S. highways, freeways, and main roads, we all here would benefit *unlike we do now*." She tossed a strand of hair over her shoulder and went on. "I realize that the government may already supply a substantial amount of money towards this cause, but this is America—our standards are changing. Our ideas are constantly evolving with the time—that's what makes us so great! We have the power now to improve the condition of our country's roads, and that's a cause deserving of the added funding. Here, I'll give you an example." Her eyes widened as she looked over the audience. "Who had a tough time getting to this debate tonight? I know we have a huge mix of people here, some traveling from the other end of the country, some driving just a couple of miles. So come on! Who had a rough time on the roads? I want a show of hands. Don't be shy!" she encouraged.

A couple of people raised their hands slowly, as if nervous to distinguish themselves. They all seemed unsure of where the conversation was going. Winifred looked unhappy with the amount of audience participation but hid her disappointment well, summoning up a phony smile as she tried again.

"Oh, *please!* Come on!" she repeated, this time with more power than before. "I know that we have a *lot* of people in from out of town!" Four or five more hands rose unsteadily, as if the weight they carried was too heavy to lift. Only one person confidently identified themselves.

I recognized it to be Nadia again. For the second time that night, her hand was quickly shot down, this time by my father.

Winifred waited another moment before she shrugged to herself, satisfied.

"See! Look at that! Some of the highways and main roads in this country need some serious work. You *know* it's time to make a change when devoted and hardworking citizens such as yourselves cannot even travel peacefully! And I am *sure* that many of you had to refill your gas tank once or twice on your way over here. Taking a simple trip these days can be so expensive—a harsh reality I'm sure you've all faced.

"Well, unlike my opponent here, I want to do something about it. You see, if we could flatten out the roads and make them an easier surface to drive and walk on, all American citizens who use bus and automotive transportation would find themselves saving money on fuel costs.

"Take schoolchildren alone, for example. Of the fifty million children in our country who attend school each day, twenty-six million regularly use bus transportation, while the other twenty-four million are driven by a private vehicle. In one day, a school bus transports an average of 54 children, while the average car carries somewhere between one and two students. Considering that the typical home is five miles away from the public school of its district, and that the standard miles-per-gallon fuel capability for a school bus is seven, while a standard car can go around twenty-one, we are able to discern the number of gallons of gasoline used for school transportation in the United States. As my research confirms, there are sixteen million privately owned vehicles bringing students to and from school each day. Assuming that both of these commutes are roundtrip, we learn that *each of these sixteen million cars consumes an average of 171 gallons of gas a year on school transportation alone!* Additionally, each of the nearly half a million public school busses in our country use 1,714 gallons over the course of the year on average. Think—if just half of these students were to walk, or say, bike ride to school because of improved roadways, parents would find themselves spending hundreds of dollars less in gasoline annually, and the public education system as a whole could save millions!

"Without having to spend thousands each year on the rising cost of fuel, Americans will have more money to devote to the purchase of consumer goods, charity organizations, and industry as well. Not only is this sure to boost our economy, but my position on this issue is also all about conservation and 'going green', if you will. As responsible Americans, it is our job to use fossil fuels responsibly, and be on the constant lookout for actions that will help to preserve our planet's natural resources. If our roads were reconstructed to make non-automotive commutes more convenient, exhaust emissions from vehicles would drop dramatically. We could be cutting a huge chunk of the pollution out of our air! Therefore, my plan benefits not only us, but our environment as well.

"Additionally, with Americans using less fuel, there will be much more gasoline around for the rest of the world. This surplus will allow for other countries to sell their fuel at lower prices, an action that will surely boost their economies as well, not to mention how good it will be for the travel industry on an international level. Having a lower global demand for gasoline would also allow scientists to concentrate on developing an alternative fuel source before the supply completely diminishes.

"As I've mentioned before, these flatter, straighter roads would also make other ways of transportation more sensible, such as walking or riding a bike. If roads were leveled out to be completely horizontal, walkers and bikers would be able to conserve more energy because they would be able to move a longer distance with shorter steps. This would enable many of our people to make their way to work or school without a machine aiding them such as a car or bus. In this way, everyday Americans will be able to work exercise into their daily lives. Your vote today will bring much more than just convenience to our country. Consider the possibilities! This could be the first step toward creating a more active community—a healthier America! The increase in walking and jogging is another surefire means to boost our economy because many people will purchase items such as running shoes, bicycles, and scooters. In fact, the demand for scooters would be sure to rise, especially for those portable ones. They help people to get around quickly, even though they're still exercising. These devices are also incredibly easy to store, so if your destination doesn't have a bike rack, you can fold it up, and bring it inside with you. Plus, they are very safe, and virtually resistant to injury!"

I thought of *my* last incident when I traveled by scooter and suppressed a snort. Winifred shot me a shameful look, before turning back to face her audience.

"As I was saying," she continued, "with all of this foot traffic, people who still choose to take cars or busses will not be on the road with that many other motorized vehicles. Therefore, my cause can eliminate a good chunk of traffic from American roads! Think of it—your commute time can be cut in half!"

At this, the crowd was launched into another round of whispering—some even clapping with approval.

"Another reason why the funding should go towards my cause is for our own safety. For starters, with flatter roads, cars traveling by will be able to see pedestrians and other obstacles from a much farther distance away. This allots the driver a longer time span to notice the obstacle and a much lengthier one to decide how to maneuver around it. Do you know what this will do? It will eliminate accidents on the road. Most importantly, it will keep our children safe."

Winifred's statement was followed with more applause, but she continued to speak over the crowd.

"Moreover, thousands of vehicles each year swerve off the road or crash into other cars because of poor road conditions in icy, harsh weather. If we were able to construct better roadways, we would be able to minimize car accidents, and maybe even the injuries and deaths that can result from them!"

Winifred stepped down from her speaking platform and away from the podium, moving towards the presentation she had brought. A stagehand rushed to her side in order to hand her a cordless microphone. She snatched it hungrily, and continued on with her speech.

"America, I have shown you all of the facts." She paused for a moment to flick the power switch on her display. Instantly, the two toy cars began making their way around the racing track. She smiled as the free world focused on the vehicles, the one on the straighter, more level track slowly beginning to take the lead. When the two cars had finally completed their lap, she wordlessly gestured towards the instruments which were recording the projected amount of gasoline each one had used. She moved aside to let the cameras focus in on the numbers, and then read them aloud for the audience to hear. With a long, drawn-out breath, she saw it fit to continue speaking.

"America, I have shown you all the facts," she repeated, her voice growing louder with each syllable, "and now it is time to make a decision! I'm sure we have all experienced the frustrations of a road that stands below our expectations. Let me just tell you now that if you vote for my cause, we can finally reach a solution for this serious issue…once and for all. America, my issue affects you no matter what you may think. It *will* save the environment, and it will save lives, not to mention time and money. Not only will it preserve your health, but protect your safety, as well. It is guaranteed to help all of us, whether you drive a car, a truck, or even if you take the bus! So now, as my speech comes to a close, I ask you America; *why not* change something that is guaranteed for the better? Thank you."

Winifred knew she had done a good job—the look on her face made it clear.

Her message was strong, and she met the applause that followed her speech with a confident smile.

My heart reminded me that it was my turn next, each beat delivering a painful blow to what I assumed was already a very bruised chest.

"Alright!" Mr. Foxwell cried into his microphone after the clapping had died down. I pressed a hand to the thudding, hoping that the pressure might quiet it.

It didn't work.

"Well done, Ms. Tigers," Jeremy continued. "Miss Greybird, since your competitor has finished speaking, you may begin with your speech when you are ready. You have fifteen minutes."

I nodded in Mr. Foxwell's direction, but couldn't bring myself to speak. My throat felt swollen and in that instant, the spotlight's heat on my neck became intensely painful. I was suffocating—unable to find the air to breathe, much less respond.

It's alright, just take a minute to gather your thoughts. I tried to reassure myself. I held my breath, then slowly let it out. When I could no longer feel the echo of my heartbeat like a base drum, I began to prepare myself for what I was about to do.

In the silence, I swallowed hard, looking into the bright light and gathering everything I had learned into what I hoped would sound somewhat like a well-rehearsed speech.

"Miss Greybird?" Mr. Foxwell squeaked, breaking my concentration. "Miss Greybird, are you ready to begin?"

"Of course," I answered. Winifred and I had been evenly matched until that point, each with just as many triumphs as we had defeats.

If this was a battle, we were in a stalemate—a standstill.

And if I had one shot to change that, it was quickly disappearing. After this, there would be no more chances. Every soldier would be stationed on the front lines, every weapon used, every risk ignored. I had everything to lose but more to gain.

The war was coming to a close, and I knew that I had to prevail in this last combat.

With one final deep breath, I took my place on the battlefield.

chapter thirty one

I stared into the sea of people sprawled out before me.

"Before I begin, I would just like to congratulate Ms. Tigers on her wonderful performance tonight." Some applause followed this, but I got the strange feeling that none of it was intended to go towards Winifred. I managed a smile. "I have to admit, she's a tough act to follow!" A few scattered chuckles or snorts were heard from around the room, the loudest of course being Nadia's over-exaggerated one. "But on a serious note, I am here tonight to talk to you about an issue of the utmost importance. And you can believe me, if I didn't truly believe that my cause is more beneficial than that of my opponent, I wouldn't be standing before you today." I smiled, eyes scanning over the now stern faces of my audience. It was strange to consider my power over them, and I realized that I would have to channel it in order to win. It was a skill Winifred had probably practiced hundreds of times, but one I had only the next fifteen minutes to master.

"Although Winifred had many excellent points and ideas," I continued, "I *do believe* that there is a better cause in which our funding should be placed. This cause is our *American animal shelters*. Now, I know that we, myself included, would all love to improve the conditions of our roads. I'm not going to pretend we don't want to make the commuting aspect of our lives ultimately easier. However, I can assure you that if government funding is not placed with the shelters, there will be *more* road-related problems than ever before. This includes *car accidents*." I paused to encourage the puzzlement that was appearing on the faces of the audience. "If the shelters that rely on government funding are denied it, they will be unable to maintain the areas in which the animals are kept, and will have inadequate financial means to feed the animals, forcing them to close down. In addition, it is not uncommon for the government to donate the land on which the shelters are built. Without these larger amounts of property, the shelters would only be able to house and provide for *a fraction* of the animals that they do today. This would leave us with *millions* of dogs and cats roaming the streets each year, causing three main problems."

I looked out into the crowd below, only to find that their full attention was on me. "The first major problem would be an increase in erratic driving." I spoke slowly, giving the crowd time to realize the contradiction between Winifred's promises and my facts. "Imagine all of those homeless dogs and cats out on the road. You are driving, not recklessly, nor even carelessly. In fact, you are concentrating on the road before you, just as a good driver should. But even to a driver such as yourself, if the government funding is not given back to the animal shelters, you will definitely be put in one very bad situation. I will illustrate this situation for you now. So, there you are driving, when suddenly, a dog runs into the middle of your lane, just feet from your car. Stunned, and not knowing what to do, three things could happen. First, you can stop your car quickly and wait for the animal to pass, maybe even getting out of your car to help it along. Although this may seem like a solution to the problem, I can tell you right now that it will do more harm than good. By stopping your car without any further indication to other drivers on the road, you are not only further endangering the animal, but yourself, as well. For instance, the vehicles driving behind you will be unprepared for your stop, and may not be able to react safely and without negative effect. The two most popular driver reactions in this scenario would be to swerve the car, or to slam on the brakes. Both of these options put you, the passengers in your car, and the animal in direct danger, while also endangering the car behind you, and all other street traffic as well.

"With this in mind, I can promise you now that Ms. Tigers' road reconstruction plan wouldn't help with animal visibility whatsoever. Before crossing a road, I have yet to see an animal walk alongside it, or pause to watch for oncoming traffic. Most of the time, they're traveling perpendicular to your vehicle, and straightening our roads won't help with that type of accident in the slightest. Automotive related accident mortality *will* increase—despite the promises of my opponent. Let me ask you this—who are you driving with? A friend, a co-worker, a spouse, a neighbor, your children? Are their *lives* something you'd be willing to risk for a shorter commute?

"The next possibility is that you can keep driving at the expense of the animal's life in order to keep yourself safe. Although this last choice may not physically damage you, hitting and ultimately killing an animal in which humans have forged bonds with for hundreds, even thousands of years, can have lasting emotional effects. Anyone who has ever had the misfortune of hitting an animal on the road will know that these effects can be devastating. Today in America approximately 1.2 million dogs and 5.4 million cats are killed on our roads each year. If we are not given the money to keep these animals away from our streets, think of how dramatically these numbers will increase! We know that over five million animals are housed in American shelters, and we know that nearly half of these shelters receive government funding. So, if all of these government funded shelters were forced to close, we would have around 2.5 million additional homeless animals roaming our streets. Knowing that of every 100 stray animals, 55 are hit by cars and trucks, we can approximate that 1,375,000 or about 1.4 million of these animals would be killed on the roads annually! Seeing as that would push our total up to over 8 million animals killed per year on American roads, I am able to tell you now that if the money is not given to the shelters, the amount of dogs and cats hit on the street will increase by twenty-one percent! Plus, if you consider that one fourth of all collisions with an animal result in human injury, we can expect that without government shelters, the number of human injuries due to stray dogs and cats will increase by 350,000 a year!

"Lastly, and arguably your most dangerous option, you could swerve out of the way of the animal. This is a reaction that many people have when an animal is on the road. Nonetheless, although this might save the animal, it could kill you. For one, you could swerve into another car, or even off the road all together, putting your safety and the safety of other drivers in jeopardy. That, to me, doesn't sound like the best idea—especially once you hear that 200 people a year are *killed* by turning sharply as they try to avoid an animal that has stepped onto the road. If the funding is taken away from the animal shelters, I can almost guarantee that the appalling percentage I have just presented to you will skyrocket—increasing by as much as 34%. That is 268 deaths *a year* –some of which we can prevent *right now!* I know that to some, adding 68 more to a statistic isn't very convincing. Who can blame you? Our brains are used to processing big numbers, impressive figures, and so what's 68 more? Well, I'll tell you. sixty-eight is an entire neighborhood. It's people with families and jobs and responsibilities. Two school busses filled with children. And when I have the opportunity to save 68 lives, you can bet I'll have no second thoughts.

"Now that I think about it, none of the circumstances or consequences I have just mentioned sound that good to me. How about you?" I watched as a couple of people shook their heads in agreement. "What about if you consider that 2,800 dollars is the average cost per insurance claim on a vehicle involved in a collision with an animal, and without the government funded animal shelters, your vehicle is over 20% more likely to see damages of this extent *each year*?" Nearly the entire audience was shaking their heads now.

"However, the previously stated statistics are not alone in supporting my issue. Think about this for a moment—what if these homeless animals were not taken to government-funded animal shelters and given shots to protect them from disease? What if, instead, they were roaming around near our homes and workplaces? I'm here to tell you now that without our government shelters, multiple deaths would occur *monthly* due to the diseases these stray animals might be carrying. Rabies especially, would be a big threat to all of us. Eventually, we would have to give the funding money back to the shelters again in order to keep disease-carrying animals from spreading the maladies to ourselves, and our own pets. Unfortunately, since that original budgeted money would already have been invested in our roads, do you know where the funding would come from? Directly from the pockets of the American citizens, that's where. Yes, I'm talking about a nation-wide tax increase here, the effects of which can virtually decimate our economy.

"Having all of these homeless animals on the streets can be dangerous in many more ways, as well. For example, people outside can be severely injured by animal bites and attacks. Just this year, over 4.5 million people have been seriously bitten by dogs alone. If the amount of stray dogs were to multiply due to the government's failure to supply funding to shelters, this issue will evolve from just a serious matter to a nationwide public hazard! In addition, multitudes of stray animals could cause harm to our personal property as well, including our gardens, homes, and yards. Public streets and parks would become unclean and unsanitary in addition to posing an increased safety threat for us, our families, and our community.

"Straightening our roads can also have its negative effects, as well." I thought back to the geography quiz I had been studying for on the day I received my first White House reply letter. Smiling, I remembered the chapter it had covered— *the importance of natural landforms.* In all my life, I don't think I have ever been so thankful to have paid attention in class. "For one, hills and all other uneven landscapes act as a natural barrier for us from storms such as hurricanes and tornadoes. Without these features, we would be enabling natural disasters to increase in destructive power and damages. It is our responsibility now to do all we can to stop the leveling of roads, as they enable a deadly force to have even more power over our lives."

I took a deep breath. The audience was still, patiently waiting for my next move. Somehow, I couldn't help but to feel that they were my allies. I couldn't let them change sides now, I was just too close. I needed them with me. It was in that moment, up on stage in front of thousands of people, that I began to realize where I had gone wrong before. My voice had been strong by itself, but it could never bring anything new. As I stood before the crowd, watching their eyes drink in my emotion, a major secret of war occurred to me. *You can't win a battle if you're fighting alone.* A voice is only as powerful as the people who listen to it.

They were listening.

"On the other hand," I continued, "none of these horrible situations *has* to occur. In order to further demonstrate this idea, I would like to call up my friend and advisor Sandy Giraffing, who will be presenting my example to us."

The air turned to ice—solid, heavy, ice—and for an instant, the room was trapped beneath it. I looked over the soundless crowd, practically able to hear Cornelia V. back in Pennsylvania, complaining that I hadn't formally addressed her sister with the proper name, *Sandra*.

The moment that followed seemed unreal, unnatural, impossible, like the world was nothing but one giant television screen in which somebody had pushed the mute button. Yet, I had somehow created it, and the audience sat wide-eyed below, the stifled victims of its silence. There was no coughing, no sneezing, no hushed whispers or the rustling of fabric. Just three thousand people holding their breath.

This is what they had been waiting for. They had not expected me to save my example until the very end, but now it was coming. It seemed to me like a tiebreaker of sorts. *The one thing that could help America decide on their vote was being walked up a ramp and onto the stage by a girl with strawberry hair and possibly the highest heeled shoes known to man.*

For the first time in weeks, my eyes met with Jawsie Hamstering. The last time this had happened, I was terrified. This time was no different, although my fear was now for a different reason.

As Sandy approached me with Jawsie, I realized that the dog at her side was not the same one I had known earlier. Of course he was still the same animal—same shabby looking dog with a fiery glow in his eyes, but something had changed.

Nothing about Jawsie had been muted or restrained—that was for sure. Just one look at him made it clear. In fact, you might say that he was showing more personality now that you weren't scared to come within ten yards of him. The fire in his eyes hadn't been toned down or put out; it was just being expressed differently. Jawsie was no longer terrifying simply because he knew that there was a better option. As I looked into the face of the dog before me, I suddenly caught sight of the animal which the Hamsterings' had seen all along. The only difference was that now, everyone else could see him too.

I watched as Sandy made her way up the stairs, with Jawsie trotting contently beside her. I extended my palm for the dog to sniff as he approached me, which he instead began to lick. Sandy held out Jawsie's leash for me to hold, and I took it in my opposite hand.

"Thank you, Sandy," I said, looking up at her once more before she began the difficult task of climbing down the steps in her heels. She was smiling, and although I didn't realize it, I was too.

"You're welcome," she answered with an even bigger grin than before.

The crowd had no idea that we were talking about much more than bringing a dog up onto a platform. *Much more.*

As good as it felt to have her with me, Sandy soon made her way back to her seat and I was left on stage to complete my mission. I took a moment to organize my thoughts, and continued to speak.

"Ladies and gentlemen," I began. "This, is *Jawsie*. A few people smiled at the dog, now panting heavily from the heat of the spotlights upon him. "Jawsie is a living example of the effects of my opponent's, as well as my own position regarding our subject of debate. Although now, Jawsie is practically a staple in my Pennsylvania neighborhood, a couple years ago, you might have been able to find him roaming along highway seventy-nine." I finished the sentence with a cold undertone, allowing the time for what I had just said to sink in. Within moments my audience was silent again.

"This dog," I continued, "managed to live without human support for nearly his entire first year of life. It was then that Jawsie, still a puppy at the time, was involved in a terrible accident. Witnesses say that Jawsie was attempting to cross the highway at around 10:15 p.m. One man, seeing the dog, called animal control and reported his location before driving away. The next time Jawsie was seen, it was by police. He was lying near the roadside, cradling his left paw in which his olecranon and radius bones had been broken. One of the carpal bones, located towards the bottom of that paw, was also seriously fractured. Officials noticed right away that the injuries were located at about the same height of a small car's bumper and reached down towards where the middle of its tire would go. Investigators assumed that Jawsie had been hit by an automobile, and that the collision had thrown him to the side of the road. The entire right side of his body had been badly scraped from the fall, with a gash over his scapula running half an inch deep by three inches wide, and roadside pebbles and debris embedded into his skin. The accident had been a hit and run. If government funding was not provided to the animal shelters, as Ms. Tigers has proposed, we would all be seeing many more accidents such as the one I just described.

"Upon sighting him, police tried to capture Jawsie so that they could bring him to an animal hospital where he could receive further medical attention for his injuries. Jawsie however, was unwilling. Despite his serious pain, the dog stood up and began to protest—scratching, jumping, and even biting. Prepared for the possibility of a *vicious* dog such as this, the police had been dressed in protective padding so that Jawsie could not cause any physical harm. After a couple moments, Jawsie had been wrestled into the back of a large rescue van and was heading towards an animal hospital where he was sedated, bandaged up, and then sent to a *government-funded* Pennsylvania animal shelter. At the shelter, Jawsie was to receive further special care until he had made what was expected to be a full recovery. Still considered a dangerous animal, Jawsie was kept in an isolated cage for the duration of his stay at the shelter.

"Then, one ordinary autumn afternoon, a woman by the name of Gina Hamstering entered the shelter and she saw in Jawsie something that the others had neglected to see. She looked beyond the dog's appearance and took the time to understand where he had come from. When she looked at Jawsie, she saw an animal in desperate need of human compassion. My neighbor saw an animal that, initially, might not be easy to love, but an animal that in time, would thankfully repay her with unconditional loyalty and affection. With one last look at this dog, Mrs. Hamstering decided that she would take him home—and she did just that. While she was signing the adoption papers, the police officer witnessing her signature offered her a sympathetic word of advice.

"'Are you sure you want to do this, ma'am?' he asked quietly. 'This dog might be awfully dangerous.'

"'I believe he's awfully misunderstood,' she answered with a smile. The policeman only shrugged before handing Jawsie's leash off to his new owner, a major turning point in the life of both the dog and its human companion.

"'Good luck, then,' he wished her blankly. 'Just don't say I didn't warn you.'

"Despite the opinions of others, Mrs. Hamstering took Jawsie home that very same day. As his new outer wounds began to heal with time, some of his older wounds, the ones found only inside, began to heal as well. Slowly but surely, Jawsie was becoming less like the dog that Mrs. Hamstering had seen at the shelter—the dog who seemed lost in his own eyes, dying to break free. The only problem now, however, was that Jawsie was still a *bit* too wild to be living in a suburban neighborhood. Once he was fully healed inside and out, this wasn't much of a problem. All it took was a few obedience classes before the spirit that used to survive in only the eyes of this dog had established its potential throughout him. Jawsie has never been happier…"

My voice trailed off and my eyes met with the animal that I had now regained faith in. Slowly, I understood what I had been debating about in the first place. *I knew the last surefire reason that the animal shelters needed to receive the money*—the one that couldn't be researched, but rather experienced. I had found a reason for America to fight on my side.

"Jawsie has never been happier, and *I have never been happier for him*. If you just take the time to look into the eyes of this dog, you will understand what a miracle these shelters can be—why they can't be taken for granted, why we can't let them go. They gave Jawsie a second chance at *life*, and in return he's become a part of somebody's home. Two big brown eyes that greet them in the morning, won't judge us for how we're dressed or the ways we style our hair. A head that doesn't care about the types of cars we drive, or the numbers on our paychecks. A wagging tail that will never grow scarce in times of need, and a heart that won't ever turn away from us. If you don't believe me, I ask you now to look into Jawsie's eyes, and I promise that you will.

"Humans tend to be selfish and may unknowingly sacrifice the well-being of others in order to better themselves. What those in favor of Ms. Tigers' funding plan fail to realize is that if the money is taken away from our shelters, we will really be doing more harm to *ourselves* than good.

"Shelter animals like Jawsie all over America have found care, and a place where they can *feel safe,* thanks to government shelters. They may come from the streets like Jawsie, or homes of abuse and neglect, but regardless, the shelters offer them a chance to find family. By giving the shelters' money to a fund for the reconstruction of our roads, we would be denying families like the Hamsterings' and dogs' like Jawsie of their right to all of that. Are we really going to put our government in the position to take those opportunities away? If anyone here watching or listening to this speech right now knows an animal in their life, I ask you to think of them right now. Remember how they've kept you company, and encouraged you, and even *inspired* you. Would you give all of that up to cut thirty seconds off of your trip to the grocery store?

"If government funding was taken away from the animal shelters in our country, nearly 10% of the dogs and 11% of the cats in our country would never have had the chance to find the loving homes that they have today. So, Mr. Foxwell, if you are asking me who the continued funding of animal shelters will benefit, I am answering not only ourselves, but the environment, millions of loyal animals like Jawsie, the *future* animals that might get a second chance, and the animals with the unconditional love that I urge you to not take for granted. It is for all of us that a portion of our government budget continues to be set aside for the animal shelters. I know, America, that you will not base your decision off of short term convenience, but that you will make the *right choice…* Thank you."

The oxygen supply in my lungs had been completely depleted at this point, but my words had been formed with certain strength. My speech had been concluded and I was caught between two forces, not knowing whether I should surrender to the tears welling up in my eyes or yield to the smile I could feel pushing at the corners of my mouth. A fantastic sound met my ears, a booming applause—and the limbo of emotions I was entangled within tightened their hold around me. The sounds of my audience thundered upon the stage like an explosion of fireworks, crashing down upon the world like an uncompromising wave with an undeniable message. I was breathless, but each passing second filled me with pride to the point of swelling.

"Thank you," I managed. "Thank you!"

My heart was alive, beating against my body as if it were trapped inside and trying to break free. When it had lain dormant, I was its cocoon. Now, it was ready to find its way out—showing the world that it had managed to become a butterfly. A true miracle.

My smile won over.

chapter thirty two

The memories that mean the most to us are always fleeting—seconds in time we must struggle to hold onto. The same was true with my applause, and as quickly as it had come, it was soon silenced by Mr. Foxwell.

"Thank you, Cara," he squawked, adjusting his glasses as he spoke. "The debating portion of this evening has finally come to a close, and it is now time to vote for the better position and argument—that of Miss Greybird, or her opponent, Ms. Tigers. I will allow five minutes for those who wish to look over their scoring rubrics to do so. There will be no conversing during this time. When your five minutes are up, I will call a vote and the winner will be chosen. You may begin."

I stood at the podium with my heart pounding in my chest, trying not to look nervous—and when that didn't work, concentrating on masking my panic. The longer I stood still at the podium, the hotter I became. I began to take big steady breaths in order to calm myself, but they proved to be of no effect.

Everything to come was completely out of my hands. I had done my part, and now the final say was left up to the audience. There was nothing more that I could do…and it bothered me to no end. Thoughts now useless were racing through my mind, twisting and mangling my memories so that they might confirm my worries. Time was an odd thing to consider, the way some moments pass by at an ungraspable speed, while some, like the one I was experiencing then, were stretched out so long that they seemed to taunt you. For a moment, this idea struck me as funny, but after another moment I decided it to be cruel.

I was trapped in a silent eternity, standing up at the platform and being judged by the world, waiting for my future to be decided for me. Finally, interrupting what had come to resemble some type of effective torture method, Mr. Foxwell began to speak. I could hear the sound of his voice distantly, but was so nervous that his words were somehow unable to register in my mind. It wasn't until Jawsie began to playfully nibble at my ankle that I drifted down to reality.

"…and now, it is time for us to vote." Mr. Foxwell finished off his sentence. "Before we get to the results tonight, I would just like to thank you all for being here. I would also like to remind you of the rules once more. You must not vote based on nepotism, and nothing but your own takes on what our competitors have said today should influence your decision. In addition, voters who may be indifferent to the outcome of our debate must vote accordingly. Once more, nobody under legal voting age will be allowed to take part in our final ballot tonight. Thank you in advance for your cooperation." Mr. Foxwell breezed through his last few sentences as if he were a stubborn schoolchild being forced to recite his classroom's rules for the third time that day.

"If there are no further questions," his voice grew somewhat deeper and a hint of curiosity was becoming evident in his eyes, "let's get on with the results…"

I felt as if my heart had shoved its way into my throat and I was now choking on it, fighting for each breath. Swallowing hard, I struggled to contain myself, giving what I hoped would appear as a confident smile.

"Firstly," Mr. Foxwell squeaked, "I am asking that any person who is indifferent to the outcome of the debate please raise your hand now and say 'I' so that you may be subtracted from the final tally of the vote. If you wish, please do so now."

"I," A man with a shaky voice called from the back of the room.

"I," A woman in a rather large purple hat repeated.

I stifled a laugh, having seen both the man and the woman enter the debate room considerably late.

"Is there anybody else?" Mr. Foxwell asked, furrowing his brow. "Anybody at all?" No more hands were raised. He sighed, "Good then, let's move on. There are two thousand three hundred and twenty-four people joining us in person for the debate today. This number minus two indifferent voters is two thousand three hundred and twenty-two. Next, taking into consideration that two people with us today are not at the age of eligibility required for voting, we should have a grand total of two thousand three hundred and twenty. This number divided by two is one thousand one hundred and sixty." He shut his eyes as he did this last bit of mental math. "The number I have just presented you with, one thousand one hundred and sixty, is the number of votes each side of the debate would have to get for the results to be tied. Therefore, the first competitor to get one thousand one hundred and *sixty-one* votes will be the winner!"

Mr. Foxwell managed a smile, loosening his tie a bit before continuing. "Twenty voting booths have been set up in the Grand Hall, the rather large corridor you have all passed through earlier this evening. A Deseo employee is stationed at every booth. Now, upon entering this debate, all eligible voters in the audience were given a ticket, each printed with its own identification number and barcode. When approaching the voting area, all he or she must do is present this ticket to a Deseo poll-worker, who will tear off the perforated strip along its edge. After this, the voter's ticket will be handed back and they will be permitted to enter the booth, where an electronic kiosk has been set up for their usage. To activate their ballot, voters merely insert their ticket, barcode face up, into the slot at the front of the machine. They will then be taken to a voting menu where the names of our debaters and their causes are listed. The voter will signify which issue they support by selecting the name of its debater and then pushing the green 'cast ballot' key, both using the kiosk touch screen. Note that each ticket will only register with our equipment for a single use, thus ensuring that each elector gets exactly one vote. A detailed list of voting instruction and procedure steps have been provided in every booth if you require any additional information.

"If you are unable to vote using this electronic method, please request the help of a Deseo employee, who has signed a confidentiality agreement to respect the privacy of your ballot. After you have voted for a competitor, the screen will revert back to its original menu for the next user, and you may go back to your seat. Your ticket must be removed from the kiosk and returned to a poll-worker as you exit the booth. A computer will alert officials once a debater's tally has reached one thousand one hundred and sixty one votes, at which time we will stop the voting process and the winner will be announced. Thank you, and let the voting begin! Good luck to each of our competitors, and may the best woman win!"

What happened next did not follow quite as expected. When picturing the scene in my mind, I had visualized the entire crowd standing up all at once and racing each other to the back of the room, rushing to cast their vote. Instead, most people remained seated in their chairs, some lost in their decisions, while others had taken to watching the rest of the crowd. A few people who I assumed to be the family or friends of Winifred stood quickly and made their way towards the Grand Hall. If I squinted, I could see my parents moving towards the back of the room as well, along with Genevieve whose pink jacket could be seen from any distance. Nervously, I shifted my gaze over to where the rest of my supporters had been sitting, only to find Nadia and Sandy amongst a cluster of empty chairs, looking as if they had been benched for a championship sports event. Feeling tense and uneasy, I gave a powerless look towards the back of the room. About twenty or thirty people lined each aisle, slowly ambling towards the voting booths. Who had received the most votes so far was anyone's guess. The majority of people, the other two-thousand and some, still didn't appear to have made up their minds yet.

It was either that, or they were afraid to show it.

I stared deeper into the crowd, their faces slowly blending into an indistinguishable mass. My body was going numb, senses slipping away. I could no longer smell the thick perfume that once hung over the motionless air, or feel the spotlight shining against my back, settling beneath my skin like a razor-sharp blade. Darkness crept over my eyes, seeping in from the corners of my foggy vision. The surrounding voices disappeared and the faint spots of black continued to multiply, consuming the world around me like a parasitic shadow. I was drowning in the sea of unmoving people, and struggling for breath. The waters were rising, filling my chest, my lungs, my throat, and anchoring me down. I was sinking, away from the shore.

It suddenly occurred to me that the room around me was getting smaller and smaller. The air was gone and the darkness was becoming absolute.

The people before me were deciding my future, but I needed to get my mind off of them—*fast*.

chapter thirty three

I managed to turn my eyes away from the crowd, drawing an uneven breath as I shifted my weight back from the podium and onto my feet. They said patience was a virtue, but I'd never been quick to acquire it. Now, as I waited for two thousand three hundred and twenty people to decide my future, I really wished I had.

As I considered this, my senses were slowly returning. There was now an evident prickle making its way across my leg—dull at first, but becoming stronger as more time went by. It began at my left knee, grazed its way down towards my ankle, and then stopped for a moment, only to repeat itself again. *It's just your nerves*, I convinced myself. The ache disagreed and became more persistent, snagging along my skin.

I sighed—this sharpness, whatever it might have been, wasn't going away on its own. Tentative, I glanced down at my leg.

My eyes met with those of a husky-rottweiler mix. Desperate for attention, he gave out a small yelp and extended its paw towards my knee, letting it slip forcefully down as he would if he were trying to push open a door.

Giving a weak smile, I crouched down to Jawsie's height, and began to run my fingers through his freshly groomed coat.

I had found my distraction.

For what must have been an hour, I remained focused on Jawsie, never once giving into the temptation of looking out into the crowd. The more time went by, the less I had the urge to face my audience at all. It seemed that the harder I concentrated on something other than the voting, the better I felt, and the more I lost track of time. In the end, only the shrill voice of Mr. Foxwell was enough to pull me back into reality.

My heart dropped like a stone in my chest.

"Attention," he called, his tone impatient. The air was thick but his voice sliced right through it, and within a moment the room had become silent. I reached out toward Jawsie and tousled his fur one last time before rising to my full height.

"Will everyone please take their seats." Mr. Foxwell's face was stern, but his command seemed to come out as more of a question. After just one look into the crowd, it wasn't difficult to see why.

From the open back doors, fifty or sixty people could still be seen waiting to cast their votes at the voting booths. The rest of the crowd was standing around the outer corners of the room, including a restless looking Sandy.

Knowing that the results would soon be disclosed, the straggling audience found their seats in a hurried silence.

For the first time after the debate, I dared to glance over at Winifred. I hadn't considered it up until that point, but she was the only one in the room who could possibly understand the pressure I felt. She was standing bolt upright, every muscle in her back and shoulders frozen stiff. Her skin was waxen and her eyes were dry, as if she had been replaced by a life-sized dummy.

Thinking about it, I realized that there was probably even more strain on her because, as much as I hated to admit it, most people expected me to fail from the start. Winifred, on the other hand, had built herself up to a height almost mountainous, believing that her foundation below was strong enough to support her weight at its peak. *Now that it had the chance to crumble, I realized that she had a much farther distance to fall from.*

Having recaptured the room's attention, Mr. Foxwell was beginning to speak. "Thank you for finding your seats so quickly." I managed a smile and turned in his direction, shaking off the thought. No matter what Winifred's first impressions of me were, I knew that I had defied them; I didn't have to win in order to make my point.

"Ladies and gentlemen, the time is now upon us to learn this evening's results. I realize that many of our eligible audience members were unable to vote this evening, but that is because one of our competitors has already reached a vote count of one thousand one hundred and sixty one, which I have already mentioned, is over the 50% mark—thus, an automatic win. Our winner tonight has been determined by means of an audience poll, which our computers report as having lasted a time-span of forty-seven minutes—one of the quickest voting periods ever held in this building. Actually, if I am remembering correctly, it is the *second fastest*—just a few minutes short of a record, which if I'm not mistaken, was set by President Deerun himself.

A chorus of whispering voices shot through the crowd. My heart skipped a beat. "Quiet, please!" squeaked Mr. Foxwell. He was flushing, his voice now curt. I knew that the results were near. "Our winner today is a hardworking, quick-thinking person, who has certainly earned her place in Washington. This woman, taking the win today is none other than…Cara Greybird!"

chapter thirty four

My body responded to the news far before my mind had the chance to grasp it. Adrenaline was in my blood, pushing through my veins, flowing through the crowd. Every feeling was crisp, every nerve at its end, buzzing with an electric current raised to a voltage I had never experienced. I didn't believe what I saw or heard, but at the same time, knew that it had to be real. My emotions were the next to catch up, but they were far from decisive. One moment I was torn between tears and laughter, the next, skepticism and elation, terror and fearlessness. It occurred to me, again, much too late, that I should act proper—restraining my emotions for humility's sake. I had never been too good at that.

"Thank you!" I called into my microphone, the tremor in my voice more than apparent. Hands unsteady, I grabbed a hold of the podium with both hands, shifting my weight off of my weakening knees. "Thank you all so much! To my audience, my family, President Deerun, my best friend, Sandy Giraffing—Sandy, I couldn't have done it without you! And to Ms. Winifred Tigers—a challenging opponent who has taught me more tonight than I ever could have asked! Thank you all!"

In all the excitement, I had dropped Jawsie's leash. Recognizing my astonishment as a chance for freedom long before I did, he was off within a moment, running to the side of a woman backstage. The stagehand was quick to capture him, giving me a thumbs-up as if to say that he was in good hands.

Before I knew it, the audience was at their feet, clapping, talking, some moving towards the stage and others for the door. More than anything, I wanted to meet them—to get to know those who had voted for me, and even those who didn't. To see the expression on Sandy's face alone was almost enough incentive to send me running down to the crowd. Nonetheless, my mind was returning in small fragments, and by some miracle, my manners came with them. Practically floating on air, I moved away from the platform and down towards center stage to shake hands with Mr. Foxwell. Winifred was still behind her pedestal, gripping the wood like a frightened child to their blanket. Her back was bent over in a way that was almost unnatural, as if her spine had collapsed inward.

"You were really great." I approached her cautiously. To my surprise, she extended her arm out towards me, taking her hand in mine.

"You were good too, *Cara*," she admitted. At a loss for words, I found myself laughing. Her voice was hard but her face was bearing an expression that *just might have been* her version of a smile. It was the biggest compliment I would receive all evening.

"Maybe we'll meet each other again in Washington sometime?" my voice trailed off, uncertain. Winifred didn't answer, and it took all the courage I had to look her in the eyes. If she was angry, or humiliated, or even sad, they hid it well. In fact, it was as if Winifred had realized something I only hoped the rest of the world would catch on to one day. She understood that the two of us were equals, not a child and an adult in this sense—just two people in a battle where neither would give in. But as in every war, one side had to lose, just as the other had to win. I hadn't humbled her or brought her down. Instead, I had proven that I wasn't fighting an uphill battle, but one on even turf.

She shrugged and her expression softened. "With you, I wouldn't expect anything less. Let's count on it."

If I wasn't already 99% sure that I was dreaming, this would have put me over the edge. I pinched my leg with my opposite hand, but despite all reason, I wasn't waking up.

Winifred seemed to understand my wordless effort to thank her in return, and let go of my hand with one final nod of acknowledgement, turning to meet the sea of people below. It felt somewhat unnatural for us to have gone our separate ways so quickly. In truth, the two of us had no real connection to each other. We had met as uniformed soldiers, enemies of opposing sides. Now that the war was over however, there was no more reason to fight, and nothing more to say. It was time for us to return home.

Balance still a little shaky, I headed for the stairs, preparing to make my own way into the crowd. My family was waiting at the bottom step.

"Cara, Cara, over here!" my mom yelled as if there was some possibility that I could miss her from three inches away. She pulled me into a hug before I reached the landing, using more force than I assumed was possible for her size. Practically crushing my cheek against her shoulder, she lifted one hand to wave over the rest of my family. In an instant, Nadia and my dad were running towards me at full speed. The earth around me was moving faster than light, spinning, acting, ever-changing—but for a moment everything was still. All I could see were the three of them, asking question after question as if there was enough time in the world to explain my past two weeks in Washington, let alone how I felt at that moment.

"I missed you so much!" My mom extended one hand to each of my shoulders and took a step back, looking me over like one person could completely change or grow, or whatever it was she thought, after just half a month. Looking back on the moment, maybe it was possible after all.

Maybe anything was.

"That was fantastic. Monumental—best thing I ever saw! I give it two thumbs up!" I looked down to find the youngest self-proclaimed political publicist in Washington.

"Nadia! Thanks so much!" It surprised me how much I missed hearing the sound of her voice in person. She practically hurled herself onto my stomach, wrapping her arms around my waist. "You helped me a lot, Nad, *I couldn't have done it without you.*" The arms tightened around me like the body of a boa constrictor but I made no effort to uncoil them.

I hadn't lied. Nadia *really had* helped me, just not in a way she might realize. Of course telling her seven year old classmates about the debate probably hadn't managed to raise an unbelievable amount of awareness. No, Nadia had helped me in a different way, by encouraging me, and always being there when I needed her. This alone was worth much more than any favor because I hadn't asked for or expected it, yet it came from the heart. Maybe it had taken a hug of life-threatening pressure to help me see that, but it should have been apparent all along.

"That was amazing, Cara! Amazing!" My father was shaking his head as if he couldn't quite believe what he had seen.

I wanted more than anything to catch up with my family, to help them attempt to comprehend my journey, but I knew that my supporters were in need of my attention too.

A couple of them broke away from the crowd, pulling me aside to offer their congratulations or thoughts on the debate. Others horded about me, yelling out their questions in a desperate attempt to be heard, and extending their hands through the masses of people in the hopes that I might shake them. I thanked them all, but for the moment my family was all that mattered to me—until I turned my head and saw where I had made my mistake.

Through the corner of my eye, I could see every one of the friends I had met in Washington standing together in a small cluster with Sandy at their head, waiting patiently for my attention. From Sunglasses to Genevieve, these were the people who had supported me to the finish. Guilt should have overpowered me, but my emotions were busting at the seams and had no room for one more feeling. I let the sensation go, turning slowly to face my best friend.

She looked as if she had been struck by lightning.

Her eyes were wide and not focusing on anything in particular, but rather, taking in the entire room. Mouth hanging slightly open, it seemed as if she had to concentrate all of her energy in order to speak.

"I…I can't believe that *you actually won!*" she stuttered, pronouncing each syllable as if they were referring to some great historic triumph. It was an odd concept to imagine, but vaguely, I understood that they were. *We had made history.*

"I wouldn't have without you," I answered softly as the thought that I had won and the debate was over slowly settled in my mind.

Quickly, I turned again, smiling towards the rest of my friends and welcoming them into our huddle. After thanking them for coming, I proudly introduced each one to my family, and vice versa. With all of these people, newly acquainted and having nothing in common but the fact that I could never repay them for all that they had done for me, you would think that they wouldn't have become as close in those few minutes as they did. Then again, miracles did seem to be the theme of the night, and as our conversations lingered on, the crowd slowly filed out. It was then that Sunglasses suggested that I go and talk to some of the reporters who were waiting impatiently by the exit, mumbling to one another about making their deadlines.

It was getting late but I wasn't tired, and decided that I would try and get through as many of the press' questions as I could. That was—only if Sandy could give the interviews with me. (She denied it, but I knew her work deserved just as much credit.)

My family would be staying at the White House that night, along with Jawsie, Sandy, and myself. We had originally planned for the six of us to leave together, but Nadia had already fallen asleep curled up on a lobby couch with Jawsie, and so my parents decided that it was best to take both of them back to their beds. Even Sandy, who in preparation for the big debate had gotten even less sleep than me, was ready for a well-deserved rest. With reluctant good-byes, they headed for the door together, leaving me to finish speaking to the media. In passing, most of the reporters greeted my sister like a casual friend, and it occurred to me that she might have been a better publicist than I originally assumed.

"Bye, Bill, didn't I tell you Cara would be great?" she yawned. "Sue, hi there. Wow, I can't believe they flew you all the way out from Tampa for this! How are those braces treating your daughter?" I smiled; fame suited her well. Genevieve was the next to leave, followed by Kate. James insisted on staying by my side until the last interview was over, and would then return to the White House with Ray and me afterwards. It didn't sound like a bad idea to me, and so he patiently waited until the last of the reporters had taken my picture and shaken my hand before the two of us headed out to the parking lot.

Together we walked past the marble columns and crystal chandeliers, the rows of empty velvet seats, and the lobby, with the fancy snacks on its tables and the Jawsie fur on its couches. All of the empty rooms we passed seemed somewhat eerie and bare, kind of like being in a library after closing hours, or a deserted amusement park. Nevertheless, it felt kind of sad to be leaving the place. I hadn't been there long, but somehow, the coliseum had become a sort of home to me. Now, I was leaving before I'd had the chance to settle in. The night outside was quiet as we stepped out onto the portico, the streets abandoned and the city lights barely-visible specks in the distance.

"Are you sad to go?" Sunglasses asked me, motioning towards the building at his back. The question caught me off-guard. I didn't want to leave, but standing on the marble balcony waiting for our car, it occurred to me for the first time that *I would be back.* I didn't know how, or under what terms, but something inside of me made it very clear that I would return and that it would be *soon.* The thought alone kept me warm outside in the ice-cold air, and I let it comfort me.

"No," I caught myself smiling. It was not over yet.

chapter thirty five

The two of us, James and I, were standing silently, staring out into the shadows of the autumn night.

Each was lost in our own train of thought when I saw the car approach.

It was a limousine, sleek and black like the one I had arrived in. As it pulled to a stop near the base of the building, a swarm of men pushed at the doors, forming a mob that began a swift and synchronized ascent up the stairs. Their faces were indistinguishable from the darkness which hid them, the suits they wore all that defined them against the night. They approached us closer, and their outlines began to sharpen. I squinted—the horde appeared to be a great number of security guards, walking closely together as if to protect something. In Washington, D.C. this could only mean one thing...*the President was coming!*

I had learned by experience that the Secret Service did not like to be surprised, and it took every ounce of restraint I had not to rush forward and meet them. Once they reached the balcony landing and were able to recognize me, the guards moved to encircle the portico. At the center of their ring was a single man in a navy blue suit, running towards me as best as he could manage in the gloom.

I recognized him immediately.

"Mr. President!" I could feel the frosty breeze biting at my body as I ran towards him, although the cold didn't seem to register with my mind. It was as if none of the chill could penetrate my body—as if I had had some sort of secret fire inside me to shield it away.

He was laughing.

"Cara Greybird…" His voice was slow, as if he were trying the name on for size. "You won! You've made history tonight. All across the world, everybody knows your name. Everybody knows what you've accomplished."

"I didn't do it alone, sir." The President smiled, but his expression seemed unfinished, as if there was something else he needed to tell me, but was waiting until the right time. Searching for more emotion, I looked up into his eyes. What I saw made me dizzy with realization.

They hadn't changed since I had met him at the hospital. He believed in me no more than he had on the first day I saw him, because *he had complete faith in me all along.*

"Thank you for everything," I whispered as the thought settled in my mind. The President shook his head.

"Thank *you,* Cara," his tone was rising with excitement. "I'm proud of all you have accomplished, but I must tell you—"

I cut him off. "Mr. President, I hope you don't mind me interrupting, but I've been wondering, if it's alright for me to ask that is, *where were you during the debat—*"

"That's what I've been trying to tell you!" His voice was loud, but the quiet of the night seemed to absorb it, sucking in the echo like a sponge. "There is something very important you should know…why I wasn't at your debate today. I should have told you, but I didn't want you to worry. I was at the hearing for the U.R.M. legislation!"

It only took a moment before my heart had found its way into my throat again.

"Please forgive me for not telling you earlier. You needed to focus on your task and I needed to focus on mine. Together, we must have done a pretty good job because…*the bill passed!*"

"IT WENT THROUGH!" I found myself screaming in disbelief. The air grabbed up my voice before it had a chance to spread.

"As of this January, Cara, it's official. You can be anybody you want to be because you will have a right to declare the opinions and ideas I know that you have! Now, just think of it—hundreds of thousands of others will be able to find their voices too…*all because of you.*"

I would have said something in return, but at the moment, I was having difficulty breathing. The world around me suddenly appeared so sharp with detail, so full of life and vibrancy that it made me dizzy just to imagine I played a part in it all.

Before I knew it, I was at the railing, staring out over a world I had only just recently become a part of. My mind was rushing, the earth was turning, the future was changing, and the President was at my side. Through it all, the night was closing in on us like a silent, inescapable force, shrouding the world in black until a time when the sun would rise again. The city slept below, and the imagination came alive in the freedom of the night. At its center, on top of the dream, the Deseo, I realized how I had come to find my home.

Our nation may have had many opinions, but I had learned the importance of voicing my own. I, Cara Greybird, had finally made a difference.

epilogue

It's funny how a simple idea can take control of a life, but scary how quickly a life can progress. Hi, it's me again, Cara Greybird. I am currently nineteen years old—and oh, yeah! I am now the *President of the United States of America!* As you may have guessed, President is what I became after the bill for the Underage Rights Movement passed. Of course, I wasn't elected into office *right away*. It took a lot of time, and even more hard work before I was ready for the job, but, as usual, I had a *lot* of help. You see, at first, it was President Deerun's idea that I run. After my first trip to Washington, the two of us remained close friends, and, unsurprisingly, he continued to envision great things for my future.

The year before I was elected, he realized that his second term was coming to a close and asked me if I would like to try for a chance at the job. I accepted his challenge, knowing that what I was about to peruse would be my greatest feat of all. Of course it was huge—nothing like it had ever happened before— but I knew it was right, and so I wholeheartedly chased it. I had developed an America project of my own in a sense. In so many ways it was different from the one which had begun my journey, but in others, it served simply as its continuation. To realize dreams, to do what's right, and to create lives free of impossibilities… The rest seemed to pass by so quickly, but to make a long story short, here I am now; *the President.*

But of course, how could I do anything without my best friend? Being her typical wonderful self, Sandy continued to encourage me, and was always there when I needed her. After awhile, she found herself loving the world of politics too, and to make *another* long story short, I realized that picking my Vice President would be an easier decision than I had originally thought.

Naturally, the families of both Sandy and me are here in Washington too. After awhile, living in the White House came to feel just like home (except of course without Jawsie). In his place however, the White House has allowed us one more resident, *our very own shelter dog.* Cornelia V. named him Lawrence Bartholomew Montgomery, but in honor of the belief that brought him to us, we call him Sparks for short.

Right now it's my third month in term and I'm doing pretty well. You would be surprised where you can go with one idea, a little work, and a lot of luck!

For me, it all started with an idea, a spark. Sometimes, it burned me, but in the end, it lit my way. I was in the dark without it, undistinguishable from every other shadow and face. When the flames became brighter, they acted as a torch that, if ever so slightly, led me away from the masses. I realize now that this element had given me something only I had the power to find: my voice.

I held the power to break my own mold.

And because of this, something that had started out so ordinary had managed to shape me into a person that defied every limit and restraint I had ever known.

It all began with a letter labeled '*Dear Mr. President.*'